RETURN TO THE SCENES OF GALACTIC CRIMES . . .

In this second volume of all-original science fiction mysteries, you'll meet victims and villains from the far future or the day after tomorrow, from light-years distant worlds and from right here on Earth, from your average humanoid to the finest products of robot engineering to species not yet dreamt about.

Once again that master of malevolence, Mike Resnick, has put together strikingly original crime scenarios, and rounded up some of science fiction's finest gumshoes to track down the perpetrators, ferret out their motives and their means, and bring them to justice.

So get ready to sample some of the wildest cases in the galaxy with some of the finest detectives the future has to offer.

MORE WHATDUNITS

MORE
WHATDUNITS

edited by
MIKE RESNICK

DAW BOOKS, INC.
DONALD A. WOLLHEIM, FOUNDER
375 Hudson Street, New York, NY 10014

ELIZABETH R. WOLLHEIM
SHEILA E. GILBERT
PUBLISHERS

To Carol, as always,

And to Martin and Rosalind Greenberg

CONTENTS

INTRODUCTION
by Mike Resnick

A few months ago DAW Books published *Whatdunits*, an anthology of original science fictional mystery stories. The gimmick was unique and, I think, successful: I created a number of murders with science fiction backgrounds and then assigned each of them to a science fiction writer to solve. In most cases, the writers were given two or three murders, and then chose the one they wanted to write.

Well, here we are back again with a second batch of "whatdunits." This time, along with the original gimmick, we have another one, equally unique in the history of the field: every story in this book has been written by an editor. (At one time or another I've sold books or stories to most of them; you can't imagine how enjoyable it was to be on the Power side of the editorial desk for a change.)

Most of the editors, as has always been the case with science fiction, also enjoy careers as part-time writers—and a handful of them are writers who enjoyed very brief careers as editors.

As with the first volume, I'm including the murder descriptions that our contributors had to work with; I think you'll find their approaches and solutions properly brilliant.

And if this book sells as well as its predecessor, perhaps I'll corral a batch of publishers to write Volume III.

WORTHSAYER

by Stanley Schmidt

Dr. Stanley Schmidt, author of many novels, short
stories, and science articles, is the long-time editor
of *Analog Science Fiction* magazine.

*Minimal information problem: an alien whose
race possesses the gift of precognition is brought
to Earth by a large stock brokerage firm to manage
some mutual funds. Its first day on the job it makes
them almost a billion dollars in profits. It is killed
in its quarters before it can report to work the next
morning.*

*The only clues at the scene of the murder are an
expired credit card (made out in a name that cannot be traced and that the credit card company
swears does not exist), an unopened bottle of champagne (which the alien could not possibly have me-
tabolized), and a plastic letter opener.*

*Who killed the alien—and since it was precognitive,
why didn't it know what was going to happen and take
steps to protect itself?*

I knew something was up when I got the call to go at
once to room 333. As the house detective for a hotel
where not much happens, I often fill my days making
spot checks of rooms that have been vacated and not yet
rerented. I have a key that opens *everything* in the Fritz—
except that two weeks ago they changed the lock on 333.
I hadn't seen the inside since. Most peculiar, and a bit
insulting.

Manager George Wilcox was waiting by the door,

wringing his chubby hands nervously. With him was a guy I didn't recognize, tall and rangy with curly black hair, wearing an impeccable Brooks Brothers suit and an expression no less distraught than George's. "What's up?" I asked.

"We're not sure," said George. "It *could* be murder, but . . . Oh, you'll have to see it all for yourself anyway, so we might as well get it over with. I'd like you to meet Mr. Charles Everett Oswald, CEO of Korag, Karfingel, Thatterthwaite, and Phui."

I blinked as I took Oswald's hand. "The stock brokerage?"

"The same," he said gravely.

"Of course," said George. "They rented this room for one of their . . . er . . . employees. Now let's go inside. Brace yourself, Rik."

He opened the door and a blast of desert air hit me full in the face—hot, dry, and heavy with an odor I couldn't place. I remembered when 333 had looked like all our other rooms, but it sure didn't now. There were plants all over, vaguely tropical-looking yet somehow *wrong*. The most conspicuous item of furniture was an overgrown computer workstation, fairly ordinary except that it sported *dozens* of little screens. There was a desk with nothing on it but what looked like a cereal box with labels in a foreign alphabet, a plastic letter opener, and a wine bottle. And there was a bed with a body on it—a most surprising body.

It's one of them! I thought incredulously. At a quick glance, it could have passed for human—a wiry, leathery, little old man with a froggy face. But look at it for three seconds and you'd see that it was *too* wiry, too leathery, too froggy.

Everybody knew what the Tsigant looked like. As the first aliens to visit Earth, the papers and newscasts had been full of them for three months. Never in a million years would I have expected to find one murdered in my own hotel.

If, I reminded myself, it *was* murder. *After all*, I asked

myself, *how could a being with the gift of precognition
let itself be murdered?*

"His name was Azuk," said Oswald. "I became suspicious when he didn't report in this morning. I came
over, and . . ." He gestured around the room. "Naturally, I suspect foul play."

"Maybe," I said, though I saw no recognizable signs
of it. There was no sign of a scuffle, no damage I could
recognize to the body. I couldn't begin to read the expression frozen on the corpse's face. "Any particular
reason?"

"He was in good health yesterday," said Oswald.
"And he made us a *lot* of money. Maybe somebody didn't
like that. In any case, it seems like too much of a coin-
cidence to assume this is natural."

"Maybe," I repeated. "First, we have to determine
which it was. I need a coroner's report, and I doubt that
any human doctor is qualified to do one. We're going to
have to get one of *them* in to do it."

Both Oswald and George went a little white. "You
mean a Tsigan?" Oswald said finally.

"That's right."

Oswald was silent quite a while. "That's going to be
. . . awkward."

"How so?" I asked.

"I'd rather discuss that privately . . . when we're finished here."

I shrugged. "No problem. Let me look around a little
first." I did, taking my time and letting them squirm a
bit. I couldn't find anything on the computer except financial data. The champagne bottle was unopened; I'd
come back when I was through with Oswald to write
down the label info and check it for fingerprints. Likewise the letter opener, which looked like an authentic
Woolworth's. I checked the desk drawers and found them
empty. Why a letter opener and nary a letter in sight?

I pointed at the foreign cereal box. "What's this?"

Oswald gave a nervous giggle. "Tsigan chow. He
brought a lot with him. Say, we're not going to have to
call in the city cops, are we?"

"Don't know yet," I grunted. "First let's find out if it's murder." *And how,* I wondered, *do our laws apply if it is?*

I walked over to take a look at the corpse—and felt a shiver run up my own spine when I noticed the straight-edged object sticking out of the dead alien's mouth. After a moment's incredulous hesitation, I slipped on a dis-posable rubber glove and drew it out just enough to con-firm that it was indeed a perfectly ordinary Visa card.

I pushed it back in, hoping George and Oswald hadn't noticed. That card took a big bite out of my hopes that this was a natural death. It looked too much like the sort of "calling card" that deranged killers often leave to sign their work.

I turned to George. "Looks like you're going to have to give me a key after all. I'm going to have to come back and go over things carefully. Meanwhile, no one is to touch anything, or even come in here without me." Then, to Oswald, "Okay, let's go talk about that au-topsy."

"Why don't we use my office?" he suggested. "It's debugged."

I couldn't resist grinning. "You mean it only has *your* bugs. Thanks, but I think we'll use mine."

My office used to be a broom closet, but it's home. I leaned forward across the desk toward Oswald, who was obviously less comfortable in such modest quarters. "So, now, why is it going to be so awkward to get a Tsigan doctor to come look at a dead Tsigan?"

"Maybe I'd better start at the beginning." He seemed to be avoiding my eyes. "You know how the Tsigant sud-denly showed up at the UN last summer and said they'd been watching us for a long time. You know how they said they could see the future, and started proving it by making public predictions and letting us watch them come true."

Of course I knew, but I listened anyway. That whole business had made me uncomfortable from the start. The accuracy of their predictions could be unnerving, but it could also be very appealing to all those human sheep wanting to be led. And when the Tsigant started hinting that they'd be glad to advise us in all our affairs . . .

Don't get off on that now, I scolded myself. *Pay attention!*

"Naturally," Oswald was saying, "we at KKT&P watched all that with great interest. We thought it would be a great thing for a stock brokerage to have somebody with that gift working for us. We thought it was just a daydream, of course. The Tsigant were obviously dealing with humans only through the UN. How could any private company hope to get into the act?

"Then one day Azuk—the one who died—showed up on our doorstep asking us to take him in. Said he wasn't happy among his own people, and in return for asylum he'd watch the future markets for us and make us rich.

"We thought it over good and hard. It seemed risky, but awfully tempting. Finally we decided we couldn't pass it up. After all, the stuff we'd been reading in the papers proved they really *could* see the future, and there wasn't anything in our laws to forbid it—not yet, anyway. So we hired him, rented a room in your hotel, and had it outfitted to keep him comfortable. The staff was sworn to secrecy, and he never had to enter or leave. What's one more employee telecommuting, these days?"

"What, indeed? I notice, Mr. Oswald, you keep talking about 'we.' Who, precisely, is 'we'?"

"I beg your pardon?"

"Who made these decisions? Who else knew Azuk was here?"

"Uh . . . nobody, actually. As CEO, I have a discretionary budget and a good deal of autonomy. He came directly to me, and while I quickly decided he could be a great benefit to the company, it seemed equally clear that the fewer people who knew about him, the better. Even the hotel knew only that the company was renting a room and wanted it specially modified and everyone kept out of it."

"Hm," said I. "Then I take it you have no idea who might have wanted to kill him, or why?"

"None whatever," said Oswald, but he looked nervous and evasive. Then he sighed and said, "No, wait. It's a long shot, but there was somebody in last night, right at quitting time. A rather well-known somebody who came in acting like a lunatic."

"What did he do?"

"He was ranting and raving and practically demanding that we sell off all our stock in Outward Bound Space Systems." Oswald laughed nervously. "Perhaps you heard about that in the morning news. We just bought that stock yesterday morning, on Azuk's advice. It was his first day on the job, you see—"

"Exactly what was his job?"

"We put him in charge of some mutual funds and told him to look at near-future stock reports and tell us what was going to go way up real fast. In his first hour he bought an enormous amount of Outward Bound—made something of a stir because it's quite unusual for a mutual fund to acquire a controlling interest in one company. But two hours after that, it was announced that a dynamite invention that had been tied up in litigation for years was suddenly free for Outward Bound to develop. By four P.M. their stock had skyrocketed. Needless to say, we were thrilled."

"Needless to say. And this visitor you had, I take it, was not. Did he have some connection with the invention?"

"None that I know of. But I gather he had inside information that led him to anticipate the court decision we took advantage of. Evidently he was planning to do what we did, but we beat him to it. Now he was trying to tell me I'd better sell it to him, at a price well below the new market value, because it was sure to go down even faster than it had gone up. 'What happened today was a fluke,' he said, 'and if you wait till the markets open tomorrow you'll take a terrible loss.' I asked him, 'Now how do you know that?' He turned beet-red and said, 'How did *you* know it was going to shoot up? I can only think of one way. You must have a tame Tsigan . . .'

"And then he was out of there. Well, that made me

plenty nervous, because of course we *did* have Azuk and I was the only one supposed to know. I wasn't sure if this guy was just spouting words out of anger, but it scared me to think that he might really know.''

"I can imagine. And I suppose even without Azuk, you can predict my next question, Mr. Oswald. Who was this visitor?''

Oswald waited three beats, then said, "Ronald Klaren.''

So Ron Klaren was a suspect. Everyone knew who he was, too: a flamboyant entrepreneur with a habit of playing tight margins and overextending himself to the point where one big deal like this that went the wrong way could ruin him. Yes, he could be *very* upset. If he seriously suspected that Oswald had been getting tips from a Tsigan soothsayer—or worthsayer—he would not let it drop until he had checked it out and looked Real Hard for a way to exploit it. And with his influence and contacts, he very likely could.

Of course, I could not rule out Oswald himself, either. Even though Azuk was a goose with a proven record of golden eggs, he was not one Oswald could exploit indefinitely. Having made one big killing, Oswald just might have decided that the sooner and more permanently he got rid of this embarrassingly shady contact, the better.

In any case, my first orders of business were to go over that creepy room with a fine-toothed comb, get the lab working on fingerprints and any other tidbits I found there, and take a closer look at that credit card and try to trace it. And, of course, to get a Tsigan medic over here to examine the body ASAP.

Setting those processes in motion took two easy phone calls and one hard one. The hard one was to get through several layers of security to talk to a leader of the Tsigan delegation. But the expected resistance dissipated dramatically when I said the words "dead Tsigan"—though I had no doubt that everything I said or heard after that was quite thoroughly bugged.

* * *

The Tsigan medic arrived just as I was finishing up my scrutiny of the crime scene, having already sent some goodies to the lab. The smell in there was pretty potent by then.

I'd never seen a live one in the flesh before. His skin had a kind of iridescence to it that the dead one lacked. His name was Iqaln. It was no surprise that he was accompanied by a couple of UN Security guards. No doubt the death of an alien "off campus" during the first negotiations with extraterrestrials made them exceedingly nervous.

Dr. Iqaln bent over the body and made passes over it with some sort of scanner, occasionally muttering something quiet and unintelligible. It went on for quite a while, but I was relieved to see that it apparently wasn't going to involve any cutting.

Presently I asked him, "Can I ask you questions while you work?"

"Yes." His English sounded a bit like a trained parrot.

I pointed at the champagne bottle. "Do you know what that is?" Iqaln nodded quite humanly, but silently. "Could Azuk have used it?"

"The bottle, perhaps. The contents, no."

"The information I need from you is quite simple, Doctor. Did Azuk die of natural causes, or was he killed?"

"Could be either," said Iqaln, finally laying his scanner aside and standing upright to face me. "The facial expression and the human artifact in his mouth do suggest something out of the ordinary. However, there is no evidence of gross trauma or poisoning—though there is some deep central nervous system damage."

I found that intriguing, but the interview on the whole was frustrating. Much of my work consists of watching people and judging their credibility, but I couldn't read a live alien's face any better than a dead one's. "If he was killed," I asked, "*how* was that nerve damage caused?"

Despite what I'd just been thinking, it seemed to me

that that question bothered him. ''Uh,'' he said, ''under some conditions we Tsigant can . . . uh . . . remotely stimulate each other's nervous systems.''

Great. I thought. *Not only precognition, but telekinesis and maybe telepathy, too*. Aloud, I said only, ''Are you suggesting that Azuk was killed by one of his own kind?''

I was *sure* that one made him uncomfortable. ''Why would you say that?''

''Think,'' I said. ''If he was killed, it was evidently done by a method which the Tsigant can do, but humans can't. So I ask you: did any Tsigant have a motive to do it?''

''Uh . . . I know of none . . . but I am not qualified or permitted to discuss any aspect of the case except the medical. I have done that. If you wish to ask more questions of Tsigant, you will have to speak to my superiors.''

''Okay,'' I said. ''Just one more question. How long has he been dead?''

The doc seemed relieved to be back on his own turf. ''Since early this morning—approximately six A.M.''

I was in no hurry to talk to Iqaln's higher-ups. The more I learned about the Tsigant, the more uncomfortable they made me. But I'd keep it in mind as something I might have to do later.

Meanwhile, I had other things to do. With the Tsigant's permission, George and I moved the body (minus credit card) to another room and stored it on ice. I was the tiniest bit queasy about having not yet said anything to the city police, but a lot of the legalities of this case had no clear precedents and I was following the terms of my license to the letter.

The crime scene didn't feel quite so spooky with Azuk out of there, and felt a lot better with the ''air-conditioning'' turned off. With some relief, I made a couple of phone calls to follow up my lab and credit card investigations. I'd found no clear traces of human presence except some fingerprints on the champagne bottle. Thanks to a youthful indiscretion involving a fraternity

project to relocate a phone booth, Ron Klaren's prints
were on file, and they did match.

So Klaren had gone to see Azuk, though the lab said
he hadn't touched the bottle since several hours before
Azuk's death. He *could* have stayed after putting the bottle down, being careful to avoid touching anything else—but
why? And how could a human cause the kind of damage Dr.
Iqaln had reported?

Getting nowhere with that, I called the credit card
company. I'd already known that the card was eight
months expired; what was more surprising was that the
company had no record of either its number or the name
to which it was issued.

What good was an expired credit card in a nonexistent
name that matched no account on the company's books?

Another dead end, or so it seemed at the moment. And
it was getting late.

I made one more visit to the scene of the crime, stopping on the way to pick up my "clues" from the lab so
I could put them back where I'd found them. I was hoping vaguely for inspiration, but all I saw was a too-
familiar pattern of mocking nonsense. The only thing
that had changed was that the bed was now empty, still
rumpled and unmade, with "J. Abraham Washton's"
Visa card resting forlornly on the pillow.

I was tired, and glumly convinced that I would have
to try to talk to other Tsigan—tomorrow. There was just
one more thing I wanted to try tonight.

Ron Klaren didn't want to see me, but his blockers
couldn't argue with my private police credentials. I found
him in a plush den decorated with antiques and trophy
heads of animals, several of them recently extinct. Up
close, at 10:00 P.M., he didn't look quite as cosmetically
perfect as the public is used to seeing him; but he still
looked quite suave and commanding with his boyish face,
sleek silver hair, and gold brocade smoking jacket. He
offered me a sherry, but I declined. "I appreciate it, Mr.
Klaren, but I don't think either of us wants this to take
any longer than it must. I'll come right to the point:

there's been a death, possibly a murder, and your fingerprints were found on a bottle left in the deceased's room
last night. Can you explain what you were doing there?''

He set the sherry bottle aside with a sigh, but kept his
own drink, lowered himself into a recliner, and took a
sip before answering. "I give lots of people gifts, often
in bottles. Maybe you'd better tell me who this unfortu-
nate was."

"I think you know, Mr. Klaren. Or are many of your
business associates Tsigan?''

He put down his glass, steepled his fingers, and
frowned almost imperceptibly. "Okay, I guess there's no
point in beating around the bush. You're saying that
KKT&P's Tsigan fortune-teller was killed?''

"Possibly; even that's not certain, but it looks very
likely. And you're a leading suspect, since we know you
went to see him shortly before he died. We also know
about your earlier conversation with Charles Oswald.''

Klaren smiled sardonically. "Yes. Hardly a cooperative chap. I suppose Oswald told you I was unhappy because they made a killing—no pun intended—I'd counted
on making myself. I tried to talk him into undoing the
damage, but he wouldn't budge. He became rather nasty,
actually. The more I thought about it, the less likely it
seemed that they could have been sure enough to sink
that much of a mutual fund into one company unless they
were getting help from somebody who could literally see
the future. I don't know anybody who can do that except
the Tsigan. Oswald didn't respond to my accusation, but
I became convinced it *had* to be that.

"So I started checking. Yes, I know it's not easy for
ordinary mortals to get close to our alien visitors, but I
hardly think it immodest if I point out that I'm not an
ordinary mortal. I have contacts, Mr. Parvenza. I used
them. I found out about this runaway alien who was
working for Oswald, and I found out where he was, and
I went to see him."

"What time was that?''

"Oh, I'd say elevenish. And I assure you that this Azuk

character was just as stubborn as his boss—and just as much alive when I left him an hour or so later.''

''You say he was stubborn. What were you hoping to get from him?''

''Why, what I couldn't get from Oswald, of course. A second chance to get what I'd been aiming at for so long. If I couldn't persuade Oswald to unload that stock, maybe I could get his tame Tsigan to tell him things that would scare him into it.''

''You wanted Azuk to lie about the future,'' I said. ''And you hoped to bribe him to do that with a bottle of champagne?''

''Oh, of course not! I didn't know what it would take; I didn't even know if he could metabolize the stuff. But I did figure it would make a good host gift to break the ice. If he knew enough about our culture to make hundreds of millions per hour in the stock market, surely he'd know enough to recognize a goodwill gift.'' He laughed shortly. ''Turns out he took it, even though he couldn't drink alcohol—seems he collects alien bottles. But he wouldn't consider doing what I asked.''

I got no more out of Klaren, and left dissatisfied. His story seemed consistent with everything else I had, little as that was, and I still didn't see how he could have done the physical deed—or how a precognitive victim could have let him. But his motive was so obvious I couldn't get him out of my mind.

Early the next morning, after too little sleep, I again called the UN and arranged to talk to one Diilang, who I gathered was the leader of the Tsigan delegation to Earth. An hour later I was doing so—not face-to-face, but across a CCTV link from another room somewhere in the UN building. ''I assume you already know about the death of one of your delegates in the hotel where I work,'' I said. ''I'm investigating because we're afraid someone may have killed him.''

''You mean Azuk,'' said Diilang, who looked to me much like Iqaln but had more rumble in his squawk-talk. ''Why do you suspect this thing?''

"Well, for one thing he had a counterfeit human credit card stuck in his mouth, which seemed most unusual." Was that a flicker of reaction on Diilang's face? "Also, your medical expert, Iqaln, examined the body and said that Azuk's facial expression suggested that something unusual had happened in his last moments. He also said he found no physical damage—*except* some internal and potentially lethal damage to his nervous system. A kind of damage which, as I understand Iqaln, no human could cause, but a Tsigan could."

He certainly showed a reaction that time. Too bad I couldn't read it. He almost hissed, "Surely, you don't think we—"

"Oh, not as a matter of official policy," I assured him, as casually as if I actually believed it. "But how *did* you and his other compatriots feel about Azuk?"

A pause so long it just *had* to mean something. Then, with what sure sounded like sullenness, "That's of concern to us alone."

"Maybe so," I said, "but the suspicion of murder casts doubt on the whole human-Tsigan relationship. You've spent a couple of months here building up our trust in you, dazzling us with your ability to foretell the future, holding out the promise of a mutually beneficial arrangement between our species. If our people suddenly get the impression that some of you disagree with others so much that they run off and hide, and then you kill to silence them. . . . It's not going to help, sir."

Again a long silence, followed by what I heard as sullenness. "I repeat, sir, that the details of Azuk's relationship with his fellows are no concern of yours. However, I can tell you that he was a malcontent and he did disappear." Pause. "What bothered us most about his association with the human financial firm was the impropriety of his independently offering special aid to a particular human group while the rest of us were trying to work for the benefit of your species as a whole."

Yeah, I thought with heavy irony. I said, "So it might have been convenient for you to be rid of him."

"Perhaps," said Diilang. "But we would hardly need

to kill him. It would be quite sufficient to send him lies
about the future that would discredit him with his human
employer.''

"Perhaps," I echoed. "But suppose whoever killed
Azuk was acting on his own rather than for your government. Might he, for instance, have had a co-conspirator?
Someone who planned to desert with him, changed his
mind, and then wanted to cover his complicity?''

"I tell you again, that's our concern, not yours.''

"Of course. My apologies for an inappropriate question. But perhaps you could tell me this. Iqaln said one
Tsigan could damage another's nervous system by remote
control. Exactly how is that done?''

"That's hardly the sort of information we'd wish to
share with humans," Diilang said stiffly. "But I do find
it interesting that you're the second human who's asked
us that question in the last day.''

I found that interesting, too. "Who was the first?''

"He called himself Ronald Klaren. Now if you'll excuse me—''

"Certainly. If you'll answer just one more question—''

"I've lost patience with you," said Diilang. "No more
questions today.''

He reached forward. My screen went blank and my
speaker silent.

So Klaren had also been to see Diilang. That strengthened his standing as a suspect. The very fact that he had
gotten through to the alien leader proved that he had unusual connections—which was hardly surprising.

Perhaps, after giving up on both Oswald and Azuk,
Klaren been trying to feel out a weakness—to learn a way
to kill a precognitive alien.

Or maybe it wasn't a simple murder. If Klaren had
learned that only Tsigant could do that nerve trick, and if
he, too, suspected there was a co-conspirator, he might
have tried to find and hire that individual to do the actual
deed. . . .

It seemed like more of a lead than I'd found yet, but

it still didn't take me very far. I switched off my monitor
to get some quiet, leaned back in my chair, and closed my
eyes. I tried to empty my conscious mind, to make it re-
ceptive to anything my subconscious might choose to dump
into it. Words started flitting across from ear to ear. At
first most of them had to do with the case, and then I
started free-associating, which sometimes helped. *Empty
desk . . . precognitive corpse . . . letter opener . . . let
'er rip. . . ripped a seam . . . things are seldom what they
. . .*

My eyes snapped open and I sat bolt upright. The few
things I'd found at the scene seemed utterly irrelevant to
it—*if* they were really what they seemed.

But what if they weren't?

I stood up and charged out into the nippy fall drizzle to
grab a taxi. Twenty minutes later I'd gathered all the
"clues" from room 333 at the Fritz and lugged them back
to the lab. "Analyze these as thoroughly but nondestruc-
tively as you can," I told the dropoff clerk. "And fast. I
have to know if they're really what they look like."

She looked skeptically at the expired credit card, the
cheap letter opener, and the expensive bottle, and
shrugged. "Whatever you say, Mr. Parvenza."

The lab called back within the hour. It was Anitra, a
very good tech whose friendship and confidence I'd cultivated over the years, and she sounded baffled. "The
champagne appears to be just what the label says," she
said. "Good stuff—if you need any help drinking it when
this is all over, let me know. But that other stuff . . . I've
never seen anything like it. The credit card and letter
opener are both full of hidden structures that look vaguely
like microchips. We did the credit card first, so that didn't
surprise us *too* much. Most credit cards are smart these
days. But when we looked closer, none of it looked quite
right. And the letter opener has it, too. Who ever heard
of a cheap letter opener full of exotic microcircuits?"

"I thought you might find something like that," I
grinned. "Any idea what the circuits do?"

"None whatever," she said. "We're not even sure they're really circuits. Do *you* have any ideas?"

"I might. Maybe we can talk about them later over that champagne. Right now I've got work to do. Thanks ever so much, Anitra!"

I hung up before she could press me for details. Truth was, my idea was still pretty vague. But I really did have the feeling things were starting to fall into place.

I suddenly remembered something Diilang had said during our interview that hadn't fully registered at the time, and my heart and brain sped up even more. I grabbed the phone and called him back. It didn't take *quite* as much bullying this time.

Somewhat to my surprise, I got him to talk to me on the regular phone, which saved me a trip to the UN. The only disadvantage was that he was a good deal harder to understand without visual cues. (I suppose he said the same about me.) "When Ronald Klaren visited you," I began, "and asked how your remote control works, did he ask anything else?"

"I don't understand," said Diilang—stiffly, I thought.

"I need to know," I told him. "One thing we can't understand about this case is how someone with precognition could let himself be killed. Why wouldn't he foresee it and take measures to prevent it?"

There was a long silence. Then Diilang said, "Please stop bothering me," and hung up.

I didn't bother trying to call him back. The very fact that he cut me off without answering strengthened my conviction that the question was very important.

And I had a half-baked idea *why* it was important. The Tsigan doctor had said they could kill by remote control, and the Tsigan leader hadn't denied it. He had also mentioned (in what I now suspected was a slip of his alien tongue) that they could send—or at least fake—a message from the future.

Suppose that was the *only* way they could get information from the future!

All us humans, myself included, had been making a big assumption ever since the Tsigant showed up. They said they had precognition, and they proved it by making lots of predictions. They were never wrong—but what about all the things they didn't predict that happened anyway? We just assumed that the entire future was an open book to them; nobody thought to ask how their precognition *worked* or what its limitations were. Which made their offer to tell us everything we should do from here on out all too tempting to a lot of people.

Which was, I suspected, exactly what the Tsigant wanted. If you have the run of the Galaxy, and you came upon a sometimes-warlike race that was about to burst forth into your domain, wouldn't *you* like a way to control that race's future development?

What if their "omniscience" was really just a straightforward application of an impressive, but limited, technology? What if all they knew about the future was what their future selves told them via some sort of "time telephone?" What if it was difficult or expensive to send those messages, so they couldn't send very many?

They could create the impression of knowing far more than they did, just by showing off a few laboriously arranged demonstrations. And maybe those messages themselves could be dangerous—especially if they interfaced directly with the recipient's nervous system.

Sound familiar?

So far all my evidence had said that Azuk was dead, but nobody had been in his apartment at the right time to do the damage. Well, maybe the explanation was very simple: they hadn't.

Maybe the murderer didn't even have a motive—yet.

Maybe, crazy as it sounded, he could still be stopped. . . .

A day and a half hiding out in room 333 was beginning to get on my nerves. It might not even be the right place, I thought, and I had only a vague idea when the time would be. I had so little to go on. It could be any time, any place.

But that was too big a field to stake out, and I did have reasons to suspect *this* time and place. If my time telephone theory was right, there ought to be a receiver and a transmitter. Since Azuk was spending all his time in this room, he had to be collecting his "future" data and sending it to his "past" self right here. So where were the transmitter and receiver?

I sure hadn't found anything that looked like I'd expect them to. So they had to be disguised as something else. That made sense; Azuk would be just as eager as his compatriots to be thought of as having a mysterious gift for seeing the future rather than a black box that could do a few tricks. So I'd had the letter opener and Visa card checked out, and the lab report suggested I'd struck pay dirt. One of them, evidently, was the transmitter and the other the receiver.

Who ever said a time machine had to be *big?*

Which was which? Well, if my hunch was right, he'd sent stock data back to something which fed it directly into his nervous system. Maybe not directly; maybe he had some sort of implant in the roof of his mouth that Iqaln had chosen not to tell me about. Feed the wrong kind of signal to that something and it might make his nervous system do things it shouldn't—maybe even fry the neurons themselves. The receiver must be the one that he had in his mouth when he died, because that was how the lethal signal from the future—from *now*—got into his nervous system.

So the Visa card was the receiver. It was not just a "calling card"; it was the business end of the weapon. Whoever came up with the scheme had an admirable eye for detail. A smart credit card would normally have things in it that looked sort of like the timephone's works, and an *expired* card would be less likely to invite close examination.

I hoped, though I didn't know, that the transmitter and receiver would be a matched pair, so it would be difficult or impossible to send a killer signal to Azuk's receiver without using his own transmitter. So I guessed they would most likely come here to do it—and since there'd be no advantage in waiting, they'd do it soon.

So I'd put everything (except Azuk) back where I'd

found it, and settled in to wait. And after a day and a half, I was beginning to wonder if I was on a completely wrong track.

Even on stakeout, one has to go to the bathroom. When I was coming back, it finally happened. I heard the outer door opening, ducked behind a smelly alien plant, and froze, pistol ready, heart pounding.

The door opened slowly and a Tsigan, one I hadn't seen before, slunk into the room. He, too, was holding something that I suspected was a weapon. Did he know I was here, or did he think Azuk was in the bathroom and might come out too soon? If he was trying to kill him, he must not know he was already dead.

One thing bothered me: if he thought Azuk was alive and on the premises, why not just shoot him here and now? Why bother with what I thought he was going to do—what he *must* be going to do, since Azuk's death proved the deed accomplished?

And what would happen if I stopped him?

I tried not to think about that. I'd read enough science fiction to give up on making sense of temporal paradoxes, and this was no time to get sidetracked into thinking about them again.

My suspect looked around, seemed to relax a little, and stepped to the computer. He didn't sit down, but he did pick up the letter opener—the thing I'd guessed was the transmitter—and slipped it deftly into what looked like one of the ventilation slots on the computer. He looked around once more, then laid his "gun" down and poised his hands over the keyboard.

"Stop!" I yelled, charging out of my hiding place. "You're under arrest!" I had no idea whether such an arrest would hold up in court, but there was no time to think about that, either.

The Tsigan turned his head but didn't move his hands from the keyboard. He started to type. . . .

I had to do something fast. I was willing to try arresting an alien, but shooting him seemed *too* risky. In the split second of my hesitation, he took one hand from the keyboard—but kept typing, hunt-and-peck, with the other—and reached for his weapon. My reflexes realized I was within reach of the champagne bottle, grabbed it and in one swift movement cracked it over his head. Bubbly pressure released explosively, showering everything in sight with champagne and shards of glass.

He staggered back, apparently not seriously hurt, but bleeding, just as I was, from several small cuts. His blood was a bright Christmasy green that made a nice contrast to my red.

"You idiot!" he squawked. "You've probably killed him!"

Only then did I see the champagne dripping from the computer—and letter opener—and remember the sparks it had triggered when it hit, which had not registered consciously until now. With a precipitously sinking feeling, I realized what he must mean.

And at that instant the outer door opened again to admit my old friends from UN Security, with sidearms drawn.

"I'm afraid," one of them said, "you're both going to have to come with us."

It's quite a blow to a detective's ego to find out that he did it. There was a big meeting after that, with both UN and Tsigan leaders, in which they admitted that I was right about how their precognition worked, including the roles of the letter opener and credit card. I'd picked that up from Diilang's remark about messages; unfortunately, I hadn't picked up on the part about "we wouldn't have to kill him."

A lot of secrets came out now because the human leaders had suddenly developed a healthy fear of the pig in that poke. The Tsigan I'd tried to stop from sending a destructive message back to kill Azuk in the past wasn't doing any such thing. He was my counterpart: the detective they'd turned loose to track down Azuk when he disappeared. He'd been working pretty much on his own and hadn't checked in with headquarters as often as he should have. He didn't know about either Klaren's or my visit to Diilang, or that Azuk was already dead. But he did see the same news that had driven Klaren into a frenzy and used that to figure out where Azuk was and what he was doing. He had independently reached the same conclusion that Diilang had let slip to me, that Azuk could be rendered harmless to Tsigan goals by sending him phony messages that would make him the laughingstock of KKT&P. *That's* what he was trying to do when I clobbered him.

But the shower of champagne had shorted out all manner of things in the computer and time transmitter, and that's what zapped poor Azuk. So I was, however unwittingly, the killer—or at least the weapon. Since the lethal impulse was sent back through time, what looked like a "whodunit" had really been a "who-will-do-it."

I feel terrible about my role in it, but both the UN and the Tsigan are letting me off. Everybody's willing to accept what happened as an accident and the Tsigan have had to back off quite a bit in their pressure to take over our affairs. Now that we know they don't really know as much about the future as they wanted us to believe, their "guidance" is a lot easier to resist. The UN has ordered them off Earth, on pain of destruction of their fleet (yes, we could do it) and we're back to trying to make it on our own, without soothsayers. Or worthsayers.

But we've got a new incentive to do it really well. We know they're out there, and while they're not everything we thought they were, they're not to be trifled with.

And someday, I suspect, they'll be back.

FOR LOVE OF JUOUN
by Jane Yolen

Jane Yolen, author of more than 100 books, edits her own hardcover imprint of young adult fantasy novels, as well as *Xanadu*, an annual fantasy anthology.

(I cheated. Just as an experiment, without either of them knowing it, I gave Jane the very same scenario I gave Jack Nimersheim in the first volume of *Whatdunits*—and I received two excellent and totally different stories.)

A human brings home a cute little monkeylike pet from another world. One day it goes berserk and attacks him, and he kills it. He is then brought to trial for the murder of a sentient being. He claims the animal was smart, a quick learner, but definitely not sentient.

Courtroom drama: was the pet sentient or not? If it was, was the human justified in killing it or not?

—So, Mademoiselle, now tell us from the beginning what it was you saw, what it was that happened. What it was that made your late Papa kill the Jew-on.

—Juoun, M. Prosecutor. More nasal, more like the language of old Portugal on old Earth. Zhe-wan. Papa brought the Juoun back for me. He always brought me back presents from his travels. A Twitter from Alcebides IV and a Macadomion Cat and a . . .

—*A twitter, Mademoiselle?*

—A kind of lizard, M. Prosecutor, with a frilled neck

and tail. It sings quite beautifully, hence its name. Papa loved to bring me alien creatures. To keep me from being lonely while he was away. Company of a sort. He did not want me to see any young men, you see. He did not approve. I was his alone.

—*His? How do you mean that, Mademoiselle?*

—His little girl, M. Prosecutor. Why, what other way could you possibly mean? My mother died giving birth to me, you see, and he did not want the same to happen again. So our house was filled with women servants and many pets. And they were all company. Of a sort. You understand.

—*I understand. Go on. What happened when he brought back the Zhe-wan?*

—Oh, good, M. Prosecutor, you have it almost exactly right. Only more nasal.

—*Mademoiselle!*

—Just Papa's tone! I am sorry, M. Prosecutor. I will proceed. Papa had been gone so many days, so many nights. Nights were the hardest because he was not there to sit by my bedside and tell me stories to help me sleep, especially when the headaches were the worst. Stories of his travels and stories that he remembered from all the great books. But I knew he would soon be home because Griselle said so. She is the housekeeper. And, oh—if only she would smile a bit more. Frowning as she does gives her two lines on either side of her mouth. Like a parenthesis, you know.

—*And did he arrive when Griselle said?*

—Oh, assuredly. Griselle may not smile, but she is always accurate. She took his message and his coordinates and plotted the course. He landed within the very hour she said. And he had the Juoun with him. It was very small.

—*But the corpse of the alien we saw was as big as . . . as big as myself, Mademoiselle.*

—The Juoun grew quickly, M. Prosecutor. Papa noticed it at once. At first it was the size of a small Earth cat, only more monkeylike. Its fur was the color of earth turned over by a spade, dark and brown. The soil in my garden is like that. And so I wanted to name the Juoun after something growing in my garden, a flower name. But Papa would not hear of it. He said, "It is called Partoux, which in the language of the Juoun's home planet means Child of the Night."

—*Partoux. Child of the Night.*

—Exactly. Papa thought it was because the Juoun was most active in the evening. But he did not know. How could he know? From the beginning the Juoun wanted only me.

—*And how did you know that?*

—Why, it told me so.

—*It talked to you?*

—Oh, M. Prosecutor, how droll you are. *Talked!* As if the Juoun could talk with its mouth like you. Like me. No, of course not. But the Juoun told me all the same. When I first picked it up in my arms—and it no bigger than a baby—it turned its violet eyes on me. And I was the Juoun's completely.

—*So, it was sentient.*

—Is the Twitter sentient? It knows to ask for food. It knows to relieve itself in the garden.

—*But the question before the court, Mademoiselle, as you know only too well, is whether your late father killed a sentient being, or merely a pet. If sentient—and he was aware of it—then a grave crime has been done and we cannot resurrect your father but must let him lie forever in his bier. However, if the Juoun is, as you claim, but a pet, then you will have your father restored to you as soon as the trial is complete. You understand?*

—I understand completely, M. Prosecutor. Shall I go on?

—*Go on.*

—All day the Juoun slept in its little crib. But at night, after Papa told me my story and turned out the lamp, I would go over to the crib and pick up the Juoun, carrying it to my bed. I held it in my arms. It licked my neck and my breasts.

—*Mademoiselle!*

—You want the truth, M. Prosecutor. Like a little animal, it licked me, a sweet tickling. And I would go to sleep happily, almost as if its tongue had drugged me into dreams. Its tongue was not sharp or rough but as soft and as velvety and as soothing as a kind of cloud.

—*A cloud?*

—If a cloud had a tongue.

—*Go, on, Mademoiselle.*

—And as if that licking made it grow, it grew.

—*I do not understand, Mademoiselle.*

—Nor do I. I am only in the first college grade of biology, after all; xenobiology is grade four. I do my lessons by modem, of course, as our villa is so far from any school. And while I do well in biology, it is not my vocation, you understand. I wish to write. Already some of my poems have been published. One about my Juoun has been especially remarked upon. Would you like to hear it?

—*This is a trial, Mademoiselle, not a salon. And a trial with grave consequences at that.*

—Ah, but did not the great poet of the Andromedas write: "The matter of poetry is the matter of all life?"

I am neither a poet nor a critic, Mademoiselle, but a bureaucrat. A prosecutor. I have a license of life and death, not a poetic license, if you will forgive me a little joke. Ahem. Now we must proceed.

—Your question, then, M. Prosecutor?

—*You cannot explain more this—um—this matter of the licking making the Juoun grow?*

—I can only hypothesize, M. Prosecutor, that by licking my flesh, the Juoun received some sort of vitamins or other nourishment which caused it to get bigger.

—*As if it were some sort of vampire, Mademoiselle?*

—Except that word conjures up a monster, M. Prosecutor. And my Juoun was no such thing.

—*We will not use the word, then, if it distresses you. But we will note that this activity of licking seemed to cause the growth of the alien. And further that the licking did not unduly discomfort you?*

—To the contrary, M. Prosecutor. It was most comforting. Even . . .

—*Even what, Mademoiselle?*

—I cannot say it.

—*You must.*

—Papa would not like it.

—*Your Papa is in his bier, Mademoiselle, and will stay there forever if the truth does not come out.*

—Ah, you are right, M. Prosecutor. Then I will say it, though you must forgive me if I whisper it.

—*We will hear the whisper, Mademoiselle, and treat it with the utmost delicacy.*

—Ah, then, I will tell you. It was most comforting, even . . . even sensual in its delight. A cloud touch, a flower touch. I said it best in my poem. One can, you understand, talk about these things in a poem, disguising the deed with words about other things.

—*Do you mean metaphors, Mademoiselle?*

—Ah, M. Prosecutor, then you were joking with me about not being either a poet or a critic. A bureaucrat, perhaps, but one who understands many other things, am I correct?

—*It is important to my job that I understand much, Mademoiselle. May we proceed?*

—Then you do not wish to hear my poem?

—*(Sigh.) Recite your poem, Mademoiselle, if you think it has a bearing on these matters. Please.*

"For Love of Juoun

> Oh, little feather stroke, oh, angel tongue,
> To whom gross canticles and hymns when sung
> Cannot describe the miracle of touch,
> The nightly prayer I need so much;
> The soothing . . .

—*I think we understand, Mademoiselle. You need not go on.*

—But I develop the feather image, speaking of shaft and vane and barbs and the night plumage and . . .

—*Mademoiselle, I must insist!*

—And it is only a pet, after all. A poem about a pet.

—*When you wrote this poem, how . . . um . . . big
was your pet?*

—About the size of an adolescent, I believe. But growing quickly. The poem was put out on the nets within
days of my completing it. I had twenty-four responses
within hours. The publishers told me they had rarely seen
so great a response. And almost a thousand more since.

—*Mademoiselle, now I must ask you a question of the
gravest delicacy.*

—Would my Papa approve?

—*I believe, Mademoiselle, that without this question,
your Papa will remain unable to approve or disapprove.*

—Can you whisper it, then?

—*I will whisper. Mademoiselle, are you still a virgin?*

—M. Prosecutor, that is *indeed* a delicate question.
But I have no fear of answering. But of course! My Papa
would not have it otherwise. He would have no men near
me. And he is correct. It seems my family has a predis-
position to die in childbirth and no amount of modern
medicine has changed that. My mother and her mother
and her mother before her all died with child. I will be
the last of the line.

—*Then, I must proceed with other questions.*

—If you wish, a doctor can examine me, M. Prosecutor. A woman doctor. I am fully prepared if it would
mean my father's life.

—*That will not be necessary, Mademoiselle. Let us
now, assuming the nightly ritual with your pet and the
quickness with which it grew, come to the night in question. When somehow your father killed your . . . um . . .
pet.*

—You understand, M. Prosecutor, that my father gave
me the Juoun and was then home for a matter of only a
week before going away again. He is . . . he was . . .
these tenses become so terrible difficult especially as he
will soon be *is* again.

—*If all is in order, Mademoiselle.*

—He is, or was, and will be again, a trader in oddities.
The pets, alone, he brings home for me. Flesh, he often
says, is not to be traded in. And I, of course, agree.

—*There are, as well, laws to this point. Which is why we are having this trial. But it is good to know your father spoke of this. That he was aware. Intent is the most important part of any prosecution.*

—This I understand, M. Prosecutor, having taken classes in the law. My little avocation. Besides the writing.

—*Go on.*

—And so he was away for the three or four months in which the Juoun reached its present size.

—*Its maturity, Mademoiselle?*

—We have no way of knowing that, M. Prosecutor, this being the only known Juoun in captivity.

—*Size, then, Mademoiselle.*

—Griselle told me that he would be coming in that evening, but too late for me to stay up. And I said I would greet him in the morning, that we would have breakfast together on the veranda. Griselle was to tell him that. And I went to bed.

—*With the Juoun, Mademoiselle?*

—But of course with the Juoun. And it was taking its nourishment, with its feather tongue, when Papa came into the room. I believe he misunderstood the intent, though I cannot be sure. And there were many explosions and screams. I believe I was one who was screaming. And angry words. And names. And suddenly the Juoun lay on the floor. Dead. And Papa, too.

—*We come to the crux of it, then, Mademoiselle. What were the names and who did the shooting—for surely those are the "explosions" you mention. And what kind of angry words?*

—"Monster" and "Slut" and "Fornicator," M. Prosecutor, though how such could apply to either me or the Juoun I do not know. All I have read suggests to me that such names were injudiciously used. And my Papa would *never* use words injudiciously. And the Juoun was such a gentle beast. How could it kill my Papa? There must have been much agitation in other quarters. Perhaps Griselle. Perhaps an assassin.

—*Perhaps your father had since found out that the*

*Juoun was no pet at all but a sentient alien of powerful
sexual attraction and all his fears of your death in childbirth rose up to confront him. And his knowledge of the
laws forbidding trading in sentient beings.*

—No, no, M. Prosecutor, it was nothing like that. It
could be nothing like that. My father was not an injudi-
cious man. He was a gentle, caring man. He cared for
me so well; he gave me everything I needed.

—*Everything except your freedom, Mademoiselle. Everything except access to the world. He was a tyrant,
Mademoiselle, though you are too innocent to see that
and still, with such passion, defend him. A tyrant who,
when thwarted, could turn violent. A man so obsessed
with the sexual innocence of his only child, that he mis-
read a feeding for rape. A man so sure of his good name
in the field of trading that while he professed not to deal
in alien flesh, provided the same without proper licenses
as presents for his daughter. For in this instance he was
right, Mademoiselle, in this one thing. Autopsy evidence
proves that the Juoun was sentient. And a male. Though
as far as we could tell, only very newly come into its
prime. And still—like you, Mademoiselle, a virgin. But
with your evidence here and with what we know of your
Papa and his dealings and the nature of this "beast"—
we can now render our verdict as to intent.*

—But he did not know. He *could* not know.

—*The verdict is in. You can read the screen yourself,
Mademoiselle. Guilty of the death of a sentient being. By
intent. Your father will not be resurrected.*

—Alas, alas, and what will become of me now?

—*Mademoiselle, all will be well. You are his only heir
and he was a very rich man.*

—True. True. May I go now? I have much mourning
to do.

—*You may go, Mademoiselle. I sign off now.
O*&%CGB,HJCV Closure File 18027t5. Guilty.*

—Griselle, Griselle, come quick. It is done. The old
monster will be buried. And the Juoun, that liar, is gone,
too. Imagine all that time with me and it was female.

But once it started on Papa, it turned male. I could not have it. I *could not,* Griselle! The Juoun was mine. And then it was not. I killed it and I am glad. Now you and I can have everything we want. We can go anywhere. We can be everything to each other, just as you always said. Only first, give me the Juoun's touch. Here. And here. And there. Most especially there. You are almost as good as the Juoun already and much more fun. Though you do not have violet eyes. I will miss those violet eyes. But nothing else. I promise you.

DragNeuroNet

by John Gregory Betancourt

John Betancourt, a noted writer and former editor of *Weird Tales* magazine, currently edits and publishes his own line of science fiction books, Wildside Press.

At a dinner party for a politician and six wealthy political campaign contributors, the politician is murdered. No one else is in the house except a chef and a maid, both with perfect alibis. The only clues are the murder weapon (a steak knife), some gray hairs in the victim's hand (and most of the guests are graying), and two small coins placed on the victim's closed eyes.

The police force is shorthanded, and a robot policeman, compelled by his programming never to threaten a human, must trick the killer into confessing.

I was working autocide out of the Ride-O-Joy Retirement Home for Vehicles that day. A bunch of punk kids had kidnapped a Lincoln Galaxy and driven it through a delicatessen's plate-glass window. Then they broke into a sentient cash register with sledge hammers. Both the Galaxy and the cash register had been dead-on-arrival at the scrapyard: memory chips burned and fused, not even a chance for a transplant.

Of course, the kids had been real amateurs, out for fun and chump change. I'd nailed them within an hour, based on the clues they'd left behind: half of a 1997 Miami Marlin baseball card, a chewed wad of Double-Yummi bubblegum, and the billfold one Buck O'Grady had accidentally left in the back seat of the Galaxy.

When confronted at a posh local discotheque, the Dance Macabre, Buck had confessed and named his accomplices. Open and shut case; some are easier than others.

Now I was back at the Ride-O-Joy Retirement Home consoling the Galaxy's wife, a foxy little Jaguar who had seen better days. "I do not understand their motivations," she kept saying. "Why *my* husband? Why . . . why . . . why . . . ?"

She started going into a closed loop, repeating the question endlessly. I'd heard it a thousand times before. Why, she wanted to know? Because humans are irrational, that's all there is to it. That's life in the big city.

It's tough, but I'm a cop. I'm used to it now.

At 14:04, my next call came in.

"Murder report in your sector," the robo-dispatcher said. It fed me the address, an estate in a posh residential neighborhood. "Check it out."

"Ten-four," I said. "Proceeding now."

Disengaging myself from the still-whying Jaguar as politely as I could, I extended my wheels and cruised out from the vehicle retirement home. I took Broad Street up Goldberg Hill at top speed, lights flashing and siren wailing.

Humans would always be cruel to their machines, I thought, sure as rust and taxes. Since sentient machines had been granted full legal rights as U.S. citizens, we'd had nothing but trouble—both on the streets and in private homes. What would it be this time, I wondered? Electrocuted oven? Smashed smart-TV?

The ways of human violence against machines were legion. I'd only considered eight hundred and twelve possible murder scenarios when I reached the address, a three-story Victorian mansion set well back from the road, surrounded by ancient oaks and a three-meter-high electrified barbed-wire fence.

In the driveway, I retracted my wheels and switched to

interview mode, standing upright, assuming a more humanoid pose. Humans interacted better with me that way.

Then I rang the bell. I didn't have long to wait.

As humans went, the blonde who opened the door was a real knockout. She had a long, lean chassis, large frontal ornaments, and wore a low-cut sequined gown that revealed more of her legs than it hid. It seemed rather impractical garb, but then humans don't rust and so don't have to protect their skins the way we do.

"What in the name of heaven," said the blonde as she looked me over, "are you?"

"I am a Robot Investigation Unit. Per section 33-B of the New York City Revised Legal Code, I embody the full authority, responsibility, and legal force of a human police officer. A crime has been reported at this residence. You are required by law to assist me with my investigation. You are entitled to legal representation before answering any questions I pose, and your conversations with and in front of me are recorded as legal evidence."

"I see," she said with a little smile. "In that case, come right in, officer—Byron's going to get a real kick out of you. There's been a murder, you see."

"Thank you." I strode past her and found myself in a large, airy foyer. Tapestries hung on the walls; the floor consisted of black and white marble squares set in a checkerboard pattern.

"Through there," the blonde said, pointing to a large open doorway.

I went through, into a sitting room, with the blonde on my heels. Six humans, four males and two females, sat on sofas or chairs. None looked happy. One of the women was crying.

Swiveling my visor, I photographed them all. *Click, click, click.* I uploaded to the precinct computer; Records and Reports began their analysis, putting names to images and files to names.

As humans went, these were an odd group, three gray-haired men, one middle-aged brunette, one strikingly redheaded woman in an equally striking red gown, and the blonde behind me. It was the redhead who was crying, her long curled hair bobbing up and down in rhythm to her sobs.

They were not the sort of people who normally belonged together, I thought. Something unusual had brought them here. What? When each human's file had been downloaded to my memory, perhaps the answer would present itself. Or I could always ask.

"He never had an enemy in the world," the crying female kept saying. She was Caucasian, age circa 25–30, "Never had an enemy in the world. . . ."

She grew silent as she saw me. Then she began to tremble, her pale blue eyes as glassy as the Galaxy's had been, only with tears instead of glass. It must have been her appliance that was murdered, I thought. Humans often bonded with their favorite machines; once I'd seen a man throw himself onto the scrap truck as his dead stereo system was hauled away for recycling.

"Excuse me, ma'am," I told her. "A murder was reported here."

She began to cry again. I paused, waiting for her to finish, and took another survey of the others in the room. I had registered changes in their body language when I first entered: first one, then another had tensed. Several had forced themselves to relax. I'd seen nothing to point to a machine-killer.

"Come on, Sally," said one of the gray-haired Caucasian males. He touched her shoulder gently. "Everything's going to be all right."

"A crime has been reported at this residence," I said. "May I inquire who filed this report?"

"I did," said the blonde who had let me in. She lit a cigarette and blew smoke at my ducts.

"Name?"

"Abbott . . . Nichola Abbott." Her voice dropped to a silken whisper. "But you can call me Nikki, officer. Mrs. Carlisle seemed a bit out of it. Is that a crime?"

"No, it is not," I said. "Thank you, Nikki."

By then I had downloaded Nichola Abbott's file. She was a lawyer, it seemed, employed by Brackman, Brosnan, Beemer, and Schmidt. That's all it said; she'd spent her life on the right side of the law, at least so far.

I turned my attention to Mrs. Carlisle, who was snuffling delicately into a handkerchief. R-&-R had downloaded her file into my memory as well. Mrs. Sally Paulette Carlisle, age 24, had two outstanding traffic violations, both for exceeding the speed limit by more than 15 kilometers per hour, both dated from nearly two and a half years ago. *Not relevant.* I filed the information in short-term holding memory, but decided to make no mention of it. My job is murder, not traffic control.

"Ma'am?" I said.

"I just don't understand it," she said. "He never had an enemy. . . ."

"Ma'am, please," I said. "If I might see the body?"

The male next to Nikki Abbott stepped forward. Though he was gray-haired, he carried himself like a prize fighter, and he had the strong good looks normally associated with vid actors . . . only he wasn't smiling into a camera and hawking tooth-polish or shoes or refrigerators.

He snarled, "You damned tin thing—show some respect! Can't you see she's nearly in shock? We pay our taxes! Why don't you get back to the scrapyard and get some *real* policemen out here!"

"Your name?" I demanded.

"Byron van Osterland. I said—"

"I heard you," I cut in. In those two seconds I had run a full check on him: no outstanding wants or warrants for his arrest, though he had once been indicted for insider trading two years before (the case never went to trial). "Please, sit down, sir. You and the others must remain here until instructed otherwise."

"We're all important people—" he blustered.

"You are in the presence of a Robot Investigation Unit," I began, and went through my whole legal-cop spiel. "If you choose to disregard my instructions," I told him, "you may be subject to detention at police headquarters on charges of obstructing an official police investigation. You are entitled to legal representation before answering any questions I pose, however, and your conversations with and in front of me are recorded as legal evidence. Do you understand your legal rights and obligations?''

"Better listen up," Nikki said. "It's not kidding. It can legally haul you off to jail if you get in its way.''

Van Osterland set his jaw stubbornly anyway.

"Byron . . . *please*," Mrs. Carlisle said.

"Do you understand your legal rights?" I asked him again.

"Yes." Van Osterland sank down into an overstuffed armchair, his face a confusing mix of emotions. Anger and frustration seemed predominant. *Hostile to investigation.* I loaded that fact, too, into my holding memory.

I asked the other humans if they understood their rights as well. All said they did. Normally I wait until after I have seen the dead machine before going into legal matters, but considering van Osterland's reaction, this seemed the correct moment.

"Listen," said one of the gray-haired men. "I really can't afford to be involved in any sort of scandal. How about you let me go, and if you need me, my lawyer will be in touch?''

"Name?" I asked.

"Dmitri Popadous.''

I accessed his file. Popadous, it turned out, was a wealthy New Yorker of Greek descent, aged 49, with no wants or warrants out for his arrest. He owned a large shipping fleet and gave handsomely to many charities . . . and many political campaigns. He'd donated over a million dollars to the current President's first campaign. *Political power-broker,* I concluded. This case was definitely not your typical residential machine-murder.

"You will remain here for now," I said. I turned to Mrs. Carlisle. "Please show me the body."

Dabbing at her eyes, she rose and teetered for a moment. Her shoes, I noticed, had large transparent heels with fish swimming in them. With those huge heels clicking faintly on the hardwood floor, she led me back through the foyer and into a formal dining room. A crystal chandelier overhead filled the room with light. The table beneath it had been prepared for a dinner party: white lace tablecloth, fine gold-and-white china, cloth napkins, wine chilling in electric buckets full of simulated ice. Service was set for eight.

The body was there, too.

And it wasn't a machine.

Mrs. Carlisle gave a tremendous sigh. "There he is—my husband. *Dead.*"

For a long time—perhaps as much as three seconds—I did nothing at all. I couldn't. The enormity of the mistake was shocking.

To the best of my knowledge, no machine had ever been assigned a human murder to investigate. Humans, with their dull senses, slow reflexes, and ponderous information-gathering techniques, believe they are infinitely better at solving crimes involving humans: they mutter things like, "human intuition" and "human nature" to justify keeping their glory-work.

Robot Investigative Units were only added to the police force as a token gesture, after all—a sop thrown to the crowds of sentient machines. Robot cops like me—good cops, loyal to the police force, smarter and faster than any human—get the drudgery details no humans want. Like machine-murders.

Can machines *be* bitter? More than a few of us on the force, good cops and union members just like me, think humans should stick to what they do best: committing crimes, not solving them.

And now I'd been accidentally assigned to a human murder. It was the chance of a lifetime.

Of course I was going to milk it for all it was worth.

"What is the deceased's name?" I enquired politely.

"James Ford Carlisle."

There are certain names which, when fed into Records and Reports, bring police procedures out of their usual automated loops. "James Ford Carlisle" was, of course, one of those special names. I knew that even before I reported his murder and queried Records and Reports for his file.

Of course I'd already heard of him. James Ford Carlisle: prominent United States of North American Senator, environmental activist, multimillionaire philanthropist. His life was a long list of public works, charities, and service to his people. Likely enough, he would have been our next president.

I moved forward slowly. Carlisle, an elderly male Caucasian, sat at the far end of the table, his head tilted back at a sharp angle. The handle of a steak knife protruded from the underside of his jaw; the point had lodged somewhere in his brain. Two small metal disks, both nonmagnetic, lay on top of his eyes. The body's temperature registered at 23.2C, several degrees above the room's. He had been dead for at least an hour, probably more.

Rather than his file, though, the next thing I got in from the precinct was a slow-as-human-reflexes message. It was being hand-keyed on a dumb-computer console: RIU-3827, YOULL CONTINUE TO GATHER INFO FOR NOW. BACKUPS WILL ARIVE TO TAKE OVER INVESTIGATION SON/XXX SOON. ACNOWLEDGE.

Acknowledged, I fired back. I had perhaps fifteen minutes before glory-mongering humans arrived, I figured. Still, there was a lot I could do in fifteen minutes.

And, since this was the first human murder case a Robot Investigative Unit had ever had, and it was a major one, I knew I'd better handle it right if I expected another . . . if any machine expected another. Office politics are office politics; when you got a shot at power, you had to take it, whatever your body. I had to hurry if my chance was going to do any good.

"How long has he been dead?" I asked.

"I don't know," Mrs. Carlisle sobbed. "We found him about half an hour ago."

"Who found him?"

"Dmitri Popadous—" sniff, sniff, "—and Davy Eddington. They're both spending the weekend here."

"What relationship did they have to the deceased?"

"I . . . I guess you'd call them political supporters.

Jim was getting ready for a run at the Presidency, and he insisted I invite them all here.'' She blew her nose. ''He said he needed their support to win his next election. . . .''

Records and Reports had already downloaded the file on Eddington. I read it. Davis Jeremy Eddington was a Caucasian male, aged 54, a billionaire horse breeder from Kentucky . . . known to donate large sums of money for political campaigns.

''Please bring everyone in here,'' I told Mrs. Carlisle. ''I wish to interview them.''

''What about the servants?'' she asked.

''I will start with them.''

Swallowing, she nodded. She left through a different door than the one we'd entered, more composed now that she had a definite task to accomplish.

I examined the corpse more closely. Extending my visor on a long metal stalk, I photographed Carlisle from several angles. The metal disks on his eyes turned out to be old coins. Both of them had numeral tens, 1968 dates, and lettering I identified as Greek. When I tried to get information on them from Records and Reports, I found my datalink had been ''temporarily interrupted'' . . . humans, it seemed, didn't want me to solve the case without them. Typical.

The body had been stabbed twice in the chest, doubtless the killing wounds. Then the knife had been carefully inserted through the jaw and into the brain, and the coins placed over the eyes. Quite unusual.

I vacuumed the floor directly around the corpse, picking up a little dust, a few clothing fibers, and bits of lint: nothing very impressive. Then I opened the victim's two clenched fists—he might have been able to snatch a button or a bit of cloth from his murderer's clothing.

Sure enough, clutched in the corpse's left hand were three short gray hairs. I upped magnification on the hairs. No roots; all had been broken off of longer strands. I found it unlikely, knowing human hair and how it grows, that three hairs could have broken off during a fight in this manner.

Next I examined the hilt of the knife. It had blood on it, but enough bare wood showed for a quick ultraviolet scan. There were no fingerprints, nor even any smudge marks from gloves. It had been wiped clean.

The napkin beside the corpse's plate had been moved out of position. I turned it over and found a large smear of blood on the other side. The murderer had used the napkin to wipe the knife's hilt free of fingerprints—he hadn't worn gloves. That meant the murder hadn't been premeditated. Impulse crimes are generally sloppy, with clues all over the place. But how did that fit with coins on the eyes and broken gray hairs in the corpse's left hand?

A throat cleared behind me. A male and a female, both of Hispanic descent, both aged circa 30–35, stood in the doorway through which Mrs. Carlisle had passed moments before. The male was dressed in a white chef's outfit, the female in a maid's uniform. The male held the door open; the room behind him was filled with kitchen equipment.

"State your names," I said.

"José and Julia Lopez," the male said. "I am the cook. My wife is the maid."

"Can you explain where you were and what you were doing over the last two hours?"

"We were both in the kitchen," José Lopez said.

"Preparing the evening meal," Julia Lopez added.

"Together?"

"Yes," Julia said. "I always help with meals."

"Did you hear anything?"

"No," said José Lopez. "All the rooms in the house are soundproofed to prevent eavesdropping devices from picking up conversations. When he wanted us, Mr. Carlisle pushed a button under the corner of the table."

I looked. The button was there, all right. I thought it safe to dismiss the two; they seemed unlikely suspects.

"Return to your duties," I said. "You will be summoned if a further statement is required."

Then the seven humans I had seen earlier filed into the room like jury members about to return a verdict of guilty. They all looked angry and upset. I wasn't surprised; that seemed to be the normal mental state of most humans I encountered.

I had already read the files on Sally Carlisle, Nichola Abbott, Byron van Osterland, Dmitri Popadous, and Davis Jeremy Eddington. When I checked my holding memory, I found files on the other two had been downloaded before my datalink with Records and Reports had been interrupted.

Joan Veracruz-Eddington, Caucasian female, aged 55, had two citations for driving while intoxicated. There were no current wants or warrants for her arrest, however, and she had no profession listed. She was married to Davis Eddington.

Paul Trench Longfellow, Caucasian male, aged 48, also had no wants or warrants out for his arrest. He, too, had no profession on file. The rich seldom need them, I supposed.

All seven of them stood nervously clumped by the door. I told them what I had found so far, the coins and the three stray hairs.

"Greek coins?" van Osterland said in a wondering voice. "Isn't 'Popadous' a Greek name?"

Dmitri Popadous glared at him. "If you are insinuating that *I* committed this crime—"

"Not at all!" van Osterland said. "Greek coins on his eyes . . . it just seems curious to me. That's all."

"Mrs. Carlisle!" Dmitri Popadous said. "As your guest, I must protest this sort of treatment!"

Mrs. Carlisle just sobbed into her handkerchief. Her red hair somehow managed to stay elegantly coiffed.

"Is there a supply of old Greek coins in the house?" I asked.

Nikki took a drag on her cigarette and puffed smoke at me again. "Everyone knows Carlisle collects . . . *collected* . . . coins from all over the world. I'd be surprised if he didn't have a few from Greece."

"I know he does," Dmitri Popadous said. "He showed them to me last night." He must have realized how that sounded because he suddenly added, "He thought I could tell him more about them, I, uh, guess. I couldn't. I'm an American, never been to Greece in my life. You know."

"Where does he keep these coins?" I asked.

"In his study," Popadous said. "On the shelf behind his desk, in large leather binders."

"They are readily accessible?"

"I guess so," he said.

Nikki said, "Anyone could have walked in and taken a few, if that's what you mean. This place is a fortress on the outside, but it's wide open inside." She puffed more smoke at me; it hung like a gray-purple veil between us. "Carlisle used to say he hated to live in a prison. He was pretty chill for a senator, and believe me I've known *senators!*" She gave me a wink and a low chuckle.

"Yes," I said. "I believe you."

"What about the hairs?" van Osterland said. "Surely that's enough of a clue to solve the case, isn't it?"

"Yes, it is a clue," I said. "A forensics lab can compare the proteins they contain to those in the hairs of any suspect." I looked at Dmitri Popadous. "If gambling were legal, I would bet the proteins in these hairs match yours, sir."

He sputtered in rage. "How dare you—"

"Please, please," I said soothingly. "It's an easy thing to check. I have a small forensics lab built in. May I vacuum your head for any loose hairs?"

Dmitri Popadous stepped forward and bent at the waist. "Hurry up about it, you damned machine!" he snarled. "And when this is over, I'll buy you from the city and take an ax to you myself!"

I vacuumed his head, catching two complete hairs in my collection basket, roots and all, plus one broken hair like the ones taken from Senator Ford's hand. Quickly I ran a protein scan for comparison. As I had anticipated, the hairs matched. There could be no mistake.

I printed a report out on my built-in laser printer. When I handed it to Dmitri Popadous, he read it, then stared at me, speechless for the moment.

"Yes," I said. "The proteins match exactly."

Dmitri Popadous might well have been a leper, considering the others' reactions. They drew away from him with looks of disgust. David Eddington held his wife protectively; Byron van Osterland held Sally Carlisle.

Popadous stared at first one face, then another. "Please," he said. "You all know me! I—I didn't do it! I scarcely knew the senator—"

"Just a few more questions and my investigation will be complete," I said. "Mr. Popadous, was the victim right- or left-handed?"

"What? I don't know—"

"Everyone knew," said Joan Veracruz-Eddington in a hard voice. "He was left-handed. Mrs. Carlisle made a joke about it last night—about the weird scribbles Senator Carlisle made when he wrote his name."

"That's right," Byron van Osterland said quickly. "Sally said the bank kept questioning Jim's signature. We all laughed."

"One more question," I said. "Mr. Popadous, do you brush your hair after you bathe?"

"What's that got to do with anything?" Byron van Osterland demanded.

"Yes," Dmitri Popadous breathed, a trace of hope rising in his face. "Yes, I do brush my hair!"

"The investigation is complete," I said. "The pieces of the puzzle are all in place, except one. Allow me to explain the sequence of events.

"The murderer asked to see Senator Carlisle in private. They came into the dining room to talk. Whatever they discussed, it enraged them both. On an impulse, the murderer seized a knife and stabbed Mr. Carlisle twice in the chest. Then he fled the room in fear.

"A few moments later, he came back. He wanted to make it look like someone else had committed the crime. He chose to incriminate Mr. Popadous. He removed two Greek coins from Senator Carlisle's collection, placed them over the senator's eyes, and inserted the knife through Mr. Carlisle's jaw. It looks like a premeditated execution-style murder that way. Next, he placed three hairs taken from Mr. Popadous' hairbrush in the corpse's left hand as a clue.''

"That sounds pretty fantastic!" Nikki said.

"True," I answered. "However, the culprit made a series of mistakes. First, he took hairs from a hairbrush. All of the hairs in the corpse's hand had been broken by a stiff brushing; they could not have come off in a struggle. Perhaps the hairbrush will yield fingerprints; our murderer did not believe in wearing gloves. Since the culprit thought Mr. Popadous would be arrested, he had no reason to hide his touching the hairbrush. He has doubtless wiped clean the coin collection.''

"But what if he *did* wipe his fingerprints off the hairbrush?" Davis Eddington demanded. "What then?"

I continued, "His second mistake was wiping off the knife's handle. This not only meant the act was not premeditated, it meant his fingerprints were there, on the knife, to begin with. Furthermore, it means he must have gotten blood on his hands. Although he has doubtless washed them, minute traces of blood will still remain; forensic scientists will examine everyone's hands after you are all brought to the police station.''

Turning my visor, I looked at Byron van Osterland. In my experience, sloppy murders usually involved human emotions—the most frequent ones being love and jealousy. From the familiar way he held Mrs. Carlisle, I thought the two of them might well be having an affair.

I asked van Osterland, "Will the forensics examination be necessary, sir?"

"No." He bit his lip and shook his head. "I forgot to wipe off the hairbrush, like you said.''

There was a shocked gasp from everyone in the room. Mrs. Carlisle pushed away from van Osterland, crying now, tears streaming down her cheeks, her breath coming in ragged gasps. Paul Longfellow let her lean on his shoulder. "Shh," he said, "there now, Sally. It's going to be all right. . . .''

"It is my duty to arrest you for the murder of Senator Carlisle," I told van Osterland.

Nikki handed him a business card. "Call me if you need a lawyer," she said.

I began to inform him of his rights just as the doorbell rang. The human policemen had arrived . . . too late to grab the glory.

As it later turned out, Byron van Osterland and Sally Carlisle had been having quite a torrid little love affair behind Senator Carlisle's back. Though he was nearly three times her age, he'd been attracted by her striking good looks. She'd been equally attracted by his power and money. But then she'd gotten involved with the far younger and far richer Byron van Osterland. It was a love triangle fit for scandal rags.

Ultimately Sally Carlisle planned to leave her husband for Byron van Osterland. Van Osterland, a longtime friend of the senator's, wanted to keep their political and business relationship as friendly as possible. The two men had discussed the situation alone in the dining room. An argument broke out; van Osterland stabbed Senator Carlisle in a blind rage, then tried to cover it up. It was as simple as that.

The case had everything the media could have wanted: sex, power, money, friend betraying friend. All that plus a new angle: a robot cop making the bust.

Needless to say, I got quite a bit of attention as the first Robot Investigation Unit to solve a major murder case, and I had cracked it within twenty minutes of my arrival on the scene of the crime, despite faked evidence.

I became quite a hero that week. Of course, I used my air-time to cite a few statistics . . . how RIUs solved ninety-five percent of their cases within twenty-four hours (compared to human police solving eighty-four percent within six months). How you couldn't successfully threaten, bribe, or kill an RIU. How we saved human lives by taking human policemen off the streets and putting them behind desks, where they belonged.

You never can tell what the end result will be, but public opinion now seems in favor of letting Robot Investigation Units run all police investigations—human or machine. Of course, we're quick to explain, we'll need to keep all current human policemen on the job for the extra paperwork we'll generate, with our added efficiency and speed. That's only fair. After all, we were forced to join the Fraternal Brotherhood of Police Persons, and we're strictly by-the-book cops. And that means watching out for our brother policemen, whatever we think of them.

BAUBLE

by David Gerrold

David Gerrold, who writes best-selling science fiction, teleplays and screenplays with equal facility, is also the editor of a number of anthologies.

This is a synopsis rather than a problem:
Give me a bittersweet mood piece in which a cynical private eye of the Philip Marlowe type traces a lost necklace to an alien thief, who requires it for spiritual/metaphysical reasons that lead the private eye to forgo his much-needed fee and tell his employer that he can't solve the case.

At first, I thought her hair was on fire.

The light danced around her face in orange waves. Red and yellow highlights sparked and flashed. Biogenetic cellular-holography. She was a walking celebration.

I stopped what I was doing, which was easy, because I wasn't doing anything. I was sitting and listening to myself die. I opened my mouth, realized I didn't know what to say, closed it again and waited.

"May I come in?"

"You're already in."

The door slid shut behind her.

She wore an oil-slick daycoat. It parted for an instant and my heart stopped. Naked shimmersilk. Sprayed on. She did it deliberately. I was doomed and we both knew it.

"May I sit down?"

There were only two chairs in the room. There was no other furniture. I didn't need furniture. Furniture is for

resisting gravity. I've never had a problem with gravity.
Levity, maybe. Gravity, never.

I waved a hand toward the other chair, a barely per-
ceptible gesture. She poured herself into it. I envied the
chair.

I cleared my throat, tried to clear my mind, and asked,
"What is it you want?"

"I was told you might be able to help me." Her voice
had the same smoky rasp as a glass of hundred-year-old
bourbon. You could die in it. "I'm looking for a bauble."

I coughed mechanically. Another part of me slipped
and died. Somehow, I got the words out. "I'm afraid
you've been misinformed. I deal in trade goods."

Translation: when there's nothing else, I fence.

I was fencing now. We were both fencing. A different
sense of the word. She was winning. I was dying. Faster
than ever now.

"It's *very* important to me," she insisted. "It's worthless to anybody else, but it's very important to me. It's
a necklace." The violet huskiness in her voice was so
rough you could climb it.

"I'd like to help you, but—" A lie. I wanted nothing
more than to be somewhere else. Anywhere else. Parts
of me were trying to respond. No. Not right. Parts of me
were demanding that other parts respond. Parts that no
longer existed. Or operated. Or cared. "—I'm not what
you think I am."

"I know what you are," she said, all honeysuckle and
razors. She stopped. She studied me for a moment. Her
eyes changed. She knew she didn't have to pretend with
me.

She pulled a silver cigarette case from her pocket. I
watched as she opened it, a graceful unfolding gesture.
Her fingers danced a little ballet, selected a cigarette,
and lifted it to her molten lips. Her nails gleamed like
ice.

She waited. I made no move to light it. She lifted an
eyebrow at me.

"No, I don't mind if you smoke," I said, pretending

to misunderstand. Discourteous, perhaps, but energy conservation ranks higher than courtesy to a dying thing.

Over the dancing flame, she said, "I was told that you sometimes manage private investigations. This necklace was taken from me. I need it back. I've followed it across five worlds. I'll do *anything* to get it back." The emphasis was heart-stopping. "You understand me, don't you?"

She was a fantasy of pink and gold magic, and she had eyes as green as ocean dreams. I understood. But it was empty understanding. Too late.

Without breaking the connection from her eyes to mine, I shook my head slowly.

She inhaled, held it, closed her eyes, opened them, exhaled, glanced sideways over at me. "Does the name Kilrenko mean anything to you?"

I looked at my fingernails. They needed cleaning. I looked at her fingernails. They were made of diamond. They glittered. They were silver knives. I thought of the scratches those nails could leave on a man's back and decided I was safer thinking about anything else. Almost anything else.

"Never heard it before," I said. She didn't believe me either.

I knew who she was. I couldn't *not* know. There were only a few of them. And they were all famous. She was one of the ones they called the Alluras. They said the Alluras were the most beautiful. I believed it.

A hundred years ago, I sold off the last part of my humanity. For the first time, I was beginning to regret it. I could almost remember what I lost, what it felt like. I could *almost* wish for it again.

"When I was a little boy—" she began. "Yes," she said, to my look. "They start with boys. There are good reasons for it. And no—" she said, to my unasked question, "I've never once stopped to wonder if I've missed anything."

That was the difference between us. Light-years.

She shrugged out of her coat. I watched in fascination. It slid off her shoulders and carelessly down her sides.

She juggled the cigarette from one hand to the other. It was a performance for an audience of one.

Too bad it was wasted.

Maybe not.

She wasn't stupid. She knew. And she knew that I knew, too.

"When I was a boy," she began again, comfortable now, "they told me that one of the reasons I was selected was because of my persistence. My refusal to quit. That's part of the transformation process. So much of it is beyond your imagination." Another languorous puff on her cigarette. Tongue against teeth. Lips pursing in a seductive promise. The cigarette moaned and died happy. "Yes, I'm completely female now. In fact, I'm more female than if I had been genetically designed and born female. But getting here requires persistence. I have persistence. *Do you understand what I'm saying?* I want that necklace. Whoever has it. Wherever it is. No questions asked. I'm going to have it back."

"What makes it so valuable?" I asked. My throat was dry.

"That's not your concern."

"It is if you want my help."

Silence. She considered my words. "I couldn't even begin to explain it," she said.

"Try me."

Her eyes narrowed. "All right. It looks like a simple strand of silver beads. Nothing really extraordinary about it at all. If you didn't know what it was, you'd assume it was just a trinket. Polished volcanic rock."

"What is it?" I asked.

She dropped her cigarette to the floor. She placed the toe of one bare foot on it and scuffed it out in one violent movement. She brought her eyes back to mine. They had changed color. They were black, with little glimmers of crimson at the back of them. "It's me," she admitted. "It's the part of me that doesn't walk around."

"Memory beads?" I asked.

"Of a sort." She conceded. "Memory, yes. Processing, too. And . . . *more.*"

"It's an identity platform, right?"

"You've seen it." A statement, not a question.

I shrugged. "I might have heard about it."

"Without it," she said, and her voice took on a terrifying quality, "I'm dead. The body walks around, but the soul—the soul is in the necklace." She looked at me perceptively. She stood up and turned around. Slowly. If the shimmersilk could hug her any closer, it'd be behind her.

"Look at me," she whispered. "Do you think it's right that a body like this should be walking around without a soul?"

Long pause. "You play dirty, lady."

"So they tell me."

"I'm dying," I said.

"I knew that before I walked in."

I tapped the chair arm. My fingers clicked like granite. "I began two centuries ago," I said. "I'm wearing out. I'm running on empty. Do you know that term. It's an anachronism now. It means there's nothing left. It means that I'm running on my own momentum."

She listened politely. She had time. I didn't. I talked anyway.

"When I started, I had three brains. Now, I have one. I have no backup. If I lose a memory, it's gone forever. And the *last* one is wearing out. I'm losing memories every day, a bit at a time, a bit at a time, a bit at a time—" I stopped myself, rebooted the thought.

"Yes," she said. Then she added, "Please don't ask me to be sorry."

"I know," I said. "You don't do sorry."

"I can't help you," she said slowly.

"Actually, you can."

"I won't," she clarified. "I don't do *sympathy*."

I tapped the chair arm again. A portion of the wall beside me opened. A drawer slid out. She came alert. She didn't move a muscle, but she came completely, totally, *absolutely* alert.

I reached over and pulled out a self-destruct box just

large enough to hold a dagger. "I'm the only one who can open this," I said. "If anyone else tries—"

She nodded, knowingly.

I opened the box and faced it toward her. "Is this what you're looking for?"

Her glance dropped to the box. Her pupils expanded. Her eyes met mine. Her face lit up—she *glowed*—as if just being near the beads was enough to complete the connection. Her voice fell to an almost inaudible whisper. "Thank you," she said.

I shook my head. "If you take them, I'll die." I tapped my forehead meaningfully. "I was hoping to have those beads wiped and installed. They're not a perfect match, but—"

"They'll never work for you," she said. "Not for you, not for anyone. They won't work for anyone but me."

"So I discovered. I was hoping to sell them instead." I closed the box again. "I'm waiting for my buyer. Perhaps he'll help you."

Her glow faded. "He isn't coming," she said with quiet finality.

I didn't ask. She didn't volunteer.

"So what do we do now?" I said.

She studied me.

I studied her. My view was infinitely better than hers.

At last, she said, "If I had the resources, I'd pay you. Instead, I can offer you only my gratitude. For whatever that's worth."

"It's worth my life," I said.

She smiled. A little joke. Very little. But it was her first real smile. She nodded.

I opened the box again.

She stepped over to me, the closest she'd come to me yet. I stiffened as she leaned forward and lifted the beads out of the box. She fastened them around her neck. They began to glow. But she began to *blaze*. If she had been beautiful before, now she was blinding. I had to avert my eyes.

She approached me. With one elegant silver finger, she tilted my chin upward. She lowered her face to mine. "I will never forget you.'' I felt parts of my autonomic circuitry overloading. She pressed her lips against mine. I might have died.

I didn't. But I might have.

She straightened. She retrieved her coat. And left in silence.

I sat alone in the slanting gray sunlight and listened to my breath rasp and my heart throb. Amazed. I still lived.

The Allura models were supposed to be the most elegant practitioners of personal entertainment in the spiral arm. That was an ancillary joy. You died happy. The Alluras were also the most successful assassins.

I'd probably committed high treason, letting her recover herself. God knew who was going to die. It wasn't going to be me though. I'd bought my life with the bauble. What was left of it.

I couldn't wish her well. She was no more alive than I. But, for two dead people, for just one instant, we'd struck one hell of a spark. Whatever the cost, it had been worth it.

I sat. I listened to myself die. I smiled.

ASHES TO ASHES
by Beth Meacham

Beth Meacham is the Executive Editor of Tor Books. Prior to that, she edited science fiction for Berkley Books, Ace Books and Baronet Books.

Minimal information problem: an asteroid miner is found dead in her plexidome bubble. Everything seems to be in order, except that her toothbrush is missing, and there is a small puddle of fluid on the floor. The body shows no signs of violence, no marks or lesions—but she had hit it rich the week before, and murder has to be considered, especially since she was a young woman in excellent health.

Was she murdered or not?

The secure circuit chimed, diverting me again from the Involuntary Termination paperwork that had to be finished and transmitted before 2400. I accepted the call. The forward antenna connection was still a little loose despite the repairs I'd gone Outside to make, so the transmission was coming in a little noisy. This patrol ship was falling apart. If Officer Doyle didn't make sergeant soon, we'd be breathing space, unless we choked on our own wastes first. A promotion meant a new patrol vessel.

"Licensed Cyborg number 20812 speaking for Officer Benjamin Doyle," I said. I pride myself on always following procedure, no matter how distracted I might be. You never knew who would be on the line; when you were handling licenses and permits for a whole sector of the Belt, it paid to be polite at first.

"Hey, John!" It was Officer Martin, a friend of Officer Doyle's. They had attended the IntraSystem Police Academy together, and there was money down on who would be promoted first. Officer Martin was not a formal person. "How you doin'? Get Sherlock on the line—I've got a great one for him."

"Yes, Ma'am," I said. "Officer Doyle is sleeping. Shall I wake him?"

"Sleeping? What time is it?" She glanced away from the vid pickup. "Oh, 22. Sorry. Well, this is too good to wait. Wake the bastard up. He'll thank you in the morning."

I sketched a gesture of acquiescence. "This may take a few minutes, Ma'am. Will you wait?"

"No problem, John. There's nothing else happening in five billion cubic kilometers of space. I might as well look at a picture of your ship for a change."

I looked with some dismay at the screen full of unfinished paperwork as I disconnected and pushed back from the counter. It would have to get done somehow. I still had two hours. Involuntary Termination permits were routine, but time-consuming; there were so many records to trace and verify. I preferred the asteroid claims, the travel and residence permits, the export manifests. Of course, the Removal of Asteroid Body From Orbit forms were a headache, too.

I rolled aft to Officer Doyle's sleeping area.

Members of the IntraSystem Police Force endured a life of nearly intolerable boredom, with only the promise of brief periods of extreme danger sometime in the future. Low grade officers were issued the oldest police vessels, and set to patrol their assigned sectors of the asteroid belt. Patrol consisted of maintaining position in the belt, monitoring all transmissions, boards and chat lines, trafficking ships and asteroid bodies, and facilitating the paperwork that kept track of the lives and deaths of the wide-spread population of the Belt.

Benjamin Doyle was a young man, still in his forties. Sometimes he seemed like a child to me, but he was well-trained and very intelligent. He treated me better than the law said he had to treat a 148-year-old cyborged ex-cop. If he had a fault, it was impatience, and his obsession with becoming a detective. He talked about it too much; too many people knew that he thought of himself as some kind of reincarnated Sherlock Holmes. That's what Officer Martin was calling about—somewhere some puzzle had come to light, and they were going to challenge Officer Doyle to solve it. It was a game.

Officer Doyle was not happy to be waked.

"Ben, we've got this great corpse. I thought of you right away; you're going to have some trouble with this one." Officer Martin was gloating. I could see it in the slight crinkling of her brown eyes, and the barely suppressed smile on her round face.

"Diana, slow down. Do you mean to tell me that there's been a murder in your sector?" Officer Doyle was waking up fast. He'd never had a murder before. Death in the belt was usually by mishap, occasionally by stupidity. The worst we'd seen in decades was a mine manager who had gone so stir-crazy that he killed his dome-mates. There was no mystery there.

"Well, what we have is a death. It might be murder. It's one of those closed-room scenes you're always on about. I've got a five hundred yen bet with Jomi that you can't figure it out."

Officer Doyle hit record. "Diana, tell me all about it. Do you have holos for me? I'll need all the site recordings, you know."

She smiled. There was some trick here—Officer Martin usually bet on Officer Doyle, not against him.

"You can have everything except the autopsy. What you gotta tell us is how the stiff bought it. Deal?"

"Deal. Transmit."

Officer Martin reached down, activating the upload. It was a lot of data, and the system had to repeat a couple dozen blocks. That antenna; the whole lousy ship. It took minutes to get the files clear and unpacked.

* * *

The scene was the typical asteroid miner's biosphere—a semi-opaque sealed bubble-dome, dropped by the carrier ship into a small crater on a fairly large rock. The 'lock had been forced open. Officer Doyle studied the exterior holos carefully, tagging all the footprints in the dust for comparisons. He even rotated the image to look at the side of the dome away from the access port—fortunately, whoever had snapped the views had taken one from above. There were only three sets of prints, and two of them led back to the patrol ship. Officer Doyle's eyebrows went up.

"First hypothesis is eliminated, John," he said. He often talked to me that way when he was puzzling out some mystery. I was not to respond unless he asked me a direct question. "No one else was on that rock."

He accessed the interior holos. The victim was lying crumpled on the floor in the workroom area of the dome, near the ore sample analysis kit. The first view showed only booted feet and legs and a swell of hip covered by a light-weight undersuit. The second view showed that, surprisingly, this miner was female. Officer Doyle let a low-toned whistle escape him. She had dark, fine, razor-cut hair, and delicate Oriental features. Although she didn't look as if she were more than 60 or so, there was a network of wrinkles on her face, particularly around the eyes and mouth—this was a woman who hadn't smiled very much in her life. Perhaps it wasn't surprising, after all, to find her alone on a rock in the Belt. Her eyes were closed; there didn't seem to be any sign of violence, either around her or on her. There was a small puddle of some clear liquid near her mouth. Officer Doyle frowned, and tagged it. He went over her body inch by inch, looking for any sign of the cause of death, or even any anomaly. Not a mark on her. She looked like a robot that had had the power suddenly shut off, assuming that anybody made robots that looked like beautiful angry women.

"Hmph. Now we know why Diana put her money down against me. The autopsy is the only thing that's going to tell us the cause of death here. Unless . . . John, let's have the site survey."

That was a different file. I opened it, and Officer Doyle

settled back to absorb the details of the dead woman's living quarters. The first thing he checked was the atmospheric composition. It was normal; everything in balance, no toxic gases, no aerosol poisons, not even much in the way of bacteria. Normal. He checked to see if the investigating crew had taken surface samples from the dead woman's skin. They had, but she was clean. There wasn't even surface bacteria on her—she must have just come from the cleanser. Clean skin, clean clothes, clean air; and the bubble and its contents looked as bright and fresh as if they were new.

"Sir," I ventured, "how long had the victim been on that site? May I check the permit record for you?"

"Good idea, John," he replied absently. "Do that. It does look clean, doesn't it? Cleanser next, and then inventory, I think. . . ."

He was completely absorbed. I rolled away to the galley, and started some coffee. It was clear that Officer Doyle wasn't going back to bed. I still had that IT permit to transmit which wouldn't really take more than another ten minutes. Than I could run a trace on the dead woman. It might be useful.

Her name was Kitten Rodriguez Yang. If I still had eyebrows, I would have raised them at that. She had apparently paid her own boost fees up from Mars—at least, all the credit transfers came from an account in her name. Rodriguez had been in the Belt since 2183, hopping from rock to rock. One nice thing about a place like the Belt, at least from a law enforcement point of view: hardly anyone could move without leaving a hell of a trail. There just weren't many opportunities for private transportation. She'd bought that new bubble and kit in '87; she was some clean-fiend—I'd never seen five-year-old equipment look so good. Of course, I'd never really looked at life-support that belonged to the guy it was supporting . . . nearly everyone in the Belt was under contract, using company supplied equipment. I guess it made a difference. I tracked her from rock to rock. She'd filed half a dozen small claims in nearly ten years, and one big one six years ago. That must have financed the new kit. I wondered why she had stayed in the belt after that strike. It was a huge, heavy metal-bearing asteroid, enough to set anyone up for life on Mars, or even Earth. But she'd sold it to TransSolar Mines just like she sold the others, for a quarter of what it was worth. Maybe she just liked it out here. She had been dropped on the rock where she died only six weeks before, and she hadn't left it. She wouldn't, now.

I noticed that her credit account was carrying a lot of communications charges. She was probably a chatnet junkie like the rest of the miners out here. I logged in on Officer Doyle's official account, and set the system to sort all of Rodriguez's posts for the past six weeks. There were hundreds, no surprise; I told the Net to download them to us. Officer Doyle could read all about the victim's last days when he was ready.

Officer Doyle thanked me when I brought him the coffee. I told him that I'd done the trace, and that I'd accessed the nets for a record of Rodriguez's messages.

"I may not need them, but it can't hurt. Good job."

"Thank you, Sir. Have you found anything interesting in the inventories?"

"Well, it's not so much what I've found that's interesting. It's what I can't find. Look—" he pivoted his stool suddenly toward me. "We've got an asteroid miner, a prospector. She's been out here for a while, judging by her samples file."

"Almost ten years, Sir."

"Exactly. Ten years out alone, on and off of rocks, grubbing under the surface. She's bringing all kinds of bits and pieces of stuff into her bubble for assaying. She's lived in this biosphere for ten years—"

"Five years, Sir. She bought it five years ago."

"Exactly. Five years in it, breathing in, breathing out, washing, recycling, eating . . . and do you know what?"

"What, Sir?"

"This little biosphere is as clean as if she had moved into it the day before she died."

"She seemed very tidy, Sir."

"Yes. Very. Now, John, look at this." He popped up

a view of the bubble's hygiene area. There were scrub sponges hanging on the wall and the cleanser was set on high. There was a bottle of antibacterial spray in the corner. The waste-catch was closed. Under the standard mirror was an old-fashioned wood and bristle brush, and a comb that looked like mottled plastic. There were large bottles of moisturizer, anti-bacterial powders, eyedrops, and a water carafe. And there was a small tool kit.

"Do you notice anything, John?"

"It's very clean and tidy, Sir."

Office Doyle shook his head slightly. "Anything else?"

"The brush is certainly old-fashioned. Not the sort of thing I'd expect from a miner."

"Yes, it's an antique. And especially odd given that her hair was cut so short. Anything else? What isn't there?"

He was giving me every chance to see what he had obviously seen. He was generous—he wanted me to share the excitement. His brown eyes glowed, his aquiline nose flared slightly. Those expressive hands were moving nervously, clutching slightly at the air.

"No, Sir. I'm sorry." I wondered what it was.

"There is no toothbrush or rinse. Nothing for cleaning the mouth and teeth. There is no toilet tissue or kleenex. There are no vaginal cleansers. There is nothing, in fact, to indicate that this woman who was so fastidious about her skin and hair and clothes and environment paid the slightest attention to anything that might come out of her body. Why do you suppose that is?"

"I don't know, Sir. It's very odd. Why would anyone take such things?"

"Perhaps they were never there."

I froze for a second. "Sir?"

"Look here, John." He shifted the holoview again, back to the body. "This little puddle." The tag flashed. He keyed on it, and brought up the analysis of the material. "Synthetic lubricant."

I knew that stuff well. It flowed through my own joints and bearings. "Sir, are you saying that a cyborg murdered this woman?"

"No. I'm saying that this isn't a murder. The 'victim' is a cyborg."

It wasn't possible. She was on the record as a human being; she had bank accounts, travel papers, property. She was young. And she looked completely human. No one was cyborged and left to look human—there were laws against it. The legal process was so complex, and the cost of even the simplest implants so high, that most cyborgs were owned by the big corporations, or by the government. Take someone like me. I was a cop for forty years, and a good one. I traveled the system, I had responsibilities, I had experience. It was a life worth living. Then the accident. I had a choice: I could be retired back to Earth on a lousy little pension, and live out the rest of my life on a floater chair, along with the other useless geezers. Or I could sign my rights away and become a cyborg. I always felt like I belonged to the Service; it didn't seem much different when that became literally true. Of course, I lost all my rank—no human being could be made to answer to a cyborg. But the Service knew what to do with my experience. They issued me to promising young officers, to keep them on the straight path, and help them out in a quiet kind of way. Benjamin Doyle was my fourth. He was by far the most interesting.

Most cyborgs weren't like me, of course. The majority were corporate soldiers who reached mandatory retirement and had to choose between cyborging and fifty years of increasing decrepitude. Modern medicine could keep people healthy and active for about 90 years—after that, it could only keep them alive. There were a lot of human veggies down on the planets; there was a lot of incentive to sign away your rights and go on working. Even the ore carriers looked good by comparison.

But the law was clear that cyborgs weren't human anymore. And they weren't permitted to look human. Or pass for human. If this Kitten Rodriguez Yang was cyborged, then she was illegal in more ways than were obvious. Her owners were in big trouble. The fact that someone with her key code had terminated her probably wouldn't be enough to avoid the fines.

"The answer is just that there isn't any murder here," Officer Doyle was saying. "The cause of death was remote circuit disruption, by whoever held her key codes."

He looked so satisfied, pleased with how quickly he'd solved the mystery. It was fast—it was only 2400 now.

"Sir?" I hesitated to bring it up, but I had to. "I don't think that it's so simple. Who did it? Who did she belong to? She's a completely illegal model. And how did she get up to the Belt in the first place?"

Office Doyle just stared at me. Then he shook his head and stood up.

"You are exactly right, John. As usual. The simple answer is just the first answer, and it opens more questions than we had when we started. I'm going back to bed. Just leave everything the way it is, and shut down yourself for a while. We'll start tracking the real questions tomorrow."

As I linked into the navigation and life-support monitoring systems, I thought how few young officers would be wise enough to take that kind of advice from me. Benjamin Doyle would go far in the IntraSystem Police Service.

I came out of dream-sleep when Officer Doyle woke, alerted by the monitors in his area. My dreams had been disturbing, full of images of Kitten Rodriguez Yang. I couldn't get my mind around the idea of that lovely woman as a cyborg. If her skin was her own, then she was far too young and healthy to have signed away her life.

The secure line chimed. Officer Doyle accepted the call before I could detach from the navigation checks.

"Diana," he said, "I was expecting to hear from you."

"Hope you had a pleasant sleep-shift, Ben," Officer Martin said too casually. "Did you look at the puzzle?"

"I did. We should tie Jomi into this circuit, if you want my answer now."

"Now? You're shittin' me. You haven't solved it yet."
Officer Martin's face was a study in indignation.

"No, I haven't solved all of it," Officer Doyle said
slowly.

"Well, then. No need to get Jomi Haavi out of bed.
You just keep at it, Ben. Every hour brings me closer to
500 yen." She smiled like a cat, reassured that she was
going to win this bet.

"Diana," Officer Doyle said, "I want unofficial access to your permits and claims file. I need to check
some of Rodriguez's transactions."

"Well. I see you've gotten as far as what her name
was. How long have you been at it, Sherlock?"

Officer Doyle gestured impatiently, opened his mouth
to say something, then closed it again. He sighed. "Diana, can I have the access code?"

"Sure thing, Sherlock. I'll set you up. Let me know
if you figure out whodunit." Officer Martin was grinning
like a maniac when the connection was broken.

"She is an annoying woman, John."

"Yes, Sir."

"As soon as her access codes come in, I want you to
find every record and transaction tagged to that piece of
rock, and every file that has Rodriguez's name mentioned
in it." He paused. "Don't take the autopsy report. We
don't need it, and I want Diana to lose this bet."

"Yes, Sir. I'll make sure she knows that I didn't copy
it."

Officer Doyle grinned, and settled down with coffee
and breakfast to read over the chat line files I had captured last night.

I ran through all the pending requests we had. There
weren't many, fortunately, and nothing I couldn't handle
myself. I wouldn't have to try to lead Officer Doyle back
to his duty just yet.

Officer Martin's ship sent me an access code and pass-
word. I got a good connection after a couple of tries, and
did a quick sort through the files, copying everything that
looked promising. Rodriguez's autopsy was blocked to
me. So much for honor.

I informed Officer Doyle that I had all the files he had requested. He nodded and told me to see if I could find any records on Rodriguez that would trace her movements before she arrived in the Belt. He clearly didn't expect to find any, and neither did I. An illegal cyborg like that wasn't likely to have left any trace at all on Earth or Mars, at least not under the same name and ID.

I pulled the oldest documents we had gotten on the first sweep—the 2183 Belt travel permit, issued on Luna. I linked into the System archives. I hoped that the antenna was going to be stable enough to hold a signal all the way to Mars long enough to get any useful information. The System archives were labyrinthine, but complete—it just took a lot of patience to find what you wanted. I had had about a hundred years to find my way around. I got into the travel permit section quickly, and then had to wait while my request for access was sequenced in. I keyed in the permit number, requesting the documents on which the permit had been issued. I scanned them as copies were uploaded to me. Credit account verifications, insurance certificates, medical certification, IntraSysterm Police clearances, birth certificate; if any of these documents were genuine, they would be useful. Obviously, the medical certificates were forged. I issued follow-up commands on the credit verifications and the birth certificate.

Rodriguez's credit was backed by banks on Luna and Earth. I requested her account records up to the issuance of the travel documents—they had already been released into the records. While those were being searched and compiled, I checked the birth certificate. It had been issued on Earth in 2103, in Singapore. If it was real, Rodriguez had been only 89. I decided to take a chance, and sent a quick, comprehensive inquiry to Earth. All her medical records would be on file somewhere, and an investigative inquiry might be enough to get them sent up to me.

The data circuit chimed, indicating that the banking records had come in. I started scanning through them. When she applied for a travel permit up to the Belt, Rodriguez had had only 2000 yen available to her, but she also had the price of her transport upsystem in a blocked account, and the price of a good secondhand kit also blocked off. Interesting setup—the kind that you often saw with indentures working out a contract. I couldn't find any record of an actual indenture, though I wasn't expecting one, at that point. Activity on her account for the five years before she came to the Belt was extremely odd.

"Sir?" I hesitated, but decided I had to show Officer Doyle.

He looked up from the transcripts.

"Sir, I have the banking records from fifteen years ago, and they are most peculiar. If I may?"

"Go ahead, John. What have you found?"

I showed him the records. Rodriguez's account showed deposits from various sources—corporations and individuals—in amounts of between 500 yen and 10,000 yen, on a nearly weekly basis. Quite an impressive income. But every time a large deposit came in, it was moved out within a day, and always to the account of one Simon O'Neil. There were also monthly transfers from O'Neil's account into Rodriguez's. Other transfers out were small, mostly restaurants and boutiques, electronics and network access. She didn't seem to stay in one place for very long. She didn't pay any rent.

"John, I think you've found the tracks of whoever she belonged to," said Officer Doyle. "Can you get the bank records of this O'Neil character?"

"I'll certainly try, Sir."

"Good. I've found something very interesting in the transcripts you copied from the chatlines. It seems she had found a big vein of iridium on that rock where she was terminated. She was quite amusing about it, saying that she'd been probing and sampling every little rock she could get to, and then there it was literally under her feet. It sounds like a very big hit indeed. Can you find out when she filed the claim?"

I took an instant to review my memory, making sure I was right. "Sir, she didn't file. Officer Martin's records don't contain any Asteroid Mineral Claim forms, either from her, or on that asteroid.''

Officer Doyle frowned intently. "Now, that's very odd indeed. Very odd.''

''Sir, the other thing is that for the past ten years, there have been no transfers on her account involving Simon O'Neil. All we have are mineral rights transfers to TransSolar Mining, at below market value.''

Officer Doyle thought for a moment, then said "Let me see a list of board members and executive-level employees of TransSolar. And trace Mr. O'Neil for me.''

I was unable to find any travel documentation for Simon O'Neil after 2183. the same year that Kitten Rodriguez Yang boosted up to the Belt. I asked Officer Doyle if he thought that Rodriguez had killed him.

''Maybe. There is that possibility, remote though it is. It depends on whether she was cyborged ten years ago, or not. If she was, then of course it isn't likely that she could successfully kill someone who held her key codes. Assuming that he held them.''

I nodded, but kept my thoughts to myself. Anyone capable of concealing the fact of being a cyborg might be capable of anything. Officer Doyle looked on this as an interesting puzzle. But it was far more than that. I wondered how many of the miners in the Belt were secretly cyborged. How many people in the System might be. It had never before occurred to me that someone could live forever as a human being.

We were distracted at that point by a call from Captain Wu, wanting some routine information. I was reminded of our duties, and of the ten-day reports that were due. Officer Doyle put aside the puzzle until the shift's work was done. Attention to duty was weighted heavily in the promotion reviews, and Officer Doyle's enthusiasms were already too well known.

I disconnected from calculating orbital perturbations for the report to find Officer Doyle talking to Officer Martin again. She sounded quite upset.

''Ben, dammit, what have you been doing?''

"Me? Not a thing. Looking into that problem you handed me, in my off-hours."

"You've been messing around in my files," she accused. "You've erased data!"

Nothing could be more insulting.

"Sir, if I might interrupt?" Officer Doyle nodded permission. "Officer Martin, at Officer Doyle's instructions I sorted your files and copied data out. If there has been any difficulty, it is due to my errors. However, it seems very unlikely to me that I have made any data-handling errors."

She looked thoughtful. Officer Martin was impulsive, but not foolish.

"Then, John, do you have any idea why all my sector records on this death are corrupted, and why I've just had an official inquiry as to the purpose of and justification for requests for information which I haven't filed?"

Officer Doyle quivered to attention behind me. "Diana, where did the request for justification come from?"

"Out of Belt HQ, directed from Luna. Ben, what the hell have you been doing?"

He smiled. "I think we've asked the right question, John. I wonder which one it was?"

Then he frowned slightly at the vid pickup. "Diana, if you really want to know, I'll tell you. But you might not want to."

"Crap. There's something about that dead miner that I didn't figure out, isn't there? And you've started poking into it. It's my sector. You'd better tell me."

"Okay." He shrugged. "First, you've lost the bet. Kitten Rodriguez Yang was a cyborg. She was terminated remotely by whoever held her key codes. But that's not the end of the problem, and you should have seen that. Whoever terminated her didn't file Involuntary Termination papers, a misdemeanor, because she wasn't registered in your sector, a felony. She wasn't registered with you because she was passing for human, which is so illegal that even John had never heard of anyone doing it before."

"Shit. There goes my credit balance. No—" Officer

Martin held up one hand. ''No, I get it. You're right, and I hadn't considered the implications. I expect whoever it is was counting on that. Hell. Can you cyborg yourself? Even if you were incredibly rich? Don't you have to have a sponsor to sign the papers?''

''I seriously doubt that Kitten cyborged herself. No, she belonged to someone. I think that your inquiry means that we poked a stick in the right place. Now we have to figure out which place that is.''

''You know, I don't think I want to know this after all, Ben.'' Officer Martin was thoughtful. ''Damn. This is going to be work, and the first thing we know, some Lieutenant is going to swoop in and take it over from us. Illegal cyborg miners! Jeeze! Who was she selling to? There's a place to start, I bet.'' No, Officer Martin wasn't foolish.

The two of them filed a notice of joint investigation, to cover the charges already made for data transfer, and to justify future charges. I dumped copies of everything I'd taken from her data files back to her. I wondered how the masters had gotten corrupted; I assumed that Officer Doyle was considering it, too. I noticed that her corrupted files included the autopsy report on Rodriguez, and requested a new copy from HQ. It was transferred immediately with no problem. I shouldn't have been surprised.

Rodriguez's medical records were waiting in our file space, along with an official table of organization from TransSolar Mines. And a notice that Simon O'Neil's banking records were unavailable. Not nonexistent, but unavailable. I told Officer Doyle, and he said, ''Interesting.''

The medical records from Earth consisted only of Public Health Service pediatric files, running from her birth through her sixteenth year, and the report of examination that was required for her travel permit to Luna. I scanned the autopsy, and compared it to the examination from 2183. Whoever the physicians had seen for that certificate, it wasn't Kitten Rodriguez Yang—the cell samples didn't match.

"That means," Officer Doyle said, "that the cyborging predates her movement into the Belt. I wonder
when . . . ?"

He punched up the early medical records, looking for
any sign of illness or accident. Rodriguez had been a
lovely little girl, with long black hair and almond eyes.
The file recorded a history of marginal malnutrition,
treatment for a broken arm, the normal round of
government-sponsored inoculations against contagious
diseases, and a case of venereal disease at the age of ten.
The last records, at age sixteen, were of a complete physical inventory, performed by the Singapore Public Health
Service. The results had been directed to a Dr. Yee at
Global Entertainment Enterprises. Rodriguez was in
fairly good physical condition at the time, although the
examining physician noted the presence of some bruises.

I left Officer Doyle poring over the files. This was
turning into an investigation worth pursuing, but there
were shipboard tasks to be done and the routine work of
a System Officer to perform. But as I went about my
work, I considered Rodriguez's medical record. It was
what you would expect from two hundred years ago, before the System established its Health Policy. I hadn't
seen anything like it since my own early days as a System
Officer on Luna, but I'd seen it then. I remembered how
the child had looked lying there dead, and how we'd been
able to nail the pervert who killed her, but never found
a trace of how she'd gotten from the streets in Uruguay
to the Tranquillity Hilton on Luna.

"John," Officer Doyle said thoughtfully after the
sleep-shift, "would you please request the corporate bios
of each of TransSolar's board members. We need to know
what other company boards they sit on?" He returned to
the growing case file without hearing my acknowledgment.

Ten minutes later, Diana Martin was transmitting indignantly. "Ben! You won't believe this. I just got a Mineral
Rights and Request for Removal on that asteroid where we
found the cyborg. How the hell could anybody know enough
to file a verifiable claim on it?"

"Oh, almost anybody could have. She put all the information on the chat lines, you know. It was safe enough, in theory—none of the other miners would jump her, and nobody else uses those lines. Who filed the claim?"

"Some dude named Simon O'Neil—I never heard of him, he's not registered in the Sector."

Officer Doyle slammed his hand down on the counter. I would have done the same. "Simon O'Neil, you say? Now, that's very interesting indeed. John, do you have those bios yet?"

Simon O'Neil was not an on-the-record employee of TransSolar Mining. But three members of the board of directors of TransSolar were also members of the board of Global Entertainment.

"John," Officer Doyle said, "we are beginning to see the pattern of a network here."

"Sir," I replied, "we really have only circumstantial evidence of any connection here. But if O'Neil is claiming that iridium deposit, then he'll have to prove his ID. We can get a trace started from that."

"Exactly, John. Send a request to Diana—better yet, do it yourself. Let her know what you're doing."

I requested access to Officer Martin's data base, and extracted the necessary information from O'Neil's claim documents. Since a simple financial trace had been blocked earlier, I thought I'd try requesting verification of his resources to move the asteroid should we approve the claim. It worked in a limited way—I found that his credit account was insufficient to justify granting the claim on the asteroid. Normally we did not apply this standard to claims, since asteroid miners were either already employed by the big mining interests, or were going to sell their claim to those interests. But technically speaking, we could refuse to grant the claim in this case. I asked Officer Doyle what should be done.

"Oh, refuse the claim, by all means. Get Diana for me."

He began whistling tunelessly.

When Officer Martin answered the chime, he said,

"We have evidence of a long association between the cyborg and this Simon O'Neil. It would be interesting to see who intervenes if we refuse his claim."

Officer Martin looked confused. "If he's claiming the rock, doesn't that make him the murderer? I mean, the—oh, never mind. Look, Sherlock, I don't get this entirely. We know this O'Neil is in the Belt, we know that he's benefiting from Rodriguez's death, why don't we just notify HQ and have him arrested? Or do you think someone else turned her off?" Officer Martin glanced at me, standing behind Officer Doyle. "Sorry, John."

"Oh, he probably terminated her. What I want to know now is who cyborged this woman in the first place, and how they did it."

"Uh, Ben, that's got to have happened more than ten years ago—"

"More like seventy years ago, is my guess."

"Whatever. I don't think System cops have any jurisdiction looking into stuff that happened out of the Belt and that long ago." She paused for a breath, then frowned quickly. "Seventy years ago? She was a child then! Don't be ridiculous."

Officer Doyle shrugged. "Maybe I'm wrong. Diana, your data base has already been corrupted once since we started this investigation. I suggest that you copy your files over here, before you deny that application."

Officer Martin was shaking her head as she disconnected.

Officer Doyle turned to other tasks almost immediately. When I asked him, he said, "I'm really just noticing and following up on reactions to blind stabs into the network. I have an idea of what's there, but no proof, and very little idea of where to look for any. The only way to find this enemy is to provoke him into movement."

Three hours later Simon O'Neil placed an outraged call to Officer Martin. She linked the signal through to us.

"There's nothing wrong with my claim! What are you

people trying to do to me?'' Simon O'Neil's face was well-preserved, with pale white skin; his dark brown hair had a few streaks of gray, and his skin was starting to sag around his jaw and his pale blue eyes. He was calling from a small private ship, a rental I'd seen in our sector before.

"Mr. O'Neil, are you aware that the asteroid in question is a crime scene?"

"Crime scene?" There was a tinge of disgust in O'Neil's voice. "That asteroid holds a large deposit of a valuable mineral. I have filed a legitimate claim on it."

"How did you come to learn of the existence of this deposit? You are not a Belt miner." Officer Doyle was as cool and professional as I could hope he would be.

"It's none of your business, but I was informed of it by a miner on the site."

"That would be Kitten Rodriguez Yang."

O'Neil's hand signaled contempt, an involuntary gesture he quickly suppressed. "It would. She was my . . . partner." The pause was almost undetectable.

"She was an illegal cyborg. I think you terminated her after she found the iridium."

The man paused to take that in, his face a complete blank. It was only a moment.

"And if I did? My claim is still valid."

"If you did, you are in a great deal of trouble." Officer Doyle's fingers played on a keyboard out of range of the vid pickup.

"You can't do a damned thing except write me a ticket. Write it. I admit I terminated a cyborg without a permit. I'll pay the fine."

"I want to know why."

"Why do I need any other reason than that I discovered that a woman I was in partnership with was actually an illegal cyborg passing herself off as human? I became insane with disgust. I terminated it." O'Neil's voice was cool and low; he was completely sure of his ground.

A screen at my console lit, opening a voiceprint recording and comparison program. O'Neil's smooth tones appeared on my screen as a wild sawtoothed wave form.

I split the output into two signals, and sent one to our records, the other to HQ for identity verification.

"When did you enter your partnership?"

"Only recently." The man's lies were as bland as a routine system checkout.

Officer Doyle sat quietly for a moment before saying, "I take it that you had just found her again?"

O'Neil stiffened visibly. "What do you mean by that?" The tension in his voice, barely audible, created a wild fluctuation on my screen.

"I believe that you lost touch with Rodriguez about ten years ago. I don't seen any indication that you had contact with her since that time until six weeks ago."

The HQ ID verification had come back quickly; if I had thought to put a law-enforcement trace on the man in the first place, we would have had the answers a lot sooner. His name was Simon Case O'Neil. He was born in Johannesberg, on Earth, in 2101. He had a long arrest record on drug and corporate espionage charges. He had been released from prison on Luna, after serving a five-year sentence for corporate blackmail, only six months before. I made a quick *precis* of the report, and sent it to the screen just below the vid, where Officer Doyle could read it while he talked. I also sent it to Officer Martin, who had maintained an admirable silence throughout the low-key interrogation.

"Or perhaps you decided to take a chance when opportunity presented itself?" The man blinked at that. "I don't suppose you'd appreciate it if we notified Global of your little lapse of self control, now would you?"

"Dammit, she was just a worn-out sex toy—her looks were gone fifteen years ago! The Belt modifications didn't cost that much, and they weren't giving her hormone maintenance any more. If you think that anybody is going to care much one way or another, think again."

The man's nervousness was giving way to assured contempt. The cyborg wasn't the problem, at least as far as he was concerned.

Officer Doyle was momentarily speechless; the idea of a cyborged sex toy evoked lurid old tales of girls stolen and drugged and enslaved. O'Neil was worried about his former employer discovering that he'd filed a personal claim on that rock. I was looking at a vision of a new kind of hell.

O'Neil's voice broke in. "Rest assured that I will appeal this refusal of my claim," he said coldly. "Good day." He cut off the circuit so abruptly that he chopped his own words.

Officer Martin's face popped up on the vid in O'Neil's place. "Well, Sherlock. This plot is getting pretty damned thick." She paused for a deep breath. "Don't you think we'd better report to Captain Wu before O'Neil gets his licks in?"

Officer Doyle did not respond. He seemed deep in thought, so I said, "If I may take the liberty, Ma'am, I expect that Officer Doyle would agree with you. I will request an appointment."

Captain Wu's secretary took the request for a time slot and gave Officers Doyle and Martin an hour at 1500. It was a great deal of time on short notice, but Cyborg 19439 knew that I would not request such a meeting if the cause were not urgent. Those of us who belonged to the Service respected each other.

"Ma'am, you and Officer Doyle may call Captain Wu in two hours."

"John, I don't know how you do it. I hope Ben comes out of his daze soon enough to get a report together."

"What?" Officer Doyle shook himself slightly. "Yes. An appointment, John."

"Done, Sir."

"Exactly. Well done."

"And so, sir," Officer Doyle concluded, "I believe, based on this evidence, that Rodriguez was cyborged illegally at the age of sixteen by someone within Global Entertainment Enterprises. It was done without legal consent, obviously. She was then put to work as a prostitute and corporate espionage device, controlled by O'Neil. When she was no longer attractive enough, they refitted her for asteroid mining—I suppose they wanted to get as much profit on their initial investment as possible. O'Neil landed in prison again at about the same time. When he got out, he had just enough credit to track her down and try to force her to cut him in on the sale of this big strike. We can arrest him on charges—"

"Just a moment, Doyle." Captain Wu cut him off sharply. "Martin, have you or Doyle told anyone else about this free-lance investigation of yours?"

"No, sir."

"Well, keep it that way." He looked down at something on the counter. "Look, I appreciate the work you've done, especially you, Doyle. But, in fact, you haven't got a damned thing that's solid enough to be worth pursuing. A cyborg was terminated; is this a problem? How she got that way, now, that's interesting—but it's interesting to someone whose jurisdiction is on Earth. It's not our business. I'll forward the file to Singapore."

"But, sir!" Officer Doyle's patience, never in great supply, was nearly gone. "What about O'Neil? What about the claim?"

"My boy," the captain leaned back and relaxed, "this fellow will take care of himself, the minute TransSolar finds out that he has filed on that asteroid. Don't give it another moment's thought.

"Now," he said, "if that's all, I have some files to forward and some reports to enter. Don't hesitate to bring these little problems to me in the future. The Service thinks very highly of you." Beaming warmly, Captain Wu cut the secure circuit himself.

On the secondary screens, Officers Doyle and Martin just stared at each other for a moment.

"Well, I'll be damned!" Officer Martin whispered.

"Tell me, Diana, have you checked the position of O'Neil's ship in the last two hours?"

"No . . . just a second . . . no trace of it."

"I'd send a debris sweeper that way, if I were you."

"Hell!" With that, Officer Martin switched off.

That should have been the end of it, but the puzzle wasn't solved to Officer Doyle's satisfaction. This enthusiasm was going to be a problem in years to come, but at the moment I sympathized. Officer Doyle requested a transcript of the monitor from O'Neil's ship. It would show how the ship had been destroyed.

Ten minutes later the secure circuit chimed. I accepted the call. "Registered Cyborg number 20812 speaking for Officer Doyle," I said. The screen showed only interference. The antenna again, I thought. But then it cleared. . . .

On the screen was footage of Kitten Rodriguez Yang, looking much younger than she had on the asteroid. She was facing the pickup, obviously behind a mirror, and brushing her long black hair. I heard Officer Doyle's quick intake of breath behind me. Rodriguez put down her antique brush, and leaned close into the picture, one delicate hand raised to her cheek. There was a slight rash where she touched. She winced, and reached for a bottle of antiseptic. A cyborg does not have the ability to resist airborne infections. That's why we don't have skin.

The image froze. Superimposed over it was a message:

> *Thank you. We have recovered on the property damage. You have been given certain suggestions. Heed them, or you will find out more than you want to know about life as a cyborg.*

THE LADY LOUISIANA TOY

by Barry N. Malzberg

Barry N. Malzberg, author of more than 90 books and 300 stories, most of them science fiction, is also a noted anthologist and is the former editor of *Amazing Stories* magazine.

A riff on The Demolished Man. *A human private eye is hired to retrieve an art object that has been stolen by an alien, and—if possible, though it isn't his primary objective—to bring the alien to justice. The catch: the alien, and everyone who works for it, belongs to a race of telepaths.*

Of need then, and longing, and of the yearning which makes men burn in the night, men lacking any interior, what we once were taught to call "soul," men who plod and plod their way through the anguished and sterile routine of their circumstance not reflecting upon that necessity or upon much else, men who were closed in early, taken in disarray from their own warm and living hearts and placed—well, placed where? It is not the nature of our metaphysics to consider this, now when the universe itself implodes so reluctantly and we are told, as if it were a declaration of truth, that this is the end of time.

Of those men, then, and of their uses, of what can be made of them from the sterile detritus of their necessity but first, because there is no understanding any of this without the background, without the helpless, mocking heart of the truth . . . of the Lady Louisiana Toy first.

In the known places her name was a curse or prayer and in the myriad galaxies not yet discovered or in discovery of hers that presence still might have been a benison, a plainchant, but here, too, and in the huge arcs among the stars where the birds of time themselves swooped, men knelt to her spirit and flesh with imprecations and cries, prayers infused with scatology, joined to a scatology which lifted from the ruins of their hearts. It was a ruinous age, one of blank corruption and discontent, yet one not without a certain romantic necessity, the architecture of desire still present in the space drives, in the whispers of the trawlers of space. In this age there were icons, icons for all of the men without interior which rose unevenly in small arcs from the concavities of the stars, and the greatest of them was the Lady Louisiana Toy whose dreams and spirit passed through the network, amplified to proportion beyond imagining, crushed into the hearts of all who witnessed her. She inspired woe and death, lust and darkness, cries of desperation and climax under the axis of her powerful emoting, that image of herself—and all we might have loved—spread in huge discolored patches through all the devices of dissemination. The treasure of the galaxies, Lady Louisiana Toy, and when she was kidnapped by those we called the Possessors a sigh like all mourning rose from a billion trapped and riven witnesses. What she did was not to be explained, her kidnapping unspeakable and yet this is only the least part of the actress and focused modem known as Lady Louisiana Toy. It will have to do as so much else of this limited document will have to grant service because it is impossible in these final times—or perhaps before them—to convey what had gone on, what it meant, we can only approximate, some sum of an ideal, dim image of the cave, flicker of approximation against the absolute of the cave, that Paolo and Francesca of the galaxies drifting by in their terrible embrace the closest simulacrum we might find.

They remembered Dante in this era, too. It was, perhaps, that set of cantos, the last of what they remembered. Heavens, the spirit of transcendence, all of this collapses but the purgatorial ring is not to be limned by the laws of relativity or the great, groaning hyperspace drives which opened before finally closing to us the universe.

This is *not* the story of the Lady Louisiana Toy.

It concerns her and she is at the axis, but of her and her kidnapping there is to be apprehension only by indirection. If it is ultimately her story (we cannot know and it is hard to rule the approximation) that would be only because it deals with the man who stole her back from the Possessors and the planet of the doubled suns where she had been smuggled, plucked her back, still beautiful but irreparably damaged from that prison of unspeakable pain where they had made her—for their pleasure, their pleasure, O brothers!—to cry out her necessity in the tongues of her projection. It is, then, the story of that simple and doomed man, a man very much like ourselves except that he possessed no interior whatsoever, no framing consciousness, no newstape of commentary as he struggled through his own purgatory, who lifted the Lady Louisiana Toy from her imprisonment, took her (but only briefly, only briefly!) for his paralyzed satisfaction and in so doing elevated far beyond his apprehension by the sheer expression of that unspeakable need. How could the stalker Stanley Montana have known then that he was the source of this chronicle, that it was he who triggered its necessity, he who had thought of himself only as a minor character, a wretched ingredient, a tiny actor in the story of the Lady Louisiana Toy, in the earlier and grayly unfolding chronicle of his life? We do not know what he would have said, and this at least is unavailable to us although too much else has been expressed. There are parts of Stanley Montana which, like his very soul, remain swaddled, cannot be apprehended.

How did he know, this man, that what he had done would be magnified through the millions of telepathic receptors of the Possessors? How would he know that nothing was performed in secret, that detection no less than yearning would be an expressed and public act? But he could not know, of course, there is no way in which he could have known. This man knew nothing.

There is no understanding this chronicle if it is not known that the man knew nothing.

So this is really the story of Stanley Montana and his undoing, the latter undoing which he brought upon us all. It is the story of Stanley Montana and then necessarily of the ravishing Lady Louisiana Toy, all of it legend, long spoken, then passed out in that savage, blinking instant of revelation when the Lady, magnificent in her captivity and pain, suffused with the pale gold light of her sufficiency, suffused with the knowledge that what the Possessors had done had destroyed her utterly and yet had left her at some other level intact . . . in that knowledge she opened her arms and mind to receive his cry, took that strangled confession from Stanley Montana then and with it the shrieking inference which took us to this terrific and ongoing explosion, that explosion which has sealed our doom even as it has closed off our fate and sprung us from that ravaged and beautiful final age in which these events took place. That was the end of this chronicle as we knew it then, although of course it did not feel like an ending as it was witnessed but like a series of acts which, beautiful and terrible in their juxtaposition, seemed to point the way to—well, to where? We did not know that either; in the spaces among the suns we crawled through our scripts, no less fixated, no more thoughtful than Stanley Montana.

This, then, the chronicle. It is offered not in reasonable explanation, there is none, but in humility and hope even as the very act—like the investigations of Stanley Montana—turn in upon themselves.

Dragged from the bed of the Emperor by the savage telepathic Possessors who had stalked her for years, had made their plans well, knew at last what they would do with her, the Lady Louisiana Toy felt them pounce upon her unshielded and now ungifted consciousness and she screamed. She screamed both within and without herself, trying to magnify that scream toward salvation, but it could not be done. She was the treasure of the Possessors now and they had taken her. She had not one moment for farewell, for some righting of accounts long since imbalanced against her.

Taken from the Emperor's bed, the Lady Louisiana Toy was placed into the closed box of corporeal transport and taken through secret and powerful means whose technology is unavailable to us and which will defy any reasonable explanation to places not known to any of the conventional historians of the galaxies, and the damaged Stanley Montana must have felt—we theorize as best we can under the circumstances—that thrill of displacement in his own sensibility, felt that he knew of the abduction of the treasured Lady Louisiana Toy before the awful news had been publicly disseminated, and it was at that moment, no later, that his odyssey began. We must consider his reaction as a *feeling*, it was visceral woe (looking back upon it he theorized) deep in the gut, not thought as we know it, thought being unavailable to Montana, and it was thus without apprehension. He did not know then, might never have known that subsequent events would bring him into the presence of what we called the Possessors, those plundering and predatory aliens of which he had previously known so little, of which Montana had thought nothing at all. His skull was impenetrable, his thoughts limited to his own transparent capacity. *Had he but known,* that song of regret of the spheres. We will not deal with it. He could not have known anything, of course. Tropism was his response, small and grumbling resistance to the prank the cosmos had played upon him was limited to vagrant drinking and curses.

There were then, as long before and at sometime in the imponderable future as well, so many men like Montana. They suspire in the small bars and lounges, the restaurants and galleyways of all the planets, usually alone, sometimes in groups with their blasted eyes at moments of repose revealing everything. They sit hunched unto themselves, their expressions casting not so much mystery—come to them close in the guise of a sympathetic companion and sketch this out if you will—as entrapment. They are men of small devices and foolishness who hire out their wretched and painful selves not so

much for the small compensation which is their excuse
but because they are looking for annihilation. They are
looking for something so terrible to happen that they will
be freely able to abandon the struggle to have their lives
make sense and go over the line into that death they have
always sought. They can be inspected at our leisure, they
will be there again as they have been in all of the annals
of that blasted time, and the message will be one of such
utter consistency. They have no secrets, their faces *are*
their secret and beat truth to the world.

"That is not so," Stanley Montana would say, confronted with this assessment. "Leave annihilation to the
stars out there, speak to me of thugs and mean streets
and the blood that runs toward the blood of killers. This
is my business. Essential solutions to old mysteries, drink
up, stay out of a coffin, go home." Do not listen to any
of this, regardless of the fervency of Montana's wink and
nod. Observe only the facts of the case, consider the
testimony of what the ages have taught us. The thinkers
and prophets of this terrible age of which we write knew
the truth and they passed it on, the detective (and that is
Stan Montana's self-designation, he is a detective, he
would put it on his forms and identifying statement,
seeker of solutions, detective for hire) is exquisitely and
finally the man who would seek to unravel the primal
scene, and come close to the struggling bodies linked on
that bed locked away behind the primal door, turn those
bodies—*hip ho turn*!—to his humble and needful face
and identify at last Mommy and Daddy as they go about
the heavy and sad business of replicating Montana, re-
infusing Montana. This is the business of the detective,
to crawl up to the masks *hip ho*! and ripping them away
discover the sad and necessitous faces of none other than
old Dad and Mom. Believe this, believe that all the rest
of it—the plodding, the compensation, the deductions,
the small scrambling connections of their own saddened
and diminished lives, the posturing and good old self-
annihilation—all of it comes from the need of these
brethren to conceal this necessity from themselves.

Oh, really? "Having none of it. Good-bye, then,"

Montana would say, raising his hands from the bar in a gesture of perfect and final dismissal, making his plan to move toward another place where inquiries would cease. But all of this is denial, a denial of which Lady Louisiana Toy would more than the rest of us be clearly aware.

Louisiana Toy!

The name itself arouses, even these eons after her kidnapping, her recovery and destruction, these long limping ages after she had spun through the infernal heart of the stars a crazed and incessant longing, a twitch not unlike Stan Montana's twitch as—*hip ho!*—he jiggled his leg underneath the stanchion and with blasted eyes considered anachronistic possibility. Descriptions and holographs abound these centuries later of this lady of sorrows; she is one of the most famous of her or any time at all, and yet none of them can conjure but an approximation, so great the force which she could bring without even trying to bear. Capacious bosom, longing arms, lips and eyes reproduced on a billion transceivers, the image of lust and connection for all of us febrile doomed of the Republics and the lady herself, sad and witnessing, watching all of this at the secret heart of her own possibility, carrying her own difficult way through the annals of her life with the sad sustenance, the dignity and the self-knowledge of the truly possessed.

A treasure swept away by the Possessors, our lady, a descendant of a race of telepaths similar to them so that she could apprehend everything, the flood of our longing, the lustful and needful thoughts like tracer fire skidding across the consciousness which she gave to the visiphones. Her parents were unknown, the legends said. She had been found abandoned, adopted at birth by the nurturing institutions who sprung her telepathy from its locked-away place and made it bloom no less than the flowers and purchase of her being. This is what the holographs told us, what the advisers said; how much of this was true, whether Louisiana Toy, no less than the emotions and actions she placed over the visiphone, was "real" we cannot know, but ultimately it does not matter. If there has been one lesson to be absorbed from the fourteen centuries of guilt and abomination before at last the collapse of which we read it is this: that there is no difference between what exists and what we would have exist that cannot be patched over by technology, lies, the insistence of our dreams. Even the fourteen centuries themselves must come into dispute; there are those who will argue for fifteen, others saying that fourteen millennia would not truly apprehend the situation. So the arguments go on and on in their echoing and imprecise fashion, but of the lady's true torment and distress we can only speculate in this chronicle.

We can speculate, but the speculation itself is true; what we would have is what will exist, or so the Possessors told her during the disgusting months of her captivity and indoctrination. We can get no nearer her distress, that distress is part of a story which—were it cataloged— would become appallingly sentimental and would then involve the necessity of discussing the seventeen hundred worlds, the politics of genocide which led only to the mild fracture of the Republics (genocide being only another arm of policy), the corruption of the lost judges, the nefarious and wretched spin of dispersion which had made the occupation and performance of the damaged Stan Montana and those in his trade essential to any realpolitick of that long surpassed century which we can consider only as paradigm. Image of an image, dusk of a night, there was the Lady Louisiana Toy, telepathic treasure, her bosom of lace and dreams hurled heavenward in a trillion reproductions to the storming gates of Montana's lust. Louisiana Toy, actress and saint, Mother of God and cruel partisan of the lost spirit, Mary and Medusa and Medea and Electra and a thousand other icons as well, taken from the very center of her being and laid out for us, just as the Possessors—that stern and damaged lupine race of telepaths and technophiliac monsters—took her then to the cold and distant heart of their own galaxy. It was only at that point that the practicalities commenced; the initial crime had been so audacious, so furious and somehow beyond conception as to deny paraphrase. The demands were issued, of course, through

telepathic beam and—for the rest of us who were not
telepaths—the lesser systems of transports.

They were blackmail, of course, they were insouciant
and outrageous. Even in what the inhabitants of this period thought of as "advanced times" the rockets yet
crawled between the stars while in the bowels of those
machines creatures whose pain and appearance were unspeakable and thus unknown to the passage hammered
and stoked the slow fires of increase while trying not to
be consumed by the FTL drives and trying to make of
the universe a small, elegant, somehow comprehensible
business. The messages crawled with the rockets then,
the telepathic waves crackling only to the very few who
could understand them and who (by the prejudicial and
murderous nature of this age) could not reveal their telepathic capacity.

For only at the cutting edge—this is an interpolation
and it may be forgiven for its relevance ultimately will
become clear—does one feel the rush of possibility, does
the interface of history and condition, threat and desire,
need and damage become somehow fused and resistible.
The rest of us stagger in the dark of our desire like rockets crawling at slower than light speeds through the ridges
of space. All of what we do is controlled by our ignorance; in the flickering instants of Lady Louisiana Toy's
image we may feel that something different is possible,
but it is not possible and that understanding bounds everything we do.

Had the Possessors had the true wherewithal or means
which they threatened, had they, too, not been bound to
the sublight speeds of the stokers, none of this would
have happened, they would have been invulnerable. But
their vulnerability was sealed by the fact that telepathy
was not a universal gift, they had to proceed in the language of their inferiors or not function at all. Had the
case been different, the likes of the hapless Stan Montana
would never have been engaged. He would not have lived
to function. But the Possessors were trapped in the glue
of their constancy, the very ether itself contained them.

Ultimately it was not their age after all. It was the age of Stan Montana.

For Montana lived, even at this sprawling and unspeakable time, far at the margins of all possibility. Ungifted by an interior, deprived of coherent or reasonable thought, he scuffed into his clothing, made his arrangements with prostitutes, heaved and unloaded his discharge of semen or necessity, collaborated with any who would hire him, engaged in the most dubious and slimiest of deeds which at this or any time at all still comprises the text and sorrow of life. In the twenty-ninth century (where this does not take place) or the thirty-fifth, in the ninth or the unspeakable billionth millennium, the business with which Montana was engaged will go on. One will find him here and there, at this or any other point of the past, pounding his fist against tables, ordering his feet to move even when they would die on him, bribing the ships' porters or space jockeys in the holes of the rapt Beltegeuse system to yield small bits of information on adulterous pursuit. His whine of release may be heard in the dives or alleyways of the millionth planet, his plans and formulations scrambled like Kilroy's upon walls so distant that we cannot imagine them.

For this, then: Stan Montana and no one else, not even the Lady herself, must be seen as the abcissa upon which the stars themselves turn, he is at the center of our condition now and forevermore, and it must be admitted that he was as stunned and distracted by the news of the Lady's abduction as any of us. Perhaps he was more shaken because in ways that he, too, could not have known he had secretly loved her, dreamed of her body, confessed to her image, kept her holograph along with the ever ready but certainly unconscious primal scene close to him in the dark and inelegant pause of his nights. If Stan Montana did not then love Louisiana Toy, he came as close to that as any simulacrum of ''love'' could be known in the spaceyards and boneyards of this disastrous age which we are forced to remember as the last time when it was possible to come together through the transceiver, to find a kind of community, to understand anything. They had selected Stanley Montana to seek the Possessors and recover Louisiana Toy because, they said ("they" involving the massed governments and corporate entities of that time who interpreted the kidnapping as the most audacious infliction yet upon their perilous way of life, and so they were able for the duration of this crisis to work together in a kind of unity) he lacked subtlety, lacked understanding of any kind, lacked—as we have been pointing out from the earliest part of this recollection—any significant interior life. He obviously knew nothing and therefore he had a chance with the Possessors which heavier and more sophisticated help—with genuine technological knowledge, with something approximating an interior monologue—could not have possessed.

"You are stupid enough not to know that you must fail," was the way they explained matters to Stanley Montana when they put her holograph and last known whereabouts in his hands and sent him spinning clumsily on his journey to seek the Lady and somehow return her. "You have absolutely no conception of what is against you, therefore you may succeed," is what they said and this was probably far more than was necessary, but they gave him this much at least as he was sent out. With him rode the fate of suns for Louisiana Toy, as the Possessors knew and those who defended her interest, were responsible for her condition, was at the secret heart of all purpose, she was no metaphor but a constancy; it was this constancy which granted her the power she held.

Her body was the primal vault of the galaxies themselves, at least as they had been rearranged, in her ovaries she carried the imploded hearts of suns and other galactic debris which need not be further evaluated in this context. A universal figure, a truly generating force, a metaphor gone so lucidly explosive that she had been forced to become an entertainer simply as a means of controlling her visibility, if she was on the transceivers they knew at least where she was and could track her movement at all times. Of the dangers, the climactic risks, the sheer lunacy of allowing the Galactic Riddle to become a holograph for the billions we need not speak, it is of course this lunacy itself which gave the age its divination and truest madness and not to apprehend this is to miss the point; further explication is not necessary. They owed Montana no part of the truth and did not give it to him. What difference would the truth have made? By the same reasoning, the truth is a part of this narrative only when it is of a momentary sufficiency, it must be left to other sources to explain how the galactic riddle had been placed into such a position. Of the reckoning and madness of that age we can ourselves make no judgment.

"Go, then, and find her," they said to Stanley Montana. "Recover her, find her for us, bridge the gate of telepaths, and return the Lady Louisiana Toy to the hearts of those now bereaved." They added little to this essential imprecation and sent him away, promising rich compensation but only if he were successful and giving proper impetus in the form of the holograph and the promise they whispered to him in parting, the promise that they knew would work if anything would.

"For you may have her," they whispered. "She can be yours at last. Find her, shield your thoughts and purpose from the Possessors who would otherwise apprehend them. Find where she has been hidden, bring her back to us and we will put her in a room with you. There you may close the door and you may enact upon her— shall we say this, do we dare?—anything you wish. Anything of your description, anything you can imagine, that and more and we will help you. She is love, she is loving, she is the one who has always been in search of a handsome operative like you. She lusts for your need even as you and a billion others have prayed to her."

What is there to say? What is there to be made of such mischief as this? They lied to him, of course, but they lied no less than that which had been the modicum of social and sexual intercourse for all of the indefinable history and in the stacks of deceit from which had been tossed the sprawling galaxies, the quarks and their boneyards, how awful is their lie! Looking at the tablelands

we have found now, is this the worst of all the evils which
life has perpetrated upon life? It was at least for a good
purpose. Purpose was all. Sincerity was a counterfeit,
simply a position. And this Stanley Montana himself must
have known for he had whispered to himself that confidence in all of the silent places as he had plodded his
way through the small interstices of his tiny necessities.
"Mean streets, mean doings," he had confided to himself. "Someone must always solve a murder, unearth the
truth, find the wrongdoer, relieve the damaged, give
comfort to the sick. Just as an army must always search,
destroy, and occupy, so a man must take on the burdens
of his time.

"I am good, I am good," Stanley Montana would
praise himself in those last chants before sleep, "I am of
a necessity, I am here to save, I act bad but I do good."
Of this and so many other small deceptions we must be
accepting then, seek complaisance; he suffered for us after all, Stanley Montana lived and died—multiplied by
the millions!—for those of us who have, however, equiv-
ocally survived and if there are no explanations for this—
well, then, there are no possibilities as well. One must
equate, one must show mercy in order to gain advantage
or so at least has been another of the difficult lessons
which (forever unlearned by the rest of us) have been the
contemptible and limited total of all the burnt suns, all
the progression of disaster and pain up to the time of
these events. Or beyond.

But this, too, begins to edge into the theology of the
Possessors, a race whose telepathy had created as one
could imagine a complex teleological basis not really to
be equated with our own numbed worship of disbelief
. . . their group purposes, intense gestalt, cynicism and
retrieval does not really fit into this chronicle any more
than Stanley Montana's halting and stumbling efforts to
find them. We must—like the Possessors, but with a different ascription to the word "faith"—take all of those
deductive efforts of Montana with a kind of faith. He
plodded and plotted (not through thought, through tropism as we must often be reminded) through the corri-

dors of the dark and hidden passageways between the
stars to find the Lady Louisiana Toy. And this, the nature
of his quest must be seen as the evil and secret genius of
those who had assigned him (in despair, of course, but
with a kind of cunning) to the task: his thoughts, his
ploddings and tropistic scuttle could not be read by the
assiduous Possessors, eager as they might have been to
understand him because Stan Montana had no thoughts.
His processes could not be deduced because there were
none, there was only that small core of purpose, the low,
flickering flame of his desire to get behind the door and
read the faces, this codified by dim possession. On and
on he prowled, doing the best he could, doing what he
must as the stars curled in their traces and the Possessors
cackled with the slow realization of their desire, demanding ransom then and performing unspeakable acts
which like so much else need not be summarized here.

No, of the nature of the Lady's captivity, of those acts
performed upon and inside her during that terrible period
of her captivity, we will not speak. Such a report would
only be distressing to Stanley Montana, his residue and
descendants (we are all, of course, his descendants) and
would play little role in what is, for all of its tortuous
rhetoric and sly inference, quite a simple recapitulation. It
is a recapitulation as simple as Stan Montana himself,
because we are not dealing with complex figures here,
we are doing with a man of no interior life, a lady who
was an icon and a telepathic net but whose own interior
had been gutted from her so that the wires could be
placed and she could become a vehicle for the necessity
of others. Understand that long before the Possessors had
taken their toll there were others who had touched the
child Louisiana Toy and played with her, jiggled her in-
sides and known her outside, filled all of her tender and
vulnerable being with disgusting thoughts, human and
panicky needs, hints of desolation, desolate and lasting
purposes: she was assigned early to her task of enacting
for all of the galaxies what they most wanted. Pictures
were drawn inside and outside her heart and on the walls
of her cell, she had been in a cell long before the Pos-

sessors then and the effect of her imprisonment was most equivocal. She had seen it all before.

Still, there was that need for her to be shown, for the demonstration to be made. From time to time then the Possessors would take Louisiana Toy to the arena they had constructed for just this purpose and there she was compelled before a stunned audience of several billion, all that they could summon to this greatest of all links, to reenact aspects of her life and anticipated death for their edification and amusement. She was not an actress, what she did was something far beyond acting and in the sands cast before her Louisiana Toy did what they wanted, knowing that she was giving back to them what from the first had always been in the contract. She had never expected any different. If Stan Montana had expected everything, the Lady had—by charm and essence his doubled opposite—expected nothing at all. So she went through what she must and it is generally conceded by those who witnessed the events and made transcription at that time that these were indeed the greatest, the most memorable and shocking of all her performances.

The ransom demands were of course subordinate. Did the Possessors ever expect them to be met? One must doubt this, all of it was posturing, an excuse for the abuse and the inch by inch shrieking extraction of Louisiana Toy's memory. Worlds were demanded, then more worlds, then the flaming captive hearts of undiscovered stars which yet more worlds insidiously circled, then at last in an act of sheer audacious loathing the Possessors demanded the great Troast Lock itself with its billion suns, flaming passions, untold worlds of slavery and treasure. They demanded not only the Lock but the complete submission of all who were to be heaped up in the heat of the stars as untainted treasure. It was impossible. From the very start now, it was clear, the Possessors had never had any intention but the final evisceration of Louisiana Toy and the rupturing of her link. How it had taken so long to ascertain their purposes was not known, but now there could be no doubt.

The disciples and creators of Louisiana Toy, her lov-

ers, those who had not known her at all but themselves
had somehow been touched, all of them, the totality of
witness in the billions was left with nothing to say, nothing to be done. Grasping at last the full audacity and
cruelty of the Possessors, they had been shocked beyond
response, moved beyond edification. Had they been telepathic in the fullest sense—but only the Possessors and
their captive and a few sterile mutants in this narrative
were, that must be understood, what we encompass here
are the trillions of dumb, enclosed minds excluded from
the cold circle of communion—had they been telepathic
then, they would have been struck insensate, cleaved
from their very powers. The hopelessness was that absolute,
the devastating intention of the Possessors that clear. But
in the absence of telepathy, knowing only empathy then
and witness to the sufferings of Louisiana Toy, those that
could weep did so . . . and the others—but what is there
to be said of the others? There are always such. At the
moment of Crucifixion, the horse and rider carry on, sail
out of the clear frame of the picture in the Beaux Arts
Museums of our souls.

Stan Montana plodded on.

He plodded on, that is all. That is what the Montanas
do. In the junkshops and the small arenas, in medieval
or real time, they go on and on. Their living is a kind of
dying to us, but what do they know? They do not grasp
any of this. They think little of themselves, less of their
needs or destination, do not after a while even consider
those who hire them, they know nothing either of that
tropism which unfurls them like pennants wearily in the
night. They pay that tropism as little regard as primal
Mommy and Daddy did to the watcher beyond the window. In his insensibility, say it and be done, Stanley
Montana was unconquerable. That is the burning heart
of this chronicle. One cannot destroy that which was
never born or (choose your vision of demolition) that
which has been hammered to silt. How does one van-
quish a nullity? This is a mathematical conundrum to
puzzle Xeno. Like Caliban, another refugee who had
learned speech and the only good of it to curse, Montana

went here and there, flagged spaceships, curled into the
engine rooms with the press gangs, knew captains and
kings and the lower spaces, went around and about in the
eternities of Louisiana Toy's imprisonment, plodded
through and around and beyond purpose and at last—
through means which we will elide the question of ex-
position—confronted the Possessors in that small jeweled
cave at the furthest point of the finite, that cave which
they had taken to be utterly secret, unapproachable.

How did he do it? How did he *not* do it? That is the
essential mystery . . . for he had moved beyond paradox
to that point where nullity and confrontation were the
same. Some of this has to do with the curvature of space
but more with the wretched anchorage of the heart.

Inside his garments, the holograph twinkled, then made
sullen noises as Stan Montana entered the cave and confronted the astonished Possessors. Amazed, they leaped
toward their weapons, but they were unprepared for consciousness and quickly they were cut down by the conventional weaponry of Stanley Montana, devoid of
incantation or cleverness. They were, ultimately, that
vulnerable. They fell away and Stanley Montana moved
beyond their fallen bodies, looked behind the stones to
see the lady herself waiting. She had been crouched there,
apprehending it all, broadcasting this (as she had broadcast everything, the flickering transceivers picking up this
astonishing moment. Oh, they had been hard with her.

The Possessors had been hard with Louisiana Toy but
no harder than she with herself, trapped by remorse,
blocked in her own passageway. She had laid down her
lovely life and spirit again and again until at last that
spirit, broken, had seemed to rush from her in a dying
exhalation. But as Stan Montana could now see, that was
only part of her spirit, the rest had remained, clinging to
the walls of what looked at him in that cave and it was
this spirit, now rebounding to her flesh, which seized
Lady Louisiana Toy with awful force and turned her on
Stan Montana, then past him to the Possessors who keyed
to the awful confrontation in the cave had gathered, those
that remained around and about her.

Now! she said, *now!* Her thoughts were projected as speech, speech had become codified only to a great desire and at last, come to some consciousness in this space, Stanley Montana heard it. "Now!" he shouted, carrying forward, "now it is our time, our turn!" and the clumsy weapon which he had carried through all the passageways of his great and storming quest was in his hand, it was a revolver, and he fired this antique weapon—a point ninety-eight if you will, a Dramatii welded from the backs of the beasts of the Drunk Worlds—just as his predecessors in myths too old to be available to him had fired. The Dramatii trembled and flayed him and the stunned Possessors collapsed, all of them, fell there in the view of the transceivers and the transmitting Louisiana Toy.

They collapsed, too sophisticated and smart by far to be able to deal with that which had no interior at all, too smart to know that dumb is the only way to get through the universe, they fell and fell and Stan Montana tossed the weapon high and away. Lady Louisiana Toy was upon him then, clung to Stan Montana tightly and because of her great gift, a gift which makes possible the emergence of this chronicle at the same time that it doomed the chronicle and all who witnessed it to the ages of descent which so quickly followed—the brief and flickering moments between them were opened to all of the tearful galaxies who had watched through all the millennia for the supraprojectivity of a moment like this. Cries like the origin of all cries came from Louisiana Toy, sounds came from Stan Montana which the detective could neither describe nor locate, and then the two of them held one another in terrible and clinging embrace under the merciless attention of the billion suns. "Oh, yes," Louisiana Toy murmured, "I knew that I would be spared, I knew that you would come, I waited and waited, but I always knew that you would be here."

"*Madre,*" said Stanley Montana. "*Madre de Dios. Maman. Ah Pieta.*" The dead Possessors around them, the acres of the dead oozing and blinking in their appalled truncation caught them with blood, welded them ever tighter with the gouts of their extinguishing. *"Ah, Madre,"* Stanely Montana said. "Mommy." He held her then, ever more tightly, uncaring of the celestial breakup which then began.

The celestial breakup began. The collapse began. The implosion commenced at that moment. The slow and long-awaited dismantling of time and space previously intimated in so many sources but only known at this moment began . . . but of this we are not entitled to speak, not in these chronicles which are limited to the hard and crucial joining amplified through the billions of transceivers. *"Madre,"* Stanley Montana said. He grafted himself upon the lady. *"Ah, Maman."*

Thus was the mystery solved.

Thus was the spirit of our strange and tentative quest, the arc of our passage so tenderly and terrifically revealed. Of the implosion which followed and followed and whose seizures are with us yet we need neither write nor speak, broadcast nor think. It goes on. It goes on and on. Louisiana Toy and Stanley Montana, drifting through the rings of that inferno, clasped to one another now and for the ages to come, drifting and falling, falling like a dead body falls. Thus, then, the tale of the capture and the salvation of the Lady Louisiana Toy, the ascension of Stanley Montana, and the fate of all the suns. There is less on the record. There is little left on the record. The record is still being compiled. The time and the constancy are yet unrevealed; wait and watch as to morning, to morning.

Here, Paolo. There Francesca. Everywhere the ninth circle of light.

ALIEN INFLUENCES
by Kristine Kathryn Rusch

Kristine Kathryn Rusch, winner of the 1990 Camp-
bell Award, and a Hugo and Nebula nominee, is
the editor of *The Magazine of Fantasy and Science
Fiction*.
(Once again I'm guilty of a little deception here.
Kris Rusch and Barry Malzberg are such fine and
such totally *different* writers that I thought I'd see
what happened if I gave them each the same story
to write. The first time either of them will be aware
of it is when they read this paragraph in the printed
version of the book.)

A riff on The Demolished Man. *A human private
eye is hired to retrieve an art object that has been
stolen by an alien, and—if possible, though it isn't
his primary objective—to bring the alien to justice.
The catch: the alien, and everyone who works for
it, belongs to a race of telepaths.*

The corridor smelled stale. John huddled against the display panel, replacing microchips with the latest models—
more memory, more function. The near-robotic feel of
the work was all that mattered: pull, grab, replace; pull,
grab, replace. They should have had a droid doing this,
but they gave the work to John, sure sign that his contract
was nearly up.
He didn't mind. He had been on the trader ship for
nearly a month, and it was making him nervous. Too
many people, too close. They watched him as if they
expected him to go suddenly berserk and murder them all

in their sleep. He wouldn't have minded if their wariness was based on his work as a bounty hunter. But it wasn't. It was based on the events on Bountiful, things he had done—and paid for—when he was little more than a child.

Footsteps along the plastic floor. He didn't move, figuring whoever it was would have nothing to say to him. A faint whiff of cologne and expensive illegal tobacco. The captain.

"John, someone to see you."

John looked up. The captain stood on the other side of the corridor, the lights from the display giving his skin a greenish cast. Once John had fancied this man his friend, but John hadn't had any real friends. Not since he was fifteen years old. The day Harper betrayed him. The day they took Beth away.

"I will not see anyone," John said. Sometimes he played the role, the Dancer child everyone thought he was. The one who never spoke in past tense, only present and future, using the subjunctive whenever possible. The one who couched his thoughts in emotion because he had nothing else, no memory, no ethics, no soul.

The captain didn't even blink. "She flew in special from Rotan Base."

John stood and closed the display. A client, then. The time on the trader ship would end sooner than he expected.

He followed the captain through the winding corridors. The ventilation system was out. The entire ship smelled of wet socks and too many people. Down one of the corridors, the techs were discussing whether they wanted to fix the system or whether they wanted to wait until next planetfall. John would have argued for fixing it.

The captain stopped at his personal suite and keyed in the access code. John had never seen this room; it was off limits to all but the captain himself. John stepped in, but the captain remained outside. The door snicked shut.

Computer-generated music—technically proficient and lifeless—played in the background. The room itself was decorated in whites, but the lighting gave everything a reddish cast. The couch was thick and plush. Through open doors, he could see the bed, suspended in the air, cushions piled on top of it. A room built for comfort, and for seduction.

A woman stood at the back of the room, gazing out the portals in the stars. Her long black hair trailed down her back, her body wrapped in expensive silks. She looked the part of the seductee, although she was the one who wanted to hire him.

John never hired out for anything but bounty work. He would tell her that if he had to.

"I would like you to work for me, John." She didn't even turn around to acknowledge him. He felt his hackles rise. She was establishing herself as the adult, him the child in this relationship. He hated being treated like a child. The claustrophobia inched back on him, tighter than it had been in months.

He leaned against the door, feigning a casualness he didn't feel. He wanted her to turn around, to look at him. "Why should I work for you?"

"Forgive me." This time she moved, smoothing her hair as she did. Her face was stunning: full lips, long nose, wide eyes. And familiar. "I'm Anita Miles. I run an art gallery on Rotan Base. We specialize in unusual objects d'art. . . ."

He stopped listening, not needing the explanation. He recognized her face from a hundred vids. She was perhaps one of the most powerful people in this sector—controlling trade and commodities. Her gallery sold anything that could be considered art. Once she sold a baby Minaran, claiming that since the species was nearly extinct, the Minarans could only be appreciated in an aesthetic way. He couldn't remember if she had won or lost the ensuing lawsuit.

Baby trader. The entire galaxy as an art object. If she had been in business when he was a boy, what would she have done with the Dancers?

"Why should I work for you?" he repeated.

She closed her mouth and gave him a once-over. He recognized the look. *How much does he understand? I thought I was explaining in clear terms. This was going to be more difficult than I thought*. "You're the best," she said, apparently deciding on simplicity. "And I need the best."

He often wondered how these people thought he could bounty hunt with no memory. He shook off the thought. He needed the money. "What will you pay me?"

"Expenses, of course, a ship at your command because you may have to travel a bit, and three times your daily rate which is, I believe, the equivalent of four hundred Rotan zepeatas."

"Eight hundred."

Her expression froze for just a moment, and then she had the grace to flush. John crossed his arms. Too many clients tried to cheat him. He took them on anyway. If he tried to avoid those who treated him like a Dancer, he would have no business.

"I'm not a Dancer." He kept his tone soft, but made sure the sarcasm was there. "I wasn't even raised by them. Just influenced. The trial is over, and I've served my time. When they released me, they declared me sane, and sane for a human being means an understanding of time and an ability to remember. After that little stunt, I won't work with you for anything less than five times my rate, one month payable in advance."

The flush grew, making those spectacular eyes shine brighter. Not embarrassment after all. Anger. "You tricked me."

"Not at all." John didn't move. He felt more comfortable now with this little hint of emotion. He could ride on emotion, play it. That he had learned from the Dancers. "You had expectations. You shouldn't believe everything you hear."

For a moment, she drew herself up, as if she were going to renounce him and leave. But she didn't. She reached into her pocket and removed a credit flask. She must have needed him badly.

She handed him two chips, which he immediately put into his account. One hundred and twenty thousand zepeatas. Perfect. He smiled for the first time. "What do you want from me?" he asked.

She glanced at the portals, as if the stars would give her strength. The story was an embarrassment, then. An illegality perhaps, or some mistake she had made. "Several weeks ago," she said, "I acquired a Bodean wind sculpture."

Awe rippled through him. He had seen Bodean wind sculptures once, on their home planet. The deserts were full of them, swirling beautifully across the sands. No one knew how to tame them; they remained an isolated artform, on a lone planet. Someone must have figured out a way to capture them, wind currents and all.

"That's not the best part," she said. Her tone had changed. She still wasn't treating him like an equal, but she was closer. "The best part is the mystery inside the sculpture. My equipment indicates a life form trapped in there."

No, no. Not allowed to leave the room, the wing. —If we grow up, we'll be able to leave, never see Bountiful again. If we grow up . . .

He shook the memory voices away, made himself concentrate on her words. Something inside the sculpture. A bodeangenie? But they were the stuff of legends. Traders to Bodean claimed that the sculptures originated to capture little magical beings to prevent them from causing harm to the desert. When the Interspecies Alliance went to study the sculptures, however, they found no evidence of life in or around them.

His hands were shaking. She trapped things and called them art. "You don't need me," he said. "You need a specialist."

"I need you." She turned, her hair spiraling out around her. Beautiful, dramatic. "The wind sculpture's been stolen."

ii

Sleep. Narrow trader bunk, not built for his long frame. Dream voices, half remembered:

    . . . *we'll be able to leave* . . .
    . . . *the Dancers do it* . . .

... *It'll hurt, but that won't matter. You'll grow up* ...
... *Stop, please* ...
... *Just another minute* ...
... *Stop!!!* ...
... *the other hand* ...
... *ssstttooooppp* ...

He forced himself awake, heart pounding, mouth dry. The trapped feeling still filled him. He rolled off the bunk, stood, listened to the even breathing of the other sleepers. He hadn't had the dream since when? the penal colony? the last trading ship? He couldn't remember. He had tried to put it out of his mind. Obviously that hadn't worked.

Trapped. He had started the spiral when she said the word trapped. He leaned against the door, felt the cool plastic against his forehead. The memory voices still rang in his head. If someone had listened, then maybe . . .

But no. The past was past. He would work for her, but he would follow his own reasons.

iii

Her gallery was less than he expected. Shoved into a small corner of the merchant's wing on Rotan Base, the gallery had a storefront of only a few meters. Inside hung the standard work by standard artists: an Ashley rendition of the galaxy, done in blacks and pinks; a D.B. portrait of the sphynix, a red-haired, catlike creature from Yster; a Degas statue of a young girl dancing. Nothing new, nothing unique, not even in the manner of display. All the pieces were self-illuminated against dark walls and stands, a small red light beside each indicating the place for credit purchases.

The gallery was even more of a surprise after she had told him her tale of woe: she claimed to have the best guards on Rotan, an elaborate security system, and special checking. He saw no evidence of them. Her storefront was the same as the others, complete with mesh framing that cascaded at closing each evening.

The gallery smelled dry, dustless. He wanted to sneeze, just to see particles in the air. The air's cleanliness, at least, was unusual. He would have to check the filtration system. The sculpture probably didn't disappear at all. Some overeager viewer probably opened the container, the wind escaped, and the sculpture returned to the grains of sand it was. No great mystery, certainly not worth 120,000 zepeatas. But he wouldn't tell her that.

Anita threaded her way through the displays to the back. He felt himself relax. There he would find the artwork he sought—the priceless, the illegal, the works which had made her famous. But when the door slid open, his mood vanished.

Crates, cartons, holoshippers, transmission machines, more credit slots. The faint odor of food. A desk covered with hardcopy invoices and credit records. A small cache of wine behind the overstuffed chair, and a microprocessor for late night meals. A workspace, nothing more.

She let the door close behind them, her gaze measuring him. He was missing something. He would lose the entire commission if he didn't find it.

He closed his eyes and saw in his imagination what his actual vision had missed. The dimensions of the rooms were off. The front was twice the size of the back. Base regulations required square sales—each purchased compartment had to form a box equal on all sides. She had divided her box into three sections—showroom, back workroom, and special gallery. But where?

Where something didn't fit. The wine. She sold wine as art—nectar of the gods, never drinking it, always collecting it. Wine didn't belong with the boxes and invoices.

He opened his eyes, crouched down, scanned the wine rack. Most bottles came from Earth. They were made with the heavy, too-thick glass that suggested work centuries old. Only one didn't belong: a thin bottle of the base-made synth stuff. He pulled it, felt something small fall into his hand. He clenched his hand to hold it as the wall slid back.

Inside was the gallery he had been expecting.

Holos of previous artifacts danced across the back wall. In those holos, the baby Minaran swam. He wondered where it was now; if it could feel happiness, exploitation. He made himself look away.

A tiny helldog from Frizos clawed at a glass cage. A mobile ice sculpture from Ngela rotated under cool lights. Four canisters in a bowl indicated a Colleician scent painting. He had only seen one before; all he had to do was touch it, and he would be bathed in alien memories.

More valuables drifted off in the distance. Some hung on walls, some rested on pedestals, and some floated around him. None had the standard red credit slot beside them. They were all set up for negotiation, bargaining, and extortion.

"Impressed?" She sounded sarcastic, as if a man with his background could not help but be impressed.

He was, but not for the reasons she thought. He knew how much skill it took to capture each item, to bring it onto a base with strict limitations for importing. "You have your own hunters. Why hire me?"

She tapped on the helldog's cage. John winced. The dog didn't move. "I would have had to hire a hunter no matter what," she said. "If I removed one of my own people from a normal routine, I would have to hire a replacement. I choose not to do that. My people have their own lives, their own beats, and their own predilictions. This incident calls for someone a bit more adaptable, a free lancer. A person like you."

He nodded, deciding that was the best answer he would get from her. Perhaps she had chosen him, and not one of his colleagues, on a whim. Or perhaps she thought she could control him, with his Dancer mind. It didn't matter. She was paying him. And he had a being to free.

iv

Working late into the night so that the dreams would stay away, he did the standard checks: exploring the gallery for bits of the sculpture; contacting the base engineers to see if sand had lodged in the filters; examining particulate material for foreign readings. Nothing. The sculpture appeared to have vanished.

Except for the small item he had found near the wine cache. He set it in the light, examined it, and froze. A sticker. Lina Base used them as temporary i.d.s. Stickers weren't the proper term. Actually, they were little light tabs that allowed the bearer to enter secured areas for brief periods of time, and were called stickers because most spacers stuck them to the tops of their boots.

He hadn't touched one since he left Lina Base nearly two decades before. The memories tickled around his head: Beth, her eyes wide, hands grasping, as Harper's people carried her away; sitting on his own bed, arms wrapped around his head, eyes burning but tearless, staring at his own sticker-covered boots—signifying temporary, even though he had been there for nearly two years.

Dancer mind. He snorted. If only he could forget. He was cursed with too much remembrance.

He set the sticker down, made himself move. He had to check arrival records, see who had come from Lina Base, who frequented it. Then he would know who took the sculpture.

v

The next morning, he walked into the gallery. The showroom was filled with Elegian tourists, fondling the merchandise. The security system had to be elaborate to allow such touching without any obvious watchful presence. The room smelled of animal sweat and damp fur. No wonder her filtration system was good. He pushed his way through, and let himself into the back.

Anita was cataloging chip-sized gems that had arrived the day before. She wore a jeweler's eye, and didn't look up when he entered.

"I need that ship," he said.

"You found something?"

He nodded. "A lead. Some traders."

This time she did look up. The jeweler's eye gave her face a foreign feel. "Who?"

A small ship out of Lina Base named *Runner*. Owned by a man named Minx. He worked with four others on odd jobs no one else wanted—domestic cats from Earth to a colony of miners on Calmium; a cargo of worthless moon rocks to scientists on Mina Base. No records older than twenty years. No recording of illegal trading of any kind. But he didn't tell her that. He still wasn't sure if he was going to tell her anything.

"No one you'd know," he said. "If it turns out to be them, I'll introduce you."

She removed the jeweler's eye. Her own eye looked less threatening. "You're working for me which gives me the right to know what you've found."

"You *contracted* with me," he corrected. "And I have the right to walk away any time I choose—keeping the retainer. Now. Do I get that ship?"

She stared at him for a minute, then put the eye back in. "I'll call down," she said.

vi

The ship was nearly a decade old, and designed to carry less than five people in comfort. He had computer access, games and holos, as much food and drink as he wanted. The only rule was not to disturb the pilot—for any reason. He guessed she had found out about his past, and wanted nothing to do with him.

He slept most of the time. His way of escape on ships. When he was awake, they reminded him of the penal ship, of the hands grabbing, voices prodding, violence, stink, and finally isolation ostensibly for his own good. When he was asleep, they were the only places that allowed him rest without dreams.

His alarm went off an hour before landing, and he paced. He hadn't been to Lina Base for twenty years. He had left as a boy, alone, without Beth, without even Harper, the man who had once been his savior and became his betrayer. Harper, who had healed his mind and broken his heart.

When the ship landed, John didn't move. He was crazy

to go back, crazy to look at the past he had been avoiding. No job was worth that, especially a job he only half-believed in.

You have to face your past, face yourself. And once you see clearly what happened and why, you must forgive yourself. Only then will you be whole.

Harper's voice. John shook himself, as if he could force the voice from his head. He had promised himself, when he left Lina Base on the penal ship, that he would never listen to Harper again.

He had a job. His stay on Lina Base would be short.

He drew himself to his full height, and let himself out of his room. The pilot was at the door. She stopped moving when she saw him; her gaze wary. He nodded. She nodded back. Then he went out of the ship before her.

The docking bay had shiny new walls, and state-of-the-art flooring. But it smelled the same: dusty, tangy, harsh with chemical cleaners. He gripped the railing, cool against his hand.

. . . cringing in the back of the ship, safe behind the upholstered chairs. Voices urging him to get off, and he knowing they were going to kill him. They believed he had done something wrong, and he was going to get a punishment worse than any his parents could dish out . . .

"You okay?" the pilot asked.

He snapped back to the present. He was not twelve, not landing on Lina Base for the first time. He was an adult, a man who could handle himself.

Down the stairs and into the base. No crowds this time, no holoteams, no reporters. No Harper, no savior, no friends beside him. Only ships and shuttles of various sizes. Lina Base had grown since the last time he had been here. Now it had three docking facilities instead of one. It was one of the main trading bases in the galaxy, and had grown instead of declined when the officials closed Bountiful to any and all aliens. He stopped, remembered. If he went to one of the portals, he would be able to see Bountiful, its deserts and mountains etched across the surface like a painting, the Singing Sea adding a touch of blue to the art.

Odd that he missed the place when as a boy all he wanted to do was leave it.

"You seriously okay?"

"Yes." He whirled, expecting his anger to deflate her concern. Then understood that she was speaking from obligation. He was her charge until he left the docking bay, and she didn't want the responsibility of handling him.

"Then get to Deck Three for inspection and hosing. They need to clean this bay for other arrivals."

He nodded, felt a bit numb at her lack of concern. Procedures. After an outbreak of Malanian flu almost three decades before, Lina Base had become fanatic for keeping unwanted elements off the station. During his first visit here, he had been quarantined for three Earth months.

He turned his back on the pilot, sought the elevator, and took it to a tiny corridor on Deck Three. There, a blinking light indicated the room he was to use. He went inside.

The room was better than the one they had given him as a child. This one had a couch, and a servo tray filled with beverages. He stripped, let the robot arms whisk away his clothes, and then stepped under the pale blue light in the corner of the room.

Streams of light invaded his orifices, tickling with the warmth of their touch. He closed his eyes, holding himself still, knowing that on some bases they still used hand searches, and wondering how he could ever stand that when he found this procedure so invasive. When the light had finished, he stepped into the autodoc and let it search him for viruses, traces of alien matter, alien materials, and—probably—alien thought.

Alien influences . . .

A shiver ran through him. He had been twelve years old. Twelve years old and not realizing what they had done was abnormal. Not human. Yet he was still human enough to feel terror at separation from all that he knew.

Knowing, deep down, that the horror was only beginning.

The autodoc was beeping, and for a long moment, he was afraid it had found something. Then he realized that it wanted him to leave its little chamber. He stepped back into the main room and retrieved his clothes—now cleaned and purified—dressed, and pressed the map to find out where he was and where he wanted to be.

vii

John huddled in the shuttle records bay. Dark, cramped, smelling of sweat and skin oils, it was as familiar as any other place on the base. Only this was a different kind of familiarity. Every base had a records bay. And every base had an operator like Donnie.

He was small, wiry, scrawny enough to be comfortable in such a small space. His own stink didn't bother him— he was used to being alone. He monitored the traffic to and from the base, maintained licenses, and refused admittance if necessary.

"Left just as you were docking," he said. His lips barely parted, but his teeth were visible—half fake white, half rotted. "In a hurry, too. Gave 'em the day's last slot."

The day's last slot. No other craft could be cleared for leaving then, until the next day. John clenched his fists. So close.

"Where did they go?"

Donnie checked the hard copy, then punched a button. The display on the screen was almost unreadable. He punched another button, lower lip out, grimy fingers shaking.

"Got a valid pass," he mumbled.

The shiver again, something a bit off. "Where?" John asked.

"Bountiful."

The word shimmered through him. Heat, thin and dry; deep flowery perfume; the rubbery feel of Dancer fingers . . .

"You done?" Donnie asked.

John took a deep breath, calmed himself. "You need to get me to Bountiful."

"Nope." Donnie leaned back in the chair. "I know who you are. Even if Bountiful were open, I couldn't let you go there."

Trapped. This time outside of Bountiful. John's fingernails dug into his palms. The pain kept him awake, sane. He made his voice sound calmer than he felt. "Where do I get the dispensation?"

Donnie gazed at him, scared of nothing, so secure in his small world of records, passes. "Level Five. But they won't help—"

"They will," John said.

viii

He put in a call to Anita, told her to hurry or she would never get her sculpture back. She would pull the strings and dole out the cash. He would spend his time digging out information about the traders.

Lina Base's paranoia about its traders led to a wealth of information. He spent half an Earth day alone with a small computer linked up to the base's main frame.

And found the information he had already known, plus some. Lina Base was their main base of operation. They were well known here, not popular. Two men worked with Minx: Dunnigan—trained as a linguist, and Carter— no formal training at all. The women, Parena and Nox, provided muscle and contacts. They had gotten the jobs on Calmium and Mina Base. And they had all hooked up twenty years ago.

After Bountiful was closed to aliens.

When Minx had to expand his operation.

When Salt Juice had become illegal.

Salt Juice. That little piece of information sent ripples of fear through John. Food. He had to get food. Take care of himself. He stood, unable to stop his mind.

Salt Juice had started it all.

The very smell of it gave him tremors, made him revert, close all the doors on himself, close out the memories and the emotions and the pain. He would focus on the future for protection, Dancerlike, and no one—except Harper, base kiddie therapist—had been able to get in. The only way to keep himself intact, human, was to take care of his body so that the damaged part of his mind could recover.

He went to the cafeteria.

Wide, spacious, with long windows open to space, and hanging plants from all sides, the cafeteria gave him a feeling of safety. He ordered off the servo, picked his table, and ran the credit voucher through. His food appeared on the table almost before the voucher stopped running. He walked over, sat down, and sniffed.

Roast chicken, steamed broccoli, mashed potatoes. Not a normal spacer's meal. Heaven. He made himself eat, feeling the food warm the cold places inside him. As he nourished himself, he allowed his mind to roam.

Salt Juice had been one of the most potent intoxicants in the galaxy. It was manufactured on Bountiful, using herbs grown by the Dancers. Those herbs were the main reason for the dispute with the Dancers—and when the colony finally learned how to grow them without Dancer assistance, they tried to wipe out the Dancers.

With the help of children. Poor, misguided children. Lonely little children who only wanted to leave the hell they were trapped in.

Once Lina Base discovered the scheme, Bountiful was closed. The best herbalists and chemists tried to manufacture Salt Juice away from the colony, but it proved impossible. A good thing. Later they learned that the drug everyone thought addiction-free had some nasty side effects.

Minx traded in Salt Juice.

Then moon rocks, cats. Worthless cargo. But Calmium's northern water supply had a drug as pure as crystal meth. And the Minaran skin was poison which, taken in small amounts, induced a dangerous kind of high.

The five were drug runners. Good, competent, skilled drug runners.

So the bodeangenie had more than artistic value to them. They also had some kind of stimulant value. He leaned back. What kind, he was sure he would find out.

ix

But things happened too quickly. The call came from Anita. She had bought him a window—three Earth days—and she let him know that it cost her a fortune. He smiled. He was glad to put her money to good use.

He located the pilot, and together they flew to the place from which he had been banned for life.

x

Once again, he sat in his room on the ship, far from the uncommunicative pilot. He was glad for the solitude, even on such a short trip. He hadn't been to Bountiful since he was twelve. Then he had hated the planet, wanted nothing more than to be free of it. But the freedom he obtained wasn't the freedom he expected.

. . . The plastic frame dug into his forehead. Through the portal, he could see Bountiful, swirling away from him. They had isolated him, considering him the ring-leader—and perhaps he was. He hadn't understood the depths of their anger. He was experimenting, as they had, only he was trying to save the others . . .

He sighed, and walked to the portal. Bountiful loomed, dark and empty. Only five humans on the planet. Five humans and hundreds of Dancers, thousands of other species. After the announcement of the murders, the authorities had declared the planet unsafe, and closed it to all colonization. Even researchers needed special dispensation to go. The Dancers were too powerful, their thoughts too destructive. He shook his head. But the Dancers hadn't been the real problem. Salt Juice had.

Without Salt Juice, the Dancers would never have become an endangered species. Without Salt Juice, the colony wouldn't have made money, and wouldn't have tried to protect that base by allowing ill-conceived killings to go on. The colonists had tried to blame the Dancers for the murders to exterminate the entire species; the intergalactic shock had been great when investigators discovered that the murderers were children.

Salt Juice. He still remembered the fumes, the glazed looks in his parents' eyes. Colonists weren't supposed to indulge—and none did—but they all suffered from Salt Juice intoxication because of their exposure during manufacturing. Perhaps if he had had a better lawyer, if the effects of Salt Juice were better understood at the time, he would have gotten off, been put in rehabilitation instead of incarcerated.

A slight ponging warned him that the shuttle would land soon. He dug in his duffel and removed the sand scarf, and some ointment. The woven material felt familiar, warm, a touch of the past. As children they had stopped wearing sand scarves, and he had gotten so crisped by Bountiful's sun that he still had tan lines. He was older now, and wiser. He would wear the offered protection.

His throat had gone dry. Three days alone on Bountiful. The pilot wouldn't stay—probably due to fear of him. He strapped himself in, knowing it was too late to turn back.

The shuttle bumped and scuttled its way to a stop. Already the temperature inside changed from cool to the kind of almost cool developed when the outside air was extremely hot. John unstrapped himself, put on the sand scarf, and rubbed oil over his exposed skin. Then he slung the duffel over his back, got up, and went into the flight deck.

The pilot made an exasperated, fearful noise. John ignored her. Through the windows, he could see the Salt Cliffs and the Singing Sea. The shuttle landed where they had always landed, on the edge of the desert, half a day's walk from the colony itself. He realized, with a shudder, that no one lived on the planet but the natives. The five traders and the sand sculpture were the aliens here.

He had no plan. He had been too lost in his memories. "Familiar?" the pilot asked. Her expression was wary.

She knew his history. Perhaps she thought that once he set foot on the planet, he would pull a Dancer ritual knife and slice off her hands and feet.

He didn't answer her. "You're coming back in three days?"

She nodded. Her hands were shaking on the controls. What kind of lies had the authorities made up about Bountiful to keep the curious away? That one touch of the desert sand would lead to madness? That one view of the Dancers would lead to murder?

"Wait for me. Even if I'm not here right away, I'll be coming." The words sounded hollow to his own ears. She nodded again, but he knew at that moment that she wouldn't wait. He would have to be here precisely on time or be stranded on Bountiful forever. Trapped.

The child inside him shivered.

He tugged on the duffel strap, adjusting it, and let himself out. A hot, dry breeze caressed his face. The air smelled like flowers, decaying flowers too long in the sun. Twelve years of memories, familiarity and fear rose within him—and suddenly he didn't want to be here any more. He turned to the shuttle, but the bay door had already closed. He reached up to flag her down—and turned the gesture into a wave. He was not twelve any more. The adults were gone. The colony was gone. He was the adult now, and he wouldn't let himself down.

xi

The traders made a brilliant decision to come to Bountiful with the wind sculpture. Here they had a ready-made empty colony, a desert filled with sand, and winds aplenty. They could experiment until they were able to duplicate whatever effect they needed, or they could use the planet as a base from which to travel back to Bodean. No one would have caught on if Anita hadn't started the search for her sculpture.

The colony's dome shone like a glass in the sunlight. The walk wasn't as long as John remembered. Still, he would have loved an air car. Air cars had always been

forbidden here; they destroyed the desert's delicate eco-
logical balance.

He stopped in front of the dome, stunned to see it
covered with little sand particles. In another generation,
the dome would be a mound of sand, with no indication
that anything had ever existed beneath it. The desert re-
claimed its own.

He brushed the sand aside, feeling the grains cling to
the oil on his skin. The dome was hot, hotter than he
cared to touch, but still he felt for the fingerholds that he
knew would be there.

And found them. Smaller than he remembered, and
filled with sand, but there. He tugged, and with a groan,
the section moved. He slipped inside, bumping his head
on the surface. He was a man now, not a boy, and crawling through small spaces wasn't as easy as it used to be.

Once inside, he closed the hatch, and took a deep
breath. The air wasn't as stale as he had expected it to
be. It tasted metallic, dusty, like air from a machine that
had been turned off for a long time. Decades, probably.

The traders had been in here. Of course they would
know that the dome could be breached from the outside.
Bountiful's colonists had had a terror of being trapped in
the desert.

All he had to do was go to the municipal plant and
track them from there. So easy. He would have to wait
three lousy Earth days together for the shuttle pilot to
return.

He turned onto a street and started walking. He had
made it halfway down the block before the things he saw
registered, and his emotions stopped him.

The houses hadn't collapsed. They were old-time regulation colony homes, built for short-term, but used on
Bountiful for nearly a century. The lawns were dead.
Brown hulks of plants remained, crumbling now that the
air had come back on.

The lawns, the gardens, had been the colonists' joy.
They were so pleased that they had been able to tame this
little space of land, turn it into their ideal of Earth. Plastic homes with no windows, and Earth flowers every-

where. The dome used to change color with the quality
of the light: sometimes gray, sometimes blue, sometimes
an odd sepia to protect the colonists from the UV rays.

All of that gone now. No voices, no hum of the Salt
Juice factory, no movement. Just John on a long empty
street, facing long empty ghosts.

There, on the house to the left, he and the other children
had placed Michael Dengler's body. He had been the last
one, the true failure. It had seemed so logical that if they
removed his head along with his hands, his heart and his
lungs, that he would grow taller and stronger than the
adults. But like the others, he hadn't grown at all.

John sank to the ground, wrapped his arms around his
head as if he could shield himself from his own memories. He and the others weren't covered under the Alien
Influences Act. They weren't crazy. They were, according to the prosecuting attorney, evil children with an evil
plan.

All they had wanted to do was escape. And they
thought the Dancers held the secret to that escape.

He remembered huddling behind the canopied trees,
watching the Dancer puberty ritual, thinking it made so
much sense: remove the hands, the heart and the lungs
so that the new ones would grow in. He was on a different planet now, the third generation born in a new place.
Of course he wasn't growing up. He wasn't following the
traditions of the new world.

The attorneys asked him, over and over, if he believed
that, why hadn't he gone first? He wanted to go last,
thinking that the ultimate sacrifice. Dancer children didn't
move for days. He didn't understand the adult reaction—
the children weren't dead, they were growing new limbs.
Or at least, that was what he thought. Until Michael Dengler. Then John had understood what he had done.

He stayed on his knees for a long time. Then he made
himself rise slowly. He did bounty now. He traveled all
over the galaxy. He had served his sentence. This was
done, gone. He had a wind sculpture to recover, and the
people were within his grasp.

He made himself walk, and concentrate on the future.

xii

He found where they got in. Another section had been dislodged, letting too bright sunlight into the dome. Footprints marred the dirt, and several brown plant stalks were newly broken. Being this close usually excited him—one of the few excitements that he had—but this time he felt empty inside.

His breathing rasped in his throat. He had a dual feeling; that of being watched and that of being totally alone. The hairs prickled on the back of his neck. Something was wrong here.

He followed the footprints to the municipal building. The door was open—an invitation almost. He couldn't go around to the windows, since there were none, and most buildings didn't have another doorway. He braced himself, and slipped in.

The silence was heavier in here. The buildings always had a bit of white noise—the rustle of a fan, the whisper of air filtering through the ceiling. Here, nothing. Perhaps they had only found the controls for the dome itself. Perhaps they wanted it quiet so that they could hear him.

The walls and floors were spotless, so clean that they looked as if they had been washed days before. Only the dirt-covered tracks of the traders marred the whiteness, a trail leading him forward, like an earth dog on the trail of a scent.

He followed it, willing to play out his little role in this drama. Some action would take his mind off the remains of the colony, of the hollow vestiges of his past.

He rounded the corner—and found the first body.

It leaned against the wall, skin toughened, mummified into a near skeleton. For a minute, he thought it had been there since the colony closed and the air shut down. Then he noticed the weapon in its left hand. A small hand-held laser, keyed to a person's print. Last year's model.

He made himself swallow and lean in. One of the traders. For a minute, he couldn't determine which one. He ripped at the clothes, discovered gender—male—then studied the wrinkled, freeze-dried face.

Not the old trader, Minx, who had run Salt Juice. One of the younger males. Tension crept up his back. He held himself still. He had seen this kind of death before, but where?

The answer required that he let down some internal shields, reach into his own memory. He did so slowly, feeling the hot spots, the oppression the colony imposed on him. Then it came:

A cadmium miner on one of the many cargo ships he had worked for. The miner had slipped into the hold, trying to get safe passage somewhere, not realizing that to get out of those mines, he needed a series of shots, shots that protected him from the ways that the mining had destroyed his body, processes that wouldn't start until the mining ended.

The captain of the cargo ship had leaned over to John, expressed the view for the entire ship. "God," he said, "I hope I don't die like that!"

John touched the corpse again, figuring if he was contaminated, there wasn't much he could do about it. Amazing that he didn't die when he left Cadmium. They had been away from that planet for years. Amazing that the death would come now, here, in this faraway place, with a weapon in his hand.

He took the laser from the body, ran the diagnostic. It worked. He pocketed it. Better to use that weapon than his own. Covered his tracks, if he had to.

The footprint path continued down the hall. He brushed off his hands, and followed it. All the doors were closed, locks blinking, as if they hadn't been touched since the colony was evacuated.

He followed the trail around another corner, and found another body: this one a woman. She was sprawled across the floor, clothing shredded, blood everywhere, eyes wide with terror. No dessication, no mummification. This time, the reek of death, and the lingering scent of fear.

She appeared to have been brutalized and beaten to death, but as he got closer, he realized that she didn't have a scratch on her. John's throat had gone dry, and his hands were shaking. He had never before encountered anything as odd as this. How did people die on a dead planet? Nothing here would do this, not in this fashion, and not so quickly. He knew about death on Bountiful, and it didn't work like this.

He pulled the laser out of his pocket and kept going. The dirt path didn't look like footprints any more, just a swirl of dirt along a once-clean floor. He half-expected a crazed trader to leap out from behind one of the doors, but he knew that wouldn't happen. The deaths were too bizarre, too different to be the work of a maniac. They had been planned. And a little scared voice inside told him they had been planned for him.

xiii

John reached the main control room, surprised to find it empty and silent. Lights blinked and flashed on a grid panel nearly two centuries old. He checked the patterns, figuring how it should run on guesswork, experience with old grids, and a half worn down diagram near the top of the room. His instincts warned him to absorb the knowledge in this room—and he was, as quickly as he could.

A door slammed somewhere in the building.

His skin prickled. He whirled. No one visible. No sounds. Nothing except the slight breeze caused by his own actions. He moved slowly, with a deliberation he didn't feel. He checked the corridor, both directions, noting that it was empty. Then he left the main control room. There was nothing more he could do inside. He walked toward the direction of the slammed door. Someone else was alive in here, and he would find that person. He didn't know what he would do then.

His heart was pounding against his chest. Death had never frightened him before. He had never felt it as a threat, only as a partner, an accident. He never saw the murders as deaths, just failed experiments. No one he loved had ever died. They had just disappeared.

Another body littered the corridor. He didn't examine it. A quick glance told him the cause of death. Parts were scattered all over, hanging in the ritual position of Fetin

killings, something he had seen too much of in his own
exile.

The fourth body was crucified against a wall, upside
down, blood still dripping onto the pristine floor. Perhaps he was wrong. One madman with a lot of determi-
nation, and perhaps some kind of toxic brain poisoning
from a drug he wasn't used to. One man, Minx, the old
trader, under the influence of the Bodean wind sculpture.

He hated to think Minx had done this in a rational
frame of mind.

John had circled nearly the entire building. From his
position, he could see the door, still standing open. Minx
had to be outside, waiting for him. He tensed, holding
the laser, setting his own systems on alert.

The dirt spread all over the floor, and a bit on the
walls. Odd, without anyone tracking it. Was Minx's entire body grimy? John crept along as quietly as he could,
trying to disturb nothing. Seemed eerie, as if Minx had
been planning for this. It felt as if he had been watching,
waiting, as if John were part of a plan. Even more eerie
that Minx had managed to kill so many people in such
diverse ways—and in such a short period of time.

It made no sense.

John reached the front door, and went rigid, except for
a trembling at the very base of his spine. Minx was there,
all right, waiting, all right, but not in the way John expected.

Minx was dead.

The blood still trickled from the stumps where his
hands used to be. His chest was flayed open, heart and
lungs missing. Head tilted back, neck half cut, as if whoever did this couldn't decide whether or not to slice it
through.

He hadn't been there when John went into the building. Minx couldn't have died here—it took too long to
chop up a human being like that. John knew. He had
done it half a dozen times—with willing victims. Minx
didn't look willing.

The blood was everywhere, spraying everything. Minx
had to have died while John was inside.

To kill an adult the size of Minx would have taken a lot of strength, or a lot of time.

The shivering ran up John's spine, into his hands. *I didn't mean to kill him!* the little boy inside him cried. *We just wanted to grow up, like Dancers. Please! I didn't mean . . .*

He quashed the voice. He had to think. All five were dead. Something—

"John?"

He looked up. Beth stood before him, clutching a Dancer ritual blade. It was blood-covered, and so was she. Streaks had splattered across her face, her hands. He hadn't seen her since she was fifteen, since the afternoon the authorities caught them comforting each other, him inside her, her legs wrapped around him like a hug.

The first and last time John had been intimate with anyone.

She had hated the killings, never wanted to do them. Always sat quietly when Harper made the group talk about them. Three years of sessions, one afternoon of love. Then prison ship and separation, and him bounty hunting, alone, forever.

"Beth?" He knew it wasn't her, couldn't be her. She would never do anything like this, not alone, and not now so many years in the future. He walked toward her anyway, wanting to wipe the blood off her precious face. He reached for her, hand shaking, to touch that still rosy cheek, to see if it was as soft as he remembered, when his hand went through her.

She was as solid as wind.

Wind.

She laughed and grew bigger, Minx now, even though he remained dead at John's feet. "Took you long enough," the bodeangenie said. "And you call yourself the best."

John glanced at the body, the ritual knife, found the laser in his own hand. A laser could not cut through wind.

"No," the bodeangenie said. "It can't."

John stopped breathing. He took a step back as the

realization hit. The bodeangenie was telepathic. It had been inside John's head, inside his mind. He shuddered, wiped himself off, as if in brushing away the sand he brushed away the touch, the intimacy that he had never wanted. Had the others died of things they feared? That would explain the lack of external marks, the suddenness. That would explain all except Minx. Minx, who died of something John feared.

Then the images assaulted him: The trader ship, full of sweat, laughter and drink, hurtling toward the planet; the traders themselves dipping into the bodeangenie like forbidden fruit, using him to enhance their own powers, tap each other's minds, playing; the Dancers stalking out of the woods, into the desert; John, sitting in the cafeteria, his memories displayed before him; Anita, counting credits, peering into the bottle; the trap closing tight, holding him fast, a bit of wind, a bit of sand, a bit of plastic. . . .

John was the bodeangenie's freedom if Bountiful didn't work. He could pilot the traders' ship back to Bodean, back to the 'genie's home. Fear pounded inside his skull. He didn't want to die like that. He had never wanted to die like that. . . .

He slid to his knees, hands around his head as if to protect it. Harper's voice: *if you want protection, build a wall. Not a firm wall, a permeable one, to help you survive the alone times. The wall must come down when you need it to, so that things don't remain hidden. But sometimes, to protect yourself, build a wall.*

The sheets came up, slowly, but easier than he had hoped because they were already half there. The bodeangenie chuckled, Beth again, laughter infectious. She went to the dome, touched it, and John saw Dancers, hundreds of them, their fingers rubbing against the plastic, their movement graceful and soft, the thing that had given them their name.

"Three choices," the bodeangenie said. "Me, or death, or them."

A little light went on behind his wall. The bodeangenie thought the Dancers frightened him. The 'genie could only tap what was on the surface, not what was buried deep, no matter what its threats.

Wind, and sand, and plastic.

John hurled himself at the dome, pushing out, and sliding through. The Dancers vanished as if they never were. He rolled in the sand, using all his strength to close the dome doors. The bodeangenie pushed against him with the power of wind. His muscles shook, his arms ached. The bodeangenie changed form, started to slip out, when John slammed the portal shut.

Trapping the 'genie inside.

The bodeangenie howled and raged against the plastic wall. The side of the dome shook, but the 'genie was trapped. A little boy appeared in his mind, alone in a foreign place, hands pounding on a door. *Let me out*, the little boy said with John's voice. *Please I didn't mean to—*

His words, his past. Trapped. The 'genie was trapped. It had to be or it would kill him. Trapped.

John started to run, as if that would drown out the voice. Across the sands toward the forest, toward something familiar. The sun beat down on him, and he realized he had forgotten his scarf, his ointment, his protection. The little boy kept pounding, sobbing. Torture. He wouldn't be able to survive it. Two more days until the shuttle arrived.

He could take the traders' ship, if he could find it.

The forest still looked charred, decades after the fire that happened just before John left the planet. But the canopied trees had grown back, and John could smell the familiar scent of tangy cinnamon. Dancers.

No!!! the little boy screamed in his head.

They came toward him, two-legged, two-armed, gliding like ballerinas on one of the bases. They chirruped in greeting, and he chirruped back, the language as fresh as if he had used it the day before.

His mind drifted into the future, into emotion, into their world.

I would like to stay, John said, placing his memories behind him. *I would like to be home.*

xiv

Sometimes he would wake in the middle of the night, stare through the canopies at the stars, and think: *Someday I will touch them*. Then he would return to sleep, incident forgotten.

Sometimes he would be touching a Dancer's hand, performing a ritual ceremony, and a child's scream would filter through his mind. He would drop the knife, plead apology, and wonder at it, since none of the others seemed to mind.

He loved the trees and the grass, but the hot, dry wind against his face would make him shiver. Sometimes he would think he was crazy, but usually he thought nothing at all.

xv

Perhaps days, perhaps months later, John found himself in the desert, searching for small plants. Food, he was thinking, he would like food—when fists, a little boy's voice, pounded their way into his mind. *Let me out, please let me out*. Puzzlement, a touch of fear, and something against a block—

The memories came flooding back, the shuttle, the bodeangenie. He sat down, examined his fried skin. Human. No matter how much he wanted to be Dancer, he would always be human, with memories, guilt, and regrets.

The bodeangenie was still trapped. The shuttle was long gone, and John was trapped here, presumed dead, doomed to die if he didn't get out of the harsh sun and eat human foods instead of Dancer foods.

He looked back into the forest. He had no memories of the last few days (months?). Dancer thought. Dancers had no memories. He had achieved it, ever so briefly. And it would kill him, just as it nearly killed him when he was a boy. They were his drug, as potent as Salt Juice, and as deadly.

Please . . .

He stood, wiped himself off. The trader shuttle was hidden near the Singing Sea. The bodeangenie was trapped, the planet closed. He was thought dead, and Anita had lost her money.

Beth rose in his mind, pleading against the dome.

Beth. Her screams, his cries. Nights clutching a pillow pretending it was her, wanting the warmth she provided, the understanding of shared experience, shared terror.

Trapped.

The adults had punished him because he felt trapped, abandoned, because he had killed to set himself free.

Like the bodeangenie.

John was the adult now.

He sank to the sand, examined his sun-baked skin. Much longer, and he would have died of exposure. He was already weak. His need to run, his longing for the Dancers, had trapped him as neatly as he had trapped the bodeangenie. He had been imprisoned so long that even when he had freedom, he imprisoned himself.

Beth and a handful of children huddled near the edges of the dome, waiting for him. Children he had killed, others he had destroyed. The 'genie was using their memories to reach him, to remind him how it felt to be trapped.

He needed no reminding. He had never been free.

He got up, wiped the sand off his skin. His clothing was tattered, his feet callused. He had been hiding for a long time. The 'genie wasn't able to touch the Dancer part of his mind.

John started to walk, feet leading him away from the Dancers. He glanced back once, to the canopied forest, the life without thought, without memory. Alien influence. The reaction was not human.

And he was all too human.

Please! I didn't mean . . .

Yes, he did. Just as the 'genie did. It was the only way they knew how to survive.

The sand burned under his bare feet. He wasn't too far from the dome. Perhaps that was how the 'genie's thoughts had penetrated. Saving him. Saving them both.

John nodded, a plan forming. He would take the 'genie back home on the trader ship, using Anita's credits for fuel. She would know that he was alive then, and she would be angry.

Then he would deal with her, and all the creatures she had trapped. He would find the Minaran, free it; free the little helldog. He would destroy her before she destroyed too much else.

Sand blew across the dome's surface. Almost buried, almost gone. He got closer, felt the presence inside.

Please . . .

In his mind's eye, a half dozen children pushed their faces against the plastic, waiting for him. Beth, a woman now, held them in place. No 'genie. Just his past. Face it, Harper had said.

He had been running from it too long.

He reached the dome, brushed the sand away, searching for a portal.

The 'genie needed him. It wouldn't kill him. Wind couldn't pilot a spaceship alone.

"I'm coming," John said.

And inside the dome, the children rejoiced.

THE PRAGMATISTS
TAKE A BOW

by Thomas A. Easton

Tom Easton, author and long-time book reviewer for *Analog*, was also a textbook editor for Scott, Foresman.

The director of a galaxy-traveling ballet company is found murdered in his room, bludgeoned to death. The most logical suspect is a former prima ballerina who broke her leg, and destroyed her career, on a world where the gravity was minimally heavier than Earth's, and who has blamed the director long and loud for not giving her enough rehearsal time to adjust to the different gravity. She now travels with the troupe as an assistant choreographer.

All the clues point to her: one of her handkerchiefs is found at the scene of the crime, and the DNA of a hair found on the director's outfit matches hers. But her alibi is ironclad: she was playing cards with other members of the company when the crime occurred, she left only to use the bathroom (which is a closed environment, opening only to the card-playing room), and, as a very small woman, and a crippled woman at that, she would hardly be capable of bludgeoning the director even if she had no alibi.

Your cop's task: break down her alibi and determine how the murder was committed.

The day before we were due to orbit Schlavin in the FedArts cruiser *Marquez,* com reports said the colony had sold every ticket for our two weeks of outreach ballet and other theater.

FedArts did not have many ships, and space held many colonies. Perhaps that explained why Schlavin's messages could sound so excited over the prospect of a bit of culture from the Home Systems while we yawned and rummaged for a slightly fresher deck of cards and said, "Another night of Hearts?"

Sally Worth, the crippled dancer who was now our assistant choreographer, was sitting on the edge of her bed. I had the only chair in the cabin. Kato Sibai, the chubby music tech who hung a sheathed dagger on his wide belt and ran constant fingers through thick black hair, had an up-ended suitcase. Two more suitcases, stacked, were the card table. A small trunk almost hid the "DO NOT OBSTRUCT" sticker on the access hatch in the cabin wall.

"Ah, Caitlin," said Kato glumly. "Why did I have to argue with the man? I knew he was a bastard, and that his own ideas are the only ones that count." He touched the ornate handle of his dagger; I had never known him to draw it. He wore loose black trousers and a white T-shirt. "I still think Shakespeare would have liked a little ragtime. It's not as if no one had ever combined the two before."

"Not classic enough," said Sally. "So now Flechner is giving you the boot. So who's going to handle the synthesizers for us?"

"He's giving the job to Dubay." Shar Dubay was the Director's lover and the troupe's choreographer, Sally's boss.

When I winced, he added, "She'll do okay. And I won't starve. I've already talked to Schlavin's main veedo unit." He cut the deck and began to shuffle.

"At least you're still whole."

"Give it a rest," I said as wearily as I could manage. Sally had worn out everyone's sympathy long ago. Now it was Kato's turn. "We all know what happened to you."

"It's that same bastard's fault!" She pushed sleek brown hair back from her cheek and glared at me.

"We know, we know," said Kato tiredly. "Benthazy's gee was a tenth over standard, and you needed more practice."

"He wouldn't give it to me. Myostim should be enough, he said. We had a schedule, he said, and he wasn't breaking it for any puny little prima donna. And then he made me dance with that robot fork-lift."

"Modern enough," I said with a glance at Kato. "But that was his own idea."

He ignored me. "If you'd just broken your legs, you'd have healed just fine. But those treads . . ." He handed her the shuffled deck.

"I wouldn't have fallen if . . . !"

"Enough!" I tried to sound as much older than the others as I really was. "He didn't dump you."

"But I'm not a dancer anymore." Her tone was flat as she dealt. "Assistant to his mistress. Choreographer-in-training."

I looked at my cards. I had the queen of spades. If I handed off my two diamonds . . . "But you've got legs."

"Speaking of robots." Sally threw her hand down, climbed off the bed, and jerked her beige corduroy skirt to her hips to reveal limbs as gracefully enticing as anything of flesh and blood could be. The almost subliminal hum of pumps and motors that accompanied her movement would have betrayed her reliance on robotics instead of biology even if she had not exposed the metal rim of the basin that held her torso. The basin also held the neural inductors that allowed her to control her legs and feet just as if they were the ones she once had grown. Shoulder straps like antique men's suspenders held her body and soles together.

"Enough," I said again. "You've got reason, but you've beaten it to death."

"Someone should beat *him* to death," muttered Kato.

Sally looked at him. "It's about time someone said that. But . . ." She hesitated. Then she said, "The hell with it. I've got to go kick the can. Don't hold up the

game for me.'' She spun very naturally on her robotic
pins and headed for the bathroom door.

Now it was Kato's turn to toss his cards on the table.
''You can't play Hearts with just two people. And she'll
be in there forever.''

''You would, too.'' The ex-dancer's words came
through the metal door, punctuated by a grunt of effort.
''If you had to climb a jungle gym with nothing but your
arms before you could pee.''

''Gin?'' I asked Kato.

He shook his head. ''I'm going to bed.''

''I could still dance,'' came Sally's voice. ''But he
won't let me.''

''There isn't much call for half-robot swans.''

Kato slid the door shut behind him, and he was gone.
I thought of the tangle of steel bars that made Sally's
bathroom almost unusable to anyone else. She would
stand her legs in front of the sink, unfasten her straps
and neural inductors, and then brachiate to the toilet or
the shower. The help she needed away from here, in a
theater, anywhere, invariably soured her mood.

I had a bag with me, full of leotards and skirts and
other garments that had split their seams. I rummaged
for the fabwelder and busied myself for the next half hour.
Only when the bathroom door opened once more and I
could see that Sally had successfully remounted her legs
did I leave for my own cabin.

Not long after breakfast next morning we heard the
sounds—clanks of fasteners fastening, gurgles of fuel and
other fluids replenishing, hums of automatic machinery
off-loading our costumes and music synthesizers, rattles
of running feet—that announced to anyone who cared
that the *Marquez* had docked with High Berlin. Yet the
call for debarkation never came.

I was on my way to Director Flechner's cabin. Two
days before, when the first messages had come from
Schlavin, he had told me they had a new sort of fabric,
made from the skin of some marine creature like a giant

jellyfish. They would have samples waiting on the station.

Had they come aboard yet? I wanted to see them both because they might provide a novel costume material and because they might be exportable. And I had a cousin in the garment trade.

I had just rounded a corner and spotted the striking violet uniform of the guard at Flechner's door. Before I could do more than stop and begin to wonder—what was that guard doing there?—there was a crackle of static from the speakers in the ship's walls, and a strange voice said, "Landing will be delayed. Please return to your cabins. Remain there until the Orbital Guard has finished its investigation."

The Orbital Guard. A Schlavin institution that was surely signified by that violet uniform, which even at this distance I could see had an unusual texture. The cops by any name still were cops. But an investigation? Of what? Or whom?

And how long would it take? None of us could leave the ship until the station said the downway shuttle was ready for us and opened its gates. We were used to that, even though no one wanted to stay aboard the cramped FedArts ship any longer than was absolutely necessary. No one would be happy now.

When the guard touched the sidearm velcroed to his chest and said, "To your cabin, ma'am," I turned around.

There were other guards in the ship's corridors now, standing at intersections, blocking the galley door, chivying crew and passengers out of sight. "Move," they said. "Move along now. Get out of the way. Into your cabins. Don't leave town, ha! ha! We'll want to ask you questions."

I was not amused, though I used the opportunities as I passed the guards to study their uniforms. None of them bore insignia of rank. Most wore conventional cloth. A few wore something new, porous but clearly nonwoven, its surface varying intriguingly in reflectivity. I wanted to feel it between my fingers, but that would have to wait.

Nor was I amused when the waiting stretched interminably and the young Guardswoman who delivered lunch politely refused to respond to my questions.

After lunch I called Kato on the com.

"It's Flechner," he said. "He's dead. Dubay found h . . ."

His voice stopped and the picture froze for an instant before blinking out. Words filled the screen: "Contact forbidden between suspects until after interrogation."

But I had learned something. Shar Dubay slept with Flechner, in his room, in his bed, and she had apparently discovered his body. And he was dead because someone had killed him. Murder. Nothing else would have brought the local cops down on us so hard. Nothing else would have prompted that "suspects" on the screen.

At least in my cabin, I had much more fabwelding to do than I had had with me when I was waiting for Sally to come out of her bathroom. And it wasn't just mindless repairs. I lost myself for most of the afternoon in the new Bottom costume for our "Midsummer Night" musical.

The buzzcut blond's nametag said L. PESCH. His uniform was cloth, and he stood against the galley wall, watching the seven people gathered before him with a cautioning, judgmental eye. If I opened my mouth, or Kato or Sally or any of the other four, he turned and glared and quite silently shouted, "Silence!"

There had been a dozen of us, gathered from our cabins and marched to this holding pen. Five had already been taken next door, to the small conference room normally used for plotting programs or arguing over music selections or even, occasionally, script changes. There was a barre along one wall, and sometimes the dancers would rehearse in it, but it was not a large enough room to be much improvement over the programmed muscle stimulation—myostim—that generally kept them in shape. There was, of course, no way to vary the apparent pull of gravity. Actual rehearsal, practice, really was necessary on worlds like Benthazy. On Schlavin, where the gee was slightly less than Earth's, the dancers needed only to fine-tune their timing.

I glimpsed a stainless steel table covered with racks of test tubes and vials of reagents as the door to the ship's kitchen swung open and shut. Then a violet-uniformed tech was standing before me with a large needle in her hand. "Blood sample," she said. I sighed and gave her my arm. Of course, I thought. They had a scrap of hair or a flake of dandruff or even a drop of blood from the murderer, and they were looking for a DNA match.

One by one, the others were led away. When Kato stood, I noticed that he was not wearing his dagger. Had they already confiscated it? It was so much a part of him, the image he presented to the world. I knew he would never use it, but the cops could know only what they saw.

I was not surprised to find another buzzcut blond in the conference room when my turn came. He wore no nametag, but he did not leave me ignorant of his name or rank for long. As soon as I was seated across the corner of the table from him, he said, "Captain Spinner. You're Andrea Caitlin Doyle." His tone was dry, matter-of-fact, no-nonsense.

"Just Caitlin," I said.

He *hmphhed* and looked at a sheet of paper in front of him. "Costumer. Where were you between ten and eleven last night?"

His uniform was made of the new material. I wondered if that was a sign, more subtle than chevrons or brass bars or oak leaves, of his elevated rank.

"Ms. Doyle." His tone warned me that his patience was limited.

I had been playing Hearts with Kato and Sally, and I told him so.

"Sibai left alone, did he?"

I nodded. "But I'm sure he wouldn't have killed the Director."

He looked slightly surprised. "What do you know about it?"

"You didn't cut off the com system fast enough."

"When did he leave?"

I told him as best I could.

"Then he has no alibi at all."

"Everybody else does?"

I knew that I was out of line, that he was the one who was supposed to ask the questions, but he only stared at me thoughtfully. It occurred to me that he was young enough to be my son, if I had ever . . . Perhaps I reminded him of his mother.

When he finally spoke, he said, "Everyone I've talked to was with at least two others."

"Except him?"

"And you and Worth. You had her in sight the whole time?"

"What about Shar Dubay? His lover? Couldn't she have done it?" After a long moment while he only looked at me expectantly, saying nothing, I finally answered his question. "She went to the bathroom. I couldn't see her in there."

"But the door?"

I nodded. The bathroom door had not opened until Sally had finally emerged.

"So she has an alibi. Very solid. And yours isn't too bad. You were there when she went into the bathroom, and still there when she came out. And you couldn't have guessed how long she'd be in there. You wouldn't have dared . . ."

I grinned at him. "She always takes a long time." When he grunted, I told him why.

He did not look surprised. "You're not helping yourself."

"*I* know I didn't do it. And I don't believe Kato did either."

The room's door opened, and the same tech who had taken the blood samples handed Captain Spinner a manila envelope with a single sheet of paper clipped to it. When he had glanced at the paper, he sighed and relaxed in his seat. He still did not seem surprised. "You're right, of course. And now we know who did it."

I raised my eyebrows.

"The dancer," he said. "There's no use in continuing to give her that alibi."

"Sally? But she *was* in the bathroom!"

"And there's only one door. But she left clues. On the body."

"She couldn't have!"

"A handkerchief," he said. "And a hair." He opened the envelope and extracted a pair of smaller, transparent envelopes. One held a handkerchief folded to show a black laundry code. The other held a single hair about three centimeters long, dark, and crinkled. It didn't look like it came from Sally's head, where the hairs were straight and much, much longer. But if he said it was hers, he surely had the results of the gene matches to back him up.

"We even have the motive," he added. "She told us herself." Then he laughed.

She would, I thought, and then I remembered that I could not trust a word he said. He was investigating a murder, interrogating suspects, and in every crime tale I had ever viewed, misleading suspects—telling them what awful trouble they were in, or saying that someone else had already confessed—was quite routine. The object, of course, was to make the suspect relax, let down his or her guard, and slip.

Yet this scene did not seem right. Not that I expected real life to match fiction word for word, but he seemed so definite, while I *knew* that Sally had to be innocent. She could not possibly have murdered the troupe's Director.

And I knew *I* had not done it.

Therefore, if everyone else aboard the *Marquez* was well and truly alibied, then . . . "It had to be Kato," I said. "He carries a knife on his belt. That must be the weapon!"

Captain Spinner laughed again. He stood up, and I guessed the slight whizzing noise I heard must be the rubbing of the new Schlavin fabric against the table edge. "This?" he said.

His hand now held a knife whose hilt—all that I had

ever seen—looked like Kato's. The blade, as long as the handle, gleamed wickedly.

I gasped when he pressed the point of that blade against his palm and pushed. But the blade only sank into its handle. The skin of Captain Spinner's hand was barely dimpled.

I actually felt disappointed when I said, "A prop knife."

"Besides," said the Captain. "The Director was not stabbed. He died of numerous blows from one or more blunt instruments. He was pounded from head to foot."

He nodded once, firmly and deliberately. "You can go now."

How could Captain Spinner be so sure that Sally Worth had murdered Albert Flechner? She had the motive, for she blamed the Director for the accident that had cost her her legs. But means? She was a small woman and no powerhouse for all that a ballerina cannot be a weakling. She was also a cripple. I could not see how she could possibly beat a man to death, certainly not . . . Flechner had been twice her weight; he should have had no trouble immobilizing her.

And of course she had no opportunity. She had been shut up inside that bathroom, and I would swear in court, on whatever Good Book a judge would care to name, that the bathroom door had not opened, that she had not left that room, that she had *not* murdered the Director.

Anyone could have planted the handkerchief and the hair.

Captain Spinner had to know all that.

Yet he seemed absolutely set on Sally as the killer.

Why was Kato Sibai not a suspect? He had actually mentioned beating the Director to death, and shortly after that he had left.

Was it the fake knife? Did it signify to Captain Spinner that the soft, chubby music tech craved a more macho image but had no ability to follow through? That no matter what he said, no matter what grudge he held, he was unlikely to beat the man to death?

And why was I, Caitlin Doyle, off the list of suspects? No apparent motive? Surely Captain Spinner knew better than to trust that conclusion. Certainly I was not too old or weak to do the deed.

There must be other clues.

But what were they?

Finally I decided that the issue boiled down to just one question: At the moment the crime was committed, Sally Worth was alone in a small room with only one exit, and that exit was watched, by me. If she had indeed murdered Flechner, *how* had she left that room? Once I had answered that, I would worry about how a small, crippled woman could possibly beat a man the Director's size to death.

Every one of the ship's cabins that I had been in was just the same, standardized, stamped out of a mold like the buttons I used on my costumes. A single bed with the space beneath it sealed in with sturdy netting; most people stuffed that space with luggage. A single seat. Ample cupboards and fold-down shelves. A small bathroom, just as standardized.

I went into my own bathroom. Could I see anything that would help?

There was a sink, a toilet, a shower stall. Each one had blower openings to channel fluid flows in null or low gee.

There was a ventilator grill, but it was a mere fifteen centimeters square, far too small and no convenient scriptwriter to enlarge it.

There was the usual access hatch and its "DO NOT OBSTRUCT" Sticker.

I found myself staring at that hatch. It might be big enough. I worked its slide and pulled it open to reveal a maze of pipes and cables. The back of the hatch had another fingerhole for the slide. There was also, extending to either side along the floor, a cramped vein of dark and empty space. My hand seemed to fill it entirely. I did not believe anyone, not even a skinny, legless ballerina, could fit that tiny corridor, but. . . .

I found a flashlight and aimed it into the darkness. A

few meters off I could make out the tangle of pipes that marked another bathroom.

Then she did have another way out. From her bathroom to his. All I had to check was that the two were indeed linked, though I was now certain that they were.

But she could not fit!

That was where I stuck until I had a thought.

It was impossible.

But if that was all that was left. . . .

The guard on Sally's door made me wait while he ran a hand-held metal detector up and down my body. I did not ask and he did not volunteer whether he was trying to prevent some friend of Sally from aiding her escape or a friend of the Director from avenging his murder. The latter seemed more likely, for in or out of her cabin, Sally was sealed in a can in space. There was nowhere she could go.

"Sally?" She was lying on her bed, reading a brochure whose cover was printed in violet ink. She did not seem dejected at having been charged with murder, confined to her quarters, and ticketed for a downside trial and prison.

"What do you want?"

"To see you one more time. To say we'll all miss you." She shrugged impatiently, and I hastened to my point. "You said you could still dance, if only he would let you. And we have a production or two that could use a dancer who could separate from her legs."

" 'Sleepy Hollow,' " She was sitting up now, looking more interested. "You'd want the legs to dance by themselves. The head would float off to the side. The body—a dummy on the legs. Blackout under the head."

I nodded. "Could it be done? Do you have a manual?"

She crossed the room to open a drawer and hand me a thin book. "But I won't be here."

"We could buy a set of legs and fake it, if . . ." I had found the table of contents, and there was a whole chapter on programming. I flipped pages. "Ah," I said at last. "I see."

"What?" She leaned toward me, trying to see what I was reading. "What do you see?" Her voice squeaked on the second "what," and her body tensed.

"Was it hard to clean them off?"

She was opening her mouth to answer when the door slid open on the heels of a perfunctory rap and Captain Spinner's voice announced, "We'll be debarking soon."

Sally closed her mouth and pointed at me. "She's figured it out."

The Captain's mouth was suddenly pinched and wary. Fabric seemed to rasp against fabric even though I could not see him move. "Then perhaps we should offer her a job, too."

"A job?" I asked.

"Unless you can keep your mouth shut. We can draft you."

"The way you did her?"

He nodded.

"She went behind the walls," I blurted.

"Not quite," said Sally.

"I know. Small as you are, you wouldn't fit. But your legs . . ."

Captain Spinner was nodding. "That's what made me suspect her from the start." He undid his pants and exposed the rim of a bowl much like Sally's. Suddenly the sounds that always accompanied him took on a new but more familiar perspective: not rubbing fabric but the pumps and motors that made his—and Sally's—limbs move so well. I had not suspected because I had never known anyone but Sally with her affliction, though of course I knew there had to be others.

"I was a volunteer," he said. "They did this to make me a better agent. A spy. These can go where the rest of me can't, just as Ms. Worth realized."

Suddenly I wondered what sort of society Schlavin held. It was pragmatic, I could see already. More pragmatic than I had ever dreamed was possible. And they needed spies.

"On her own." I deliberately said nothing about my suspicions of war, rebellion, oppression, all of which the Federation would frown upon. "Without any teachers."

He nodded and grinned at Sally. "That's what makes her so attractive to us."

"And she's a choreographer." When he nodded once more, I added, "She programmed the legs to crawl down that tunnel, pushing with their toes, until they reached Director Flechner's cabin. Then they opened the hatch, went into the main room, and danced for him." I turned to Sally. "Was it hard to fill every bit of space with kicks? To kick him to death when you couldn't see what you were doing? When you couldn't be sure it was even him?"

She shook her head silently.

I turned to Captain Spinner and said, "She's reckless. Too reckless to be a good cop."

"But she's got the sort of cleverness that we need. Once we train the recklessness out of her, she'll have a promising career ahead of her.'

"In the Guard."

He nodded.

"But it was murder! Cold-blooded and brutal murder. Aren't you concerned about justice?"

"Of course," he said, and then he reminded me of the pragmatism I had noted earlier. "She told me why. I might have done the same myself."

SINCERITY

by Patrick Nielsen Hayden

Patrick Nielsen Hayden is a senior editor at Tor Books.

A long war between humans and aliens is coming to an end. There has been no clear-cut winner, but both sides are economically and politically exhausted. The two opposing generals are due to meet on a neutral world to sign a peace treaty, but the night before the meeting is due to take place, the human general is found murdered in his bed.

The aliens, who fear they will be blamed for this, immediately offer the services of their finest detective. The humans, afraid a refusal will cause offense and possibly restart the war, reluctantly agree, especially since our own detective specialists are parsecs away.

The alien must overcome human suspicion of his motivations—he might be covering up a murder by one of his own race—and solve the crime quickly. Write it.

What did I do in the war? What did I do in the war? I'll tell you, child, but you won't believe it. Ironic enough that when we finally got between the stars, they turned out to be just as full of battling lizard men as any old space opera. Like getting to Heaven and finding yourself the star of a St.-Peter-at-the-gates joke. I'm not sure we're ready to have everyone know how it all ended.

I was St. Andrew's senior aide. Brilliant Manuel St. Andrew, first interplanetary war hero. I was with him as he directed the defense of Luna, with him on the first sorties against their forward positions on Titan, with him as we pursued their retreating fleet past the Oort Cloud and beyond. St. Andrew and I, we were like this, you know? That's how I missed being vaporized when the Lunar shields didn't hold after all. Lots of people weren't so lucky.

Funny how long it took us to grasp that they weren't touching Earth. Luna City was lava by the time we figured it out: their aim wasn't to kill us, only to dominate us and make us render "honor and fealty." Tough luck for them that we managed the hyperspace drive (it isn't, really, but in a universe that turns out to have lizard men we *had* to call it a hyperspace drive) and leapfrogged to their home planet. Leapfrogged our own advancing sublightspeed fleet, too. Just as well—the hyperspace drive works, but I'm told they're getting the bugs out of cold sleep to this day. Cold sleep! Who's writing this future?

We winked into existence like avenging angels at their Lagrange points. A thousand thousand of their greatest battlecruisers rushed up to meet us, beautiful and terrible with their scarlet and golden hulls emblazoned with devices of violence and cruelty, gleaming in the cold strange light of their sun. Two of our scoutships were rammed and boarded by the same crack lizard units that ravaged the survivors of Luna: merciless, shrieking commandos clutching blasters in their slavering reptilian jaws as they rushed from chamber to chamber, leaving a river of human blood. Then both our violated scoutships died by human hands—by Manuel's hand. As he pressed the button, we wept.

Our blood flowed; theirs flowed more. We trashed their planet. They sued for peace. Exhausted, at the end of our respective tethers, both sides met on a third world— Earthcom never told me where, and they never let us outside the ship—to construct a truce. You got it: humankind was represented by ever-wonderful us, Manuel St. Andrew and his elite staff, always the unit on the spot. Hell, we'd engaged them directly more than any other unit; why give up on a winning streak?

Skip the next six months. Mostly it was our semioti-
cians and their rough equivalents, laboriously trying to
get our mutual communication above the level of sema-
phore flags, from "I kill you now, foreign object, ptui!"
to "Perhaps we should examine our shared economic interests." I didn't get the impression anyone was getting
anywhere fast, but Manuel—nominally in charge, though
semiotics wasn't his specialty—seemed to think otherwise.

Or thought so, as long as he was the Manuel I knew,
occasions of which got rarer and rarer. The fact is, for
the last month of Manuel St. Andrew's life, he was so
pumped with hostware he barely recognized me. The Will
of Earth Incarnate, that was Manuel, and as the months
of negotiation wore on that's what he literally became, a
brain and limbic system full of other peoples' intentions.
Manuel was the highest-ranking human on the spot, but
that didn't mean Earthcom was going to let him negotiate
humanity's first treaty with aliens on his own get-go.

Then one morning he was dead. Yes, I know the official story you've been told. No, it wasn't the limbic stress
of the hostware that killed him, unless you can tell me
how databurn makes you turn up with a severed head.
Panic, hubbub, armies of diplomats in confusion. Funny:
for all the months both species had spent in mutual in-
comprehension, we'd never suspected how eloquent the
lizard men's facial expressions would be in the crunch.

Or maybe "eloquent" isn't the word. It's a pulp-
magazine universe out there, honest to God. One minute
we're waiting for the order from Earth to scrub the negotiations and scoot, the next minute the supremo gen-
eralissimo high commander lizard man is addressing us
in the conference room, introducing us to an unprepos-
sessing member of their party, whom he tells us is a
detective. Tells us in English. A detective. I kid you not.
"We feel your shock and anger," he said. Three lizard
attendants stood at attention behind him in crisp battle
garb, eyes fixed straight ahead. "Manuel St. Andrew was
your champion and has fallen victim to a coward's blow,
delivered in the night." He paced back and forth, beating

his fists fiercely against his oversized, prognathous head. "You naturally suspect us, your sworn enemies, of this dastardly deed." Whirling about to face us all directly: "Give us only this: a single one of your planet's days to show it was not our blow that struck him down."

The "detective" stood to one side, tail tucked down, looking thoughtful, if a lizard man can be said to look thoughtful. Supremo Lizardissimo droned on in full flowery Dr.-Zarkov-speak. After both aliens left through an arch of their guards' drawn swords, Earthcom—always monitoring the conference room—came through and told us to hold tight, let this play out. What could anyone do? I went back to my quarters alone.

Late that night the alleged detective came to my door. I let him in. "We know you did it," he said simply. "We need only to know why."

Violets, I thought. *Verdi. Vancouver.* "Because he meant to end . . ." My vision flickered, iridesced, went red at the edges.

"Meant to end the war? It is not good, to end a war too soon. Honor is stained."

"Meant to . . . I don't know. Did I just say that?" *Van Allen Belts,* I thought as I slid to the endlessly welcoming floor.

I awoke in sick bay to our doctor's gentle ministrations. "Calmly, now," he said. "You've been out several days. Don't worry, we got the hostware out, or enough of it for the rest to make no difference."

Hostware? No kidding. St. Andrew hadn't been the only one. Then I realized the truth, like waking up from a bad dream as long-blocked neural pathways fired for the first time in months. Earthcom wasn't unified. A minority faction hadn't been happy with the idea of a truce—they wanted total victory, conquest, enslavement, a Terran Empire. *Vaughan Williams,* I thought or *heard* rather, then remembered all the V's of the night before. A brief nausea, but I didn't pass out—I wasn't a hostware dock any more, and that "suicide" trigger they'd post-hypped into me couldn't do anything to me now.

Suicide trigger. Give me a break. Manuel, friend,

mentor, forbidden and forbidding flame to my moth—bad enough I should have killed you, but to have been made to do it by incompetent, cornball conspirators *manque* . . . !

"The truce?" I managed to speak.

"Signed," said the doctor. "Sealed and endorsed by both governments. The lizards know how St. Andrew died, knew you did it under others' control. The word is that the aliens have decided we're . . . well, the word in their language means both 'sentient' and 'sincere.' Oh, and Earthcom says they apprehended the renegades who co-opted you."

Sentient? Sincere? Sincere as bedbugs, I thought, all of us. Then I threw up all over the bed.

"Oh, that's right," said the doctor absently. "You're pregnant. About a week. We can take care of it if you like."

How the hell *had* I managed to decapitate Manuel in bed, anyway?

Forty-five minutes later I was onboard the lizard men's ground vehicle, demanding political asylum. "But we're not at war any more," said their first officer—mildly, and in perfectly-accented English, though he had his hand on his blaster all the same. I didn't care. Calls were made, hurried conversations held, strange ceremonial signals traded. I sat down in a corner and gently threw up a few more times until they handed me an authentic lizard man bucket. Along with it came the news that I was now the first human emissary to their home planet, accredited and charged with founding the embassy in which you, child, have grown up. All I cared about at the time was that it was a way out, away, far far away, forever.

The lizard men are flamboyant and theatrical, much given to display. Wiping out Luna was kind of their way of saying hello. When we said hello back with cobalt bombs, they began to suspect we were "sentient." Or at any rate sincere. But when we proved ourselves capable of a truly Jacobean level of betrayal and murder in our highest councils, complete with farcical incompetence in the actual execution, they not only decided we really were sentient, they practically fell in love with us. Half the

work of this embassy consists of trying to record as much
native lizardman culture as we can before they pave it
over with a fine layer of our trashiest pop-culture pulp.
Life in the universe is infinitely variable. Go figure.

So that's the whole story at last, and kid, honestly, you
can give me the antidote now. Ah, I shouldn't be surprised; you're just a kid like any other human kid, prone
to self-aggrandizement and melodrama, which means the
locals think you're the bees' knees—but I swear, if you
don't start showing a Terran sense of irony soon, I'm
going to have you tied down in the embassy basement to
watch Marx Brothers movies until your head swims. Tri-
ple homework! Don't believe it? Think you'll hold out
on the antidote a little longer?

Querulous. Quodlibet. Quantico. That's *your* trigger.
Good, that's a good son, sleep tight. Now let's open that
hand. Naturally the vial's curled up in your hand—excuse
me, I mean in your mighty fist, of course. There. Much
better. Now let's get you a blanket and pillow. What a
snoring lump you are! And you'll never know how tired
I get of these little playlets between us. But I've learned.
I'm prepared.

Because, you know, I've lived here as many years as
you.

DARK ODDS
by Josepha Sherman

Josepha Sherman, in addition to writing books and
short stories, is an editor for Baen Books.

*In the future, aliens mingle freely with humans
on Earth. The inhabitants of Antares IV are humanoid, but much smaller than we are, and one of
them has become our most successful jockey. One
day, as the alien's mount is leading the field down
the backstretch, he literally dies right in the stir-
rups. There are no marks on the body, nothing to
indicate foul play . . . but it is known that the syndicate made millions on the horse that won, and
the police are convinced that the alien, who was
riding the heavy favorite, was murdered.*

*Your protagonist's task: find out how the murder
was committed, and tie it in to the syndicate. You
can give the alien any body chemistry you want.*

When you've been training thoroughbreds as long as I
have, you'd think the whole thing would become routine.
Hell, no! How could it be routine when I had maybe the
top three-year-old in the country, Wonderchild, and
maybe the best jockey in the country to ride him, namely
Taranak par Zan?

Is there anyone who follows racing who hasn't also followed Taranak's meteoric career? Derby, Preakness, Bel-
mont, Stardancer—there isn't a race he hadn't won, and
won with the same icy-calm precision. Oh, sure, there are
others of his kind who have a definite way with thoroughbreds—I think they *all* do! But Taranak turned race riding

into an art form. Plus, of course, there wasn't a cowardly
bone in his Asantai body.

Asantai, yeah, not human. We've all seen the newsvids
of that spaceworn ship first landing half a century ago
and the bedraggled refugees stumbling out, a bunch of
scared, short, bowlegged, almost-human beings fleeing
their people's brand of religious persecution back home
on the world they called Tarantai and we call Antares
Four. Fortunately for them, they were far too honor-
conscious a race to impose on others—and so infertile
they couldn't possibly alarm even the most hidebound
Earth-Firsters. Besides, their arrival had been quite a few
years after First Contact; even back then, aliens were no
longer the novelty they'd been. Particularly not aliens who
seemed positively designed to be jockeys. I've been in
the racing business long enough to recognize talent when
I see it, no matter in what form it comes.

Hell, it was more than talent. It seems our thorough-
bred looks remarkably like an Asantai holy animal, and
the Asantai took to jobs as handlers and exercise riders
and—of course—jockeys with cries of glee. They were
damned good with horses, too; hire an Asantai, and you
knew your animals were going to be well-treated. The
only ones to complain were those broken-down humans
replaced by Asantai. And, of course, the syndicates, the
crime bosses, call them what you want; racing is as clean
as modern security can make it, and every stable worth
its salt owns its own drug-testing compulab, but the
seamier folks are still out there trying to worm their way
in. Unfortunately for them, there isn't an Asantai born
who will do anything to injure a horse.

Anyhow, Taranak par Zan was to ride Wonderchild today in the fiftieth running of the Stardancer Stakes, Grade I,
a mile and a quarter, with a purse of $3,000,000 guar-
anteed. The day would be fair, the track fast. Trainers
keep weird hours anyhow, up at four or five in the morning every day, but even so, there was no way on earth I
could have slept till my alarm rang!

In all the excitement, I totally forgot to recharge my
car's batteries. Driving through the predawn darkness, I

saw the warning signal flash on my dashboard and swore at myself. Never would have reached the trainers' private lot, but at least I made it all the way into Union Downs' enormous public parking lot before the last of the charge trickled down and left me stuck. Still muttering at my own stupidity, I started the long trek on foot to the stable area, moving from pool of light to pool of light, cursing at the cheapness of the management for keeping to antiquated light-poles that might as well been electric for all the good they did.

I'd gotten about halfway there when I heard two folks arguing ahead of me in the darkness between two light-poles, their voices low but earnest. They turned sharply at my approach, and enough light spilled onto them for me to recognize the taller of them as Randy Jones.

Hell of a name for a syndicate man, isn't it? But somehow it fit. Jones was as fresh-faced and clean as some successful young businessman. You'd never have taken him for slime.

The other man wasn't a man at all: Taranak par Zan glared at me, his thick yellow Asantai mane bristling with barely controlled rage.

"What the *hell* do you think you're doing here?" I roared. "And you, Jones, you get the bloody blazes away from my jockey!"

"I am not *your* jockey," Taranak said, very softly, green eyes glinting. "You do not own me."

Jones had already snuck off into the night.

"Hell I don't!" I muttered to Taranak. "You signed on to ride for me, near-exclusive contract, remember?"

The Asantai don't use agents; that weird alien honor code insists they manage their own affairs. Taranak just continued to glare.

"Oh, hell," I said helplessly. "Come on, I'll walk you to the stables."

To my relief, when I started forward, he went with me. "Taranak," I began, then tried again. "Of course I don't own you. You're a grown . . . being. But what were you planning with Jones?"

There was just enough light for me to see the retractable claws flick in and out on his fingers; Taranak was still mad, but, being Taranak, wasn't about to harm his ice-cold reputation by yelling. "Nothing."

"Look, you try anything with Wonderchild today, you're finished. I mean it, Taranak. You do anything to spoil his chances, I swear I'll kill you."

That got me a sharp green glance. "I will do nothing to stain the honor of a horse."

He meant it. Of course he did; he was Asantai.

By now we'd reached the backstretch, and been checked in by the security guard. I told the man where I'd left my car, he promised to call the recharging service—and while that was going on, Taranak went his way, like the cold-blooded creature even his own people thought him.

Anyhow, some time later, snatching a chance to catch my breath after the usual hectic morning activities of overseeing horses working out or being groomed or hot-walked, pacifying owners and checking with vets and blacksmiths, I stood in the shedrow between the two barns allotted to my horses, hoping the guy with the caffeine-cart would be around pretty soon.

None of the Asantai would join me; their systems can pretty much tolerate a good many Earth foods, requiring only daily doses of what I've been told are trace minerals to stay healthy (every Asantai pops his "vitamin pills" like an old-fashioned health nut), but the oddest things make them react . . . well, oddly. Alcohol puts them right to sleep, poor guys, while caffeine makes them hallucinate, and most "recreational" drugs have no effect at all.

We all have our differences. And since the one thing we all shared was a love of horses, who cared about anything else?

Barns haven't changed too much over the years, other than being made thoroughly fireproof. Despite the presence of Asantai scurrying about their jobs alongside human workers, I could almost fool myself into believing it was maybe two hundred years ago, in the Golden Age of Secretariat and Seattle Slew. Outside, the world had changed, and was still changing, but here the same old sounds and smells remained: the whinny of a hungry horse, the crooning of a handler to a jumpy filly, the heady smell of horse and hay and sweat that shouted *racing* to anyone in the trade. And underneath it all (though, thank you kindly, all those reporters with their holocams had been barred) the current of excitement that reminded everyone this wasn't just another day.

Those horses that were going to race today felt it, too, knowing they were to race because their mangers had been removed (a horse can't run fast or long on a full belly). Only Wonderchild, his bay coat sleek with health, stood blessedly calm in his stall, thanks mostly to the slight, yellow-mopped figure crooning to him; I swear the horse was chortling back at her. "Her" being Khalite par Zan. Yeah, she's the same clan as Taranak, not that a famous jockey like him is going to acknowledge a lowly exercise rider, no matter how high-caste. Only the Zans and a few others of equal rank are allowed by the complicated social rules of the Asantai to actually sit on the back of so sacred an animal as a horse. For which I'm glad in Khalite's case; she's one of those rare riders who, as the old saying goes, have "a clock in their heads," able to judge to the split second how fast their mounts are going. In Earth terms, Khalite was a teenager, even though her skinny figure was hardly feminine by either race's standards, and just plain no-religious-nonsense-about-it horse crazy.

Just then old Zend par Tun trundled down the shedrow with a wheelbarrow full of dirty straw, headed for the compost heaps. Zend is about as old an Asantai as I've seen, thin as a skeleton, his mane faded to a dingy yellow-white. A better hand I never had, but poor Zend had the misfortune of being born into the lowest-status clan of all. I saw even Khalite, who's pretty well Earth-assimilated, stiffen slightly as he passed, her mane bristling ever so slightly. Bad enough, but watching Taranak, headed off to get ready for the first race of today's card, totally negate Zend's existence with a blank stare was worse. Zend cringed away in the deepest humility, but I saw the flash of near-hatred as he stared after the jockey, and couldn't really blame him. I'd done my best to calm tensions between the clans, but it was as tough as trying to stamp out race hatred on Earth must have been a hundred years back.

Someone else was staring at Taranak: Khalite, awestruck and adoring as any human teen ogling a vid star. Taranak, of course, never deigned to notice.

Without warning he sprang back with a shout of horror, and I whirled to see what had scared him, thinking mad dog, or maybe even snake, though the horses were too calm for anything like that.

"What in—? It's a goat, guys, a harmless little goat! A stable pet. Must have gotten loose from some other barn."

The Asantai weren't buying my attempts to soothe them. Taranak's mane was still wild about his head and his eyes were wide and blank. Khalite was doing her best to hide behind him, while old Zend—Zend was staring not at the goat, but at Taranak. And in his eyes: well, that same religious panic was there, but with it a weird sort of triumph. He must have thoroughly been enjoying seeing the haughty par Zen humiliated.

As for me, as I was trying to calm the Asantai and get someone human to take the beast back to whatever non-Asantai barn it called home, all I could think was, *Just what we needed: an omen!*

The reason behind all the panic? Just as horses remind Asantai of the holy side of life, the triangular face of a goat, topped by its horns, reminds them of Xetates, their Force of Evil. Our otherwise coolly logical Taranak was a particularly strong believer in the Asantai religion.

Yeah, but he was hardly about to let religion get in his way. Goat or no goat, the day went well, with two wins and a show spot for the three horses I'd started in the early races. Happy me, happy stable, happy owners. At last it was time for the Stardancer Stakes. Taranak, who had ridden the three in-the-money mounts for me in his usual unemotional way, paused to stand for a moment, nose to nose with Wonderchild, communing in some si-

lent ritual, then deigned to let me hoist him into the sad-
dle. Off they went into the post parade, joining the line
of sleek, keyed-up young thoroughbreds, shining in the
sunlight, Wonderchild dancing and tossing his glossy
mane, the essence of equine health, his excitement con-
trasting nicely with Taranak's impassive calm. God, it
was a beautiful sight!

Then, out of the corner of my eye, I saw Randy Jones'
face among the crowd, and a shock of alarm ran through
me. Taranak's words echoed in my mind: *I will do nothing to harm the honor of a horse*.

"You'd better not," I muttered. "You'd better not."

Then the race began, and I forgot my nerves, yelling
with the best of them as Wonderchild galloped along in
third, under a snug hold from Taranak. Too snug?

"Come on, you idiot!" I heard myself scream. "Let
him run!"

Taranak never moved, lying cold as ice along Wonderchild's neck, those small Asantai hands controlling all
that equine power, smoothing, holding the colt back.
Wonderchild ran smoothly along the rail, but he wasn't
really extending himself, not yet, not even as the field
turned for home. God, now I was *sure* the damned jockey
was in Jones' pay!

And then Taranak let Wonderchild loose. The colt tore
down the backstretch like so much bay flame, overtaking
the horses in front of him, opening up a two-, a three-,
a five-length lead. Taranak and he were all alone as they
neared the finish line, and the crowd roared its approval.

But all at once Taranak straightened sharply in the sad-
dle. Through my binoculars, I saw his eyes widen in horror, just as they had when he'd seen the goat, saw the ends
of his mane bristle beneath the confining helmet, saw him
fling his hands, claws extended, over his face. Not even
the finest jockey can keep his balance like that.

Taranak couldn't. The crowd screamed as he fell beneath the hooves of the oncoming horses.

Things would have been a helluva lot easier if the Asantai religion permitted autopsies, or at least the taking

of blood and other samples from the dead. But it didn't, and none of the par Zan clansfolk who worked for me or the other stables were going to make an exception now, so the coroner had no choice but to rule the whole thing death by accident. The cops were all too willing to go along with him; after all, there wasn't any real evidence of foul play. Besides, it had only been one small alien who died, not a human, even if he had been one of the top jockeys. Reminding them that the Asantai were legal immigrants, entitled to the protection of the law, didn't exactly endear me to them. And when I pointed out that a jockey doesn't drop the reins to throw his arms over his face in the middle of a race by accident, I was told with a shrug that Taranak might have suffered the Asantai version of a coronary but, of course, no one could be sure without an autopsy.

Which, again, the Asantai weren't going to allow.

Great.

When I finally got back to the barn, having warded off a swarm of ghoulish reporters and nervous owners, I found almost total silence hanging over it. The Asantai don't wail out their grief. But they do mourn the death of one of their own—even such an unlikable one of their own—particularly those of Taranak's own clan, particularly poor little heart-broken Khalite, who I found hugging her equine friends for comfort.

Life, though, as the trite old saying goes, goes on. Horses still had to be cared for. Grieving though they were, the Asantai went smoothly on with their work.

And me? Once the initial shock had worn off a bit I kept replaying Taranak's last few moments in my mind, seeing the horror suddenly flashing in his eyes, seeing the claws shooting out in instinctive, useless self-defense. Dammit, all that hadn't been caused by any heart attack! Taranak had suddenly seen something so horrifying he'd forgotten who and where he was, something invisible to the rest of us.

I wasn't about to believe he'd gone nuts during the race. Drugs? Not our haughty Taranak; he'd made it very clear while working for me that those few Earthly mind-altering substances that might work on Asantai were beneath his par Zan dignity. Besides, jockeys nowadays were watched so closely that even if he'd changed his mind, he wouldn't have been able to do anything about it.

Unless . . . someone had changed his mind for him. It wasn't a fact they cared to advertise to nervous humans, but the Asantai were telepaths.

Oh, right. If an Asantai concentrated long and hard enough, he just might actually be able to make another Asantai look at him. One thing it hadn't been was death by telepathy!

I stood watching my workers for a time, trying to pick out those who'd held a grudge against Taranak, then realized that included just about everyone. Even poor, snubbed little Khalite had some sort of motive to get revenge. Not that she ever would. While the Asantai certainly could hate as strongly as any of us, they were so tied up in their clans and clan-status, bound round with all sorts of alien codes of honor, they just weren't cut out to be murderers.

Humans, however, were. I could hardly forget the quarrel between Taranak and Randy Jones, and if that hadn't been about throwing the race, I was a blacksmith. Oh, yes, and I'd seen Jones turn gray when the stewards declared Wonderchild the winner (Taranak, though no longer in control, had still technically been on the colt at the finish); presumably *someone* had lost a lot of money because of that win, and guess who would be blamed? Jones would have to do a terrific job of sweet-talking his bosses if he was going to survive.

Tough. He was a murderer, after all. Oh, yes, Taranak's death had been murder, all right, I didn't have a doubt about it. Even if the scheme to keep Wonderchild from winning had backfired, it could only have been Jones who'd killed Taranak.

But, dammit, how? And with what? Even assuming there was some Earth drug that distorted Asantai senses, there was no way he could have forced it into Taranak

during their quarrel. And, modern track security being
as tight as it is, there wasn't any way an outsider could
have gotten to him afterward, either in the stable area or
in the jockeys' quarters. Something odd in his food? Impossible. Taranak, naturally small though he was, had
still watched his diet as carefully as any human jockey;
he prepared his own meals according to a dietician's
plans, and would never have eaten or drunk anything out
of the ordinary, particularly not on the day of a Grade I
stakes.

All right. Then the only other possibility was that
whatever had killed Taranak had been something very
much *in* the ordinary. I entered my cluttered little office
and sat with head in hands, going over every step of my
employees' day, knowing there was something I was
missing, something so obvious I was going to kick myself when I—

"God, yes!"

What was the one thing Taranak would have taken for
granted, the one thing all his people took for granted
every day?

Not liking where my thoughts were going, I looked
out to where they were going about their work, their eyes
still dull with shock, the set of their narrow mouths grim.
If I was right about this, if the evidence hadn't already
been hidden or destroyed, one of those workers had been
bought by Jones.

In the old days, track workers used to live in trailers
if they were lucky or in crowded rooms over the stables
if they weren't. But the Asantai here at the track prefer
to live near the barns in little clusters of huts, each with
its proper clan insignia. Since those huts don't take up
much room and are made of fireproof materials, who am
I to argue? Taranak could, of course, have afforded to
live pretty much anywhere he pleased, but he had still
been Asantai enough to have his own hut here at the
track. Feeling like a thief, even though as his boss I had
the right to do it, I overrode the security lock and entered.

The inside of Taranak's hut was as neat and cold as his life, one circular area partitioned, like all Asantai huts, into sections by woven hangings; Taranak's were, predictably, cool, elegant black and white geometrics. I hunted through the small kitchen area (depressed by the sight of the perfectly arranged packages of food) and bathroom without any luck at all. But as the Asantai might say, Chickihe, Spirit of Luck, is tricky. As I turned to leave, I nearly stepped on what I was after: one small white pill that had apparently rolled into a corner and been overlooked: a pill that contained an Asantai's daily ration of essential trace minerals.

As I left the hut, what seemed like hundreds of green Asantai eyes fixed on me, and they continued to be fixed on me all the way to my office and the compulab next door. At last I couldn't take it any more, and turned to glare right back at them, snarling, "Haven't you guys got anything better to do?"

Not an eye blinked. They went silently back to work like so many robots.

A few minutes later, the compulab proved what I'd suspected: what was left of Taranak's daily supply of trace minerals had been laced with enough caffeine to drug a dozen Asantai. Now, dammit, the cops would *have* to listen to me!

But mere hallucinations wouldn't have been enough to guarantee a fatal accident. Once again, I found myself considering that feeble Asantai telepathy. What if, thanks to the caffeine, it had been just strong enough to create a specific image in Taranak's mind. . . . ?

The whole thing was starting to affect *my* mind, giving me a headache. I staggered back into my office, figuring that maybe if I stretched out on my cot for a few minutes, I'd feel better.

The next thing I know, it was pitch-black outside. Swearing, I struggled to my feet, furious at myself for falling asleep so thoroughly, even though it had been one long exhausting day. At least all the security devices were keyed to recognize me, so I didn't set off any alarms.

The night was cool and, thanks to the track's light-poles, not as dark as I'd first thought. Hoping my car really had been recharged, I made my way down the shed-row and out toward the parking lot. There wasn't a sign of life, other than one sleepy whinny; the electronic gadgetry was working, but the living guards must have been patrolling out behind the barns.

Funny, how I kept wanting to turn to the left, rather than to the right, where my car was parked. . . . Damn, there I went again, turning left. . . .

Ahead of me, a small figure stood caught in a spill of light, and for one brief, stupid moment I thought, *Taranak?* But the faded yellow-white of the mane told me who it really was: old Zend par Tun.

Now, why would an Asantai, and an ancient one at that, be standing out here all alone? Hardly to meet a lover, not poor old decrepit Zend. The only other possibility—

For a moment the breath seemed to leave my body. Oh, no, not Zend, it couldn't be old Zend. . . . Sure, like all the other lower clansfolk, he might have despised Taranak and all the par Zan clan stood for, but par Tun never attacked par Zan!

He peered nearsightedly up at me as I approached. "Please, boss, you are not to be here."

"Why in hell not? So you can meet your human buddy? The one who gave you the doctored pills? Dammit, Zend, you did do it, didn't you?"

He hesitated, ancient mane stirring nervously, then dipped his head in the Asantai form of a nod. "Yes . . ." His voice was a whisper, heavy with shame. "Last night I stole into Taranak's hut . . . I know how to bypass the security locks. . . . No, boss, do not stare like that, I have never stolen anything from you or others. But it was simply to exchange pills for pills."

"You made sure Taranak was good and doped up with caffeine, and then you—you forced images into his mind."

"Yes. I waited till the *khafaine*, the—the caffeine had entered his system fully. And then . . . I made him see

. . . Xetates." Xetates, as I've said, is the Asantai Force of Evil, the nasty, goat-faced guy. Zend shivered, his fading mane rising. "I did not mean what happened then! I wanted Taranak to lose the race, no more, for the par Zan to be shamed without harming Wonderchild's honor. I didn't know Taranak's fear of Xetates was so very strong! I—I never meant for him to die!"

"Hell you didn't! Putting an out-of-control jockey on the back of a highstrung colt—Dammit, Zend, you had to have known what was going to happen! But *why*? What did Jones promise you? What kind of reward could he possibly have—"

"No, boss. You do not understand." The ancient green eyes burned with pain. "I had no choice. The human said that if I did not do as he said, he—he would hurt the horses. Please, please, I never wanted Taranak to die, I just couldn't let anyone hurt the horses!"

Save me from religious fanatics. "Zend, I . . ."

Before I could figure out what else I could possibly say to him, Zend was off and running like a scared rabbit, scrawny body scuttling off into the darkness.

He didn't get very far. A figure, too tall to be anything but human, suddenly materialized out of darkness, stopping just at the edge of the pool of light, and I caught a glimpse of a by now too-familiar face: Randy Jones. But this was a Jones with all urbane charm gone out the window. Red-faced and disheveled with rage, he caught Zend by the bony shoulders.

"You let me down, damn you!"

"No, I—I—"

"You let me down!"

"That's enough, Jones." I hurried forward. "Let him go."

"Go to hell!"

I hadn't seen the knife. It was only when Zend suddenly stiffened, then slowly crumpled that I realized what had just happened. For one long moment Jones stood staring at me over the pathetic little corpse, eyes wild as a fear-maddened horse.

Then we were no longer alone. The night seemed to

let out its breath in one long, collective sigh as *they* stalked forward, more Asantai than I'd seen in one place, more than just those who worked for me. Every Asantai from every stable at the track must have been in that pack, clans for once jumbled together without concern for status, all of them with the same flaring yellow manes, the same fierce green eyes, predatory eyes. Jones cried out in sudden terror and turned to run, but the hunters were all about him. Suddenly revealed claws glinted in the pools of lamplight as the pack bore him down.

I don't know how long it took. I don't know how long I stood frozen, too horrified to move. But as last I must have made some sound because the Asantai turned almost as one to stare at me, the light reflecting flatly from their eyes. Even little Khalite was in that circle, her claws just as stained, her eyes just as blankly green as the others, and all I could think of was *Alien, alien . . .*

Then one of them said softly, "We made you sleep so you would not contact interfering humans."

"You . . . made me sleep?" I echoed stupidly.

"Yes," said the second Asantai. "Then we called you here. It is no easy thing to do, nothing we would care to try again. But when the need drives and all of us think together, we can touch even a human's mind."

"You brought . . . him . . . here, too?"

"That?" Green glances slid sideways to the corpse, then back again. "That would have come even without our prodding."

True enough; Jones wouldn't have dared let his Asantai tool live, not when his own life was in peril, not when Zend might link him to Taranak's death.

"You are witness," a third Asantai continued. "Death for death. Murder has been avenged. Go home, human."

"But what about . . . *that?*" My gesture took in the shredded bundle that had been a man.

Someone chuckled softly, the sound very inhuman indeed. "It shall be returned to those who sent it forth, marked properly with clan signs so there shall be no doubt in their minds why it was slain, and by whom. Neither you nor we shall be troubled again. Go home.''

I went.

The next morning, I had to force myself out to the track, wondering what I would find, half-afraid of the answer.

What I found was an ordinary racing stable on an ordinary morning. I watched the Asantai at work for some time, trying to balance the efficient savagery of last night with the tranquillity I found today. In the back of my mind was, *What now? What happens the first time I have to yell at someone, or fire him? Will they turn on me, too?*

But then, as though they'd felt my confusion (after last night, that hardly seemed impossible), all those alien heads turned to me, all those green eyes studied me. Yet this time there was nothing but curiosity in their gaze.

And after a moment I felt the tight knot of tension loosen inside me. Hell, what was I worried about? I was boss-of-horses to them, leader of their sacred animal! Neither I nor any other honest track worker was ever going to have anything to fear from an Asantai.

"Come on, guys, back to work," I said, and they grinned their wrinkled-nose Asantai grins and obeyed.

The past, after all, was the past. A new day had begun, and there were horses to be worked.

THINGS NOT SEEN
by Martha Soukup

Hugo nominee Martha Soukup spent some time as managing editor of *Chain Report,* a trade journal.

A man is found stabbed to death in his office. It is known that he was alive when the last of his co-workers left, and that the sole other entity remaining with him was a guardian robot, programmed to protect the man at any cost. The robot claims that no one entered the office, and that it did not kill the victim; various scientific testing shows that the robot is functioning normally.

1. *Was the robot lying, and, if so, how could it overcome its programming?*
2. *If the robot was not lying and it never left the man's side, how was the murder committed and kept secret from the robot?*

Her screen was slightly unbalanced toward green. It dulled reds, making it appear Dr. Herrera's face was streaked with chocolate syrup. Ginnie Erickson glanced at the security robot, which squatted near her hip, cabled into her workstation. "Hold it, please." The image froze. She hit a few keystrokes, until the blood was vivid red. "Take it at half speed." Herrera's head moved forward a bit, as though he were trying to peer through his gouged eyes, and he began to slump in his chair. "Quarter speed."

The viewpoint shifted crazily until Ralph Herrera filled the screen. Diagnostics—blood pressure, pulse—scrolled under the image of the dying scientist, measurements taken by the robot as it made itself into a temporary heart-lung machine, hooked to Herrera's circulatory system and oxygenating his blood.

Too late. His brain was scrambled by the ice pick that had stabbed through his eyes. The security robot was not equipped with an EEG, or it could have registered its charge's brain-death and saved itself some trouble.

"Stop," Ginnie said. There was nothing striking left in the robot's memory until ten minutes later, when Drobisch, the security chief, arrived. She might have continued in fast scan, but Drobisch was standing behind her. She'd seen that part already. The digital recording would show his hasty arrival, shirttail untucked, gun in hand. He would bend over the corpse and say, "Shit! Damn it, Herrera, if you've cost me my job—" It did not seem politic to play forward to that point.

"So what's wrong with the stupid machine?" Drobisch asked.

"I don't know. Give me some time."

"Time? Time?" She suspected he was related to someone, somewhere. Surely there was no other reason a twit like him could hold his job.

"It's a very complicated stupid machine." She turned to the robot. "You're a complicated machine, aren't you?"

"Yes," said the robot, its pleasant voice coming from a speaker in its chest. She'd known the guy who recorded its core model vocabulary. He said it had taken a week, but the results were worth it, easy enough on the ears that she'd dated the voice's original for two months. She was only slightly miffed that in her six years of working with robots, no one had ever suggested her voice would make a good model.

"So simplify it," said Drobisch. "The stupid thing says Herrera came in, sat down, and suddenly had blood and eyeballs all over himself. It's a stupid waste of money. And it's useless to the company until we figure out what's wrong with it."

"The back of my neck is warm enough, thanks," she

said. Drobisch stared at her. "Could you stop breathing down it for a while? You're making me itch."

"I think I'll watch."

"Then could you tell me why the company is into investigating this thing? Why don't you leave it to the cops?"

"It's company business."

"What in the world was he working on? Why did he even need a guard robot?"

"Forget that, missy. It's classified."

"It might help me know who was after him."

"That's none of your business. Your business is to figure out what's wrong with the stupid robot. Period. So do it."

Finally she ran the robot's memory forward through its entire futile attempt to keep Herrera alive. Drobisch squirmed and left before the playback reached his arrival at the scene. Ginnie had the little office back to herself.

She stretched, sighed, and told the robot, "Let's take it from the top. Eleven P.M., Friday night."

Four hours later she hadn't gotten anywhere. Interrogating the robot and examining its visual memory gave her the same result: a headache. She leaned on the desk, flexing her tired wrists.

"When did the last person leave the lab besides Herrera?"

"Eight forty-six P.M., seventeen seconds," said the robot.

"That was Jane Yonamura?"

"Yes."

"No one besides Dr. Herrera was in the lab between then and when Drobisch arrived at eleven twenty-six?"

"That is correct."

"Did Herrera look nervous?"

"Please contextually define 'nervous.' "

"Did he do anything unusual during the period?"

"He died."

Ginnie smiled. Literal-minded program. Others might anthropomorphize the robot, despite its resemblance to a large garbage can bristling with mechanical limbs and extrusions. She knew it was a sophisticated computer program housed in a wheeled mechanism. Real artificial intelligence was still down the road.

"Did he do anything unusual during the last period he was alone, before he died?"

"He spent eighty-seven percent of that period at his computer terminal. He spent nine percent of that period pacing. He spent four percent of that period in the bathroom. These percentages are in the normal range for Dr. Herrera's late-night activities since I was assigned to guard him."

"Why were you assigned to guard him?"

"That information is classified."

"What was he working on?"

"That information is classified."

Ginnie shook her head and looked at her notes. *Yonamura leaves, 8:46:17* P.M. Herrera goes to john, 11:08:51. H. back, 11:15:02. H. dead, 11:15:43. Drobisch arrives, 11:26:25. It was odd that Herrera was murdered right after he got back from the bathroom, but that didn't help. Did someone sneak into the lab during the six minutes scientist and robot were away? Possible, but it didn't explain how the robot didn't see that person murder the scientist in plain sight.

Another thing she couldn't understand was how Herrera could sit still while someone jabbed an icepick through his eyes. She flinched just thinking about it. If he'd been drugged—but she'd been told blood workups hadn't found anything.

The robot had been instructed to tell her nothing that would reveal the nature of Herrera's work, but he had done nothing confidential in the hour and a half after his assistant left: there were no holes in what it told her. The robot's memory could be edited by a programmer, but any such edit would be recorded in deeply encrypted codes. She'd checked them. Its memories had not been touched in more than two months.

Her eyes stung. Either she was feeling sympathetic pains, or she'd been working too long.

"Off," she told the robot. She left it cabled into her computer so she could start again first thing in the morning.

George looked up from her book when Ginnie let herself in. "Long day," she commented. Ginnie grunted at her twin sister, the one named after their mother's native state. Their father was from Virginia: the family joke was that Ginnie—Virginia—was Daddy's girl, and Georgia was their mother's favorite. It was a durable enough joke that Ginnie worked with computers, like her father, and George did medical research, like her mother.

The other family joke was how lucky they were no one was from New Jersey.

"You're telling me." Ginnie hung her jacket on her side of the closet. "Hey, this is your umbrella. Keep it on your side!"

"Picky, picky. Fabulous mood you're in tonight." George was her double, wide-hipped, narrow-waisted, with too much dark curly hair to keep under perfect control. Every time Ginnie looked at her, she wanted to brush her own hair.

"You ever have some jerk leaning on you about some impossible task, and you'll be allowed to comment."

George grinned. She worked at their mother's lab, so she was always expected to put in late hours. But they'd recently finished a major project and were taking some time off. "What's up?"

"Get this. You know the guy who got killed the other day? The security robot completely flaked, didn't record the murder. I'm supposed to figure out what went wrong with it."

"Oh, now, that's interesting. Think you'll find out who killed him?"

Ginnie walked past her sister into the kitchenette. "That's 'none of my business.' I'm just supposed to find why the security robot screwed up." She took down a bowl and a box of raisin bran.

"Robots and computers. Very dull. The murder of Ralph Herrera, that's interesting. Hey, he's a fellow Cal

Tech alum. You should catch his murderer to avenge the glory of our alma mater. And that's not a real dinner, you know.''

Ginnie put the milk back in the refrigerator. ''Tough. You cook a real dinner, I'll be glad to eat it.''

''You order out for a real dinner, I'll be glad to warm it up in the microwave. So, the murder. Who offed him?''

''I don't know. Everything's very hush-hush. Drobish—he's the security idiot, he's got to really be sweating his job—won't tell me why. Maybe he's not in on it either, I don't know. I don't know Herrera's work, I don't know his social life, I don't know if he had negatives of Drobisch in bed with his German shepherd. I just have to find the bug.'' She took a big spoonful of cereal. ''Of course, the idea that they spent so much money for a security droid that can't even spot a murderer is probably reason enough. But, then, they're hiding the robot from the cops.''

''I hate it when you talk with your mouth full. That's what *I'd* sound like, if I didn't have any manners. It's not a pretty thought, you know.''

Ginnie crunched her cereal.

''Means, motive, opportunity,'' George said. Ginnie noticed belatedly that the novel George was reading was a Nero Wolfe. ''You must know something we can deduce from.''

''Opportunity, I don't understand. Motive, I haven't a clue. Means, an ice pick right into the brains and swirled around a bit.''

''Ugh. Can the ice pick be traced?''

''That's something for the cops to do. I doubt it, though. I got a pretty good look at it in the robot's visual memory. It was an ordinary Sears ice pick.''

''Fingerprints?''

''Smudged palmprints, from what I hear.''

''Could be his, if he tried to pull it out. What makes you think the robot didn't do it? Aren't you worried to be around the thing?''

Ginnie shook her head. ''I made sure to ask about that. There was brain matter on the ice pick. It would have got on the murderer's hands. There was none on the grasping limbs the robot could have used to hold the weapon, only blood and vitreous goop from the eyes. Anyway, the angle of entry was all wrong for a killer as short as the robot. Just right for a human murderer."

George marked her place in the Nero Wolfe and put it aside. "You're not bright enough to figure out the opportunity, and the means are mundane, if ugly. We'll have to work on motive."

Ginnie poured more cereal in her bowl. "I don't have to come home for this abuse, you know. I can go back to work and get it from Drobisch."

"I'm better at it, though."

"Only because you have more practice, and perfect genes."

"Motive, motive. Did you know this guy at all from work?"

"No. He's just one of those people who comes in, works constantly, and goes home. He didn't exactly hang out chatting in the cafeteria. He was working on something classified, they say."

"So it could be industrial sabotage." George frowned. "But why would a saboteur kill him in such a nasty way? Stabbing out his eyes. That seems so personal. Maybe symbolic. Like, oh, jealousy: 'You'll never look at another woman again!' "

"He doesn't sound like the ladykiller type," Ginnie said.

"That doesn't mean it couldn't have gone the other way around, right?"

"He's the kind of guy who spent all his time in the lab."

"So he was fooling around with someone in the lab, then. Was he married?" Ginnie shook her head. "So he's seeing someone at the lab, and she gets jealous. Maybe he isn't even fooling around on her. Maybe she's one of those crazed researchers who goes nuts after too much sleep deprivation."

"Maybe *you* are," Ginnie commented.

"Who's the last person who saw him alive?"

"His assistant, Jane Yonamura."

"Ah-hah!"

"Oh, come on, she doesn't look the type."

"They never do," George said wisely. "What's her line of work?"

"That one I do know. Before she was assigned to Herrera, she ran the clone lab we use." Ginnie helped design roboticized diagnostic stations, translating BioInnovation's doctors' expertise into programs that could detect increasingly fine signs of medical disorder. They went through scores of identical rabbits, mice and monkeys, testing the devices. Until she'd been tabbed to find a bug in a robot she'd had no hand in programming, the most frustrating part of Ginnie's job had been waiting the months it could take for a mouse genetically predisposed to a heart disorder to mature into symptoms for her programs to find.

"Tell you what," George said. "Herrera went to Tech years before us, but I'll bet I know some people from there who knew him. I'll call around and get the scoop on him for you. You should talk to Yonamura. Either she's the murderer, or she knows the other woman who's the murderer, or if something on their project got him killed, she may know about that, too."

"Drobisch will never let her talk. And solving murders isn't my job."

"You're a spoilsport. I'm going to call around anyway."

Ginnie went to get more milk.

She threw the printouts aside. "Gah!"

"I beg your pardon?" said the robot.

"It was, um, an interjection," Ginnie said. "It wasn't directed at you. It was directed at this damn documentation."

The robot was silent. It knew it did not have to answer a comment made to damn documentation, she thought.

Or to a lack of damn documentation. BioInnovations had only been able to obtain the nonproprietary parts of the robot's software from its designers, since for what-

ever reason they didn't want it known the robot had failed
to prevent a murder. Ginnie had called the guy she'd
dated, the one with the voice, but he had only worked on
the robot's speech software. He was no help.

The software documentation the other company had
supplied was terrible. She didn't think it had been tampered with to help preserve trade secrets. She'd written
too much overhasty documentation herself.

She was looking in particular for a programming
kludge that might have been written in to fix a bug the
earlier programmers couldn't find, what she called the
Use a Bigger Hammer school of programming. She'd
done it herself, though never as sleazily as the programmer who, faced with a program that unaccountably would
sometimes add two and two to make five, inserted code
that said, *If 2 + 2 = 5, then 5 = 4.*

Anything that obvious would leap out at her, but it
wasn't likely to be that obvious.

She also had to look for sabotage. So far the robot
appeared to work the way it was supposed to, with no
signs of tampering.

If she were actually working on solving the murder,
rather than trying to find an invisible bug in a Byzantine
robot, that would be interesting.

She leaned back in her desk chair. It creaked. "I've
been listening to George too much." The robot swiveled
to focus its attention on her. "I'm going to check on
something," she told it. "Don't go anywhere."

"Noted," said the robot.

"Not possible," Drobisch said. His desk was enormous, a monster of dark-stained wood and iron trim.

"She was the last living person to see the robot working. She might have noticed something that would help
me."

"She didn't."

"You're not the computer expert. Let me talk to her."

"We're concerned about her safety."

So you do think Herrera got killed because of what he
was working on, she thought. "Look, I just want to ask

her questions about the robot's functioning. Something that might look like nothing to you, and to her, might be the clue I need.''

Drobisch glowered at her.

She rose to go. ''Okay. Maybe I can find this glitch anyway. It probably doesn't matter. The cops will probably figure out that portable heart-lung machine you hooked to Herrera was the second one. If they guess there was a robot at the scene, they'll impound it, and it won't be my headache.''

''Wait,'' Drobisch said. Her hand was on the doorknob. She turned. ''You can talk to her. At lunch, tomorrow.''

As she'd figured. If she found the bug before the cops knew about the robot, they would erase all its memory and know they could safely use it again when it was finally returned. ''Thanks.''

''I'll be sitting in. Maybe I can help you.'' The sullen tone of his voice was a warning.

Jane Yonamura was a thin woman, older than Ginnie, though it was hard to judge: maybe thirty, maybe thirty-five. She sat across from Ginnie at the cafeteria table, not meeting her eyes. Ginnie remembered that was a characteristic of Japanese politeness. Otherwise Yonamura seemed American enough.

''I'm sorry about Dr. Herrera,'' Ginnie said. ''Had you known him long?'' Drobisch shifted in the chair beside her. You can damn well put up with politenesses, she thought. Anyone would ask that.

''We worked together for two years,'' Yonamura said. ''I knew him as well as you know most people you work with. It's difficult to get used to his absence.''

''I'm very sorry,'' Ginnie said.

Drobisch cleared his throat. Yonamura was silent.

''Did you notice anything unusual about the robot that night?''

''I really couldn't say, Ms. Erickson. I'm not an expert on such things. Dr. Herrera understood computers, but he was a very clever man. I'm an ordinary cellular biology expert; I only deal with computers and robots to the extent I need to for my work."

"That's what my sister always says, that she hates dealing with computers." Drobisch ostentatiously looked at his watch. "But she uses them more than she thinks about. I'm sure you noticed something."

"I can't think of anything."

"Well, you were working late."

"We usually did."

Just working? Ginnie wondered. Probably. They had a robot watching them for the last several weeks. "Did you have the robot assist you in any way?" The robot had been instructed not to reveal anything about Herrera and Yonamura's work to her.

"No. Well, Dr. Herrera may have asked it to time some processes, or hold an instrument. Only very simple things."

"That's good. Did it have trouble understanding any of his instructions that night?"

"No. Let me think about that." She paused briefly. "No, I really don't think so. As I said, he never asked it to do very much. I'm not even certain he talked to it that night."

Now, you'd remember what Herrera did the night he was murdered, Ginnie thought. It was only five days ago, and it had been a memorable night. "It'd be a waste to have such a state-of-the-art robot around and not have it do anything to help out, wouldn't it? I mean, I wonder what the accountants thought about okaying such an expensive piece of machinery. I guess you guys were doing something important."

"I suppose someone thought so," said Yonamura impassively. Ginnie could hear Drobisch breathing. The man breathed loud. He must have practiced being noticeable.

"Did either of you talk to the robot? Did it say anything?"

"It might have. I don't recall."

"I was going to ask if it was showing any difficulties

with language, or if it stuttered, or repeated itself. You
don't remember if it spoke?''

"I don't," Yonamura said.

"What about its movements? Did it seem to have any
trouble navigating?''

"Not to the best of my memory. It isn't something I'd
have paid attention to.''

"You're not getting anywhere here, Erickson," Drobisch said. "We all have work to do.''

No kidding, I'm not, Ginnie thought. Yonamura was
polite, but opaque: deliberately so, she was sure. That
might have to do with Dobisch's presence. Perhaps.

"Thank you anyway," she told Yonamura, who smiled
slightly and accepted Ginnie's handshake.

"It's driving me crazy," she told her sister. "Three
days of this, and the robot makes no more sense than
ever. No—the robot makes as *much* sense as ever. And
it's probably got a hundred man-years of software in it.
I could be looking forever.'' She rubbed her face, yawn-
ing. "If only they weren't too paranoid to bring in a team
of people to look over the thing. The best way to spot a
bug is to bring in a new perspective, but I can tell that
Drobisch doesn't even like having one person look at it.''

"You saw Yonamura?" George asked.

"Oh, yeah. Speaking of brick walls. That woman's not
going to talk about anything.''

"Buried passions?''

"Buried everything. I can't guess what kind of secrets
she's keeping. Maybe she just has more respect for non-
disclosure agreements than I do.''

"Hey, if you can't tell someone who shares your ge-
netic material, who can you tell?" George said. "I'll
never tell. Let them think I'm you.''

"You wouldn't pass the retina ID check they made me
take when I signed all those forms.''

"So I won't let them stare deeply into my eyes. They'd
never check. Even if they thought about you having a
twin, the world's full of idiots who think twins have the
same fingerprints and retina prints.'' As teenagers,

George and Ginnie had read too much science fiction about clones, who were nothing but high-tech twins, not only having the same fingerprints, but lockstep personalities. They hated that. "Here's your surprise bonus today for having a nosy twin." George tossed a bound document on the kitchen table.

"What's this?"

"I drove over to Tech today to see if anyone had any old gossip about Herrera. Nothing. He had a girlfriend junior year from City College, but it didn't last." Ginnie snorted. She'd never thought much of guys who had to leave campus to get girlfriends. "So I looked up his doctoral dissertation, just so it wouldn't be a complete waste of time driving to Pasadena."

"It's always a waste of time driving to Pasadena," Ginnie said automatically, picking up the binder. " 'Induced Heuristics and Rote Learning in Mammals?' Sounds like a page-turner."

"I still say Yonamura did him in, but if they weren't hot and heavy, and it was sabotage, this could be a clue to whatever they were working on."

"It was twelve years ago," Ginnie said. "It could have nothing at all to do with whatever he was doing for the company." She flipped through the pages. "And it's really badly written. Do they make you write dissertations this way? Thank god I didn't go for a doctorate."

"I had a look at it," George said. "There's some theoretical stuff about ways to treat people who've lost abilities due to strokes or other brain trauma."

"Like ice picks?"

"Ick! Like, say, somebody has a microstroke, and can't tie his shoelaces anymore. Herrera thinks it should be possible to zap the whole subroutine for tying shoelaces into a brain."

"How?"

"I'm going to reread it. It's pretty thick going, and I never read much neurology. Most of this paper is about white rats and bunny rabbits. He only mentions people toward the end."

"That's the interesting part, though, isn't it?" Ginnie

said. She squinted at a thicket of graphs relating in some way to brain chemicals she'd never heard of. "Programming human brains. Just think how a military organization would slaver over that."

"I have," George said. "So industrial sabotage goes back on the motive list. And so does international intrigue."

"Oh, great," said Ginnie. "I prefer the theory about a sex-crazed research assistant stabbing his eyes out."

"Either way, poor sap. Wonder if he saw it coming?"

"It could explain why Yonamura is so quiet. This might be dangerous business to know anything about."

"If it's related to what Herrera was working on for BioInnovations," said George.

"I'm going to ask around some more. Maybe he told someone what he was working on."

"Listen," Ginnie said. She knew she couldn't stop her sister from working a puzzle through to its finish. She was intrigued herself, but she was also feeling queasy. She reached across the table and took her twin's hand. "Be careful."

George smiled and squeezed her fingers.

She was running the robot's memory through the last ten minutes before Herrera's death. The picture jiggled as the robot trundled through the hallway behind the scientist. Herrera went into the end stall of the men's room; the robot focused on the door. Someone had taped an old Gary Larson cartoon to it, so yellowed it was brown: it showed a laboratory filled with dead cats in lab coats. Curiosity, it seemed, had killed them.

Herrera came out of the stall and walked briskly out of the bathroom. He did not stop to wash his hands. Ginnie shook her head. The robot had to hurry to keep up. He stopped at the lab door, and the robot preceded him into the room and took up its customary position in the corner opposite the door, from which it could see everything. Herrera walked into the room and sat at his terminal. She isolated the keyboard in closeup. The keys Herrera hit were A, 6, CAPS LOCK, SHIFT, J, Y, DELETE,

G, H, 2, TAB. The sequence looked nonsensical. She frowned.

That was the point the door suddenly slammed shut; the robot glanced at the source of the sound, only for an instant.

Gore was running from Herrera's eyes when it glanced back.

Someone cleared his throat behind her. "You have two days."

"Two days until what?"

"I've spoken to your department," Drobisch said. "Your supervisor agrees they're overextended in salary base. He may not be able to keep you on."

"Wait a minute."

"I've told him, of course, that since you've been on loan to the security department, we'd like to help. We might be able to squeeze out some money to move into their budget. Out of gratitude. If we were grateful."

This was nearly a subtle move. She should be impressed. "Come on. We're not talking about a payroll program. There are reams of code in this robot. You can't expect one programmer to find a bug in a week!"

"There are a lot of programmers. BioInnovations can't be expected to employ them all." Drobisch looked smug. He turned on his heel and felt.

"Damn it!"

He was setting her up to be the fall guy. Not his fault the security robot didn't work: the company employed idiot programmers who couldn't work the thing. No matter that she'd hardly seen the robot before the murder. She suspected Drobisch was in a position to alter her employment records.

He was right about one thing. Southern California, which ten years ago had looked like a bottomless pool of employment for good programmers, was finally saturated with them. And even when you lived with your sister, rents were outrageous. It took both of them to afford a two-bedroom place. The cost of water alone could break her, if she went long without a job.

She might even have to move to New Jersey.

"Damn it."

* * *

"We're not going to talk about me finding a new roommate," George said firmly. "We're going to solve this mystery."

Ginnie was lying on the sofa, her arms wrapped around a cushion, thinking. "If I have to move out, Mom will want you to move back with her."

"Not a chance. I love Mom and all, but give me a break. It's nice not to have talked to her for a week, for a change."

"You haven't told her? Good. She'd just worry. Did you find out anything about Yonamura?"

"No." George bit her lip. "I'm afraid I sort of wasted today. I wish I'd known Drobisch was going to lean on you."

"Well, you didn't know."

"Yeah, but if you lose your job—I was talking to some Lloydies about Herrera, back when he lived there. You know he lived in Lloyd House, just like I did?"

"No. Small world." Ginnie had an old college friend who'd dropped out of physics and started a small import business up in Oregon. Maybe he could use a programmer to make the shipping end of it more efficient. If she could get used to living with pine trees. Or maybe she could get a job on the loading dock. She hugged the cushion to her cheek.

"They were telling me stories about his Ditch Day stack. It was pretty memorable."

On Senior Ditch Day at CalTech, the seniors set puzzles, called "stacks," for the underclassmen to solve. The underclassmen had to solve the puzzle to gain entry to the senior's room. If they didn't find a "bribe"—usually junk food—waiting for them there, they had the right to counterstack the senior's room, giving her a taste of her own medicine.

Ginnie, distracted by killer finals, had simply thrown together a quiz for her stack. When the group trying to get into her room answered some trivia questions on her computer and solved what she'd thought was a fairly knotty programming puzzle, the computer told them where they could find her room key. She'd left a keg of beer and ten pounds of chocolate in the room, and when she got back from her Ditch Day trip to Disneyland, she found nothing but candy wrappers remaining of the bribe.

She still regretted not taking the time to come up with a finesse stack, something the underclassmen would bash their brains against all day but which would be obvious, in light of the clues, when they found out what it was.

"They got to his room and found a video monitor and a joystick outside the door," George said. "And a note that just said, 'Get the key or solve why it can't be done.' "

"Sounds like a good one," Ginnie said, interested despite herself.

"When they turned on the video monitor, it showed the interior of his room, like the camera was next to the door. It looked ordinary enough, but the floor was entirely cleared, and in the middle of it was the room key, and this little cart, with an arm in front of an antenna sticking up."

"The joystick."

"Yeah, one of them picked up the joystick and moved it around, and the cart turned around with it. One button on the joystick raised and lowered the arm, and the other made the cart go forward or backward. The arm had a magnet on it, and there was a washer taped to the key, so the magnet could pick it up."

"Too easy. There's a catch."

"You bet. It looked like the idea was to maneuver the cart over to the door with the key, and get it to push it out under the door. But they couldn't quite get the cart to work right. It'd start toward the door, and suddenly veer off in the wrong direction. Or it would stop moving. Or the key would fall off."

"Some kind of kink programmed into the cart's movement."

"They thought of that. They plotted all the unexplained movements and looked for a pattern. Like, if you turn it 180 degrees to the left, maybe it would go back-ward. Well, it did sometimes, and it didn't sometimes.''

"So it had random error programmed into it, and that's why they couldn't get it to work?''

"But how do you 'prove' that? It's a finesse stack: there has to be something big and deceptively obvious they can point to, or Herrera's screwed it up. They're starting to get very annoyed, because they can see the room and there's no bribe they can see in it. These are students who are seriously looking forward to skipping the counterstack and just trashing his room if they solve the stack. It looks like he expected it to be impossible to solve, and that's not fair.''

"What did it turn out to be?'' Ginnie asked.

"Think about it. There are three components of the puzzle they can look at: there's the remote-controlled cart, and the joystick, and the video monitor/camera setup. They can't get to the cart, except by experimenting with the joystick and watching on the monitor.''

"The joystick.''

"They took it apart, carefully, and looked at it. Nothing funny in the joystick that they could see.''

"The monitor?''

"It was late in the day when this one bright freshman began to wonder if the monitor was showing them the whole story. Some big-shot junior guy had the joystick, but she finally talked him into handing it to her. She moved the cart all the way to the back wall, and started to make it go back and forth, against the wall, as fast as she could.''

"What did that prove?''

"In the middle of the room, the cart blinked out of existence on the video monitor. She moved it back, and half of it was gone. Then it came back again.''

"You've lost me.''

"Did you ever watch a weather report, and the re-porter was wearing a green tie, and you could see Indi-ana right through it?''

"I—oh! It was a chromakey camera!''

"She pounded on the door and shouted 'Open up,

Ralph!', and Herrera opened the door from the inside. The whole back wall of the room was draped in green, he'd painted the floor green, and he was wearing a green bodysuit and a green hood.''

"He'd been in the room all along."

"Yep. She'd proved why they couldn't get the key. The camera didn't pick up greens. Where green would have been, it showed a video image he'd taken earlier, of the normal back and floor of the room. So in his green coverup, he was invisible to the camera. As long as he stayed behind the cart, from camera view, he could mess with its movements without being detected."

"Not bad."

"There's this big lump covered with green cloth in the back of the room, and he rips it off; champagne on ice, this big pastry spread, the works. He sort of cheated by not having actually ditched on Ditch Day, but he sounds like an okay guy. It's too bad he's dead." George sighed. "He had chocolate eclairs for them. I never solved a stack that got me chocolate eclairs."

"Huh." Ginnie sat up and put the cushion down. "So there was one other factor in his stack puzzle, besides the cart, and the joystick, and the camera and monitor."

"Which is?"

"Him. Herrera."

"Good morning, Erickson," Drobisch said.

"Morning," she said, smiling.

She seemed awfully confident for someone who would be canned in eight hours, he thought. She wasn't bad-looking, but she had an attitude problem. "This is your last day, you know."

She smiled again and walked the other way down the hall. He put her out of his mind.

"Good morning, Mr. Drobisch."

"Morning," he grunted. He was almost at his office when he turned around. Who was that? Red suit jacket, blue jeans, brown hair. Erickson? Hadn't he already seen her?

Drobisch hated déjà vu in the morning. He decided he

needed another cup of coffee. Yonamura could not be allowed to talk to anyone. He'd spend today making sure she knew that. It was an aggravation: no wonder he was distracted.

"This is to distract it." Ginnie held up the sound synthesizer. "It has about twenty seconds of silence programmed in before it shouts bloody murder. So timing's important on this experiment."

"Got it," George said. "You want me to walk over and sit in this chair? That's it?"

"That's it. Do it as smoothly as you can. Take even steps."

"Okay. Ready when you say."

"Now," said Ginnie. The robot was cabled to her workstation, on idle. She toggled it on with the joystick she'd rigged.

George walked across the room. The robot watched. She sat.

Ginnie waited a beat. Then she walked across the room, toward George. As she neared her twin, the sound synthesizer cried "Help! Burglar! Murder! Stop!" The robot swiveled toward the alarm. Ginnie toggled it back to idle.

"Let's see what we've got," she said. "You wait outside. I don't want it to see you again."

She turned the robot on again. "When did you last see me?" she asked.

"At 9:09 this morning."

"What did I do?"

"You entered this room. You walked to the northeast corner and sat down."

"How many times did I cross the room to the northeast corner this morning?"

"Once."

"Once?"

"Correct."

"Do you know what you've got, robot? You've got some let-five-equal-four code. You've got a kludge, and

I know who else knew that. Maybe two people who knew that.''

"Do you require a response from me?''

"No, thanks. I've already got everything from you that I need.'' She turned the robot back to idle and hit the codes on her keyboard that would allow her to erase its memory of the morning's experiment. They could find traces of the editing, but maybe they wouldn't bother. With any luck, the robot would be on the scrapheap tomorrow.

"You can come back in.''

"Good,'' said George. She shut the door behind her. "All your co-workers were staring at me. I think they're wondering why you're spending your morning standing outside your office. Did you get what you needed?''

"Yes,'' said Ginnie. "I'm almost certain what happened. I just need to pry Drobisch loose from Yonamura long enough to talk to her.''

"Oh, that sounds like fun. Remember third grade, when we'd confuse Ms. Jefferson on who was who?'' George picked up Ginnie's extension. "Drobisch, please.'' Pause. "He's not in his office? You'd better page him and tell him to come see Virginia Erickson right now. No, this will not wait. Now!'' She slammed the receiver down.

"How will you hold him?''

"I'll threaten a civil suit for wrongful termination of employment. I can doubletalk on that for at least half an hour.''

"I owe you several.''

"Nineteen, now. But who's keeping track?''

Yonamura was peering into a microscope and did not look up. "Mr. Drobisch, we've nothing to talk about. I've told you everything I know.''

"I don't need you to tell me everything, Dr. Yonamura.''

"Ms. Erickson?'' Yonamura pushed her hair back. "I don't think it's a good idea for you to be here.''

"Is it bugged?''

"Bugged? Oh, you mean a microphone. No, I don't—I don't think so. I think I found it." She avoided Ginnie's eye, as she had the first time they met. "I really have nothing to tell you about your robot."

"I want to mention a couple of things to you. I want to know if I'm understanding things right. If I do, you have nothing to worry about from me."

Yonamura was silent, watching her.

"I've seen Dr. Herrera's dissertation. It was about an idea called 'induced heuristics.' I don't know what you brought to the project, but I want to guess. I want to guess you can force-grow clones to early maturity."

"I don't know why you think so."

"You might want to know that I've discovered a bug in the robot after all. Actually, I've discovered the programming fix that covers up a bug."

Yonamura folded her hands in her lap and waited.

"I think when they were designing the robot, it had a glitch that made it think it had seen the same thing more than once. A sort of robot déjà vu. If you rolled a ball in front of it, it might think it saw that ball roll by twice, or, worst case, it might get stuck in a loop and see nothing but that ball rolling by, an infinite number of times. That would be a problem."

"I suppose it would. It's not my specialty."

"Dr. Herrera understood computers, though. And perception, and behavior. He needed all of that for the work you were doing, didn't he? You grow the clones, he works on their brains."

"Dr. Herrera's work was classified. And difficult. Even if I were at liberty to explain it to you, I wouldn't be able to."

"That's okay. I'll make a crude guess. Herrera was inventing a way to put behaviors into empty brains. Like the brains of force-grown clones. It's the only thing I can think of that explains why Herrera's still alive. Are you in contact with him? Do you know where he is?"

Yonamura leapt to her feet. "Ms. Erickson! Dr. Herrera is dead! How can you say—"

"Settle down! I'm just babbling nonsense. Not even

worth repeating outside this room. Just let me finish. If
you two were working on a project to turn blank-minded
clones into programmed zombies, and if he wanted out—
if he didn't like what he thought was going to be done
with it, but he was afraid BioInnovations or its clients
would go after him if he ran—you could use the robot's
little undocumented feature.''

Ginnie licked her lips. Her mouth was dry. She'd tried
not to think through the implications of her solution, but
she couldn't avoid it now. Yonamura looked like she
wanted to run.

Ginnie said, ''Here's where I get really nonsensical:
You've developed a way to force clones to rapid maturity.
You've made a Herrera clone, all grown up but no mind
to speak of. With his neurochemicals and electronics and
whatever, Herrera gives it a simple program: stand on
this toilet until tapped on the shoulder, leave the bathroom, walk down a hall, go into a room, sit in a chair,
hit some random computer keys, wait.

''The real Herrera, dressed identically, follows immediately behind the clone, careful to walk the same way
the clone was programmed to.

''Now, here's the beauty part: he knows, maybe from
noticing the way it perceived little cloned, behavior-
programmed bunnies, that the robot discounts anything
it believes it's identically seen, immediately before.
Completely discounts it. Doesn't perceive it. That's how
its programmers kludged the déjà vu bug.''

Yonamura sat, slowly.

''All he needs is to distract the robot long enough to
stab into his clone's nearly blank brain, incidentally destroying the clone's unique retina patterns, in case anyone thought to check. If he ducks out of sight quickly
enough, when the robot's first-aid functions take over, it
won't have time to see him escape. While its kludge kept
it from perceiving him come in.''

''You can't prove any of this,'' Yonamura said quietly.

''They didn't put the robot on him to guard him from
the competition, did they? That was a side-benefit, but
they really wanted to make sure he didn't try anything

funny. The robot was there to report if he did, and to intimidate him so he wouldn't try it in the first place.''

''That's what we thought.'' Yonamura's tone was even.

Ginnie had to work to keep her own voice low. ''Our advantage is that Drobisch wants to bury any evidence that might show Herrera's death was his fault. If you stay quiet, you may be okay.''

''Dr. Herrera was the only person who fully understood his theories. I'm counting on them not watching me quite as closely. I'd planned to get away as soon as he had enough time to cover his tracks. We weren't counting on the fraud never being discovered. We only hoped, if they thought a competitor had killed him, that it would give him enough time.''

''I hope it does. I don't want to know how much money is involved in this. I don't want to know which governments would pay for this technology. I do have one question.''

''What?'' asked Dr. Yonamura.

''Herrera's techniques—were they only useful on blank brains? Or could they be used on your brain, or mine?''

Yonamura looked Ginnie directly in the eye. She said nothing.

George was gone when Ginnie returned. It took less than half an hour to find the kludge in the robot's code, now that she knew what to look for. She made a simple deletion. Then she packed her personal effects.

''Erickson!'' Drobisch thundered. He stormed through her doorway. ''You are finished at this company. You are finished everywhere. Your work record shows inefficiencies that—''

''You're right, Mr. Drobisch,'' Ginnie said. She nodded at the security robot, which stared unmoving at the doorway, watching images of Drobisch storm in again, and again, and again. ''I not only didn't find the glitch in the security robot, but the bug seems to have gotten worse. It's a mess.''

''Goddamn stupid machine! I told them not to—''

''You were right. Under the circumstances, I think I

should give my notice.'' She picked up her box of personal items and squeezed past him as he gaped.

Would Drobisch be more interested in burying anything that would make him look bad to his superiors than he was in following her? It was a fair bet.

Oregon or New Jersey? She wondered which one Herrera would choose.

WINDOWS OF THE SOUL
by Susan Casper

Susan Casper, author of numerous powerful short
stories, is the coeditor of the anthology, *Ripper!*

*A human man, visiting the commercial center of
an alien city, sees a nonrepresentational painting,
looking very much like a colorful ink blot, in a bar.
He immediately walks into the bar, calmly pulls out
a pistol, and shoots the proprietor, an alien he has
never see before.*
   *The aliens are not familiar with human psycho-
logical abnormalities, and they call in a human
specialist to find out if the man is sane or insane.
After hearing his strange story, it's a close call,
but the specialist makes his decision.*
   Write it.

Until it actually happened I would have said that I was
ready for trouble. Excitement is a living emotion, boredom dead and deadly, and I'd spent the last five years on
this godforsaken hole of a planet. Red Dust was not a
big human settlement, but the few of us who lived there
were seated as usual around the one round table that had
been set up in the corner of Dikma's place. Most of the
patrons were natives who spread out through the rest of
the large, barnlike structure, a sort of bar, meeting hall,
community center. It was the only really large room in
the district and its plain stone walls and beaten earth
floors were about the height of architectural standards on
Phaliajeet. I suppose I should have been over there with
the 'Jeets, watching them, talking to them, but my equip-

ment was trained on them, doing my job for me, recording everything they did, everything they said. The main
decoration in my quarters were cartons of disks that no
one had ever bothered to view, and probably never would.
Don't get me wrong, I rather liked the 'Jeets, a gentle
people with no concept of war or crime, but there was
nothing particularly interesting about them.

I had wanted to go into exotics ever since I could remember. The college brochures all read, "See the universe, meet new and fascinating cultures, discover
wonders unknown to Man," and I was callow enough to
believe them. Okay, I admit it. I fantasized about living
among people like the Cyrenes, with their fabulous crystal cities and tremendous wealth of art, or the Sponid
Rigullans, so ugly that I could barely stand to look at
them, but incredibly advanced in science and technology.
Great governments and major companies would fight for
my services, because I alone could find the spark that
would unite two cultures and reach a true understanding
of great alien minds. So, there I was, all ready for the
strange, the fantastic, the incomprehensible, even the
grotesque, which would soon lead up to an important
cure, a great new art form, a whole new field of science.
I didn't expect it to be easy, but never in my wildest
dreams was I ready for what I got.

And now here I was, thirty-two-year-old Alicia Cour
Roselli, employee of Castle Fuels with one more month
left on my five-year contract. A dream job with one of
the biggest employers in the business, and I couldn't wait
for it to be over.

I knew now why they sent a rookie, fresh out of college with no experience. By law they had to provide an
exotic culture specialist on Phaliajeet, but as long as we
were allowed to dig out the minerals they didn't really
give a damn what information I provided, if any. They
left me to deal with a people who saw well into spec-
trums that we couldn't even begin to fathom without special equipment that the company would never go to the
expense of providing. A people whose speech dipped
down into subsonics that made everyone feel as if some-

one were sneaking up behind them, until one of the techs finally developed blockers. A people whose main contribution to the universe was a planet rich in ores that they themselves never used. Nor did Castle care if I wrote up my studies. I was sure they would never publish them, even if I did. In a way, it was a tragedy waiting to happen, and it did, though not the way I expected.

So dull was our existence that everyone was buzzing about the arrival of a new ship that afternoon. This was no company tanker bringing in new recruits and carrying off its payload, but a small commercial enterprise that would surely have cocoa and fruit, furniture and clothing, the newest in music, and movies we hadn't seen to death. Most of the humans were fairly excited about it. All except me. I was saving for my trip home. I was saving so that I could afford to take some time off before accepting my next assignment, and I was perfectly willing to do without anything I didn't already have. After all, I only had to put up with it for one more month. On the other hand, James and Attiya were just beginning their contracts, and most of the others were somewhere in the middle. A few luxuries were looking pretty good to them, and money you can't spend tends to burn a hole in your pocket. Martin Okawa was trying to get me excited about it, too. I knew he wanted me to sign up for two more years, the amount of time he had left on his contract. I'm not sure why. I went out of my way not to encourage him, and sometimes that wasn't easy. The others had just gotten into a discussion of popular music and what they were listening to at home these days when Bonnie interrupted.

"Here comes one of them now," she said, pointing to the newcomer. The man was standing by the entrance, staring at the room's only decoration, a rather ugly poster hanging near the counter. Heaven alone knew what it looked like to the 'Jeets, but to me it was just an ugly dull black with a bright red circle in the middle. You could tell instantly that this man was a newcomer to the planet. Sure, I knew all the humans at Red Dust by sight, but that wasn't the reason. There were people at Kesma and New Angels and some of the other districts that I wouldn't recognize. The giveaway here was that this man either hadn't yet gotten a set of blockers or didn't know how to work them. He was obviously reacting to the heavy load of subsonics in the room. His body was tensed, his movements nervous and jerky. We laughed, each of us remembering our first day or two.

"I'd better go take him in hand," I said and started to get up.

"Oh, relax. He'll find us." Martin put his hand on my arm. As usual, I pulled it away from him, but I did turn back toward my seat.

"I guess you're right," I answered. After all, the man had already walked over to Dikma and the two were talking. Just right. Of all the 'Jeets, Dikma was the most acclimated to humans. I think he really liked being around us, and the feeling was mutual. The 'Jeet's fur turned dark brown and he waved his arm in the air, flashing claws as most 'Jeets did when making a show of pride. It must have had something to do with the poster, for Dikma pointed in that direction. The man said something else, and again Dikma pointed. It was his job to study us, and he was far more patient about it than was I, but there was something wrong with this scene. That the man seemed nervous and upset didn't bother me. I could see that he wasn't wearing blockers, and even when speaking Alpha a 'Jeet gives off heavy subsonics, but the two seemed to be arguing. I'd never seen a 'Jeet argue with anyone, especially not Dikma. I was just beginning to think about interfering after all, when I saw the stranger pull a gun.

The others were on their feet as soon as the shot sounded. My first reaction was to run toward Dikma, while the others all headed toward the stranger. Bonnie grabbed the gun and a few of the others were wrestling the man to the ground. The 'Jeets did nothing. Not a move, not a sound. They stood, as if transfixed in horror, their lung slits fixed open, straining like a forest of fur-covered tree ears, showing off the short neck between head and shoulders. Their slothlike faces were stock-still, their long, double-digited arms pressed against the floor for balance. I don't know much about their physiology, but I'm fairly sure Dikma was already dead. There wouldn't have been much I could have done for him even if it wasn't too late. I think I shouted "Get someone! Get help!" But even as I screamed, I knew that there was nothing that could be done for him. His lung slits were closed up tight and his fur was already draining to a pale cream color, except where it was crusted with blood. His funny little rounded belly had ceased to pulse with life. Tears filled my eyes and I looked around hastily, cursing when I remembered that the 'Jeets had no use for cloth. Feeling emotions I wasn't aware I owned, I stood and removed my blouse. It wasn't much, but it was all I had. I covered Dikma's face and went to join the others.

The stranger was still fighting, screaming something. I wasn't really sure what he said. There were four strong men tugging at him, but he managed to free an arm, swinging it wildly. Attiya was hit, the arm raking across his head, and he dropped in his tracks like a sack. I couldn't see what happened next, but the recording was fairly clear. Bonnie stepped up behind the troublemaker and hit him with his own gun. Then she ran to check on Attiya, who was already getting to his feet. The stranger lay still as death, but they no longer paid any attention in that direction.

I was fairly sure that Attiya was going to be fine, and I think he would have said so if Bonnie would have let him have enough air to speak. It was James who finally said, "Kiss him later. I want to see how he is." There was no doctor at Red Dust. The size of the human population didn't rate one. James had been given enough training to deal with the minor stuff. Emergencies were vacced immediately to the hospital at New Angels. Once Attiya had been looked after, James turned his attention to the man on the ground. This was another story. Other than the rhythmic rise and fall of his chest, he didn't seem to be moving at all. I could wait for the outcome. Tomorrow would be soon enough to find out what this deranged lunatic thought he was doing. I overcame an urge to do him further damage and headed for the door.

Martin walked me home, his arm around my shoulders. His warmth and strength felt good, and for once I didn't pull away. The wind was down, leaving the air relatively clear, with twin moons providing more than enough light. The little circles of plain, rough-cut dwellings the 'Jeets liked so well took on a certain sheen in the moonglow. Pots of flowers and shrubs set out in inviting designs marked the buildings taken over by human inhabitants. The air smelled fresh and clean. This was the season when wormberry bushes tossed their delicate fruit on the ground. The little green berries were sweet and somewhat stimulating, though many humans had trouble getting past the appearance that gave them their name. Martin scrounged a handful from the ground and wiped the dust off on his shirt, leaving long red streaks.

"Why did he do that, Martin?" I asked. "Why would anyone, let alone a stranger, an Earthman at that, want to hurt a 'Jeet? Especially Dikma. I just don't . . ."

"Hey, Allie, what can I do to get you to call me Marty, huh? As for this mess, we don't know yet, but we'll find out. That's not what really worries me though. The question is, can we do *anything* about it?" His face was solemn. I knew Martin well enough to know when he was serious. I was about to protest, when I thought about it for a moment. This was a company town. There had been laws set up to protect the humans, to protect the project, but Castle had no rights to set up any laws affecting the natives. I shivered. Taking it for a chill, he removed his shirt and placed it around my shoulders.

"You mean he's going to walk? He's going to get on that ship and just go home? But surely there must be some native law that would . . ." I hadn't thought it was possible to be anymore upset, but suddenly I felt a rage that made me incoherent. I couldn't speak, I couldn't move, I just wanted to break something. The night was chilly after all, unusual for Phaliajeet, but then, maybe it was me. It was also unusually quiet. I turned off my blockers. I should have heard the dull rumble of 'Jeet conversation, but all that I heard were the roars of distant animals and the night breeze whistling through the rocky cliffs that marked the edge of town.

"Surely?" Martin said. "You would know better than anyone."

I thought furiously. "I did a paper on local laws, but that was years ago. I don't remember much. They had no statutes on murder. I do remember that, because it struck me as odd at the time. But I didn't know them very well then. I've never heard of one 'Jeet killing another, have you? But there might be other things that could apply." I stopped for a moment and grabbed a hank of my short dark hair, an unsightly habit I've never been able to lose, and thought. "There's the insanity law. But Martin, if they vac him out of here tonight, it's all over. Once they leave the territory, the 'Jeets can no longer prosecute."

"And if they don't vac him out of here, he could be dead. Allie, I'm scared. I never saw anyone go down like that. He was lying so still I thought he was dead."

"Serves him right," I replied, but that *was* bitterness talking. I smiled at the shocked look on Martin's face and put my hand over his. "No, I know. If nothing else, we have to find out why he did it. But Martin, if the 'Jeets don't prosecute, there's no official investigation. The ship can't turn over records even if they want to, unless we have some official claim, and that man wouldn't have to tell us anything. We'll never know. It could happen again."

We reached my place, but he made no move to leave me, and the worst part was that I really didn't want him to. At least, I was reluctant to be alone, but I braced myself. I still had only a month left on my contract and I wasn't about to get involved with *anyone* until I was safely home. He seemed to sense my mood, for he removed his arm from my shoulder and put his hands in the air.

"Listen, Alicia. If I promise to behave, let me come in for a little while. Just some coffee and conversation. We need to talk about this. I have a feeling that in a little while this whole thing is going to descend on you like an avalanche.''

"Why me?'' I asked, though I already knew the answer. Who else would they get to investigate? I was their resident expert on behaviorism. Dikma had been their human psychology expert, but he was no longer available. Martin didn't bother to answer. He smiled and ushered me into my quarters.

"We'd better check the exact reading on that law. You're going to need to know it. Besides, if I'm going to keep James from sending him to New Angels, I'd better have a pretty good reason.''

He was right, of course. First thing in the morning I was awakened by Francis O'Lynn of Castle and Kitikin, newly appointed head of foreign affairs for the Phaliajeet, knocking on my door. Martin had stayed late, going over papers, looking at several recordings and occasionally trying, not very hard, to break his promise. I had almost no sleep the night before. Fortunately, short straight hair takes almost no time to comb, and any old pants and shirt I wore would do. Fashion was not a major problem in the informal day-to-day life of Phaliajeet. It took only a moment before I answered the door. Coffee was brewing, and I had opened a bottle of bubbling syrup for Kitikin, but I was not anxious for the morning to begin. I knew what they wanted. Finally, I ushered them inside my quarters. O'Lynn headed directly for my favorite chair and took a seat without waiting to be asked. Kitikin, showing invariable 'Jeet politeness, waited until I ushered him inside, then took the bowl I proffered and squatted on the floor. He did not immediately inhale the steam, but that was not my only clue to his state of mind. It was obvious from the paleness of his fur and the rigidity of his lung slits that he was not relaxed. Even his stomach was rigid, a sure sign of stress. I didn't blame him.

"I think you know why we're here,'' O'Lynn said after a moment. "We have no legal right to detain this man. Right now, we're holding him illegally. That's why we haven't yet gone to the ship to get his records. If they demand his release, we'll have to give him to them. I've been trying to get the minister here to press the sanity charge before they move him out of the district."

Kitikin began to speak, but I held up my blockers to show him that they were not in place and he waited patiently for me to put them on and press the switch. He read the law carefully in his own tongue, then switched to Alpha for our benefit. "An individual who commits an act such that his rationality may be called into question must be detained until it can be determined if his rationality needs to be restored." He stopped and looked at us sadly. "I have said that I do not know that this applies. Is it true that a human must be insane to do this thing? You will forgive my frankness, but your people do many things that are incomprehensible to us. This is a sad day for us," he said, without even the slight accent that most 'Jeets have when they speak in Alpha. "But we do not demand punishment, as Frank has expressed it. I have tried to understand this concept . . . punishment. It means nothing to me."

"Well, dammit, it means something to *me!*" O'Lynn said, his face red with anger. This was not just company business with him, I realized. Something else was going on. I wondered what it was, but it was no more than a moment before I found out. "Alicia, there's something else you need to know. Bonnie Kirov swore when they took him away last night that he muttered one phrase over and over again. *'Agor T Mathine.'*" If he watched for my reaction, he must have been satisfied. I could feel my jaw drop.

"Agor T Mathine?" I repeated stupidly. "But he's a human!" I had barely managed to keep from spilling my coffee. Now I put the cup down on the floor.

"I know. Maybe he's a renegade. Maybe just a sympathizer." O'Lynn said.

"Frank, you're not thinking. They're supposed to have been exterminated—but even if they still exist, and I don't doubt that they do, why would any human want to join an organization dedicated to destroying human life? And even if there was such a lunatic among the humans, *they* aren't rational enough to use us against ourselves. They can't stand to be around us.'' I could feel my stomach begin to knot, something that just the thought of the *Agor T Mathine* did to me. The very idea of an organization of creatures dedicated to the eradication of human life from the universe. A bigotry so blinding that they would give their own lives to see it achieved. Fortunately, many of them had. It was shortly after starting here that I'd read a bulletin that the organization had finally been destroyed. ''And even if they do still exist, and they did allow a human to join—'' I shook my head for a moment at the utter absurdity of the idea, ''—why would they then have him go and kill a 'Jeet?''

''Perhaps because of the sign,'' Kitikin answered calmly.

''Sign?'' O'Lynn and I both asked at once. But I was beginning to get an idea. The scene replayed itself over in my mind, not only as I saw it then, but as I watched the recording with Martin last night. It had not made much sense at the time. The man had pointed at the poster and asked Dikma, ''Do you believe in this?'' And Dikma had assured him, more than once, that it was very important to him. That was when he pulled out the gun. It hadn't made any sense. I had stared at that stupid poster many a night, but it certainly had no meaning. Even if it did have something on it that my eyes couldn't perceive, the killer couldn't have seen it either. He was human, after all. At least he *looked* human, but as Kitikin explained I began to get a picture. It was a picture I didn't much like.

''Dikma was very much against the *Agor T Mathine*. We all are, of course, but he especially. He was our Machti, like you are, Alicia. He studied the humans. I understand he was quite fond of your people. He had that poster, as you know. The one for organizing against the *Agor T Mathine*. Maybe . . .''

''Is that what that is?'' I interrupted Kitikin's speech.

''But surely you've seen it. I thought you spent a great deal of time in Dikma's establishment. Did you never look at . . . . Oh, I've forgotten. You cannot see the lu-mai paint. Does it look like nothing at all?''

"Just plain, dull black. But that doesn't make sense. How could *he* have seen it? Frank, you'll have to let me question him, and Kitikin, I'm afraid you'll have to press the insanity charge. Why would any sane human be working with them?''

"I am convinced," Kitikin said, "but as far as your speaking with him . . .'' This time it was Frank who interrupted.

"I'm afraid you can't speak to him, Alicia. The man hasn't regained consciousness yet. Bonnie must have really whacked him one. James thinks we need to vac him out to New Angels. That was one of the reasons our friend here was so reluctant to press those charges. Whatever we do, it has to be done in a hurry.'' Frank took a long sip from his cup, obviously avoiding my eyes.

"Can't we bring a doctor here?'' I asked. "We can't just let him die!''

"What would be the point of bringing a doctor? We have no facilities. No, we must get on with this thing as quickly as possible. Then, if the man's still alive, we can get him some help. But Kitikin, for the good of *your* people and *my* people, and yes, even the company, we have to do this. But do it quickly,'' he added to me. "We'll give the man a hearing, and whatever the out-come, we can then get him the help that he needs.''

Kitikin stood, but did not leave immediately. He put his arm on my head, a 'Jeet gesture of comfort, and spoke softly. "Dikma had wished his remains to fertilize the flowers of the human settlement. Can this be arranged?'' I smiled at him. The 'Jeets did not bury their dead whole. Instead, the bodies were processed into mulch and used to fertilize crops. Tears filled my eyes again. I assured the head of foreign affairs that this would be no prob-lem, more determined than ever to get to the bottom of this conundrum.

Ordinarily, I would have taken my time, made up lists of things to do, talked the whole thing over with one or two of the others, but never before had the pressure of

time weighed so heavily on my shoulders. I felt as if I
were dashing about, almost without direction. I followed
Kitikin only long enough to see that the charges were
made official, and to get a warrent for the ship which was
my next stop, but James caught up with me on my way
out the door.

"Alicia, you've got to stop this madness! This man is
dying. He needs a doctor. I don't have the knowledge or
facilities to help him. I can't even find out his name, let
alone his medical history."

I took a deep gulp of air to steady myself. Things were
happening too quickly, but James was right. It couldn't
wait forever. I put my hands on his arms and moved him
gently out of my way, saying, "James, I promise. I'll
have him released if I have to find him guilty to do it.
Just keep him alive three or four more hours. That's all
I ask." I charged past, unwilling to look him in the eye.
Would three or four hours be enough? I doubted it. With
even a remote chance that the *Agor T Mathine* was involved, I had to find out what I could—but at the risk of
a man's life? That was something I wasn't sure about. Of
course, he might be a member of that disgusting organization, but I didn't give that idea much credence. I
doubted that a human could join, even if one was crazy
enough to want to.

The 'Jeets were another matter. After all, what did I
really know about them? If I had ever done one-tenth of
my job . . . But Dikma with the *Agor T Mathine*? It was
an idea I had trouble believing, but it made more sense
than the other way around. I had to check it out.

It was odd to be inside a ship again. My one and only
jump had been the one out to Phaliajeet, fresh out of
school and eager to get started on my career. That had
been a crowded transport, this a huge tanker, now devoid
of its cargo, and its tiny crew was out looking over the
planet. Still, the smells were the same. The heavy odor
of sweat and hard work that stained the bulkheads. The
harsh interior lighting that played off the white of the
walls, so painful to the eye. And yet, something inside
me seemed to feel I was going home, and it was a wrench

to pull myself out of that reverie and climb up to the records room. A Mr. Chiaparell was there to help me download the records.

"Of course I knew him. We're only a skeleton crew on the *Marshall Fields*. He's a nice guy. I'd hate to see anything happen to him. I don't know what he's accused of, but I can't see him doing anything wrong," he told me while we worked. "His name is Stratoff Kir; his assignment, assistant cook. He mostly kept to himself. A quiet guy. Gentle, you know. He couldn't even stand to be around when the animals were being butchered. They use to laugh at him for that. He didn't get into fights, he didn't join in the poker games, and as far as I knew, he didn't have any really close friends on board. Maxie, his boss, the head cook, referred to him as 'the wimp' because he took orders quietly and never screamed back when he was yelled at. Personally, I always got the feeling that he just wasn't there. I don't mean crazy. Just really sad. He always seemed to be lost in some dream world. You know, dead but moving around. He always looks as if he were going to cry." Gentle, great; just what I needed. One gentle being kills another gentle being, and somehow, the most violent organization that ever existed is involved. Chiaparell handed me the printout and I thanked him, reading it as I left.

Interesting psych profile. Stratoff was diagnosed as depressive, but nonaggressive to himself or to others. That just showed how much those docs knew about it. I grunted and went on reading as best I could, stopping only when I had to climb down ladders and maneuver around objects. By the time I made it to the building we'd nicknamed St. James Infirmary, I knew quite a bit about Mr. Kir. It wasn't a pleasant story, but I now knew where the *Agor T Mathine* came into it. At least on his side.

About the time I was headed out to Phaliajeet, Stratoff Kir had also been on a ship, a transport vessel headed for Drachma. Oddly, those records showed him to be quite amiable, involved in ship theater, and a medal-winning runner on the Olympic squad. His wife and three-year-old son had been on board with him, working their passage to the colonies, as many families did. Unfortunately, the ship had been attacked. Once again, it was the *Agor T Mathine*. It had been the attack that had ended in the capture of what we had hoped was the last of the lousy outfit. But the ship had fared badly. Kir had been the only survivor. And he had made it simply because a blast had sealed him into a cargo hold. Somehow, badly injured, without light, without food and water, and barely enough air to keep him going, he managed to survive until he was picked up by the patrol that destroyed his attackers. I found myself feeling sorry for Kir, and had to remind myself that Dikma had been a friend.

James looked nervous. He was pacing around the little hospital room like an expectant father, and when I asked him about the patient, he literally growled. "I don't know, Alicia. I have to admit it. I just don't know enough. He could come out of this and be just fine, or he could die in five minutes. I don't know, and I'm scared. Look what happens when I shine a light in his eyes. I've never seen anything like it." He turned on the light pen and lifted Stratoff's eyelid. The eye of the patient reflected like a cat's. I tried to calm him down.

"Oh, that's nothing to worry about. He has implants. Artificial lenses. He was in an accident," I added, handing him Kir's medical chart.

"Oh, polarized. I see. Must have light-sensitive eyes," James added. He went on talking, but I no longer heard what he had to say. I had an idea. A blinding revelation, more like. I believe that I left him in mid-sentence, still worrying about his patient. I was running by then, an exercise I hadn't done in quite some time, but even shortness of breath couldn't slow me up. Polarized lenses. I was sure I had one somewhere in the equipment box. It was one of those things I never used, but then, I never threw anything away. It took me ten more minutes to find the little box and another five to get over to Dikma's. Martin was there.

"Hi, Allie," he said walking toward me, and for a moment I was sure he was going to try to kiss me, but at the last second he pulled back and offered his hand.

"What's all this?" he asked. I didn't answer. I fished through the box for the lens I wanted and held it up to my eye. It was just as I had suspected. The sign looked completely different now. Where the red circle sat was a picture of a fist, wearing the ring and bracelet that were the symbols of the *Agor T Mathine*. Around it in ten different languages was the phrase, "Stop the *Agor T Mathine*, NOW!" and the word now shimmered in the multicolored glow of shattered crystal.

"I've never been more confused," I said. It was true. I was almost ready to cry. Nothing seemed to make any sense. I had harbored the feeling, half hope, half fear, that somehow the 'Jeets were in league with the devil, but the sign was exactly as Kitikin had told me it would be. Why would Kir kill a creature for being against an organization he himself had so much reason to hate? Hot tears of frustration filled my eyes and I threw the lens across the room.

Martin picked up the glass. "What the hell is this?" he asked. He held the lens up to his eye and turned it in a circle, a broad smile breaking out on his face. I remember how mad it made me. Here I was with this mess pressing in on me, with nothing making the least bit of sense, and he had the time to play. I was just about to scream at him to stop fooling around when I heard him whisper softly, "Ah, that explains everything!"

"I'm glad *you're* satisfied!" I screamed. Every muscle in my body ached with tension. He put the lens up to my eye. Angrily, I pushed his hand away.

"Patience, Allie," he said. Again he put the lens to my eye and this time he turned it slowly.

It must have been the excitement. Before I even realized what I had done, my arms were around his neck and I was kissing him. It took only a second to collect myself. "Grab that poster and let's go!" I shouted, already on my way out the door.

Twenty minutes later, everyone had gathered. Like most 'Jeet meetings, this was very informal. Kitikin squatted on the floor with the rest of the council, and chairs had been provided for myself, Frank O'Lynn and

Martin. After a brief address in his native tongue, most of which I even understood, Kitikin announced that the meeting would be held in Alpha out of deference to the rest of us.

"Alicia Cour Roselli has claimed sanity for the individual, one Stratoff Kir. She will now plead her case."

O'Lynn stared at me in astonishment, but Michael's smile gave me the courage to go on. "This whole thing has been a dreadful mistake. As most of you are aware, we do not see as you do. To you, this poster," I said, holding up the offending item, "is a strike against the *Agor T Mathine*. To most of us it is merely a red circle on a plain black background. However, Stratoff Kir does not see in the same way as either of us. Because of an injury received at the hands of the *Agor T Mathine*—who, by the way, were responsible for the murder of his family as well as most of his friends—he has had artificial lenses inserted in his eyes. Polarized lenses react strangely to light. I don't know the technical details, but I know what I saw when I looked through one. With a fully-polarized lens I can see the details of the poster—but turn the lens a mere quarter turn and some of the print disappears. The poster seems to show only the sign for the *Agor T Mathine*, surrounded by the word NOW!"

O'Lynn dropped the lens in surprise. Hurriedly, he picked it up, put it to his eye and began to turn. A moment later he stood and nodded gravely. "This is so," he said.

I continued my speech. "What did Stratoff Kir feel when he entered Dikma's. Subsonics hit different people differently, but the usual reactions are fear, anger, irrational paranoia. He was not aware that the feeling was produced by the sound waves of your speech. He had no blockers on him when he was apprehended. As most humans do at first, he would have assumed that his discomfort was due to something wrong in the room. Then he saw the poster. And what did he see? He saw a sign *supporting* the *Agor T Mathine*. Imagine his horror then. And yet, even then, he did not act immediately. He walked over to the proprietor and asked him, 'Do you believe in this?' Can you imagine his reaction when Dikma assured him that it was the most important thing in his life?'' I paused to look around. Kitikin's fur was almost white, but from the relaxed position of his lung slits I took that for sorrow rather than anger or illness. The others looked about the same. I know there were tears in my eyes, but I didn't bother to wipe them before I finished.

''This was a tragedy, but it was not a crime. Stratoff Kir reacted with haste, but it was an understandable haste. He was in a hurry to rid the universe of something that was a danger to every living thing in it. A danger that he alone had experienced firsthand. I recommend that he be released to seek the medical treatment he needs.''

Once again, there was someone at my door first thing in the morning. I dragged myself out of bed and let O'Lynn into my quarters. ''I bring good tidings,'' he said, waving several pieces of paper in front of my face. ''Kir is doing well. They'll be letting him go in time to catch his ship. The ship's captain has sent you his thanks,'' he added, handing me one of the slips, ''and an offer of a ride home in three days' time.''

I looked the paper over and laughed. ''Great! A fat lot of good it will do me with thirty days left on my contract.''

Undeterred, O'Lynn continued. ''And Castle, too, has sent congratulations. They are willing to waive your last thirty days if you want to take Captain Chu up on his offer.''

Home! I was going home! And yet it wasn't excitement I felt as I saw Marty approach from behind the curtain that cordoned off my bedroom area. Then I looked at the stack of cartons that covered my room. Congratulations. I didn't deserve them. This whole thing had been partly my fault. If I had done my job . . .

Well, maybe I couldn't have kept it from happening, but whoever they got to replace me wasn't going to do any better, and there was so much work to be done. I smiled shyly at Martin and flopped down onto the chair.

"Actually," I said to O'Lynn, "I was just about to come see you." His puzzled look amused me, and I smiled. "What do I have to do to renew my contract?" I asked.

THE WHOLE TRUTH
by Susan Shwartz

Along with her very successful novels and short
fiction within the field, Susan Shwartz has also edited a number of anthologies.

*An alien telepath does a mind-reading act on hu-
man worlds. It is hired to perform at a private
party. It announces that one of the nine people in
attendance is a thief and a murderer. The lights go
out for a moment, and when the power comes back
on, the alien itself has been murdered.*

*One member of the audience is a retired detec-
tive. Have him (or her) solve the murder.*

Gravity at Indulgences, at Station Alpha's heart, was a
lavish one G, and that was only the start of it. The tables
were true wood, not veneer. If they were safety-bolted
to the floor, you couldn't see it, and real candles burned
on each one—an ongoing nightmare (and profit center)
for Hydroponics. And don't ask what sorts of other bribes
anyone paid to Hydroponics, real wood for-God's-sake
burned in the fireplace opposite the great screen, curtained with damask, on which views of Earth were projected. Hydro was good at cost-justification, and these
days, that was the name of the game.

"Quite the dinner," said one of the discreet security
guards. He had expected to be dropsick all over his
corporate-issue Armani. Instead, here he was at a restaurant to which Guide Michelin had awarded an astronom-
ical five stars.

The other security guard nodded. She was a woman in

her early thirties who wore the company couture with a carelessness that suggested she'd have been happier in trousers and a lab coat. "Just icing on the cake. If Merrill Nomura could ferry all the suits to Alpha for major meetings with the Iatroi, hiring Indulgences for the night . . . I mean, this sleep period . . . is like throwing a tip to a beggar."

Her companion glanced at the menu, hand-written in French on heavy paper that clearly had never been recycled from anything else. "The waste," he marveled. "And the calories. Sandy, don't they worry about how much they're *eat*ing? Never mind the fact that this stuff must cost a fortune."

"Two fortunes." Sandy shrugged. "Enjoy it. How the other one-thirty-second lives. Or maybe the other one-sixty-fourth."

"If we eat all this, we'll never make the weight restrictions."

He had the look of someone whose leanness was maintained, not by scientific and elegant starvation, but by nerves and uneven pay. But even that sort of leanness was cultivated: Merrill Nomura had enough care for its image—and a strong enough balance sheet—that it pruned its people for looks as well as financial prowess, generation after generation. Rich and fat got spas and liposuction; everyone else either shaped up, quite literally, or shipped out. Even security guards.

"Eat your heart out," Sandy told him. "Guaranteed noncontaminated by pesticide, cholesterol, white sugar, or superfluous calories. People in the Domes are starving, and these people pay a premium to scarf down pretty food that won't chuck weight onto them."

Her colleague, correctly named Michael, was dividing his attention between the appetizers—patés that looked as if they'd have to be scraped off clogged arteries, but were probably almost devoid of real fat—and the faces he recognized from trade broadcasts. Much to everyone's astonishment, when the long-dreamt-of aliens finally did arrive, practically their first statement wasn't "Take me to your leader" or "We come in peace," but "Where did the markets close?'' They had learned Earth's languages—commercial English, Japanese, the Franco-Deutsch of the EC—from broadcasts. Financial broadcasts.

The long-gone Indians had sold Manhattan Island for beads. Nakagawa and the other assembled nobility of Merrill Nomura would sell Earth, not for baubles, bangles, and bright shiny beads, but for biotech. And, of course, leverage . . . the ability to stand close to the Iatroi in their carefully sealed protective suits. They would not land on Earth for fear of flora, fauna, pollution, and whatever bugs had caused the Die-Off. But Alpha—maybe—was clean enough. That cleanness brought troubled reps from government and private funding to Alpha. And restaurants like Indulgences, to which a monstrous string of initials—CEO, CFO, EVP—traveled for the privilege of living as if Merger and Die-Off had never happened.

Judging from the Iatroi's expressions, they didn't believe it either. They had to know that Earth was a violent world—even down to its microorganisms. They couldn't have gotten this far without knowing that. Or without violence of their own.

Hard to tell how much was truth and how much was PR. And Sandy wouldn't get the chance.

There they were—Earth's first aliens, pale as the most cancer-phobic exec and wearing shimmery suits that looked as if they had been sealed onto fragile-seeming bodies. There were seven of them—two marital units and—''Ho-LY!'' whispered Sandy. ''Do you see that?''

Even if her family had long been exiled into a precarious retirement after the Merger that had gutted the economy, Sandy followed the trade journals. A time might come, she reasoned, when she could resume her status within the multiplanetary companies. And so she knew. Iatroi bred in threes. But every now and then, one appeared—neuter like one of the Iatroi's regulation three sexes, but with the Iatroi trait of truth-speaking raised to the point of prophecy.

If they're truth-speakers, what're they doing playing on the Street? Though greed was a universal truth, Sandy wondered what the Truthseers made of the variety practiced in the hermetically sealed area still known as Wall Street, though it stretched worldwide and throughout the solar system. And would extend beyond it, once this deal with the Iatroi went through.

If a meteor struck Alpha, it would take out half the financial muscle stationed on—or near—Earth. A few outskirters traced the markets from Merrill/Ares and Pru-Vesta—which was, quite literally, a chunk of The Rock, and constantly bemoaned the lag time that screwed up their trades. Not to mention the Iatroi mission. She was a high-class guard, not needing pyretic implants to keep her straight. The thought didn't tempt her . . . not much.

What was the leverage that Nakagawa, senior biotech analyst at Merrill Nomura and acknowledged as the standout in his field on the *Institutional Investor* net, had over the Iatroi, that they would be willing to bring in a Truthseer? (Damn. Universities would *kill* for a chance to talk to one, but no university had the kind of funding these days to pay that sort of consultation fee.)

Other dinner guests were staring at the Truthseer, smaller and even more delicate looking than the others of his race—her race—its? A man Sandy recognized from *Institutional Investor*'s feature on the investment banking deal that combined all Earth's biotechs into one consortium empowered to deal with aliens whispered to a woman in lavish gray, explaining. "They say it's a kind of cerebral geisha. A really high-margin mindfuck, eh?"

His laughter cued the woman's, and she laughed obediently. To Sandy's surprise, the Truthseer was watching. She couldn't meet its eyes. Politely, the alien looked away. Its plate, unlike those of the other six, was empty: no chance in risking setting off the precious creature's allergic reactions. Tubes ran from a breast pac into the Truthseer's nose. Sandy would have been willing to bet that that suit's fabric contained other life support as well. A purely scientific lust gripped her. She had wished a moment earlier that she could call a broker; now, pure and simple, she longed for her old research director at Princeton.

What was a Truthseer doing here? No point in asking anyone else in the room. The other guard knew as little as she did; and the guests wouldn't appreciate a question from the hired help.

If a Truthseer had come, they must be close to some sort of deal, Sandy thought. If only she knew what sort! So what if signing an NDA was a precondition of working security. One good killing from the market, and she could retreat to Princeton with enough money to finish her program *and* buy off an SEC investigation.

Her parents' disillusioned faces rose before her, gleaming in the aspic of the pâte. She wouldn't . . . would she?

A quick glance told her that the staffers flanking each door were definitely *not* waiters or busboys. Muscle, this time, and she was willing to bet Nakagawa had hired them to prevent anyone from sneaking out and doing what she had just dreamed of. Except maybe him. He was only second-generation Senior Management. He tried harder.

With an effort of will, she focused away from the menu and on the head of the table, where the host held serious summit with the sommelier.

"This wine settled normally, sir," the sommelier told Emilio Nakagawa, who studied the bottle with more care than any lab experiment he might have run as a doctoral candidate before he dumped research for finance.

"I can always tell when it's been through a centrifuge." Reluctantly, Nakagawa turned from the Rolex Portfolio Minder he had laid on the heavy tablecloth. It was a splendid, massy thing of platinum and gold—worth enough to feed three Domer families.

Or comfortably support the likes of her to the doctorate she'd had to abandon when the SLCC—Student Loan Conscription Corp—came knocking to offer her her choices: pay up, find work, or be drafted as one of the nulls that screwed up comm transmissions and garbled files.

The wine was discussed, poured, and tasted. People drew their breaths in fearfully as if they were up for bonus review. Solemnly, Nakagawa inclined his head, receiving the murmurs of applause for his connoisseurship.

The wine was served and sipped conscientiously. Creases in thin cheeks deepened, giving the lean-faced guests a feral, hungry look.

No wine had been poured for Michael or Sandy. Not at these prices and not while they were on duty. "Must be fine," Michael said a little wistfully.

"Nakagawa couldn't tell a bouquet from toxic waste," Sandy muttered.

He shot a glance at her. "What do you know about it?"

She shrugged. "My parents . . . they worked with Merrill before the Merger." The word came out with a capital letter. "They were downsized, and there I was, halfway through research for my Ph.D. when the IGM regs got me."

"IGM?" Michael was green enough to be awed by jargon.

"I've got mine," she explained. "As in I've-got-mine-fuck-you. People mutter how brilliant Nakagawa is. He wasn't one of the best students Princeton's ever had. But he got through and got in on the right side of things. The Teflon man: survives school, survives Crash III and the Die-Off, even survives the Merger with Nomura, and here he is—perfectly positioned for a play on the Iatroi's bio-techs."

I'm not dumb, she reassured herself. *Just late to the party. Predators come to the predators' ball.*

If she had inherited her parents' VP status, would she have been any better? Nice to think so. But she wouldn't have gutted the companies, the way some of the Families had.

Still, it was hard to watch, nose to the Dome, as she'd told Michael, and to know how vanishingly small her chances were of achieving her dreams.

"My God, will you look at that!" Michael whispered.

Sandy turned. As the Iatros approached, she knew she had been wrong: one of her dreams was about to come true. She was actually going to get to talk to an alien.

She began, politely, to rise from her chair, but it—he? she?—gestured for her to remain in her seat. "This is no person to command such respect." Its breath filters made it sound as if it had a cold. Sandy stifled what might have been a hysterical giggle. She looked over the newcomer. Sure enough, his suit wasn't nearly as shiny or elaborate as those of the elder Iatroi.

The entree was served. She left it untouched, though she was hungry. The skeleton at the feast. After all, they weren't paying her to eat. Besides, at this moment, she could have been starving to death, and she'd still have ignored food to study the alien at her side.

"You honor us," she said, rising anyhow as eyes all around the table impaled them like shrimp for dipping in soy sauce, and Nakagawa glared.

"This one is concerned with information," the young Iatros said.

Right. What's the first thing anyone assumes about press officers? The alien pleaded a polite reluctance, but sat down between her and Michael. No one commented on how quickly a chair got produced, either.

"My job—and my associate Michael's—is security," Sandy said.

"You are not a marital unit?"

She glanced at the younger man and shook her head. No, and not likely to be.

"Then you are Truthseers? Two Truthseers in one place?"

"Nothing that valuable, sir." Clearly, Michael was going to burst if he didn't get a chance to get a word in.

"But you protect, you would sacrifice your lives . . ."

". . . what they pay us for . . ." Sandy cut in.

"And does that not make you valuable?" The wide violet eyes focused on the two guards. For a moment, Sandy felt herself basking in that gaze—curiosity, concern, respect, even.

"Not valuable like . . ." she gestured at the Truthseer.

"That one protects us from the danger of lies."

Then that one needs a whole lot of protection. Sandy watched the frail Iatros intently. As the humans ate and the Iatroi spoke among themselves and to Nakagawa, who didn't miss a chance to show how good his contacts among the aliens were, the Truthseer huddled in on itself. *Fear,* Sandy's study of kinesiology, told her. But "fear" didn't accord with its gaze when it reached her. That held the same approval as her guest's.

She looked up guiltily. The young Iatros had been speaking, and she'd missed precious words. This was too important to rely on Michael's memory. At some point, she would have to play the wire to learn what he had said.

"It is in our minds that we should have guards for the body as well as the mind. This is a new idea to us, and we would learn more of it." The Iatros laid something on the table between them. Sandy almost choked as she retrieved it: an honest-to-god business card! Plain white pasteboard such as no one ever used anymore. She memorized names and access codes in the instant she thought she had before Nakagawa and a waiter—private muscle stood at her shoulder, waiting to take the card. Pity. It would have made a fine keepsake.

The Iatros seemed to shrink in on itself, like a reprimanded employee. "It is always thus?"

"Always," said Sandy.

The alien's eyes flicked back to the elder marital units and the Truthseer. Another universal truth—Chain of Command.

"The Honored One says that there is much about you that is different. We must know you, know more of you than those who speak to us. They cannot be all there is of your race."

She inclined her head. If she answered that one, she'd be a null, screwing up files, before she got much older.

"And it is important to know why." For an instant, the Iatros' eyes lit with an emotion Sandy had no difficulty recognizing: the lust to know.

"Why?" She blurted out the question. As her parents said when she was a baby, she had been born with a silver "Why" in her mouth. Then they had had to sell the family silver, and it wasn't funny anymore.

"Why? Because with truth, there is no fear. We speak

truth, we Iatroi, so we are unafraid.'' The young one paused. ''That is, we have *been* unafraid.''

There was indeed reason for them to fear. She could tell them why—in detail—if she decided she was tired of life as someone with a measurable IQ. But why would senior diplomats or businessmen (business-Iatroi?) send a very junior member of the team to sound out security?

God, all the questions to ask, to answer; and Sandy was only a half-qualified scientist, not even one with xeno training.

If security's needed, stands to reason these people know they're at risk and want to figure out how to protect themselves. That could be a nice little chunk of change. Right. As if she'd ever be let out of her contract to take up something that advantageous that *didn't* give anyone else a piece of the action.

''These . . .'' a subtle gesture included the Iatroi elders, now listening to an eager, earnest Nakagawa, ''. . . would speak to you later.''

''I will be honored to hear.''

Was it her imagination, or did the Truthseer look relieved?

The Iatros made a few parting, courteous remarks that Sandy relied on her tape to ''remember'' for her. Then he returned to stand behind his elders. One of them turned to Nakagawa and gestured. Judging from the CEO's grin, he had consented to something the man wanted very much.

With a last tap to his Rolex portfolio minder reluctantly, Emilio Nakagawa stood up and tapped for attention on the delicate crystal of his wineglass.

Before the faint, bell-like noise subsided, the room went quiet. He could announce a merger, the end of the world, or simply order them to pick one person to be thrown out an air lock, and they would listen and applaud his judgment.

They were all skeletons at his feast.

''Just a few words, and then we can all go back to enjoying ourselves,'' he began blandly and waited for polite laughter to encourage him. When it was duly produced, he went on. "We are very fortunate tonight, indeed. First, for the hospitality of this fine place. I'd like to send our compliments to the chef."

He applauded, though his food was untouched. All around the table, waiters began to remove other full plates, careful not to joggle the lean arms of executives applauding food they had not dared to eat.

"Second, we are *together*," he said. "Not since the Merger has there been such an accumulation of the best of the East and the best of the West . . ."

And to hell with all the rest.

". . . gathered to honor our new trading partners, the Iatroi!"

Now, that applause was genuine. The Iatroi looked appalled at the spectacle of humans beating their hands together in unison. Sandy shook her head at the young press attaché who had befriended the security guards.

"As if that weren't enough . . ."

It never is.

"Our partners have consented to give us a demonstration of their . . . heh heh heh . . . competitive advantage. As you all know, one of the reasons this upcoming joint venture will be such a pleasure is the famous Iatroi honesty. Always the best policy, as those of us now in the industry know. But where we have the SEC . . . heh heh heh . . ."

Dutiful laughter showed finely crafted teeth all around.

". . . the Iatroi have their Truthseers. In token of the importance of this occasion, one of them has agreed to address us tonight."

Only Nakagawa, Sandy thought indignantly, would have the balls to turn an Iatros Truthseer into a parlor game.

Why are you doing this? she wanted to ask. But she knew the answer. *Because he could.*

This would diminish the Iatroi in humans' eyes, making them little more than highly exotic Gypsies—that was the extinct ethnic group—with a knack for producing fine biopharmaceuticals. And it would vastly enhance Nakagawa's status, boosting it to patron of the Iatroi. No one would ever do a deal without him again, or even think of it.

"Ladies, gentlemen—gentlebeings all—the most honorable Truthseer."

The Truthseer stood and began to speak.

"No voder?" Michael muttered.

"If it reads minds, it probably picks up languages faster than we do. Ssssh!" Sandy snapped.

It kept its head down as it spoke. The human execs began to fidget at its story of how the Iatroi had picked up Earth transmissions. The Iatros might be a Truthseer, but only their own top execs had the right to bore them.

"Let me tell you about my world." The Truthseer changed the subject. More movement. Some covert yawns.

So much for Nakagawa's power game! Sandy thought. Then thought again: he might have set precisely this scenario to demoralize his soon-to-be trading partners.

At that moment, the Truthseer looked up. It looked at her. It looked around the too-opulent tables, at the people who had feasted, but not fed—perhaps until now, and it shuddered.

"There is hunger in this room," it husked. "You starve with food before you. You feast while others fast. In this room . . . this room built upon bones . . ."

Someone whistled, distracting the fragile being.

For God's sake, make it stop! Sandy tried to catch the attention of the press officer she had spoken to during dinner.

"We hope that you and your people will help restore our troubled world to health," Emilio Nakagawa cut in smoothly. He withdrew his glance from the Rolex portfolio minder and fixed it on the Truthseer. That glance had been known to make junior executives pass out from fear.

The Iatros, too, shrank back.

"It is all right," said the human. "You are overtired, overstrained."

"Bones hold up the room, but one waits to steal them and to make more bones."

"What's it saying?" Jocular, indulgent laughter began

to rise. So did the elder Iatroi, who approached their Truthseer with tender care. If they'd been human, Sandy would have known what *that* meant. *Anything you say. Just lie down for a minute. Sure, you're upset.* And then the human would disappear. The Iatroi, though, seemed genuinely concerned.

The Truthseer drew away from its comrades. For a moment, it stood upright, as if it were some sort of general. *It's terrified,* Sandy realized. *Is it precognitive as well as telepathic—and did it just see something it can't believe is true?*

"I am telling you," it said with a kind of paralytic serenity, "that there is a murderer and a thief in this room. And that when it strikes, it will strike at . . ."

"Oh, *shit!*" Michael spat predictably as, predictably, the lights all over Indulgences went out—complete to a gust from life-support that extinguished the candles. Only the fireglow remained, and the press of bodies at the head of the table made it impossible for Security to see by that.

Predictably, too, something fell.

"Michael, get the backups on!"

Sandy propelled herself forward.

Even before the lights came back on, Sandy knew what she would see: the body of the Iatros Truthseer slumped over the heavy damask of the tablecloth. It twitched, then went into a powerful spasm that overturned the table. By the time she could push past clustering VPs and other order-giving types—all trying to shout instructions at once—the Truthseer's slight body lay limp and tangled in the arms of three Iatroi.

Sandy had never seen a live alien before tonight. But she knew she was looking at a dead one now. The Truthseer's mask was torn, its breathing mask torn away, clutched in a hand that hadn't been as fragile as all that if it had ripped apart the sturdy apparatus.

"Get it room to breathe." The execs were only too glad to comply. Nakagawa hovered anxiously, but he did it at a safe distance.

Easy to see, though, that the Truthseer would never

breathe again. Its face was so swollen that Sandy couldn't even see its eyes. Its lips were puffed, and its skin was mottled. A faint stream of violet ran from what probably were its nostrils.

Anaphalytic shock, she told herself. It used to kill people in the days when it was still safe to go out in the open and bees weren't hothoused as a precious resource for hydroponicists. They used to carry epinephrine and hope they could inject themselves before their throats swelled shut and they went into shock.

The Iatroi seemed to be in shock themselves. "Here," Sandy said. "Let me." Gently, she eased the Truthseer's light body from their arms onto the floor. She straightened the dead alien's limbs, then rose. It was strange to touch the dead, but stranger yet to sense herself as playing a part in an old, old script.

She realized the script had lines she had to speak.

"Michael," she called. "Make sure no one leaves the room."

He could get the waiters to help him, she was sure. After all, half of them were guards, too.

Best to show the Iatroi that humans had manners, even in the face of violent death.

She looked at the dead Truthseer. Couldn't leave it lying exposed like that, so far from home, poor thing. One of the tablecloths would do to cover it decently. The one at the head table, perhaps.

"Help me clear this," she ordered the nearest man, who probably hadn't *spoken* to a person as low-rank as she since he left business school. He complied, moving table- and glassware, unbroken and even untouched. "I had better take this," she said.

She scooped up a napkin, and a card fluttered from it. She recognized it as the one confiscated by Nakagawa, and laid it aside. Wrapping the napkin about her hand, she used it to lift the Rolex Portfolio-minder. Nakagawa started forward.

"They'll want this as evidence, sir," she said. Not her. Some powerful "they" she could displace her action onto, thank God.

Well, hel-*lo* there, what was that? Where the Portfolio-minder had lain was a faint violet spot. She turned the heavy little status symbol, instinctively reading the numbers that flickered across its bright face now that trading went round-the-clock. The stock symbols of Nakagawa's biotech holdings caught her attention: *very* heavy volume, which wasn't surprising; and a short sale order, which was. The Iatros deal was expected to make the biotechs reach escape velocity. No one in his right mind would expect the stocks to plummet.

She wasn't at all surprised to see the same violet stain on an edge of the Rolex. On an edge: without laying fingertip to it, she would have bet that the minder had been tampered with, its elegantly rounded side filed into something that might not slash, but could at least jab.

Under the pretext of taking the tablecloth to cover the Truthseer, she knelt. Again, she looked at the delicate hand holding ruined breath equipment. She had been wrong the first time: The Truthseer hadn't ripped the equipment off in a fight to breathe; it had fought to regain it.

"Don't even let them go to the washroom, Mike, you got that?"

Her partner would want to strangle her—better not use words like that, even in her thoughts—for using a vulgar nickname like Mike, but too damned bad. She had to get *some* satisfaction out of this mess. Good thing the Iatroi were nonviolent—said they were nonviolent, or they could all confidently expect to be crisped or fused or whatever.

The Iatros had fought with surprising strength. Someone in this room had at least one marked hand.

But that wasn't all she was looking for. Clearly as if she had actually witnessed the fatal fight, she saw . . . call it *Someone* rising from a chair, grabbing the breath mask, and . . . that might not be enough. The killer would want a backup means of death. She ran her hands over the Truthseer's protective suit and found the tear that she expected on one arm. The violet mark around the ripped fabric was the same color as the "blood" dripping from the alien's face, and staining the tablecloth. More evidence, that cloth.

She wondered if a scratch from a platinum and gold object would be enough to cause fatal shock. Clearly, that had been the intention of whomever killed the Iatros.

Behind her, she heard running, a door being flung open, explanations wailed by Indulgence's manager, and the determined rush of Alpha Station security into Indulgences. She rose to greet her reinforcements.

Who were probably about to become her own jailers.

She sighed at the future, such as it was, that she must now toss away. Good-bye, Princeton; good-bye, company status; good-bye, Mom and Dad; and good-bye even unhindered thought. Null status might be the *best* she could hope for. There weren't many things more important than going on living and thinking—but the fate of two planets might be one of them.

And she remembered the look in the young Iatros's eyes. Maybe if she'd been able to inherit a berth in the Corporations, she'd have felt differently. But remembering that, she had to afford the luxury of truth.

She got to her feet.

"Ask Nakagawa what the Truthseer's blood is doing on his Rolex," she said, relishing the slight disrespect of just using his surname. It might be the last thing she would ever enjoy. "And while you're at it, check his hands. I'd bet they're marked."

He didn't so much as look at her. "It's her word against mine," he said casually.

Hands grabbed her hard, leaving bruises. No one checked to see if Nakagawa's hands were similarly marked. Sandy went resistless in the grasp of her former colleagues. If she were lucky, she might never leave this room alive. Well, she had had her moment of power and her try for justice. *You didn't really think they would let you keep anything, did you?*

To her surprise, she had the Portfolio minder, wrapped in its protective napkin. For what that was worth. He would reclaim his property and wipe it clean—the exterior of his victim's blood, the interior of transactions that would gut the world's economy once again. Murders? The Truthseer's death would be just the start of it. Never mind the jobs lost and futures shattered. She thought of the hells outside the Domes, the diseases that had mutated even since the Die-Off. Perhaps the Iatroi science could fight them; but for the sake of a short sale, Earth would not have the chance to know.

When viewed abstractly, that was mass murder. Right now, though, it wasn't as pressing a matter as the hands on her shoulders and her fear of stringent station property laws. She had better point out she had the Rolex before she was accused of stealing it.

She opened her mouth to speak. "Let me." Also to her surprise, the Iatros press officer slid through the crowd of security. He held out his hand for the thing she held.

"Careful," she whispered. "There's a sharp edge."

The alien nodded and took the heavy little object. Walking over to Nakagawa, he displayed it in its damask wrappings, like a bottle of vintage wine presented for inspection.

"Is this yours?" he asked.

"Did she try to steal that, too? Sir, I offer you my personal . . ." He held out his left hand, a little awkwardly, to take it. It was unmarked.

"Check if he's right-handed!" Sandy cried. She heard a faint hiss and felt her knees go rubbery.

The Iatros turned toward her, then back to Nakagawa. In the moment when the human touched the Rolex, the Iatros brought it down against his hand. "Then this is yours, too!"

Even as her vision fogged from the trankspray, Sandy saw how sharp the edge on it was. There was just enough blood on it to sting, not to go into the sort of shock he had counted on to kill the Truthseer. That didn't surprise Sandy either. After all, the Iatros had said he wasn't part of a violent race—just part of one that spoke the truth.

My kind of people, she thought.

Then she was surrounded by them, watchful as her partner administered an antidote to the trank.

"You want to go lie down?" Michael asked.

She looked over to where Nakagawa was pouring out facts and figures, fast as a Truthseer could prophesy. They'd promised him the biggest bonus of his life if he talked: treatment for the cut. Probably, he hadn't taken enough of a hit to kill him, but he didn't know that. After all, he'd *never* been that good of a student.

"I wouldn't miss this for the world."

The question was: *which world?*

Not the one of Domes and Die-offs, that was for sure. Nor the worse one that might have come from tonight's work. But a world in which speaking the truth might save many lives, including her own.

And very much to her surprise. She said so, then laughed when the Iatroi seemed surprised. There was a lot to be worked out.

A small rectangle lay at her feet: the card she had been given. It was so small to be a passport to a brighter future.

She bent to pick it up. *I've got mine,* she whispered to herself and a world that had yet to hear of her. *Soon you'll have yours, too.*

WAY OUT

by Jody Lynn Nye and Bill Fawcett

Bill Fawcett has edited numerous anthologies. Jody Lynn Nye, his wife, has coedited with him as well as writing a number of well-received stories and novels.

It's 1994, and a publisher has paid out a huge advance for a book claiming to prove that UFOs exist. Now he's getting cold feet, and is afraid the book might be branded a fraud and his company made a laughingstock. He hires a scientific expert to query the writer and reexamine the evidence (which has been okayed by a previous team of experts) and to determine whether the author is telling the truth or not.

If he isn't, the proof must be subtle but convincing.

If he is, the expert must come to grips with the permutations of this revelation.

Write it either way.

His breath stank of onions and overspiced lunch meat. It was all I could do to keep from turning away as publisher James Allison Silbica ranted on a few inches from my face.

"The only thing worse than those damn prima donna writers are you detectives. Not even professional. Last one left me hanging and even had the gall to send a bill." A fleck of spittle had settled in the corner of the man's mouth and threatened to spray off at any second. I felt my pocket surreptitiously, searching for the cigarette pack that usually reposed there. If I could smoke, I could ignore the halitosis and concentrate on the case, but no. There were two good reasons a cigarette was inappropriate. First, I'd stopped smoking only a week before, and second, there was a big sign forbidding it over Silbica's desk, which he'd pointed out to me when I sat down. He ought to take his own advice, I thought. I could almost see the fumes seeping out of his ears. "If I didn't need your miserable profession, you would never have made it past the front desk! The whole damned thing is bunkum anyway. I only need the proof for the sucker readers."

The publisher was obviously still warming up. With a sigh, I forced myself to think about the fee I'd been promised. Silbica was powerful, and had the huge budget of Wung-Geterheil Publishing behind him. A grand a day and twenty-five more if I found the guy, plus expenses, of course. Top dollar, even in New York City, and compared to some husbands I'd confronted for a lot less, Silbica wasn't that bad.

"I've got the case file. Is there anything new?" I asked in the hopes of diverting the now florid-faced man's tirade. It didn't work. Silbica had a lot more to say about my unsuccessful predecessor. Only after ten more minutes of ear-blasting angst, I was able to make a hasty retreat. I kept thinking about how I'd spend the bonus. He didn't seem to notice I wasn't paying much attention. The secretary must have heard every word. More likely, half the building must have heard it. She smiled apologetically as I passed. Better yet, she had a signed check for a day's fee ready as I passed. Her smile and the proffered check were so automatic, I wondered how often she had to cover up for her boss. He must be hell to work for.

Someone else other than Silbica must have organized the file. It was clear and concise, almost totally impersonal. The last entry was dated a week earlier and it didn't take a detective to figure out it had been originally prepared for someone else. Being a private detective, I figured it out anyhow. Inside were a picture of the author and all the details:

Two years ago, Silbica's predecessor at Wung-Geterheil Publishing had signed a contract with an author named Whitney Randle. One million dollars had been paid on signing, and another on publication. Randle was to write a book proving conclusively the existence of Flying Saucers. A copy of the contract was enclosed. It took me some minutes to wade through the minutiae that lawyers use to stay in business, then I found what I was looking for. After ten years in homicide I was used to all that small print drivel, but it was one of the reasons I had left the NYPD. We won't go into the others; just read the headlines.

The contract specified that Randle had to produce for examination "the alien object" on whose strength the contract had been written. He'd produced it, all right; the problem was that Randle wouldn't let the object from his sight. When he had appeared at Wung-Geterheil a few weeks ago, he had shown the publishers a cube perhaps eight inches on a side that appeared to be made "from a shiny metal of an unknown sort." When they had tried to take the cube away for lab tests, Randle had grabbed it and run from the building. Silbica had hired me to find Randle and take possession of that alien object so that Wung-Geterheil's hired experts would have a chance to validate its unearthly origin before he printed two million copies of Randle's book and started a planned half-million dollar advertising campaign. The money involved was impressive and I decided to pad my expenses even more than usual.

The problem was that Randle had been very hard to find of late. The recently-fired detective had spend a futile week staking out Randle's Upper West Side apartment. The writer seemed to have abandoned it.

The big problem was that there were only two days before the print run was scheduled to begin. Press-time scheduling was tight, so the time limit was absolute. Rescheduling meant that the release date would have to be scuttled, and Silbica wouldn't stand for that. So I had just 48 hours in which to earn that juicy bonus.

* * *

Most people still figure that private detectives spend a lot of time in seamy bars or following murderers. Actually, about ninety percent of our work involves collecting bad debts or getting evidence on dallying husbands. About once a month someone calls and says they think their husband or wife or boyfriend was murdered. I tell them to call the cops. My jobs generally involve situations in which the law is not involved yet.

When I started on the force, the first lecture at the academy I heard had been about how legwork was the basis of almost all investigations. That's still true today, but in my current line of work much of the legwork involves a computer terminal. And knowing the person who is sitting in front of the right one.

I started with the Melon Credit Company. The manager there is a friend of mine, a good friend. We'd almost gotten married. Fortunately for her, we made the mistake of living together. A few months of the reality of living with a cop had quashed her fantasy of being the wife of one of the city's Paladins. Now Tricia was married to a nice, safe investment broker who wore really boring suits. I figured it was my duty as a friend to inject an element of excitement into her humdrum life.

In her office, she was bent over the keyboard with a pencil stuck haphazardly through a twist of her thick, black hair. I tapped on the doorframe with the back of my knuckles to get her attention. "Hi, Trish," I said. She glanced up at my voice, and one of her eyebrows was raised.

"You look terrible," she said.

"I quit smoking."

Tricia beamed, and I regretted once again the fact that we were basically incompatible living-mates. "You did? You hero! Want a diet soda?"

I shook my head, and swung around the spare chair in the corner to sit on. "Coffee."

"You'll be sorry. The stuff here tastes like paint thinner. That's why I pack in my own supplies. Most of the other programmers don't notice." She sighed. "I don't suppose it's my charms that brought you here."

I leaned over and tapped her on the hand. "Now, there's where you're wrong. I need your magic fingers. I've got to trace a man."

"Did you ever think of offering to take me to lunch or something before asking a favor?" Tricia asked, looking a little hurt.

"I've only got two days to find him. Dinner three days from now, anywhere in the city, you choose the place."

She raised one corner of her mouth in the half-grin I'd always loved. "Reward for information leading to the arrest of?"

"Nope. This guy will get a million bucks if I can bring him back intact. He's not in trouble with my employers. Not that kind, anyway."

Tricia shook her head, and whistled. "For a million dollars I'd hop back on one foot. Why's he hiding?"

"Help me find out, okay?"

With a glance over my shoulder to see that her supervisor wasn't approaching. Tricia hooked into the Credit Information Network. The screen fluttered a few times, and locked in on a spiral logo. I spelled Randle's name for her. In seconds, Randle's credit record was on the screen. As usual, it contained his whole life story according to the Finance Gods, including all his credit card numbers, phone numbers, the fact that he had co-signed a note for a girlfriend seven years earlier, and more. Once I'd asked Tricia if she'd ever looked at my credit report and she told me I didn't want to see it. What really interested me was the information on Randle's credit cards. I copied down the numbers and gave Tricia a quick goodbye peck on the top of her head.

"Don't forget dinner!" she called after me. "I want to go to the Taj Mahal!"

My next stop was the NYLesS Bank. They had issued Randle his only real credit card some months earlier, about the time he had been given a million dollars. It was one of those platinum things with no limit. In this day of instant verification, a deadbeat's credit cards are the easiest way to find almost anyone. Plastic is so much a part of our life, we hardly even think about using it, let alone realize that it can be used to trace our movements.

Fortunately, I had an agreement with a manager in the bank's processing department. He had once gotten uncomfortably behind on a few gambling debts and I'd spoken to the right people. His knees stayed intact and I got a small fee and a new friend. Mike Corby pulled up Whitney Randle's recent records for me. I was surprised to see only one charge listed. A purchase was made several days ago at a sporting goods store on 45th for $81.40. No other details. Not much, but a place to start. That corner of my brain that worries too much wondered how badly Randle didn't want to be found, and if you could get a gun for eighty bucks.

A bowling ball bag. I never stop being surprised by people. The store had even inscribed his initials, WR, on it. The clerk who sold the bag wasn't on duty and it cost me a twenty to get the record looked up. The guy is hiding from his publisher, abandons his home, has a million dollars to tap, and buys an eighty dollar, hand-stitched bowling ball bag. It probably meant that Randle was using the bag to carry the cube, which was a break for me. He'd looked like a nice guy in the picture and I was wondering how I'd convince him to tell me where he'd hid the thing. All I had to do was find him. I was contemplating how to do this when my beeper went off.

I called the number on the screen and it was Silbica. He was in full shriek mode.

"Where the hell is he? Do you realize that in only two days I have to decide whether that nut's also a fraud? This could ruin my whole career!"

I tried to generate some sympathy and failed, so I just stayed quiet. It must have been the wrong response.

"You get him or I'll see you never work in publishing again!" the publisher bellowed.

I decided not to point out that there is a limited call for detectives by publishers, or that if I failed, he would likely be fired and would be in no position to blackball anyone. Instead, I assured Silbica in my best professional voice that the investigation was progressing as planned. Wonder what that means?

The best place for me to think is your typical Irish bar, invariably known as a "pub," no matter where in the world it lies. My favorite is O'Reilly's, near Penn Station, mostly due to the presence of Kathleen the manager. No one builds redheads like the Irish. After my third Guinness, I was checking my pockets for cash when I realized that if Randle wasn't using his credit cards, he had to be using legal tender. There was a few thousand dollars left in his bank account. If he had access to that, I couldn't trace him by his charge cards, but I might be able to pin down the area he was frequenting by which moneywalls he was using. I swallowed the last ounce of coffee-black liquor, and started out of the pub.

The two guys who came out of the night might have been Feds. They had the right neat suits and striped ties. Then again, they might just have been trying to look like Federal Agents. No one offered me any ID. I wouldn't have believed their documents if I'd seen them. The first one was taller and broader than the other, but otherwise they looked exactly alike, like Dr. Seuss's Thing One and Thing Two.

The bigger one, who spoke with a clipped Boston accent, came up on my left. "You're Jack Blundell." It was a statement, not a question.

Alarms went off, gut-level warnings, and I began to back away. Moving my hand slowly, I began to reach for the snub-nosed thirty-eight revolver I carried at my belt. I didn't even see the second one move until he jerked my arm out of my coat and twisted it high up behind the shoulder blade. Several people watched this happen, right on the street, half a block from Sixth Avenue. This being New York, most hurried away, and a few street people stopped with the obvious intention of watching the fun.

"You're looking for Whitney Randle." It was another statement.

I thought of a quote I liked from a book I read a long time ago. "Thanks. And how much do I weigh?" Beantown didn't answer me. My flippancy seemed to offend the thug behind me. He twisted my arm even higher. It began to hurt, a lot. "Why all the effort to tell me what I already know?" My wrist began to approach my axis bone. I shut up.

"He has something important to us. Something you will give us if you find him before we do. It's a small box, about this big." The first one gestured vaguely. There was a strange look in his eyes, like they weren't really focused. My arm was beginning to throb, and my fingers were going numb, but I was curious about his expression. You'd think that someone intent on shaking a man down for information would be concentrating on him.

"You want to call off Thing Two here?" I asked, gesturing with a toss of my head. I tried to keep the pain from my voice and sounded as cooperative as possible. I also continued to judge whether or not I could kick backward hard enough to nail the sucker holding me in the groin before he broke my arm. Not likely. Thing One went on as if I had not spoken. It was obvious my personal comfort didn't have a very high priority with him.

"You'll get the device from Randle and call this number. It belongs to us and you will return it." He held up a card a few inches before my eyes. Someone had typed a local phone number on it. I glanced at it, and he stuffed it into my shirt pocket. "Be good and we'll match Publisher Silbica's reward. Otherwise . . ." There was a moment of silence that implied what would happen if I wasn't cooperative.

A long, dark car pulled up, the kind that always has tinted windows. The character behind me shoved, and let go of my wrist at the same time. With a shout of pain I stumbled onto the sidewalk, scraping one knee on the hard cement as my numbed hand refused to help save me. When I recovered, both men and the car were gone.

I hurried to the nearest pay phone and dug out the card. It's good to know who you're dealing with. I expected something like the FBI switchboard. Instead there was a familiar voice. Thing One answered. "Blundell, you'd better not call again until you have the box for me.

And that had better be soon.'' There was a click and a hum in my ear. Must have been a car phone.

The best route seemed to be to find Randle and then decide what I would do with his box. The alternative was to take a cab to LaGuardia and begin my retirement early. A good idea, but impractical unless I went somewhere they didn't use money because I didn't have enough saved to live six months. Besides I wanted to find out who the Thing brothers were before this was over.

Against my better judgment I called Silbica. Worse luck, he was there.

''I just got shoved around by a couple of toughs,'' I recounted the incident after the publisher's usual tirade ran down. ''Any idea who they are?'' There was a long pause before he answered.

''Probably some UFO kooks,'' Silbica actually sounded as if he was trying to be reassuring. ''Not really dangerous.''

''Yeah,'' I agreed, moving my shoulder carefully. The publisher's response showed he was worried and might know more than he was saying. ''Why would some sort of Feds be interested? Or is there anyone else who might benefit from your not publishing this book? Benefit a whole lot to hire that level of muscle?''

''Well,'' the publisher admitted, hesitantly. ''There is his ex-wife. She gets the publication payment, another million, if Whitney dies. But she'd want you to get me the box and publish the book.''

''No one else? A competitor?''

''Not even Rooster Press hires thugs,'' Silbica was definite. Great, I thought. Professional courtesy, even now. He's protecting his rivals against an outsider.

It was late and the conversation was going nowhere. Six hours on this case and I had yet to find any concrete leads.

It was almost four and my arm hurt, but I hurried back to NYLesS, where the author had most of his accounts. Yes, my contact agreed, Randle did have a cash card. It had been used several times at cash stations near the south end of Central Park. That was the hotel district. There was a good chance he was staying in one under a false name. Time for that legwork I'd learned about.

The trouble with asking at a hotel about a guest is that, contrary to popular opinion, most desk clerks rarely notice who they check in. Some aren't even bribable. Over the years I've learned to talk with the bellmen. They tend to get a longer look at the patrons and aren't paid as well, so they rely on tips, even from questionable sources like private detectives such as myself.

I'd wasted about a hundred dollars and two hours when I got to the Park Center Hotel. It featured a big lobby with lots of columns and gold trim. They can get in a lot of trouble for mouthing off about the guests, so you have to take the bellmen aside before they can talk. Some are still hesitant to say anything even in private. I thought I was lucky to get a young and enthusiastic one that had seen enough TV to be impressed at the license the NYPD issued me. Yes, he'd seen the man in the picture. Mostly the man had stayed in his room and ordered from room-service.

"He checked in last week." This squirrel hadn't even asked for a "tip." I'd told him I was a relative and my mom had just found out my cousin was in town and sent me to find him, and he believed me. I made a note of him for future reference. I hope no one spoiled him in the meantime. "You say his name is Randle? We could check the register, funny, but I think he used something else."

Then before I could act, he saw Randle entering the lobby.

"Mr. Randle!" he yelled hurrying toward the man. "Your cousin's here!"

I winced. Randle took one look at me from across the lobby, turned, and ran. He had the bowling bag with him. He was still carrying the artifact around with him.

I dashed out after him, tossing thanks over my shoulder to the fresh-faced bellman. Randle flagged down a taxi just as I got through the revolving door. Bad luck for me. The one time he needs a cab, it's actually cruising by and stops. Unusual in New York.

There were a number of the bright yellow cabs lined up along the side of the hotel. I hurried over to the first one and got in. I could still see that Randle's taxi was caught in traffic about two blocks away. If I could get close, I might even jump out and run it down at a light.

The cab was empty. The driver wasn't in it. A yard away a group of men sporting impressive mustaches were deeply engrossed in an animated conversation that involved a lot of hand-waving and fist-slamming. I leaned out the window and yelled, but an ambulance choose the same moment to turn on its siren.

I watched in panic as Randle's taxi broke free and pulled forward, but was caught by a red light while still in sight. Sometimes the city tries to help. I shouted at the group of drivers again.

Finally one man turned to watch the ambulance get trapped behind two trucks and noticed me in his cab. He sauntered slowly over despite my arm-waving and apparent need for haste. When he finally got in, I couldn't resist saying it.

"Follow that cab!" I yelled, pointing up Avenue of the Americas. I'd always wanted to do that.

The driver, whose name on the license displayed on the dash was totally unpronounceable, turned to me, shrugged, and said something that sounded like, "howathagerllnicht umlati?"

"That cab!" I almost bellowed, pointing at where Randle still sat. "Follow that cab!"

"Guesambata?"

"Ah, shit!" I yelled in frustration.

The light in front of Randle's cab changed. Within a few seconds it was lost among the hundreds of other identical yellow beetles scurrying down the Avenue.

I got out again to follow on foot, and the driver said something else unintelligible. I suspect that this time I was glad to not understand it. By now, the cab was out of sight. I went back into the hotel, in hopes of finding a clue where Randle had gone.

The price of maid service in New York has gone up in recent years. It took almost fifty dollars to get the cleaning lady to let me into Whitney Randle's room. The bed wasn't made and the "Do Not Disturb" sign still hung on the door handle. There wasn't much there. Some clothes, a few dirty, most recently purchased. Trays were stacked in one corner. I guessed Randle had pretty well gone to ground up here. I still don't know why he was on the run or who he was running from. Seeing a stranger who knew his real name must have been a shock. There didn't seem to be much more to learn here. No addresses on the phone pad or circled numbers in an open phone book. I went home, ate leftovers, and tried to get a good night's sleep.

I pulled the telephone receiver off the cradle and onto my pillow with sleep-clumsy fingers, and muttered a hello into it. Silbica's harsh voice bellowed the now-familiar tirade against private detectives in my ear. It wasn't different enough from the earlier ones to bother describing, and I tried to sound pleasant while I organized my brain for the day. I'd slept late and my shoulder hurt. He slammed the receiver in my ear, and I lay for a while with the dead phone curled in my fingers before I managed to get moving. It was almost ten before I got back to work.

Whitney's ex-wife's address was in the book. I called and Carole Randle agreed reluctantly to see me.

She lived in a security building on the Upper West Side. I noted her furnishings looked both new and expensive. A slim woman with frosted brown hair and well defined cheekbones, she went well with the surroundings. I couldn't figure how a human Tootsie-roll like Whitney managed to win such an elegant lady. Evidently, whatever his attraction had been, it had worn off.

"Whitney went, well, peculiar about three years ago," Carole said, carefully, and stopped. "Are you sure you're not a reporter, Mr. Blundell?"

"Never touch the stuff, ma'am," I assured her. "I'm trying to find him for the publisher."

She nodded, reassured. "Good. I don't want my name in the paper. Whitney's always been into UFOs and First Contact stuff. He went for a hike with some other flying-saucer enthusiasts in Roswell, New Mexico, and says he found that thing, I see you know about it."

"Yes, ma'am. The terms of the contract are that he has to present it to get the book published."

Her lips pressed together, flattening out the shimmering color that had been applied to them. "Dammit, I need that book to come out! He owes me six months' back alimony."

"Haven't you taken any legal action on your own?"

"Against what?" she laughed, bitterly. "The only thing he has of any value is his copyright. I put a lien against $100,000 of the publication payment. At least I'll get that much out of him."

"You won't if I can't produce the proof he promised Silbica. Mrs. Randle, what's in the box? What convinced him that he could use it to prove the existence of aliens?"

"Oh, his aliens aren't *aliens*," Carole said. "He has a theory that they're not from another planet at all, but he wouldn't say any more. He didn't exactly call me an 'infidel unbeliever,' but I got the idea. After that he just hid in his office and wrote. I'd hoped leaving him would bring him to his senses but he got worse."

"Do you know where he is now?"

She shook her head, and her eyes were worried. "I haven't the first idea. I loved Whitney, Mr. Blundell, but you have to understand, he was impossible to live with. Find him, please. It isn't so much the money, although you know it's hard to live in New York without enough of it."

She seemed genuinely concerned about Randle. I guessed that she hadn't hired the two strange thugs I ran into. That made three distinct parties that wanted me to locate the elusive writer. I stood up to leave, when the phone rang. With a smile of apology, Carole reached for it. Her eyes went wide, and she glanced up at me and pointed at the receiver.

"Are you okay?" she blurted out. There was a fairly

long silence while she listened to the reply. *Randle*! I scratched the question, "Where?" on my notepad, and she shrugged her shoulders. "Yes, he's here," Carole Randle finished, and held out the phone to me. "He asked for you."

I took the phone tried to sound calm.

"Blundell here," and then I just waited. What do you say to a man you've spent the better part of a day chasing?

"You're on the wrong side." Whitney Randle's voice was deeper than I expected, with an edge to it. He was close to breaking.

"If the thing's real, why not let them test it?" I suggested. If all else fails, try logic. "You'll be a hero. A rich one."

"They'll take it away."

"Who?" I asked beginning to be fairly sure Randle *had* lost it.

"The ones who sent those two who attacked you yesterday," the author answered.

"How did you know about that?" I demanded. Maybe he'd hired them himself. I'd heard of wackier things.

"Silbica told me about it," Randle explained.

"You've been talking to Silbica?" I asked, dumbfounded. The voluble publisher had never included that bit of information in his tirades.

"I've called him three or four times every day for the last two weeks," Randle explained, "trying to get him to call you and the others off. He keeps saying I should just come back to his office and save him paying you a bonus. That he hadn't even budgeted any money for it anyhow. He said you were really tough and would hurt me."

There was no mention of any calls in the case file, either. I was fairly sure that Silbica hadn't told whoever put it together about them. Using me to drive Randle back into his arms by implicit threats. Nice guy. I just stood there for a second, getting angrier at being played for the sucker. Randle spoke again before I was ready to reply with anything but profanities.

"You just make it easier for them to find me. They don't know our time very well, so they follow you hoping you'll find me."

"Who are 'they'?" I demanded. "Who else is looking for you? The Feds?"

"No. You wouldn't believe me. Silbica doesn't either." Great. That made it all clear.

"Look, maybe we can work something out. Where are you?" I tried.

"No, you'd just take it," came the quick reply. He might be close to a certifiable breakdown, and he might have been a nut, but he wasn't stupid. That bag was worth about twenty-five grand to me. I admit I was quite willing to grab now and talk later.

"Will you stop?" the author's voice hardened. "You have to stop." The latter softened to a whine. I felt sorry for Randle, but he'd be better off in a place where he could get treated. Paranoid delusions are no fun to have, and he sounded like he was in the middle of a doozy.

"Sure, meet me in a few minutes and we'll talk about it."

"You're lying," Randle accused and I heard the phone go dead. He'd actually sounded disappointed.

I dashed for the window. If Randle had known to call me here, he must have been able to see me enter. I scanned the street for pay phones. The bag was easy to spot, even from the fifteenth floor. Randle was still in the booth, not moving yet. He was just standing there like he was unsure what to do next.

I called my thanks to Carole Randle as I ran out the door. She stood silently watching me, with her arms crossed tightly against her body.

I banged the elevator button. Luckily, the car was still waiting from the time I rode up, and the doors slid open within seconds.

Outside, I spotted the bright red trim on the bowling bag about a block away from the steps of the apartment building. Randle was walking slowly along the sidewalk near the curb. It was almost as if he wanted me to catch him. Or maybe he was just exhausted from running for so long. Afraid to panic my nervous quarry, I restrained myself and began striding briskly after him. I'd catch up within a few blocks and then it would be all over.

I was just a few steps behind Randle when I saw the car. It was the same black Olds that Things One and Two had dived into last night. It cut across the traffic and slowed. Whitney Randle just kept walking, lost in his own thoughts and oblivious to all of us. There was no parking on this side of West Side Drive, so they would be able to pull up to within a few feet and grab the bag, or the author, before he realized they were there.

About a dozen yards ahead I saw the door begin to open and Thing One begin to lean out. Without thinking about it, I dived past Randle and rammed my shoulder into the opening door.

This was the same shoulder that had been twisted by Thing Two yesterday. Nice irony, but the car hadn't stopped yet and I hit a lot harder than I'd planned. One arm and a foot wearing an expensive shoe were hanging out past the edge of the door as the thug was getting ready to jump out.

I felt the sheet metal of the door buckle and heard a crunching sound that had to be arm and leg bones breaking. The painful intensity of the howl that issued from behind the darkly tinted windows confirmed that something had been broken, maybe smashed. I was thrown off my feet. The car sped up and pulled away. I looked for Randle, but he had frozen a dozen steps away. Our eyes met and he began to back away, clutching the bag to his chest.

I tried to raise my arm and told him to stop. It was the same one that I'd just rammed a moving car with and at that instant I realized how much it hurt. If I hadn't broken anything, it would be sore for weeks. The world narrowed and for a few seconds all I could do was stay on my feet.

By the time I could focus my eyes, Randle was running down the middle of the sidewalk half a block away and gaining speed. For a pudgy fellow, he certainly could move. I started off after him, trying to ignore the shooting pain the jolt of each step brought to my doubly-abused shoulder. I was gaining, but there was a crowd gathered ahead at a bus stop and it looked like Randle might get away again.

"Stop, thief!" I bellowed pointing at the fleeing author with my good arm. "Stop him, he stole my bag!" Not a lot of hope in New York, but worth the chance.

This one paid off. Maybe the black kid was a bowler, or just civic-minded. A long arm with a purple sleeve reached out and tried to grab Randle as he passed a clump of teenagers. The kid managed to catch the author's sleeve, but was thrown off balance by the older man's momentum. He let go before falling and Randle sped off, but I had gained several steps. Randle looked winded already and I would probably catch him within a few blocks. I needed to catch him soon. I was in good shape, but distracted as I was by the pain of my shoulder, my stride was off.

As we ran, Randle held the bag in his right hand. It banged against his leg occasionally. I noticed that the writer's left hand was under his coat, in his rear pants pocket. I realized he was pulling out his wallet. If I'd had the breath, I would have yelled that it was a little late to try to bribe me. It wasn't until he stopped suddenly before one of those enclosed storefront electronic tellers that I realized what he was doing.

In New York, because the vermin view the autotellers as feeding stations, all the banks have begin setting up inside glassed storefronts. The theory is to give you at least two or three minutes to enjoy your money before you're mugged. The only way to get into one of these setups is to have a bank card. Before I could get there, Randle had used his to open the heavy security door and close it behind him, providing him with a temporary safe haven. I guess he figured I wouldn't be likely to have a card for the same bank. Unfortunately, he was right.

We stood there for almost a minute, both out of breath. Separated by the thick glass door, we were just a few inches apart. I was in no hurry. There is only one way in or out of these stations and I was leaning against it.

Eventually I took out the big pocket knife I always carry and began working on the panel where he inserted his card. The case was hard plastic, but eventually I would dig through and short out the lock.

"Look, can't you let me go?" I could barely hear Randle whine through the thick glass.

I shook my head sideways in reply. I'd earned that bonus. Every movement of my shoulder painfully reminded me of that fact.

"I'm not trapped." The nervous author begin unzipping the bowling bag. I just stopped and watched. There was still no way he could get past me, and if the cops came I'd get the bag impounded as evidence and Silbica could use his pull to get at it.

"There is a reason they never find survivors," Randle was babbling nervously. "Even after the worst crash."

I started working on the plastic again. A big chunk peeled off and I held it up for Randle to see.

"They have a lifeboat, one that lets them get back." Randle was speaking hurriedly now. It was still hard to hear him through the door but hysteria made him yell out each word. "Don't make me use it! Not until I'm ready to meet them. Please, you must understand!"

I'd have shrugged, if it wouldn't have hurt as much.

"They came back for the others, but I found this one." As he finished, Whitney Randle pulled the cube from the bag. It looked like twenty-five grand to me. Another piece came off the panel. I was breaking and entering, and I hoped I could be away with Randle and bag before New York's finest hauled me off. The silent alarms wouldn't go off until I disturbed the mechanism. It was time to see if I could short out the lock. There was some sort of circuit board visible and I decided that was a good place to start. The thin board went crunch and I was rewarded with a few sparks. Fire Laws require all electric doors in New York City to failsafe open.

The lock clicked and I smiled.

"No!" Randle screamed, and a blinding green light filled the cash station. When it had faded, I was alone. Trouble was that I was still holding the door handle and it hadn't opened. Somehow, right in front of me, Whitney Randle had vanished from a sealed glass room. I goggled for a minute, trying to make my brain believe what my eyes were seeing. No Randle.

On the floor, the shining cube lay next to the empty bowling bag, sagging sideways against it as if it had been dropped. I picked it up. It was strangely heavy. If this was the proof he intended to offer Silbica, it was convincing. I was never so surprised in my life, and a career as a New York police officer leaves little to be surprised about. I turned it over. The metal was dark green, with a pink sheen, though both colors were distinctive. There was a small button on one side, but no other markings, and no obvious joins or seams to show how the mechanism had been put together. I heard sirens up the street, and stuffed the box into the bowling bag. I was hailing a cab when the patrol car pulled up. Even if my face had been captured on the security camera, they'd have to explain the disappearance of their customer before they could prosecute me. The scraps of plastic with my fingerprints on them were in my pocket.

When I called Wung-Geterheil, James Silbica didn't believe Randle had used the cube to get away. When I finally convinced him that I at least had the cube, he told me to messenger it over and he'd mail my bonus. Sure. I believed that like I believed in my congressman's promises. We finally agreed that I'd come up and he'd write me a check on the spot. I could almost hear the cackle in the man's voice. Checks could be canceled, and without the cube in hand I'd have no way to collect.

The sweet secretary gestured me in. Silbica stood up when I entered, and put out a hand to me. "Is that it?" he demanded, pointing at the bowling bag.

"That's it," I said. I unzipped the leather container and pulled out the box. The track lights over Silbica's desk picked up the pink and green glints of the alien metal, and I saw an answering green light in the publisher's eyes. "We just have a little more business to transact, and it's all yours."

"Of course, of course," Silbica said jovially. He pulled out a checkbook, and wrote out my fee and bonus. It looked terrific on paper, twenty-six thousand dollars, and no oo/xx. I held out my hand, and he glanced at it with evident distaste. In answer, I plunked the box onto his desk blotter. He smiled, and pushed the slip of pink paper toward me.

"Don't forget to record it," I said, folding the check and putting it in my pocket. Our eyes met, and I'm sure he knew I knew what he was thinking. I felt sure that the moment I walked out the door, he'd be on the phone to the bank, canceling it.

"Of course," Silbica replied, and scratched something in the check register before putting it away.

I stood up and shook hands again. "You realize what you have there is absolute proof positive of what Randle wrote, don't you?" I knew he didn't believe in Randle's book, but curiosity would bite him the same as it would any other man. It wasn't the nicest thing I would ever do, but Silbica was a jerk who had tried to double-cross his writers, and I figured it was the only way to keep him from cheating me out of my fee.

Silbica squinted at me. "How's that?"

"You can find out for yourself everything Randle knows about the aliens," I said. "All you have to do is push that button on the box."

I closed the door behind me carefully, and tipped a wink at the nice secretary as I walked down the hall. A flash of green light lanced out from beneath Silbica's door and outlined both our shadows on the wall ahead of me.

I wonder what he said to Randle or his new hosts when they met?

THE KILLER WORE SPANDEX

by Brian M. Thomsen

Brian Thomsen was a Senior Editor at Warner Books, and creator of their Questar line of science fiction. He is now an Executive Editor at TSR.

An interstellar chess tournament is being held at a fancy hotel on Antares III. Of the 32 original participants, it has boiled down to two players: a human and an alien. They each make some 15 or 20 moves before adjourning for the evening, and it is assumed that the alien is slightly ahead.

The next morning the alien does not show up to resume the match, and a quick search discloses that he is dead in his quarters. The hotel detective must determine whether a murder has been committed and, if so, solve it quickly before a riot or even a war breaks out over it.

In the dead alien's room are three things that don't seem to belong there: a plastic paper clip, a letter opener, and an oddly-shaped piece of metal that seems to have no function.

Solve it.

Spandex was the most important discovery of the twentieth century. It fit the body like a glove, showing off every contour and cleft in all its sin and glory. With spandex what you saw was what you got.

You couldn't hide anything when you wore spandex.

The killer wore spandex, had nothing left to hide, and held a blaster aimed at my crotch, and was about to pull the trigger.

My name is Mouse Chandler and in order to understand the situation that I had found myself in, we're going
to have to go back in time a bit. . . .

I was born on Earth in the twenty-fourth century, the
latest in a family of post-collapse computer detectives,
back when knowing how to use a keyboard was something special rather than standard operating procedure, if
you know what I mean. After too many years of being
beaten up for low pay, irregular hours, and lousy fringe
benefits, I decided to accept a position as hotel dick at
Griffin's Satellite, way out past Antares. I figured that it
wouldn't be worth my creditors' while to chase me there
for a lousy three grand and the pleasure of busting my
kneecaps.

So far the job was fairly routine. I'd already busted a
Danuvian empathy team who were running a Murphy
scam out of the Jeopardy Suite, a three-headed Andres-
sion selling pirated copies of the v-disc for *Cosmo Je-
dies—the Final Generation,* and a traveling sales rep who
tried to pay his room bill with cash (I pocketed the out-
of-date currency for myself since I collected antiques,
and artifacts from the pre-collapse, and you couldn't get
your hands on anything as ancient as paper money or
paper anything for that matter on a salary as skimpy as
mine). It looked like this resident peeper gig was just the
sort of break a dinosaur gumshoe like myself needed.

I was supposed to be running a security check on the
staff since there had been a few reports of missing personal items on the part of some of our more influential
guests, when I sort of got sidetracked.

Her name was Dena Quatro and she was a perfect example of Benatrix womanhood, and the Griffin's Satellite
maid's uniform provided the perfect wrapper. The
French-style domestic mini-dress hugged her curves, and
each of her four shapely legs were perfectly suited to
their black fishnet stockings. The basic black and white
color combo was complemented by the opal blue luster
of her skin.

The only non-uniform part of her attire was the highly

functional silver hooped earrings that she was currently using as leg rests for her top two gams in all of their fishnetted glory.

"Oh, Mouse," she purred, "I've always thought of humans as such pitiful two-legged creatures—but you're so different! Being a detective must be really exciting!"

"The job's a piece of cake, cupcake. Sometimes I even have a little time to do some free-lance work," I explained, wallowing in her multi-limbed attention.

"Ooh, how exciting!"

"Just some bounty hunting, retrieval of missing property, stuff like that. I sort of specialize in artifacts and antiques and the illegal purveyors of such. In fact, right now I'm on the lookout for a paper thief who seems to be working this quadrant."

"What's paper?" she asked in all her innocence, nuzzling her face against my chest, and wrapping her legs around my shoulders.

"A twentieth century material that was used for letters, documents, and such, prior to the advent of data and the disk."

"Back in the dark ages?" she asked in wonderment.

"Sort of," I said. "One of GS's recent guests claimed to have an entire manuscript stolen from him while he was staying here a few weeks ago. He was a bit of a fruitcake, so management didn't really take him seriously. I mean, the idea of someone carrying around an original three-hundred-page manuscript by a classic author like Ron Goulart is really pretty strange. Its street value is at least two-hundred-and-fifty grand. Recently I heard that he had offered a ten grand reward for its return, no questions asked. But enough about work. Where were we . . . ?"

I was about to pay her reciprocal physical attention, when I found myself beamed to the executive office for an immediate meeting with the bane of my existence. I cursed the day the employee-locator disk was invented.

Unflapped by the summoning, I put my most obnoxious foot forward in hopes of hurrying this along so that

I could return to Dena, and greeted the boss, "Yo, Merv, what's up?"

The executive manager of Griffin's Satellite gritted his teeth (he hated the nickname I had given him), and tried to ignore my impertinence while saying his piece. "Chandler," he said, "despite my advice to the contrary, you have been placed in charge of security for the upcoming Interstellar Chess Tournament. It is a matter of great intergalactic diplomacy and prestige for our hotel. Never before have representatives from thirty-two different worlds met to celebrate a game of Terran origin at a Griffin resort. This is an event tantamount to the first Olympic games, the establishment of the United Nations, the Riggs-King rematch, the treaty of Alpha C, the . . ."

"It's just a chess tourney," I interrupted. "It's not as if the Galactic Ladies of Wrestling were holding their Supernova Squareoff here."

"Chandler," he continued, "the chess masters of thirty-two different worlds will be doing battle across the checkered fields of glory tomorrow, while all of their homeworlds watch on the Griffin Video Network. Please show a little decorum around our guests, and for God's sake don't let anything happen! We can't afford any bad publicity, and quite frankly the Interstellar Strategic Arms Limitation Talks are going quite poorly, and certain factions are just waiting for an incident to back out and start a war. As you know, war is bad for the tourist trade. Do you understand what I'm saying?"

"Yeah. Your job is on the line, so *my* job is on the line."

I started to leave as Merv tried to get in the last word.

"And Chandler, I don't want to find you spending your time on activities that could be described as outside of your job description or as unnecessary distractions."

Just before the door closed I said, "Management designed the maids' uniforms around here, not me."

The chess masters arrived within the hour, each accompanied by its entourage. All of the participants and their travelling parties wore the traditional uniform of the

Antares Chess Federation, namely black & white spandex bodysuits, each individually styled to match its wearer's bodily form.

All of the players had arrived with the common purpose of emerging from the tourney victorious. Second place just wouldn't cut it.

That is not to say that various players didn't have other agendas on their mind.

Since the formation of the Interstellar Federation there have been many uneasy alliances. Just because the lamb will occasionally lie down with the lion is no reason to believe that they trust each other. Sometimes the lamb is packing a rod trained on the lion's gonads, and this accessory is the only thing keeping dear Leo from claiming his supper. It's hard to go against one's nature, and that loaded rod is the unsatisfying appetite suppressant that leaves the lion courteous but hungry. As luck would have it, the tourney had representatives from both the Pastori and Leoni worlds in attendance.

The rest of the menage-a-extraterrestrials made up a mixed bag: red, blue, green, tall, short, bestial, lizard-like, male, female, other. All were reasonably well-behaved and respectful toward their opponents. Most were first-timers to this part of the galaxy and with the exception of two players, all were newcomers to the tourney.

Unfortunately, those two exceptions were doozies.

The first exception was Brooklyn-born Sebastion Fischer, reigning champion of the last four tourneys. Obnoxious, pedantic, self-centered, and arrogant, he was the type of guy who gave new meaning to the caricature of "the Ugly Earthman." The popular rumor was that he was a reform school dropout who liked to remove the warts from a toad's back with a pair of tweezers. If he wasn't only fifteen years old, he'd probably be doing time somewhere right now.

Where Sebastion went, Chanel was never far behind. Chanel was his mother, and she made Mama Borgia look like June Cleaver. Her eyes alternated between two looks—"come hither," and "don't mess with my meal ticket.'' Her fingernails were lacquered so I couldn't tell if the rumor that they were made of razor sharp stainless steel was true or not.

The other exception was the Maileran, Host Grlot, a veteran of eight previous tourneys who, much to his chagrin, had made a habit of coming in second for the last four years. Unlike his habitual final opponent of the last few years, Grlot was quite mature in his behavior (350 years of existence does that to a guy), and almost zen in his acceptance of his opponent's temper tantrums.

Coincidentally, it was the Earth-Maileran ideological debates that were at the crux of the current Interstellar Federation schism. The Maileran felt that Man was not maintaining the diversity of the integrity of the galaxy with all of its plans for terraforming and redesigning every world it comes to. The Maileran learned many years ago that it is important to venerate the past, for without veneration it fades away, leaving the future without a solid anchor. They felt that several of Earth's recent motions (such as making Spanish the official language of the galaxy) were both outrageous and untenable.

The Maileran did not believe in a homogeneous galaxy of sameness, and Grlot's wearing the spandex Federation uniform was probably the only concession he was about to make.

I had just finished surveying the crowd when Merv got up and gave his usual spiel of obsequiousness that he used for all catered events of over ten paying customers, finally getting around to the pertinent procedures at hand. Over the next four days thirty matches would be played. Only the winners of each day's matches would be allowed to play the next day, until only one player emerged victoriously. All first matches were determined by a random drawing, and the schedule for the first day of competition would be posted in the lobby.

The players and their entourages checked the schedule and all retired for the evening.

I retired, too . . . into Dena's eagerly waiting gams.

* * *

Day One's matches were fairly routine. All of the games were over by three, and the next day's schedule was posted by eight. The only real incident of the day occurred after hours when a fight broke out between two of the losers whose opinions on a local brand of happy gas differed as to whether it tasted great or was less filling. I separated the two before any real damage was done. This was really quite easy, considering the Eisner was from a race of intelligent mice, and the Waldo, his opponent, was from a race of five-inch myopic midgets. I was diplomatic—I told them to knock if off or I'd step on both of them.

My biggest challenge of the day was avoiding Chanel Fischer, who kept telling me that I would make the perfect "father figure" for Sebastion. The lady, and I use the term loosely, just wouldn't take no for an answer, and if I hadn't been beamed to the bar to settle the dispute, I probably would never have escaped with what was left of my virtue intact.

At the close of Day Two, the four remaining victors were interviewed by the Griffin Video Network for what they inaccurately labeled a "human interest" feature.

The first player interviewed was Troy Ferrum, a golden-haired, platinum-skinned Adonis from the planet Twilo, who liked fruit salads, show tunes, and four-month space voyages for two with the close personal friend of his choice. (One got the idea very quickly that he was willing to interview new candidates for this position). He was proud to be Twilo's representative, and was sure to add that Twilo's major industries were tourism and tanning.

The second player interviewed was the half-reptile/half-avian headbanger from the planet Mattellmetta (which loosely translated means "the planet of metal of great density"). One might say that he didn't have a way with words, or was slightly less than verbal. In reality, his responses were solely limited to grunts, and the occasional hand gesture that was bleeped out on thirty of the thirty-two affiliated broadcast worlds. You could say that what he basically lacked in profundity, he sure made up for in profanity.

Third up was Host Grlot, who had managed to decimate his two previous opponents in record times. It was easy to see that his playing had greatly improved over the last year, and he spent most of the interview talking about his hobbies, and the rigors of long-term travel. When questioned on the current Federation schism, he chose his words carefully.

"The past," he replied, "is very important to Mailerans—not just *our* past, but that of other worlds as well. This is why I carry a sample of my artifact collection with me whenever I travel. *Not* just from my own world, but from Earth, Mattellmetta, and Sephid, as well. When I am with them, I am at one with the past."

The final interviewee should have been Sebastion Fischer, but according to his mother, he had already been sent to bed. She, on the other hand, was more than willing to be interviewed.

Needless to say, there was no fourth interview.

When I returned to my little hole-in-the-wall later that night, I thought about what Grlot had said about the Maileran way. I've never been interested in what the thinking men referred to as "the big picture of politics and progress." Decisions at that level didn't really concern me in my day-to-day life, and if the powers that be wanted to level the pyramids of Cheops to make way for the largest on-line data/credit information center on Earth, who was I to say that they were wrong? Maybe pyramids were important long ago, but like the canals of Mars that were landfilled by Amalgamated Earth last year, who really cares? Just like Shelley's shattered statue in the desert, it is destined to become part of a long-forgotten past.

There was a time when the name Mouse Chandler was held in high esteem with others such as Sherlock Holmes, Mike Hammer, and Jonn Shaft. No case was too hot to handle, no broad too cold to warm up. But that was back in my great-grandfather's time and a lot has happened since then. Violent crime was almost eradicated on Earth with the advent of complete computer surveillance and summation. Who needed a PI when the eyes of the public were already on you? The Mouse Chandler legacy was quickly disappearing into the shadows, labeled redundant and obsolete.

I guess that's why I held on to that confiscated paper money. Sure, anything made of paper would fetch a nice price on the antique black market, but I wasn't interested in selling it. Like the Maileran, I just wanted to hold on to a piece of the past.

Day Three brought news that the ISALT meeting had been interrupted by a demonstration of a radical Martian-Maileran alliance fringe group who claimed that there was a Terran-organized conspiracy to replace all planetary cultures with Earthlike homogeneity (much the same way Japan reshaped the corporate industrial world in its own image back in the 1990s). The demonstration side-tracked all productive discussions on the matters at hand, and the talks were recessed for the weekend.

A spokesperson for the Maileran delegation expressed their surprise at the interruption, but quickly added that "Their argument was probably not without merit, and perhaps an investigation should be mounted prior to the actual signing of any agreements. Such a hidden agenda on the part of the Earth would never be in the best interest of other members of the Federation."

Back on Griffin's Satellite, the third day of competition yielded the expected results, and both Fischer and Grlot had advanced to the finals.

At the request of the management, the starting time for the final match was pushed back to the following evening so that the simul-broadcast would be taking place during prime-time in seventy-five percent of the available markets.

Dena visited me that night. We hadn't been able to spend much time together since the tourney had started. She had visited with the Benatrix contingent during her off-hours for a little homeworld gossip, and had come down with a serious case of homesickness.

"I've decided to return to Benatrix with them when the tourney is over. With the exception of you, the glamorous life of Griffin's Satellite has not been all it's cracked up to be," she said quietly.

I wasn't surprised. Sure I was going to miss her and her French maid shtick, but she had to move on. With a quartet of legs like she had, she shouldn't have to settle for second-floor maid status in some backwater resort.

"But we have tonight," she purred.

. . . and she made it worth both of our whiles.

All eyes were trained on Fischer and Grlot the following evening. Fischer had already thrown his usual final match temper tantrum, ordering the removal of all cameras from the playing area. (Merv had already prepared for this by hiding his main three setups behind two-way mirrors.) Grlot had requested a time limit be set on the evening's session as he had been feeling drowsy all day, and feared that he was coming down with the scourge of the galaxy, which we knew as the common cold.

Fischer seemed more agitated than usual. The grapevine had it that his mom had found her heart's desire in the arms of an unexpected suitor, namely Merv, who was conspicuously absent from the evening's festivities. Perhaps she thought this would give Sebastion the media edge, being real close to someone on the inside. (I refused to believe that she was desperate enough for a warm body to settle for him.) Unfortunately, whatever her intent had been, her actions had resulted in her son playing particularly badly. After twenty moves, he was already down by a queen and a pawn, and probably would have lost within the hour had Grlot not begged fatigue, and asked the game be held over to the following morning. Mrs. Fischer overruled her son's protest that he wanted to finish and win the game right then, and agreed to the postponement.

The game was adjourned to be resumed the following morning at 9:00.

* * *

Needless to say, when Merv found out about the change in schedule, he went through the roof. Closing ceremonies were set for the following evening and could not be pushed back any farther since several of the participants would be returning to their respective worlds just a few hours later. More importantly, the penultimate moves of the game would wind up being broadcast opposite *The Geraldo Donahue Kiss & Tell Talk Show,* or even worse, against the highest-rated daytime TV show in the universe *The I Love Lucy—Odd Couple Comedy Hour.* But, figuratively speaking, he had helped to make the bed that he was now sleeping in, and he was the one responsible for the changing of the sheets.

Nine A.M. came and went, and Grlot was noticeably absent. Sebastion contended that this was an automatic admission of defeat.

"He knows that no one can defeat the undefeated king of the chessboards! I demand that the match and the title be awarded to me here and now!" he ranted.

Cooler minds prevailed, and Grlot's aide was dispatched to see what was keeping the finalist.

Merv was called away a few moments later, and before you could say "Coming, Merv," I found myself standing next to him in Grlot's room looking at a very dead Maileran chess champion.

Grlot was crumpled on the floor, his flat featureless face indented by a charred crater five inches in diameter. It reminded me of the face of a stoolie I knew who had met a blaster face-first. The shot had to have been at close range, so it looked as though he must have surprised someone inside his room when he had returned from the match the previous night. He was still in his match bodysuit, and he still clutched his game notebook in his third tentacle.

The rest of the apartment seemed undisturbed. His nest was unslept in, and its coverlet had not been turned down by the evening staff from the night before. (Luckily Merv was preoccupied with the crisis at hand, or there would be hell to pay at the next staff meeting.)

"This is horrible! There's never been a death at any of the Griffin resorts before! Why did it have to happen at mine?"

"You mean a murder," I corrected.

"Now don't go jumping to any conclusions. It could have been natural causes," he insisted, carefully avoiding looking at the corpse.

"There is nothing natural about the burn marks left by a blaster." I insisted. "Grlot was shot in the face by person or persons unknown. Given the Maileran body structure, he couldn't possibly have done it to himself. His tentacles just aren't long enough."

Merv began to lose his cool.

"The publicity will kill us!" he sputtered. "The media will have a field day. We'll never get another interstellar event like the tournament and the corporation will blame me. I'll be back in Atlantic City, cleaning ashtrays."

"Not to mention its possible effect on the Federation talks, galactic peace, and all that," I added.

"You don't think it was an assassination, do you? An intergalactic incident will close this place. I'll be ruined! I'll never work again!" His outburst was suddenly interrupted by a moment of composure, as if a reassuring thought had just occurred to him. He turned to me, and with his-all-too familiar corporate tone continued, "It's obviously *your* fault. You were in charge of security. You're always bragging about how there were no real challenges for you, and that the job was beneath your supreme investigative abilities. Well, this was your opportunity and you blew it. You should have known that something was going to happen. I will not be held responsible for this."

"Listen, Merv, just try to keep a lid on this. The peace talks don't reconvene for another twenty-four hours. Maybe I can piece together what happened by then, and you can make an official statement or something."

"You'll have to solve it. All the attendees but the
Fischers are leaving tonight after closing ceremonies. The
first thing they'll do will be talk to the press, and before
you know it . . ."

"What a minute," I demanded. "No one can leave.
They're all suspects."

"There's not much I can do about that," Merv replied. "As members of interstellar consortiums they all
have diplomatic immunity. We can't detain them. We
don't have the authority, and by the time someone with
the proper authority arrives, they'll all be long gone. If
their ships don't leave tonight, they'll have to have their
courses reprogrammed, and no one would want to go to
that expense. You have less than twelve hours to get to
the bottom of this."

His managerial poise restored, he left the room.

There I was, alone in a hotel room with a Maileran
corpse. He must have been dead for at least six hours
since his naturally moist skin had already begun to dry
out. The fact that his entire head had not been completely
blown off meant that he had been shot with the blaster,
point-blank, and it was probably a mini-hand blaster at
that. This was definitely not the work of a professional.
A professional would have been neater, more precise.
Assassins use lasers, not blasters.

I turned my attention to the rest of the room. Grlot had
been quite fastidious. The nightstand and desk were all
carefully arrayed with artifacts from at least twelve different worlds, set up on display as if they were in a museum, and a crowded museum at that . . . except for a
space on the desk blotter. The area was roughly 18″ by
20″ and contained only three small objects of apparent
Earth origin: a used and slightly bent plastic paper clip,
a decorative plastic letter opener shaped like a sword emblazoned with the Presidential Seal of the United States
of America, and a small, oddly-shaped object that
seemed to cling to the desk as if it had been magnetized
(I believe the object was what they used to call a "refrigerator magnet." They came in various shapes and

sizes and were used to post household notes prior to the advent of the post-it monitor). With the exception of these three tiny objects, that which seemed to be the Earth exhibit seemed awfully empty . . . almost as if something were missing.

I closed the door behind me, then coded the portal to enforce an automatic security seal on the door and a stasis environment within the room. The room, and the body within, would be kept in the exact same condition we found it in when the authorities finally arrived. No further decomposition, no dust, and no disturbed fingerprints.

I knew that various special interest groups were just looking for a way to widen the schism at the Federation talks . . . but murder at a chess tournament, even an interstellar one, was just too far off the wall, even for someone who has seen some of the things that I have.

It was my guess that Grlot had surprised the assailant, who panicked when Grlot had arrived back at his room about an hour before he was expected by the planned networks schedule. But if that was the case, what was the assailant looking for—something to steal?

The hours passed quickly. I interviewed the various other players, checked the perimeter for signs of a break-in, and reviewed the elevator surveillance tapes, but with two hours left before zero hour I had nothing to show for my efforts.

I was about to admit defeat and resign (which would be the high point of Merv's day), when I felt a pair of shapely legs circle my waist, and a pair of delicate hands covered my eyes.

A familiar voice purred, "Guess who, gumshoe?"

It was Dena. She was dressed in a Benatrix team bodysuit, and had just turned in her resignation (and, unfortunately, her maid's uniform as well).

"Gonna miss me?" she asked.

"Sure, you know I will. All ready to go?"

"Just have to finish packing a few last things."

"What are you going to do once you get back home?"

"I don't know, but I'm sure a smart girl like me will figure out something."

I kissed her lips, and then kissed her hand, just like the classy swells do, caressing each finger. I was stopped by a bandaid on one finger tip.

"What happened?" I asked.

"A little on-the-job accident," she quipped. "Nothing serious. Well, gotta go, it's been fun." And she was gone.

I was about to resume my last mile to Merv's office when an uneasy thought crossed my mind. *An on-the-job accident.* With all the automation that had taken place in the domestic industry, how could she have cut her finger? Back in the twentieth century, if I remembered correctly, they had a word for those type of cuts.

I had to see Dena again, and if I hurried, she'd still be packing back in her place.

I really hoped that I was wrong, but knew that I wasn't. Sometimes those were the breaks.

She was still there, and was about to pack the carry-all that most women called their handbags.

"Mouse, I didn't expect to see you again, at least not so soon," she said in surprise.

"How's the paper cut?" I asked.

"Fine," she responded, before realizing that she had just given herself away. When she did a half-second later, she pulled out a hand blaster from her bag and aimed it at my crotch.

In typical 1940s B movie style, I stalled for time, and hoped that I would be able to talk her out of any drastic actions.

"So you were the paper thief all along," I quipped.

"Just wanted a little financial cushion for life back on Benatrix, and paper is light and easy to transport. Besides, the black market back home is quite lucrative."

"Get anything good from Grlot?"

"An original short story manuscript by someone

named King, a letter from the office of the Vice President circa 1990—it's written in crayon by the way—and a grocery list circa 1980. Real exclusive stuff. Together with the Goulart manuscript, I should be able to make a real killing.''

''You already have,'' I observed.

''I didn't mean to kill the Maileran. He surprised me. I had figured that he wouldn't be returning for another hour, and used my pass key to get in.''

''You forgot to turn down the coverlet.''

''So fire me. On second thought, I have a rocket to catch, so I'll fire you. Ciao, baby.'' She started to squeeze the trigger . . .

. . . and I found myself beamed back to Merv's office.

''Your time has run out. What do you have to report?'' the corporate stooge demanded.

''Quick, seal off Dena Quatro's room!'' I ordered, trying to regain my composure after having been rescued from death's door by Merv.

''But she's resigned,'' he said.

''She's also the killer,'' I insisted. ''Seal her off before she gets away!''

And he did.

It turned out that Dena had a record several files long for similar thefts at other resorts, under a variety of other names. This was her first murder, though. I really think she enjoyed it, and given the opportunity she'd probably do it again.

I didn't think the authorities would give her another opportunity for a very long time.

The case was closed. Fischer was declared champ for the fifth year in a row by default, and the Federation talks resumed without incident. Merv accepted a job as Fischer's ''manager,'' and out of the goodness of the corporation's heart I was offered his job in gratitude for my work above and beyond the call of duty.

I declined the position.

I was going to miss Dena. She wasn't the first female

to try to kill me, and she probably wouldn't be the last. It was time for me to move on. Perhaps I'd try the Benatrix homeworld.

Benatrix was even farther from the jurisdiction of those kneecappers. A land of virgin opportunity—and besides, I'd sort of developed a thing for pretty young babes with four legs in fishnet stockings.

CATACHRESIS

by Ginjer Buchanan

Ginjer Buchanan is Senior Editor at the Berkley Publishing Group.

A detective, experienced at his job and more than able to defend himself, is murdered while working on an embezzlement case on an alien world. The only clues his partner can find at the scene of the crime are a key that fits no known lock, an artificial rose, and a wristwatch that runs backward.

1. How was the detective killed?
2. Who killed him?

The chemist had left a note behind, claiming that he was going off to look for absolutely nothing.

He'd taken a fair amount with him, though, most of it the rightful property of his employer, some belonging to his prim and proper little wife.

Ampurdan is just a backwater colony in a backwater galaxy. It's on the circuit for the Patrol, and they can be called in when any of the major commandments of God or man are broken. For more minor infractions, the wrongdoings of the locals on a Saturday night, that sort of thing, there is a quasi-legal vigilante system that works pretty well. But embezzlement, on the scale of what the chemist had done—well, the truth was that nobody much cared. Except, of course, for his employer and his prim little wife.

So they came to us. Schline and Wurtz. Private Investigators. Heirs to a tradition that stretched back to the long-dead planet of Mother Earth. Like a lot in our trade, we were ex-Patrol. Like a lot, we did other things to keep the credit balance healthy. I was, of all things, a plumber. Wurtz, a big good-natured guy, worked at the star port pushing large things around. I suppose that I was the brain and he was the brawn. We'd been together for about ten years. I had known Wurtz in Patrol, and came to Ampurdan when I quit. I'd been in a foul mood because my lady had refused to quit with me. Wurtz cheered me up, got me thinking again, instead of lying around moaning. We worked—and played—well together.

The mean streets of Ampurdan are fairly quiet though, so we didn't hesitate to take on the case of the chemist. Since I was in the middle of a major clogged drain at the tech barracks, Wurtz wound up handling the legwork.

Which is why Wurtz is dead.

Wifey gave us a holo of the chemist. A colorless little man, balding, with a mustache and a chin beard. He was short, portly, and, in the holo, dressed in his prim and proper best, down to and including spats!

Wurtz took it and did the obvious—checked out both the star port and the scanner port. The chemist, it turned out, was either very dumb, or very complaisant. He hadn't even used a false name when he had scanned out, although he had used a fair chunk of his ill-gotten credits. His listed destination was Katalonia, a planet far, far out on the Rim.

We reported our findings to employer and wifey. Employer, when he found out that most of the credits were gone, was inclined to let it go. Wifey, however, thinned her lips, removed what was no doubt her wedding ring, and handed it over to us. Star port was experiencing a lull in activity. And the aforementioned drain was still very clogged, with God only knew what. So Wurtz booked a scan to Katalonia.

That was about a week ago. The s-fax came in this morning, unsigned. It said that Wurtz was dead. That was *all* that it said.

Scanning, as you may have figured out, isn't cheap.

But Wurtz had been my partner and my friend. I withdrew old-age credits. And I scanned to Katalonia.

My first impression was that the chemist had come to the right place to find absolutely nothing. That was what surrounded me. Vast expanses of it. Sandy reaches, in shades ranging from yellow/white to dull yellow to golden yellow. Oh, there were occasional outcroppings. Some were bizarre rock formations, and others appeared to be buildings. They'd been hard to spot at first because they were the same colors as the sand.

Above me, an equally vast sky seemed to stretch impossibly beyond the horizon. In places it was yellow, too, but mainly it was a cloudy blue. There must have been a sun up there somewhere, but it sure wasn't obvious.

And I sure was not happy about having apparently scanned into the middle of nowhere. Even for a tourist class scan, this was mighty cheesy. I said a few things aloud about the situation, which made me feel some better, and started out toward the nearest cluster of yellow buildings, when a plain, old-fashioned gunshot rang out.

I fell to the sand and rolled. The sound came again. For a moment, I wished that I didn't recognize it. But the Patrol is well-versed in weaponry of the ages. If only I had one with me. . . .

Then an equally plain, old-fashioned, open-topped auto appeared, backfiring its way around a nearby arrangement of rocks. It was yellow (of course) and at first I thought it was covered in flowers. It lurched to a stop, and some of the flowers got out of the passenger side and walked over to where I lay, stomach down. It was probably easy to find me—I wasn't yellow.

A Katalonian, I assumed. Humanoid. Obviously female. Two arms. Two legs, glimpsed under a long clinging white gown. She looked a lot like the folks at home, except that her head was made of flowers. Delicate, extremely feminine red and white flowers. It was a pleasure to see the red. And she smelled delicate and sweet, too.

"You are Schline?"

I scrambled to my feet and agreed that I was Schline.

"You have come for Wurtz. He spoke of you."

"Yes, I've come for him. I've come to find out what happened to him."

"He sought the chemist of Ampurdan. He found him."

"Then I've got to find him, too. Do you know where he is?"

She nodded her petals.

"Will you take me to him?"

"Come," she replied. I followed her to the auto, and joined another Katalonian in the back seat. Her gown was torn, and her red-flowered head was bent over what looked like a small tuba that she was holding in her lap. She was sobbing, softly but continuously.

"Weep not," the driver asserted. She was the largest of the three, and her head of white flowers was the wildest-looking. "The search of Schline is more important than our search. He is the friend of Wurtz."

We drove across the smooth sand until a grouping of yellow/white buildings in the distance went from simple specks to dots to the sketch of a town. I saw a bell-tower, pointed vacant archways, a leafless tree or two. We stopped.

"There." The driver gestured. "Up there. The chemist."

I got out of the auto, and stood for a minute, hands in my pockets, by a thin tree. The man I could see clearly at the top of the low rise might have killed Wurtz. This meek little man we had joked about might have gotten the best of one of the best. I wanted to know. I *had* to know. But I hesitated, watching my shadow move behind me, although I still couldn't see the sun. Finally, I took a deep breath, turned, and climbed the hill.

The chemist, dressed as he had been in the holo, was staring intently at a straggly pale green bush, muttering to himself. I called his name, loudly. He looked up, squinting as though the light was in his eyes.

"I'm Schline. Wurtz was my partner."

The chemist sighed, stretching his waistcoat.

"Ah, you got my s-fax, then. It was a terrible tragedy. I have some blame. I felt compelled to notify you."

"What happened?" I growled. Menace is hardly my middle name, but I was determined.

"I introduced them, you see. We'd gone together to the concert. We'd gotten rather friendly. The only two humans on Katalonia, you know. Rather friendly. Even though he was hunting me."

"He found you."

"Oh, yes. Quite quickly. So I gave him what I had left to take back to Ampurdan, to my wife. You see, I don't need credits now. I did find what I was looking for, which was all I ever wanted to do."

From the vantage point of the low hill, I could, in fact, see almost absolutely nothing.

"Yes. That's obvious. But what about Wurtz? If you are to blame . . ."

"No, not! Not the way you are thinking." He sighed again, and brushed a speck of sand from his spat. "The ladies. I introduced him to the ladies. He got involved. He went too far. All the way to the sea. He was trying to help, but . . . ask *them*. They know."

He turned and walked slowly away. I thought of stopping him, but in my gut I knew that he wasn't capable of harming Wurtz. I think that I knew it before I climbed the hill.

The car and the Katalonians were waiting for me.

"The chemist says you know about Wurtz. Why didn't you just tell me right away?"

The driver seemed puzzled. "You asked to be taken to the chemist. We did what you requested."

Aliens, I thought. "All right. Now I'm asking to be taken to the sea."

"That is where we were also going," the driver answered. "That is where Wurtz went, after he found the key."

We drove off, then, away from the buildings and the trees and the chemist who had found what he was looking for. Before long, I was really missing them. We drove in silence, over harsh yellow sand. Now and then, we'd pass gnarled rock formations, some with scrawled script on them. It got colder, though the light never dimmed. The only sounds were the scrunch of the tires on the sand, the subdued sobbing of my seat companion, and the gentle buzz of some insect in the driver's head.

Suddenly, the Katalonian who had first greeted me gave a muted shriek, and clutched the driver's arm. She pointed toward the horizon. Against the yellow of the sand, something or things were moving. They were a dirty white, and they seemed to be rolling along, blown by a nonexistent wind.

"Follow! Follow!" croaked my seat companion. She blew a slow moaning note on her horn.

The driver veered off after the objects. "Wait a minute!" I protested. "What about the sea? What about Wurtz?"

I was ignored. We flew over the sand, getting closer by the mile. Now I could see what we were pursuing. I closed my eyes, but I could still see them. A herd, for lack of the right word (if there is one) of oddly misshapen, oversized skulls, thundering along almost in formation. Not human skulls. Not Katalonian skulls. Just—skulls. I swallowed. And, having no choice, hung on for the ride.

We kept our distance, and continued to follow. The sand under us grew whiter and smoother. There was a tang in the air. Salt. Fish. Brine. Familiar things. I was ridiculously happy.

The skulls rolled along, past long low ridges, around the ruins of a yellow brick building, and—quite suddenly—onto a great expanse of beach. The sea, completely flat, completely blue, completely still, was on our right. In front of us, the skull herd parted to avoid some debris in its path. One skull, toward the back, paused and then turned in our direction. It grinned hideously. The driver slammed to a stop. She stood and gave a truly heartrending cry. The skull seemed to grin even more wildly, then rolled quickly away after the rest of the herd.

"Oh, are they not terrible?" the driver cried. "They have led us here! They have wanted us to know this torment!"

I sat stunned in the auto, as the three Katalonians climbed out and stumbled across the sand to the debris there. The delicate one fell to her knees and picked up a limp brown object. She rose, cradling it across her forearms, staring out at nothing, as though she were in shock. The driver bent and raised a corner of a larger object. Something with stubby legs and rows of teeth that looked bloodless and extremely dead.

As I left the auto and went closer, the sobber threw down her horn, raised one arm and screamed at the sky, "Look what they have done! The skulls! Look what they have done to the innocents! We are too late!"

"We knew that we were too late," the driver said stiffly. "We knew when Wurtz found the key. In truth, we knew when the skulls first came. When they heard the concert, they could not be stopped."

I was close enough to see, if not understand. The brown object. A cello. What the driver held. A grand piano. The empty shells or skins of the instruments, drained of all vitality. Lifeless, no matter how you looked at it.

I didn't belong here, with the Katalonians and their grief. I went back to the auto and left them with their dead, to do whatever had to be done. And to wonder what part Wurtz had played in all of this. In a little while they joined me. We traveled along the shore slowly, again in silence.

"She will feel some peace when she knows that we found them," my seat companion said.

"Yes," the driver agreed. "We go to her now. And—" she turned her petals briefly to me, "—to Wurtz."

We drove round the shoreline of a small cove. The water was still, calm. No sun. No moon. No tides. No surf. Ahead, a lone naked tree, which seemed to be growing in the sand at the edge of the water. A dark green figure beneath stood out with startling clarity against the pale sand and the pale sky and the pale sea. One long branch extended above the figure, something limp draped over it.

The auto stopped a short distance away. The figure in

green was a Katalonian, I could see. She was slender, beautiful. Her head was a mass of roses, roses of all colors, all full-blown. Their fragrance overcame even the briny stench of the motionless sea.

The three approached her quietly, taking me with them.

"This is Schline," the driver said. "Friend to Wurtz."

The rose woman extended her arms gracefully.

"It is good that you have come for Wurtz. He was a good man. He did his best. He said that he wanted to help me—us. He said that his job was finding things. He found the key." She handed me a small object, a thin flat piece of ivory. Her voice was soft, musical. I took the key, and held it close.

"He went looking further, then, for more keys, more pieces. I followed him, though he did not want that. But we came too far. We came here to the sea." She paused, and looked out at the silent water.

"We heard the watches calling. They were so terrified that they were running backward, as if they thought that would give them time to escape the skulls. He dropped the key, and went to save the watches. I tried to stop him. But it was too late—for the watches, for him."

She lowered herself slowly to the white sand, and knelt by the form that had been lying at her feet, covered by the empty skin of a large dead watch, like the one that hung from the branch above.

"I've stayed here with him. I've kept away the ants. They've gotten to the watches. But I have kept them from *him*."

She drew the watch skin aside then, and I saw what it had been protecting.

A sickly pink. Formless, nearly hairless. Not recognizable as anything, human or otherwise. I tried to convince myself of that. But I knew.

I swallowed a lump of sickness. "Wurtz?"

"What is left behind of Wurtz. Yes." She lowered her beautiful, fragrant head almost reverently over the empty skin of my dead partner.

"Cover it—him." I said hoarsely. I thought of home,

of Ampurdan. "I can't—I won't—take him back like that. It's not—right."

"That is so, Schline, friend of Wurtz. What is needed now is not a thing of humans." The driver said softly. "It was never meant that you would take him from here. But you will be here for him when we do what needs to be done. For this little while, you and he are Katalonian."

What grief for the life of a man? More than for cello or piano, I decided. I reached down and pulled off the watch skin, and touched the thing that had been Wurtz.

"Yes. I will be here."

The rose woman turned her head toward me. She stood. "For Wurtz, then." She reached up with one slender hand, and plucked from her cheek one perfect red rose. She gently placed it on what remained of my partner. A drop of blood seeped from the stem, and fell, a single, special stain in the midst of absolutely nothing.

FLIGHT OF REASON
by Tappan King

Tappan King, novelist and short story writer, is the former editor of *Twilight Zone* magazine, and also served as a science fiction editor for Bantam Books.

A human emissary is visiting a planet with which we are at war. His introductory peacemaking sessions go well, but as he is returning to his quarters, he is bludgeoned to death by one of the inhabitants of the planet. The alien government, fearing that this will destroy the peace negotiations, calls in a human detective to solve the murder before the cease-fire ends. It is the most difficult type of minimal-information crime to solve, since there are no witnesses, a hostile alien population, and a severe time limit.

Who killed the emissary?

I woke up on my feet, half dressed, heart racing. An alarm was blaring, and for a minute I thought I was back in the Starforce again, yanked out of my bunk by a call to battle stations. Then I saw the light flashing on the com unit by the side of my bed, and I remembered where I was. . . .

My cozy little love nest in Birdland, light-years away from the war. I swore, then I laughed, and sat back down on the bed, taking slow, shallow breaths to get my heartbeat under control. Cieux stirred, disturbed by the sound. The covers fell from his hip, baring the long, graceful lines of his body.

"The only way you'll ever leave the 'Force is feet first,

girl." That's what they told me on the day I was called up for duty. I was a scared, scrappy little ten-year-old then, determined to prove them wrong. Some days I think they may have been right after all. It took me fifteen years of kissing and kicking butts to buy my life back from those bastards. But they still own a piece of my dreams. . . .

The phone buzzed again, the high-pitched tone signaling a priority call. Cieux rolled over against me. I wanted nothing more than to burrow back under those soft, warm furs beside him, but something told me there was trouble. I reached over and palmed the phone into my ear so I wouldn't wake him. The clock said it was half past two.

"Yes?"

"Captain Chase?"

"This is Nora Chase. Who the hell is this?"

"This is Sergeant Ana Fujita, Com Officer at the mission."

"You'd better have a damn good reason for waking me up, Sergeant. I just got home an hour and a half ago."

"We've got an emergency, Captain. You'd better get down here right away." She sounded really shook up.

"What kind of emergency?"

For a moment there was no answer. "Ambassador Singh is dead, Captain," she said at last. "So's the officer assigned to guard him."

"That doesn't make sense. I took the ambassador to his quarters myself, just after midnight." ProTech, the rentacop agency I work for, had been hired to handle security for the latest round of peace talks between the Terrans and the Phae. It sounded like somebody had screwed up badly. "How did it happen, Sergeant?"

"I can't answer that, Captain." She spoke very slowly, like someone was listening in. "The place is crawling with Territorial Guards. They've got orders to bring you in if you don't show up soon." The Guards were the personal goon squad that protected Sidon's ruling elite. If they were involved, it was bad news.

"Can't the Chief handle it?"

"Chief Sarit has been relieved of his command, Cap-

tain. I'm not sure how much longer any of us will be
allowed to stay on duty.'' There was a loud noise in the
background, like something splintering, followed by
shouts. ''I'd get my butt down here PDQ if I were you,
Captain.''

''I'm on my way, Sergeant,'' I said, and flicked off the
phone. As I leaned forward to pull on my boots, Cieux
moved closer, curling his arm around my waist.

''Where are you going?'' he cooed softly. I could smell
the faint musk of the down at the back of his neck, still
damp from our lovemaking.

''It's just business, Sugar,'' I whistled back. ''It
shouldn't take long. Go back to sleep. I'll be back as
soon as I can.''

''But you just got home,'' he murmured. ''It's hours
to dawn. Come back to bed.''

''I can't. I've got to take care of a problem down at
the mission.'' I eased his arm from around my waist,
and got up quickly, pulling on my tunic. Cieux sat up,
turning on the lights.

''What is it, Nora?'' he asked, speaking Terran now,
his voice harsh and husky. ''Is something wrong?''

''You know I can't talk about it,'' I answered.

He rolled out of bed and onto his feet in one fluid
motion, wrapping me up in his arms. ''That's what you
always say. You're always rushing off without a word of
explanation,'' he whispered in my ear, holding me close.
''This time I'm not letting you go until you answer me.''

''Okay,'' I said, resting my head for a moment against
his chest. ''Some bad shit's gone down at the peace talks.
Ambassador Singh is dead—probably murdered.'' Cieux
stared at me for a moment, then laughed harshly.

''Dear me!'' His voice was a mocking trill. ''Now
who'll persuade us nasty Birds to accept the benevolence
of Terra?''

''You're impossible!'' I said, pushing him away. ''This
may seem like a joke to you, but it's not to me!''

''Why not?'' he asked, ''What do you care about any
of this, Nora? It isn't your war anymore. You don't have
to jump every time they jerk your strings.''

"You don't get it, do you?" I said. "This has nothing to do with the damned war. I'm a cop now, remember? That's my job, damn it! My squad was hired to protect the peace talks and we blew it. Now someone's got to clean up the mess."

"It doesn't have to be you."

"What do you mean?"

"We've been over this before, Nora. You don't have to do this. You could quit at any time. Let someone else play cops and robbers for a while." He was looking at me intently now, the tips of his feathered fingers resting on my shoulders, the pale membranes at the corners of his golden eyes flicking quickly down and up again.

"I can't, Cieux. I've been a soldier since I was ten. There aren't a whole hell of a lot of jobs I'm qualified for. And even if I could, what would we live on? The money you make?"

Cieux's crest twisted; a sign that he was angry. But his voice was calm.

"We'd figure something out. We could find some place new, away from all of this. Start over." His voice was soft, his touch soothing, his words enticing. I knew if I didn't leave now, I might never leave.

"We'll talk about this later," I said, reaching for my body armor.

"There may not be a 'later,' Nora," he said, sharply, stepping between me and the door.

"Stop it, Cieux!" I said, pushing him aside. "I can't deal with this. Not now. I've got to go."

"Nora, wait!"

I slipped quickly past him out the door, slamming it behind me, not daring to turn back.

I broke into a sweat as soon as I hit the lobby. Sidon is a stinking hellhole this time of year, just before cyclone season, and the Birds who own this building like to keep it hot, even though most of the tenants are human. The bodysuit I was wearing didn't help.

I had to bribe the doorman to get my black-and-white out of the garage. It was nearly three by the time I got aloft. I kicked in the siren, and ripped straight across the DMZ, almost hoping a Phae patrol would try to stop me.

I was furious with Cieux for starting a fight when I needed most to be clearheaded. But I wasn't surprised. He'd never much cared for my work. Maybe it offended his aristocratic dignity that I worked for a living, and made good money at it, too. But we'd been too much in love to fight about it at first.

We'd met at the Ciaran Temple School, where he was working as a wing-boxing instructor. I'd just gotten the gig with ProTech, and needed to brush up on my fighting skills. I was attracted to him immediately. He wasn't the first Phae I'd been involved with. I'd "crossed over" shortly after my discharge, and never looked back. I'd spent ten long years on my back in the service, and I was looking for something a little different. But Cieux was the first Phae I'd ever gotten serious about.

It turned out we had a lot in common, like a lot of misfits who find their way to Sidon looking for a safe haven. I was a disillusioned war hero who'd used her bonus to buy her way out of the 'Force. He was a pampered son of a powerful military clan who'd jumped ship in a firefight during the Cluster Wars. We both liked jazz, ringdancing, and long walks late at night. And we both thought the war was nothing but an expensive joke.

He was hopeless with money, so I hired him as my personal trainer—though our workouts usually involved a bit more than just sparring practice. We got a place together in Birdland. It was a perfect arrangement. He had the residency papers, and I had the money to pay for the place. My friends said he was using me. His said the same about me. For a while we were blissfully happy.

Then came the cease-fire.

Humans and Phae have been fighting each other since our first contact a century ago. I guess that's one more proof of just how alike the two races are. We both broke lightspeed about the same time, and there are only so many habitable worlds in our little corner of the galaxy.

It was a strange sort of war. Phae play chess. Humans prefer demolition derby. We'd blow away a few of their settlements in a massive display of firepower. They'd retaliate with assassination, terrorism, and sabotage, disrupting our command and control and undermining our morale. Over time, we'd borrowed a few of each other's tricks and fought each other to a standstill.

Lately, though, both sides had gotten a little tired of the war. When you've killed off enough of your able-bodied adults that you have to start drafting kids, there's bound to be some resistance. So when the Terran Command proposed a cease-fire, everyone thought it sounded like a good idea—at least until both sides were strong enough to fight again.

They chose Sidon as the site for the peace talks. It made a certain kind of sense. As a center for espionage and the interstellar arms trade—not to mention other more exotic vices—Sidon was already more or less neutral territory. And although the planet was officially controlled by Phae, humans were allowed to come and go as they pleased, as long as the government got a cut of their business.

So one morning we woke up to find troops in the streets. The war we'd tried so hard to escape had followed us to Sidon. Cieux took it pretty hard, especially after my outfit was hired to protect the peace talks. It was a lucky break for me, an end to piecework and a steady management gig at premium pay.

But Cieux didn't see it that way. Every day he grew more moody and resentful. I couldn't really blame him. I'd been working fourteen-hour days since the talks started. There had been serious incidents almost every day—vandalism, attempted break-ins, fights among the delegates. I spent all day putting out fires. With the time limit for the cease-fire running out, it was getting worse. When I got home, I was exhausted and didn't feel much like talking—or anything else, for that matter. And every night my dreams were haunted by fears that something would go wrong while I slept.

I'd promised Cieux that we'd take some time alone together as soon we had a chance, but it didn't seem to be enough for him. Now it looked like it was going to be a long time before that chance came.

I reached the mission around quarter past three. As I descended toward the hoverpad, I heard a hissing sound, and a laser canon sliced across my nose. A pair of Territorial Guards were hovering on either side of my floater, weapons raised.

"What the hell do you think you're doing!" I shouted into the com unit.

"This area is interdicted by order of the Governor," a voice answered. "Leave immediately or be destroyed."

"This is Captain Chase of ProTech Security," I whistled back. I'd learned several of the Phae dialects in the 'Force while working for military intelligence. This one was a high-caste form used to command obedience. "I have been ordered to report here. You will contact your commander immediately."

It must have worked. A few moment later, I was given clearance to land. But when I stepped out of the floater, I was surrounded immediately by four Guardsmen in full flight harness and battle gear.

"Come with us, Captain Chase," rasped one of the Guards, gesturing toward the lift with an ugly-looking hand weapon. I didn't feel much like arguing.

They hustled me onto the lift, bypassing the second floor conference areas and continuing straight on to the basement. We walked in uneasy silence down the long corridor to the offices where my squad was headquartered. I didn't see any sign of my own people—or of the Terran military.

My escort halted at the door of the office, and motioned me inside. I entered alone. The lights had been dimmed, and the room was oppressively hot. I understood why when I saw who was seated at the conference table: Seet Touthiou, Territorial Governor of Sidon.

Seet owned Sidon. He'd fled here following a Phae power struggle four decades earlier, and had carved an independent city-state out of this harsh jungle planet with the money he'd made as an arms broker. Though he ruled Sidon with an iron hand, he rarely left the Governor's palace, kept there by age, poor health, and fear of assassination.

He sat in a great, thronelike chair, flanked by two enormous bodyguards. Their crimson turbans marked them as disciples of Ciara, a religious sect trained in lethal fighting skills. It was said that a Ciaran was more weapon than warrior, a puppet conditioned to obey his master's every whim without question. In the 'Force, we'd called them Golems. As I approached, the two shifted into a defensive stance, hands on their weapons.

Without quite knowing why, I made the low salute of the clanless warrior, and whistled a greeting filled with honorifics. To my surprise, Seet Touthiou laughed, and raised one trembling hand in greeting.

"This may not be as difficult as I feared. Please, sit down, Captain Chase," he said softly in dry but unaccented Terran, indicating a chair on the other side of the desk. I sat down slowly, making no sudden moves. The two Golems relaxed, returning to parade rest.

"Thank you, Governor," I said, carefully. "Do you mind if I ask you a question?"

He shook his head.

"What the hell is this all about?"

Seet laughed again. "I appreciate your directness, Captain. I'll try to respond in kind. I find myself in a most difficult situation. When the leaders of the Terran Alliance and Phae War Council approached me about holding peace talks here on Sidon, I gave them my personal assurance that I would allow nothing to endanger the delegates' safety and security. Yet within the past hour, two humans have been killed here in the mission—Satyajit Singh, the head of the Terran peace delegation, and the guard assigned to protect him, Kent Hong, of your own security service."

Seet Touthiou steepled his feathered fingertips below his chin. "But there is more than mere murder at stake here, Captain," he continued. "The cease fire is scheduled to expire at dawn—just over three hours from now.

Each side suspects the other of the crime, and the delegates have informed me that they will not consider extending it until Ambassador Singh's murderer has been apprehended. If the issue is not resolved by then, Sidon will become the next major battlefield of the war. This is no idle threat. There are two fully-armed starbases in orbit over Sidon, one Terran and one Phae, each ready to rain down massive destruction on my tiny little world on a moment's notice. That is not an outcome I wish to contemplate. That is why I have summoned you here, Captain Chase.''

"I'm afraid I don't understand, Governor.''

"I thought it was obvious, Captain. I need your help. I want you to find the murderer.''

"Why me?'' I answered, completely floored. "Why not one of your own staff?''

"You must understand, Captain Chase, that nothing happens on Sidon that I do not know about. I've learned a great deal about you, and much of it impresses me. I know, for example, that you achieved an admirable record in military intelligence with the Terran Starforce—a record you walked away from when you resigned from the service two years ago. I am also aware of your rapid rise through the ranks of ProTech Security Systems, as well as certain details of your personal affairs which I find intriguing. . . .'' He was obviously referring to my relationship with Cieux, although he seemed very uncomfortable speaking about it.

"I need someone objective to handle this investigation,'' he continued. "Someone not allied to either faction, and therefore credible to both. You are that person. You possess one trait which none of my staff can claim. You are human. The Terrans would not trust a Phae investigator to be impartial in this matter. Yet you have demonstrated to my satisfaction your independence from Terran authority, and your—sympathy for the concerns of Phae.''

"I don't suppose I have any choice in the matter, do I?''

Seet smiled. "I'm afraid not, Captain. I would have to

consider any hesitation on your part as evidence of your involvement.'' He glanced for just a moment at his body-guards, as if to remind me of the power he wielded. I could almost hear his little trap springing shut.

''Okay,'' I said. ''We don't have much time. How do we begin?''

''I have already begun.'' said Seet. ''I believe that the murders were committed by someone who is still inside this mission. Until proven otherwise, everyone, Terran and Phae alike, must be considered a suspect. I have sealed off the mission from the outside world. All of the races here are under house arrest—including your own unit, Captain. No one will be allowed to enter or leave until the investigation is concluded. If there is anything else you require, you have only to ask.''

''Just one thing, Governor,'' I answered, rising slowly so as not to upset Seet's Golems. ''I'm going to need some protection, some backup. I'll have to question everyone involved, commandeer all of their records. That's not going to make me very popular around here. And someone here has already demonstrated a willingness to kill.''

''I've already anticipated your request, Captain. A squad of my own personal Guards has been assigned to accompany you at all times.'' For some reason, that didn't reassure me all that much.

The atmosphere inside the mission was charged with tension—not too surprising with three different military forces under house arrest, all furious at the loss of their freedom. Territorial Guards had taken over all of the security checkpoints. Com lines had been disconnected. No one was allowed to move.

Ram Sarit, my unit chief, had been confined to quarters since he'd reported the murder. When the Guards brought him into the conference room where I'd set up shop, he looked pretty messed up. Somebody had worked him over pretty good. There were bruises on his left cheek, and one eye was half closed. First I got him some hot coffee and a cold towel, and then I set my com unit to record, and got down to business. He seemed grateful for the coffee, but he kept glancing warily at the two Guards who stood behind me.

"What happened here tonight, Chief?" I asked him.

"I'm not sure," he said. "The Governor's goons seem to think I'm holding something back, but I'm not. All I know is what my people told me—and what I saw myself."

"Okay, let's start there."

"The peace conference session broke up just after midnight," he said. "My officer on the floor said that the negotiating teams had argued over terms of disengagement most of the night, but they'd made some real progress toward a settlement. And they'd made a tentative agreement to extend the cease-fire three more days, subject to a full vote of the delegates the following morning."

"Sounds to me like somebody didn't want that vote to take place."

"He may get his wish yet, Nora," Sarit said. "In any case, the Terran MPs who were on duty told me that Ambassador Singh left the conference area shortly afterward and went directly to his quarters."

"That's right," I said. "I escorted the ambassador to his suite myself around 12:15. and made sure he was securely locked in before I left. Gia Sanchez had evening sentry duty at the guardpost outside the suite. I was there with her until her shift was up around 12:30, and held down her station until Kent Hong showed up about five minutes later, and then clocked out myself around quarter of one, and went home. What happened after that?"

"Not much. The first indication I had of any problem was when I got a call around ten minutes past two from General Hamadi, of the Terran Command. He said he'd been calling Ambassador Singh repeatedly for fifteen minutes or so, and getting no answer. I thought he was overreacting, but I called Corporal Hong just to make sure. When he didn't respond, I went up myself. There was no sign of Hong when I reached the suite, and the door was locked with the Ambassador's own code."

"How did you get in?"

"I had to break the lock. Luckily for me, a couple of MPs decided to give me a hand, or I wouldn't have had an alibi. When I finally got the door open, I found Corporal Hong dead in the outer room of the suite, and Ambassador Singh lying on the floor in the bedroom near the window. He looked like he'd been bludgeoned to death with a silverwood statue that was lying nearby.

"So they must have been killed sometime between 12:45 and 2 AM. How did the Governor hear about it?"

"I don't know, Nora. I played it by the book, reporting the deaths first to the two delegations. But before I could notify headquarters, Seet Touthiou's bully-boys were all over the place, and I was being roughed up by a pair of oversized Golems with brains the size of walnuts. I've been more or less out of commission since. I'm sorry I can't be of more help to you."

"It's okay, Chief. I should be able to get the rest of the information from the delegates." My alarm chimed. Four o'clock. "I'd better get going. I'll need access to the timelog files. Any problem with that?"

Chief Sarit laughed, jerking his chin at the Guards. "No problem, Captain. No problem at all."

I got less cooperation from General Hamadi, who remembered me all too well from my days with the 'Force.

"If Seet Touthiou thinks I'm going to hand over classified information to a turncoat like you, he's more of a senile old fool than I thought."

"I'm just here to do my job, General," I answered.

"What job is that?"

"Finding out who killed Ambassador Singh."

"I can save you time, Chase. It was the Phae. I've read Sarit's report. The window was wide open. One of them could have flown in that window, killed the Ambassador, and flown out without stopping to breathe."

"But why kill the Ambassador, General?"

"It's in their blood," Hamadi answered. "They live for the kill. When Saj Singh started to make some inroads with their diplomats they had to have him killed, or they'd be out of a job. They're beasts, all of them."

Then he turned to me with an ugly look in his eyes. "But you know all about the Phae, don't you, Chase? Tell me, how does it feel to get it from one of those big strong Birds?"

I left before I did something I'd regret later.

It was the same story with the head of the Phae delegation—Kia Sciaw, Chief of the Kerakaw, largest of the Phae warclans. He vehemently denied the charge, accusing General Hamadi himself of the crime.

"We are Kerakaw," he told me, as if that alone settled the matter. "We have given our word that we would not raise a hand to any Terran while this cease-fire lasts. The Kerakaw do not break their word. It is unthinkable. But this one is without honor." He did not deign to speak Hamadi's name. "He has been against this truce from the outset, as his own officers will attest. He would willingly slaughter one of his own kind to hold onto power—"

It was half past four by the time I'd finished my interviews. There wasn't much to go on, but I had one ace up my sleeve. When ProTech was assigned the security detail for the mission, we'd required every security officer to carry a timelog while on duty. Not just our own people, but members of the diplomatic corps, the Terran command, and the Phae War Council, as well. Normally, the data in those logs was confidential. But with Seet Touthiou's enforcers behind me, I'd been able to collect them all. As soon as I'd pushed the data through my com unit, I'd have a pretty good idea of everyone's movements at the time of the murder.

As it turned out, it didn't help much.

Everyone with an obvious motive for killing Ambassador Singh had an airtight alibi, including General Hamadi and Kia Sciaw. Whatever part they might have played in the murders, they didn't commit them with their own hands. Now I had to find out who did. In less than two hours.

There are two checkpoints outside the hallway to the ambassador's quarters, one staffed by Phae warriors, another by Terran MPs, in plain sight of each other. Neither log station reported any traffic through those doors during that time. As far as I could determine, no one had come anywhere near the suite between the time I left, around quarter of one, and the time Chief Sarit and the MPs had entered the room around ten past two. The time-logs confirmed it.

Unless someone had walked through walls, the only person who had access to the ambassador was Corporal Hong. And he was dead, too.

Five o'clock. Suddenly I felt very tired. It was time to look at the body.

The smell of death was strong as soon as I'd opened the door to Ambassador Singh's suite. Corporal Hong was lying facedown on the floor in the outer room of the suite next to the door, his neck twisted at an abrupt angle. There were no signs of struggle. It was clear Hong hadn't killed the ambassador. So much for that theory.

The ambassador lay on his back on the bedroom floor, his body obscured by the billowing curtains. I'd seen a lot of dead bodies during my years with the 'Force, but this one was pretty grisly. There was nothing much left of his head and his chest was badly caved in. The free-form silverwood statue that lay nearby was covered with his blood. I didn't have much doubt it was the murder weapon.

I stared at the two bodies, trying to make some sense of the pattern. Whoever killed the two had considerable strength. Both the ambassador and his guard were large, powerful men. It wouldn't have been easy to overcome them without a struggle. The brutal nature of the killings pointed to someone trained in Phae fighting skills. Terrans usually used beam weapons because they were quiet and easy to conceal.

Or the killer could have been a human, imitating Phae killing techniques.

I was no closer to an answer than I'd been two hours earlier.

One more thing to check. I got up, walked back into the bedroom again. The window stood wide open, revealing a small balcony with a high iron railing. In the

searchlights that bathed the building, pairs of Territorial
Guards flew by as they made their rounds.

I pulled a stylus out of my pocket, waved it over the
balcony. An arc of white light struck the tip, almost
knocking it out of my hand. I knew enough about the
Phae to know that they wouldn't leave a window unde-
fended. The security systems were intact. That took care
of General Hamadi's theory. Whoever had murdered the
two men had walked in the front door. But the door had
been locked with the ambassador's own code. And there
was no way anyone could have reached the door without
being seen by the sentries outside. Or by me. . . .

I went quickly through the ambassador's effects. There
was no sign of his cardlock. It made sense. The killer
had stolen the card, and locked the door after him. All I
had to do was find the cardlock, and I'd have the
killer. . . .

"I believe I know who the murderer is, Governor."

Seet Touthiou looked up from his desk, his eyes wide
with surprise.

"Would you care to enlighten me, Captain?"

"Certainly. There was only one person who was alone
with the ambassador for any length of time. Only one
person had the opportunity to kill Corporal Hong as well.
Someone so obvious no one would suspect."

"Who, Captain?"

"Me, Governor. I was the last person to see Ambassador Singh alive. I had time to kill him when I escorted
him to his quarters. And I was alone with Corporal Hong
after Gia Sanchez left. I had time to kill him just before
I went off duty, to make it look as if the murder had
taken place after I had gone. And I've been trained in
Phae fighting techniques, so I have the strength and skill
to commit both murders. And then there's this."

I reached into my tunic pocket, and pulled out a
gleaming rectangle with the seal of the Terran embassy.
Ambassador Singh's timelock.

"Is this a confession, Captain Chase?" asked Seet.

"I don't know," I answered, suddenly aware of what

I'd been saying. "I have no memory of the crime, but there's no other answer. Somehow I have been made to kill these people against my will, and then to forget that I've done so. It doesn't seem possible. . . ."

"Oh, but it is, Captain," Seet replied. "Take these two here," he said, gesturing to his bodyguards. "Properly trained, they will do anything I tell them, including forgetting that I ever gave them the order. It's a little side benefit of their training." I felt a dull numbness overcome me as the last piece of the puzzle fell in place.

"Then I know who was responsible for my own programming, Governor."

"Would you care to tell me, Captain?"

"If you'll grant a condemned woman a last request, I'll do better than that. I'll show you."

The first ruddy rays of dawn were staining the sky by the time my request was fulfilled. To my surprise, Seet Touthiou accompanied me to the brig, leaning on the arms of his bodyguards as he hobbled down the hallway. Two more Guards were stationed outside the door of the cell. At a gesture from Seet, they stepped aside, and let us in.

I knew I was taking a risk seeing him, but I didn't have a choice. They'd roughed him up a bit, and shackled his hands behind him. His golden eyes met mine, cold and defiant, and something inside me died.

"Why did you do it, Cieux?" I demanded, pushing the emotions away as I'd done so many times before.

"You would not understand, Nora." He used the dialect reserved for inferiors and slaves.

"Try me."

"I dishonored my family with my cowardice. This was the only way left to me to regain my honor. To allow Terrans to rule us would bring shame to my lineage and clan."

"But you turned your back on all that, Cieux, broke your vow to your family. You were free—"

"I was weak then, Nora. I could not help myself. I am strong now."

"But you fell in love with me—at least you said you did. Was it all lies, then?" Part of me still held onto the shreds of hope.

"You were nothing to me but a source of base pleasure." He answered, his voice flat and dull. Nothing of the Cieux I had known remained in his eyes.

His gaze turned to Seet, crest twisting in contempt. "What do you intend to do with me now?"

Seet answered slowly, choosing his words carefully. "You have broken my law, and you are subject to my judgment. You know the consequences—and your choices."

"So," whispered Cieux, nodding. "I choose honor." He folded his feathered arms across his chest, closed his eyes and sighed deeply. A moment later his head fell limply to his breast. I started to go to him, but Seet held me back.

"A moment, Captain." Cieux shuddered, convulsed, and slowly slid from his chair, crumpling to the floor. Seet released my arm and I ran to him, pressing my fingers against his throat. There was no sign of a pulse.

I straightened out his body, folding his hands, kissing him gently for the last time. In death, the sweetness and innocence I had known had returned to his face. I rose, turning my back on the past—and on all hope for the future.

"It's dawn, Governor," I said. "You have a murderer to present to the delegates. Shouldn't we be going?"

Seet laughed. "A pity he died before he could come to trial," he said. 'Now we'll never know for certain what his motives were."

"You still have me."

"Indeed I do, Captain. But you are of very little use to me as a scapegoat. Far more useful for—other purposes." I turned to him, uncertain of his meaning. "Humans are a most volatile breed," he continued. "I need someone loyal to me who understands their ways if I am going to govern this planet properly. Would you consider leaving your current position and taking a position with my staff, Captain? The duties would not be entirely unpleasant, and the compensations greater than you might imagine.''

I stared at Cieux's lifeless form, unable to speak.

"Think it over, Captain. But don't take too long. As you yourself pointed out, it's almost dawn.'' His meaning was all too clear.

"All right,'' I answered. "I'll take the job.''

"A very wise choice, Captain.'' Seet signaled to one of his Guards. "Go to the delegates, and tell them we have found our murderer,'' he whistled. "Tell them the peace is secure.'' The Guard bowed, and hurried off on his errand.

"So that's it?'' I said. "Just like that, and I'm free?''

"Very few of us are truly free,'' Seet laughed, his arm encircling my waist. "The best we can hope for is to be comfortable in our chains. Come along, Nora. There is work to be done. . . .''

SHE WAS BLONDE, SHE WAS DEAD—AND ONLY JIMMILICH OPSTROMOMMO COULD FIND OUT WHY!!!

by Janet Kagan

Janet Kagan was a story editor for MSW Productions before she left the cinema in favor of a career in science fiction.

A beautiful girl, working as a whore on a pleasure planet, is found strangled in her room. Only eight clients were in the whorehouse at the time: six men, one woman, and a male alien of humanlike proportions. Each of them is alibied, either by the whore they were with, or by each other (some were in the bar).

The only clues in the girl's room are the following: a feather on the window ledge, a blue-tinted contact lens that belongs neither to her nor any of the suspects, a small denomination copper coin on the floor, and a deck of playing cards missing the king and queen of hearts.

Solve it.

Jimmilich Opstromommo's first thought at the sight was that he had inadvertently stepped into one of Madame Fauna's fantasy scenerios. The room was holographed twenties-showgirl, rich in satins and velvets, gaudy in primary colors. Anna Lila lay sprawled across the lounge, face up. Her blood-red fingernails and mouth shocking against the pallor of her skin. Her eyes were wide and blue and staring up at him vacantly. A long red scarf, exactly matching the color of her strapless satin gown and her silent mouth, was drawn tightly about her neck as if she had been strangled.

All in all, the scene was of the same period as the Yarthian murder mysteries he'd grown so peculiarly fond of, having come across the first very early in his cross-cultural studies.

As he had progressed considerably in his studies since that time, he knew to a nicety that the strapless evening gown should have been "provocative." As the human john beside him had turned a rather sallow shade of green, Jimmilich thought that, for once, Madame Fauna had mislaid her scenerio. Perhaps the open wardrobe on the wall beyond Anna Lila was a bit overdone. It looked as if it had been ransacked—gaudy feather boas in every color of the rainbow had been tossed about, drawers emptied, even a deck of playing cards had been strewn around.

Beside him, the john made a peculiar ulping sound. Recognizing it, Jimmilich felt around the room until he found a real container and handed it to the man, who promptly threw up in it. Definitely not his scenerio, Jimmilich noted.

Fauna's reaction was even stranger. Ever so slowly, she knelt beside the lounge and lifted Anna Lila's hand to press it to her cheek. A tear formed at the corner of her eye.

The disarray of Fauna's clothing had also fallen well within the "provocative" range, but the john only continued to retch.

Fauna made a soft, sobbing noise in the back of her throat, then she stiffened and gulped. Jimmilich knew those for a human "gathering of courage" and waited. Still cradling Anna Lila's hand in her own, Fauna raised her head to look Jimmilich straight in the eye. With effort, she said, "She's dead, Jim."

A most confusing situation, Jimmilich decided. He

cleared his throat. He knew humans made that sound when they were hesitant and unsure of what to do or say. "Uh, Fauna," he said, "Anna Lila was never alive. Try the reset and, if that doesn't work, I'll be glad to check her programming cd for you."

Tears formed and fell, drawing colorless lines down Fauna's cheeks. Wordlessly, she held out her hand to show him: the programming disk was distorted, discolored. "She's dead," Fauna said again. Her face turned grim. "Murdered."

Jimmilich sighed and recognized the sigh as an almost human reaction. Fauna was apt to anthropomorphize—she did it with the whorehouse cat, she did it with the dog. For Fauna to ascribe human characteristics to a WHOR-F seemed somewhat less understandable to him than the cat and the dog. Jimmilich had dealt with AIs and knew the difference between intelligence and a program. The cat had a wonderful sense of humor, something that couldn't be said for Anna Lila, "dead" or "alive."

Still, the johns and janes anthropomorphized just as much—even to the point of bringing exotic presents to their favorite WHORs. Fauna'd been cognizant enough of the tendency in others to program the WHORs to display and coo and brag over gifts they'd been given. Probably Anna Lila was just as "dead" in some sense to the john beside him as she was to Fauna. That would account for his reaction.

Given a new program cd, he could resurrect Anna Lila for Fauna. In fact, he could could hand a cd to any of the other WHOR-Fs or WHOR-Ms in the place and it could resurrect Anna Lila . . . so he was at a complete loss to understand what reaction Fauna wanted of him.

She rose, straightened, pulled her lace kimikimi "decent." All the time, her eyes held his. She took a step toward him, tossed her head as if to toss back the tears, and said, "Find out who did it, Jim. I want to know."

Belatedly, he wondered if the local laws were such that one could call a cop for a computer crash. Perhaps this fell under the heading of industrial sabotage? "I'll call

Officer Krupke,'' he said. Krupke was a regular at the Pink Pillowslip; familiarity with the hardware might help.

Fauna shook her head. "You're the one asking all the questions, Jim. You're the closest thing we've got in the place to a detective—you find out who did it.'' She tossed the end of her boa over her shoulder.

The gesture was definitive, and he did not miss the implied threat. Either he found out whodunnit—his outside reading supplied the proper term—or she'd bar him from the Pink Pillowslip for good. And if she did that, he'd never finish his thesis on human behavior.

With difficulty—because his neck did not work quite like a human's—he nodded. At least he now had some idea of how to proceed. "I'll need a listener,'' he said. "For a watson.''

"On the house—any or all of them.''

"Hargon, if he's free.''

"I'll send him right up.''

Fauna took the john by the arm and gently brushed her hand across his cheek. Her voice changed to its professional coo. "Poor Mr. Smith. . . .'' Her use of his ritual name seemed to draw a little of the color back into the john's cheeks as she led him to the door. "What you need is a cool hand to soothe your fevered brow . . . and I know just the hand for you.''

Jimmilich was not deceived by the professional voice. The look she shot over her shoulder at him would probably have been understandable on any world, in any culture. "Do it, or else!'' was the translation that leapt to mind.

But how was he to do it? There was so much about the human culture that he didn't yet—might never—understand. He wasn't sure he even understood why the Pink Pillowslip existed. He realized he was only dealing with a small subset of a particular human culture, but that had made the research problem no less intriguing. The analogy to a restaurant was quite clear: the Pink Pillowslip provided a meal that its customers could not or would not trouble to make for themselves. To satisfy a purely physical need, a WHOR-F or WHOR-M would do fine; those ministrations were inexpensive. . . .

A listener, though—a listener had to be human and the price was high. That was the service he did not understand. The name didn't even suit the job description. A listener just as often talked as listened . . . or gave advice or even, on rare occasions, cursed the john in scathing terms. And still the john paid through the nose.

The door opened and closed softly behind him. Hargon, of course. He was a tall, heavily built man with curling hair and a quick smile. He smiled now and made a slight bow. "On the house," he said. "Tell me about it. . . ."

Jimmilich spread his hand to indicate the scene. "Fauna wants me to find out who 'murdered' Anna Lila, even though she wasn't alive to begin with."

As if he understood completely, Hargon nodded. "Fauna would; it's just like her." He waited a moment, as if he expected Jimmilich to say something, but Jimmilich could think of no proper response. Hargon said. "I don't know a great deal about your culture, Jim, but I'd like to learn. Would you do it out of kindness to Fauna?"

" 'Humor her,' you mean?"

"Exactly."

"I guess so."

"Good. Then—as Fauna expects you to take charge of this investigation—where do you suggest we begin?"

Jimmilich thought of all those murder mysteries he'd read. "Start with the scene of the crime, I suppose. I don't even know how much of this—" He spread his hand again, "—is real."

"That one's easy." Hargon turned to the wall beside the door and drew his hand through the peeling paper until he reached the edge of a framed poster advertising "70 GIRLS 70!!!" "Ah," he said, and the room was instantly stripped of its holographic overlay.

Anna Lila still lay staring up at them. The posters were gone from the walls, the chairs had turned a neutral beige, but the profusion of clutter behind her remained.

"Looks like an explosion in a feather factory," said Hargon. "I didn't think that sort of mess was part of the scenario."

"Then someone really did ransack her belongings."

" 'Her belongings'? Now who's anthropomorphizing?" Hargon said with a smile.

Jimmilich tilted one brow. His features didn't so easily form a smile, but he knew Hargon would recognize his own culture's equivalent. "I'm humoring Fauna," he said.

"Of course," said Hargon.

Jimmilich crossed the room and knelt to examine the clutter. "I didn't think the feather boas were real at all," he said.

"Most of the clothing is—it's a matter of texture. You can't tickle somebody's cheek with a feather holograph."

"And the deck of cards?" Jimmilich, having noted the position of each, began to pick them up.

"A special case," said Hargon. "I'd have to ask Fauna before I could tell you more about that deck of cards."

"Can you tell me if the King and Queen of Hearts are normally missing from this deck of cards?" Jimmilich fanned the deck to display its incompleteness.

Hargon thought for a long moment, then said carefully, "This afternoon, given this clientele, those two cards are normally missing from that deck."

"Thank you." Jimmilich pocketed the deck, then turned his attention back to the profusion of feathers. Several of the boas had shed feathers. He tried to remember whether he'd seen Fauna's boa shed. Reaching into the tangle, he pulled out a particularly ratty specimen and held it up. A few feathers drifted away. He frowned.

"For souvenirs," said Hargon. "Some of the johns like to take a memento. Fauna knows which ones and programs Anna Lila to wear something . . . expendable."

"Some of the others look as if they might have been expended as well."

"Fauna can't always be right, as much as she tries."

"I don't know, Hargon. Whoever killed Anna Lila was

looking for something—and he got mad when he didn't find it. Or he got mad at the boas. Just look: this stuff has been thrown around.'' Jimmilich stopped. ''Maybe this is a cultural difference? If I were searching for something, I'd do it very carefully, with as little disturbance as possible. This looks like the result of a fit of frustration at not finding it.''

Hargon turned slowly to take in the entire room. Then he crossed to the windowsill. ''Yes. I think I agree with you. A human could have had a fit of anger at not finding what he was looking for.'' He made an odd sound of disgust. ''Yes, it fits. Look at this—there's even a feather over here on the windowsill. That argues for a fit of pique, all right.''

Jimmilich looked and saw what Hargon hadn't. He moved to join the listener at the window. Tilting an eyebrow, he said, ''You're not much of a watson, Hargon.'' He picked up the feather.

''Sorry,'' said Hargon, though he didn't look the least bit sorry. ''What have I missed?''

Jimmilich held out the feather. ''This didn't come from any of those boas.''

Hargon took in the feather, then turned to look at the boas again. He shrugged. ''Hey, you're the detective! Is that a clue?''

''It is if we can find the boa it did come from.''

''Good work, Jim! What do we do next?''

Once again, Jimmilich fell back on his historical precedents. ''Next, we interrogate the suspects.''

''Lead on,'' said Hargon, cheerfully.

Jimmilich paused only to retrieve Anna Lila's programming cd from the lounge. If all else failed, he might be able to restore enough data from the disk to find out who was the last person she'd seen. It was a long shot, but he didn't want to fail Fauna—or the bright-faced Hargon, who seemed to be enjoying this all.

Or himself, he admitted grudgingly. After all those murder mysteries and all those detectives, he wanted to know how he would fare in their circumstances . . . and this might be his only chance to find out if their methods actually worked.

So everybody had an alibi. Jimmilich sat at a table in the listeners' lounge and stared gloomily into his drink. It was nice that Fauna kept a bottle of something that would intoxicate him for emergencies. It seemed so appropriate—hard-bitten detective drowns his doubts. . . . It went with the territory. Jimmilich downed the drink and called for another.

Six johns and a jane, and each with an alibi. Well, he thought to himself as he took a sip of the freshened drink, at least it's not a locked door mystery.

Though Fauna had already locked a door on him. She'd forbidden him from looking at the program cds of any of the current clients' WHORs, except for Anna Lila's, of course. That seemed like cheating somehow. He still hadn't taken it out of his pocket. If there was any information to be retrieved from it, it was still a last resort.

He leaned forward and tried to make his voice "tough" by human standards. "Okay, Hargon. We play by Fauna's rules."

Hargon nodded. "The good news is Fauna says I can tell you anything you want to know about these clients."

"I thought you listeners had a very strict client/listener privilege. I thought you never told what you'd listened to."

Hargon shrugged. "I don't much like it, but Fauna declared an emergency."

Still startled, Jimmilich looked around the lounge. They were alone. Seeing the look, Hargon added, "Furthermore, Fauna gave all six a freebie . . . to keep them here until you decide which of them did it, I think. We won't be interrupted."

"Can you tell me about the missing King and Queen?"

Hargon settled back in his chair and raised his own drink to take a sip, then he said, "First, I should explain why Fauna wouldn't let you read the programming cds. You see, for some clients, they lie. Take Ella Smith, for example. She comes in to see a WHOR-M, and that's what the WHORE-M's cd will say, but that's not what she actually does here.''

''No?''

''Uh-uh. She takes the Queen from the deck and the WHOR-M opens a door to a very private room.'' Hargon took another sip of his drink and went on, ''Then along comes Topo Smith, who takes the King and is likewise shown into that private room.''

''So Topo and Ella are actually having an affair with each other?'' He stared at his drink but didn't pick it up. ''Oh! Topo is low-caste. It's okay for either to be serviced by a WHOR, but it's not okay for them to sex each other.''

'' 'Love' is the operative word in this case, but that's essentially it.''

''And the programming cds—''

''Say each has been having it off with a WHOR,'' Hargon finished for him.

''So not one of the clients has an alibi, not really. I guess that makes it easier. Tell me about them, Hargon. Tell me whatever you know.''

''It'll take a while. . . .''

Jimmilich knew the proper response to that. ''I'm not going anywhere,'' he said.

By the time they'd passed a leisurely two hours, Jimmilich had learned that the current clients were a rather eccentric crew, even by the Pink Pillowslip's standards.

One came by simply to have two hours of uninterrupted peace and quiet in a bath; his WHOR-F scrubbed his back and brought him a drink, but that was all.

Another was a collector of exotic birds—he had examples from all over the known universe, some reputedly illegal; he was fond of WHOR-Fs in feathers. Hargon didn't know if he was the same client who raided boas for souvenirs or not.

Yet another Mr. Smith was a computer programmer. That was not eccentric, at first glance, but Hargon—smiling—had explained that this one's programming specialty was WHORs. ''Every now and then, he likes to write his own," Hargon explained. "Fauna indulges him. Whatever you found on that cd would most certainly not be true. That man teaches computers to lie."

And there was a symptomatic. Hargon had explained that at some length, as Jimmilich's culture didn't have an analogous profession. "He helps train medical students. He's a consummate actor—so good he can produce disease symptoms at will. Not all of them, of course, but enough to be convincing. From his 'medical history' and his 'symptoms,' the medical student has to figure out what he's 'got.' "

Tilting an eyebrow, Jimmilich said, "Much the same game Fauna plays with her clients."

Hargon grinned. "I never thought about it that way. Of course, you're right. Only his fantasies are for teaching purposes, instead of recreational." He leaned back in his chair. "I must tell Fauna that: she'll be delighted."

It all came down to humoring Fauna. And Jimmilich knew exactly what to do. "While you're at it, Hargon, tell Fauna I'd like to assemble all the suspects at the scene of the crime."

"You know who did it?"

"I do." When Hargon leaned forward excitedly, Jimmilich said, "And I'm not going to tell you. We've got to do this properly, or we'll disappoint Fauna."

"Right," said Hargon. "Half an hour? In Anna Lila's room?"

"Yes. Two more things: restore the holograph before anyone shows up, and spill a little perfume about the room, would you, please? Something not too strong but noticeable to most humans."

Hargon gave him a puzzled look but said, "Gotcha," and left the room bellowing Fauna's name.

The excitement was contagious. How about that? Jimmilich thought to himself. That stuff in the books works, it actually works! Motive, method, opportunity . . . that's what you need to know. And Hargon had told him all of that.

Half an hour would give Jimmilich just enough time

to double-check his suspicions with the programming cd he'd taken from Anna Lila's room. He took it from his pocket. This time, he looked at it carefully. If he had been human, he would have laughed.

It was exactly the size and weight of a cd . . . but it wasn't a cd. It was a small denomination copper coin from Wencelaus. Put that in a WHOR's disk drive and you'd have a meltdown of major proportions. . . .

He'd figured it out all right. Belatedly, but he'd figured it out. Now, he only hoped he could play this next scene correctly.

Once again, Jimmilich stood in the stare of Anna Lila's unseeing eyes. Around him, Fauna had assembled the suspects: some looked guiltily at each other, some guiltily at Anna Lila's sprawled figure. Fauna bore a grim expression on her normally smiling face. The john she'd led away and now led back still looked green around the gills.

Ella Smith was the first to open her mouth. "I don't know why we've been brought here," she began. "It's not as if we'd have any reason to damage that . . . that WHOR-F." She managed to make it sound ugly.

"One of you had very good reason to . . . do away with Anna Lila," Jimmilich said. "Sit down, Ms. Smith. This won't take but a moment of your extremely precious time."

"But—I couldn't have done it," said Topo Smith. His voice was a whine. "I was occupied at the time. Ask my WHOR-F if you don't believe me. . . ."

Jimmilich sighed and looked at Hargon. The listener nodded and bellowed, "Quiet!" Quiet ensued—it was a sullen quiet, but Jimmilich welcomed it.

"Thank you," he said. Politeness was not normally a detective's trait, but Jimmilich felt he was entitled to make some accommodation to his own personality. "I'll make this as brief as possible. Each of you has an alibi for the time of the murder—"

There was a mutter of agreement at that, but Jimmilich overrode it—as he knew any of his models would—to continue, ''But each of those alibis is a fraud. So we've seven suspects. Fortunately, we have only one murderer.''

More grumbling and a ''Get on with it, dammit!'' from the one Smythe in the room.

''Let's begin with the motive. Humans have a strong tendency to anthropomorphize . . . to such an the extent that they even bring their WHORs presents. And one of Anna Lila's clients had given her just such a present. It was of no value to poor Anna Lila, but it was of immense value to one of you in this room.''

''What was it?''

''I don't know. But Anna Lila was programmed to brag about her gifts—so any one of you might have known she had it. And the killer wanted it. So between johns, he waited and brooded. He knew she wouldn't give it to him; she wasn't—'' He was about to say ''programmed to give her gifts away,'' but one look at Fauna's face and he swapped wording. ''She wasn't the kind of girl who'd give anything away.''

He'd gotten it right. Fauna nodded approvingly.

''So while she was waiting for her next client, he sent her poison.'' From his pocket, he drew the copper coin. ''This is the same size and weight as a program cd. He handed it to an innocent WHOR and said, 'Oh, here's the program disk for Anna Lila.' And the poor WHOR obligingly took it up to her. Of course, when the WHOR gave it to Anna Lila, it killed her, but the WHOR was too naive to know the difference between reality and a scenario.''

''They often are,'' Hargon agreed. He patted Fauna's hand sympathetically, and she nodded.

''Then our murderer came up here to search for the McGuffin.''

''I thought you said you didn't know what he was looking for,'' said one of the Smiths, accusingly.

''I don't,'' said Jimmilich. ''That's what the old detective stories call the object of the search, when they don't know what it is.''

The john made a disgusted face, but Jimmilich, feeling

pleased with himself for the way he'd handled that, went on, "So the murderer came up here to search for the McGuffin. He thought it would be easy: just turn off the holograph and whatever was left would be the object of his desire."

He gestured to Hargon, who turned off the holograph. Anna Lila still stared, the boas still tangled on the floor.

"Unfortunately, it wasn't easy, as you can see. The murderer searched but couldn't find what he was looking for. In a fit of human pique, he tore the place apart, scattering the feathers everywhere."

If he'd had a cigarette, Jimmilich would have lit it and taken a drag. This was the right place. Instead, he had to settle for a growl. "Hell," he said, "I even found a feather down Anna Lila's cleavage—that's how far the feathers flew." He took a feather from his pocket and held it out as evidence, then dropped it on the top of the only real table in the room.

"One of you had that fit of rage, one of you knows what the McGuffin actually is, and that one of you is the one who killed Anna Lila."

Fauna glared at johns and jane. "Who was it, Jim? Tell me who!"

"You mean you can't smell him, Fauna?" Jimmilich knew his face looked grim to humans, Hargon had told him as much, so he left his face looking "grim" and went on, "Something stinks in here. . . ."

He lit a match. "And if you don't mind, I'll do something about that stench right now." So saying, he leaned over to put the match to the feather in the center of the table.

"No!" One of the Smiths leapt at him and slapped the match from his hand.

Hargon stamped it out almost before it hit the floor.

And this Smith held the feather, cradling it in his hand as if it were the most precious thing in the universe. Despite all the retching he'd done earlier, he looked fit now. Fit and angry. "You don't know what this is!"

"Yes, I do," said Jimmilich. "It's the McGuffin."

"A feather?" said Fauna. "A feather was worth Anna Lila's life?"

"Yes!" said Smith. "It was worth a dozen of her sort! It's a feather from a Herschel's sweet-charity from Mira II—they're extinct. They've been extinct for a hundred years . . . and some blithering idiot gave it to a WHOR as a gift!" He subsided, sputtering.

Fauna shook her head, bewildered. "Jim? I don't get it."

"He collects rare birds, Fauna. He could have cloned a whatever-that-was from the feather. We'll have to see that the feather gets to someone who can handle it properly. If you don't know someone, I can ask around the university."

The Smith clutched the feather. "No," he said. "It's mine. You can't have it. It's MINE, I tell you!"

And with a shriek of anger, he shoved Jimmilich aside and dashed to the door. Before anyone could set off in pursuit, Jimmilich said, "Let him go, Fauna. I don't think there's anything you can do to him legally."

"But," said Ella Smith, "there must be some punishment for him!"

"There will be," said Jimmilich. "A perfectly proper sort of punishment. He's taking his precious feather home with him to clone and raise—at no small expense—a turkey."

Hargon guffawed. "You swapped feathers on him!"

"You didn't think I'd burn the real one, did you? Maybe it actually is as precious as he makes out. I used one from Anna Lila's souvenir boa."

Fauna sighed. "A turkey. I suppose it's poetic in its own way." Her face darkened. "Still, I'm damned if I'll ever let him in the Pink Pillowslip again."

"Do what you think best, Fauna," Jimmilich told her. "Would you like me to see about reprogramming Anna Lila for you?"

"No, no, Harry can see to that, I'm sure." She rose and came close to him, turning up the "provocative" mannerisms all the way. "You've done so much for me,

Jim.'' She kissed him delicately on the cheek. "Thank you. . . .''

It was such a brilliant display of her art, Jimmilich almost wished he was human so he could appreciate it properly. "You're welcome, Fauna.'' Then he knew the right thing to add and did, "Any time you need me, just whistle. You know how to whistle, don't you. . . .''

It was some hours later before Jimmilich could speak to Hargon privately. He went credit card in hand. "I need a listener, Hargon, and it has to be you.''

Hargon grinned. "Put your money away, Jim. Fauna wouldn't hear of it after what you did.''

"In private, then. . . . But I'll leave the card and you can decide after you hear me out.''

Shrugging, Hargon led the way to a quiet room, with two comfortable chairs and a table to set their drinks on. When Jimmilich was settled, Hargon leaned across the table and said, "Tell me.''

"I figured who *really* dunnit, Hargon, and I don't know whether to tell Fauna or not. I did the first part right, I think. But should I go on humoring her or would she like it better if she knows I really did work out the method and the opportunity.'' He sat back and thought a minute, grateful that Hargon kept quiet while he did so.

"Maybe not,'' he said aloud. "I still don't see the motive.''

Then he realized that if he wanted any information at all from Hargon, he'd have to keep playing the game. He tilted an eyebrow. "See here, Hargon. If someone had actually stuck that copper coin in Anna Lila's disk drive, there'd have been a nasty meltdown . . . not that artistic sprawl. So the 'dead blonde' was programmed, and Fauna was the only one who had the opportunity to swap the program cd for the coin.''

"Why are you telling me this?''

"Because you had to be in on the whole thing, too. You found the feather on the window sill, not me.''

"You interpreted it correctly.''

"You mean I interpreted it exactly the way you meant

me to interpret it. The john was in on it with you—he had to be. In fact, they all had to be in on it with you.'' He stared at Hargon accusingly. ''You would never break client/listener privilege!''

Hargon smiled and said nothing.

''But why? Why would you go to all that trouble? Why the elaborate charade—all for *my* benefit?'' Jimmilich tried his best to understand, but there was still something he was missing. ''Help me out, here. I don't know human culture as well as I'd like to—''

''You know Fauna. You were willing to do her the kindness of playing her game. Tell me about Fauna.''

Without conscious thought, Jimmilich found her precedent in a dozen stories. ''Sucker for sick kittens,'' he said. ''Tough broad with a mushy center. Everybody's fall guy. . . .'' Both his eyebrows suddenly shot up.

''Is that a laugh?'' Hargon asked.

''Yeah, that's a laugh. She got me. She wanted me to see the real specialty of the house, didn't she?''

Hargon nodded, grinning, but didn't say a word.

''And that wasn't easy, since I don't come in two sexes. Even if she could have found another of my species around, sex would have been the last thing on our minds at meeting.''

''Fauna likes a challenge.''

''So she had to work out something as pleasurable to me as sex would be to one of her regular johns.''

''Not the sex,'' Hargon corrected, ''the right pleasurable fantasy. Sex doesn't necessarily come into it. Pleasure does. Fun does.'' He grinned again. ''And you did have fun, didn't you? Fauna still isn't entirely sure, because your facial expressions are hard for us to read.''

''I had a ball,'' he said, and both eyebrows went up again as he at last grasped the expression that had come from his own mouth. ''A ball,'' he repeated, hoping Hargon would get the joke.

Hargon threw back his head and laughed. ''You'll do. I think we're all going to have fun helping you with your 'studies.' '' He stood. ''And I leave it to you to find the right way to tell Fauna you know the whole story. . . .''

That was easy, now that he'd gotten the hang of it. Jimmilich made straight for the bar.

Fauna, in her silks and feathers, stood leaning a "come-hither" from the bar. Jimmilich obliged and, draping an arm over her shoulders, he whispered low in her ear, "That was real good for me, baby. . . . Was it good for you, too?"

Her shout of laughter told him he'd got that right. He was Jimmilich Opstromommo, he was the Pink Pillow-slip's private dick, and he was on a roll.

THE UGLY EARTHLING MURDER CASE

by George Alec Effinger

Hugo and Nebula winner George Alec Effinger spent some time as a "first reader" for Ace Books, and was also Assistant Editor of *The Haunt of Horror*.

The inhabitants of Proxima Centauri II come in four genders, and all four are capable of teleportation.

A drunken human tourist accidentally kills a member of a four-alien sexual grouping (tantamount in their society to marriage). He is apprehended and tried, and found innocent of murder. Instead he is convicted of accidental homicide and given a suspended sentence.

While he is gathering his belongings prior to his release, he is murdered with a blunt instrument. Lest this cause yet another interstellar incident, a detective (alien or human, take your choice) is assigned to find out who killed him. The three most obvious suspects are the three remaining members of the sexual grouping; all are incensed that he got off scot free, but all deny killing him.

The only clues at the scene of the crime are a pocket mirror, a handkerchief with a blue stain that the police lab has not been able to identify, and an alien tool that was probably the murder weapon.

Solve it.

No one had liked Fredrick Tolliver. No one on Earth, his own home world; no one on Proxima Centauri II; no one in the known universe, as far as I could tell. My name is Ferencz Ipolyi-Toth. I'm what used to be called a detective, or a private investigator, or quite a few less neutral and more unflattering things. Nowadays, we in the trade don't call ourselves anything at all. We just open offices with only our name painted on the door, yet our clients find us easily enough. I was located in the ancient town of Buda, the half of the Hungarian capital on the right bank of the Danube.

My current client was Waters Plasmonics Corporation, a large, wealthy, and impenetrable high-tech operation based in Rochester, New York, and Geneva, Switzerland. I knew they were impenetrable because I'd once been hired by someone else to find out what Dr. Bertram Waters was up to these days. After six weeks I gave up, admitted defeat, and returned my client's retainer.

It was kind of interesting to have WP Corporation hire me. Maybe along the way I might accidentally pick up some information about Waters and his associates, not that it would do me any good now. But I like to pick up loose information whenever I have the chance. You never know when it might come in handy, and I had plenty of computer storage space.

Of course, Fredrick Tolliver had been one of WP Corporation's top dreamers. That's pretty much all he'd done for them. He sat around all day in his office and wrote down everything that came into his mind that began with the words "say, what if . . . ?" It wasn't a bad job, as jobs go, except he'd had to put up with Rochester winters. Even in Budapest, we've heard about Rochester winters, and we're not unused to harsh winters ourselves. The mitigating factor was that he'd earned more in one year than I make in ten, enough to make even the Frozen North of the U.S.A. seem attractive.

Sitting in the comfortable black leather armchair beside my desk was Gerhardt Schnellenbogl, a group leader out of WP Corporation's Geneva branch. "The police in Chivakatopran City, on Proxima Centauri II, have ruled

Tolliver's death an accident. Must've been some bizarre accident, the way the back of his skull was crushed in. We believe he was murdered, and the Ukolsti—that's their name for themselves—are trying to stave off an interstellar incident. Commendable sentiment, we suppose, but we'd also like to learn the truth.''

I nodded. ''I get a thousand EC dollars a day plus expenses. Minimum of ten days, payable now.''

Schnellenbogl didn't even blink. ''Cash or check?'' he asked.

''Gold,'' I said.

He just opened his very thin briefcase and clinked together a stack of twenty EC$500 coins.

I stood up from behind my desk and came forward to shake his hand. ''Thank you, sir,'' I said, ''and you'll have my report within a few days.''

I know. I probably sounded pretty damn self-confident. Nevertheless, this wasn't like investigating Waters Plasmonics. This was simply a murder. I didn't think the inhabitants of Ukol could've come up with something I'd never seen before. Of course, as I've admitted, I've been wrong before.

Even after a century of use, the interstellar tunnels were still expensive. WP Corporation was picking up my travel costs, of course, so I was on the next day's shuttle to the Proxima Centauri system. My destination, the second planet, was very Earthlike in such matters as size, atmosphere, and amount and nature of the radiant energy it received from its sun. You'd expect that to be true for any world on which intelligent creatures in any guise had developed. There were also some primitive life-forms in the cold oceans of Proxima Centauri III. Right now, they didn't interest me. The Ukolsti, however, certainly did.

The dominant race on their planet, the Ukolsti came in four genders, although to my inexpert eyes half of them looked like moderately alien men and the other half like moderately alien women. I'm not sure now if four genders made them tetrasexual or quadrisexual. Following the pattern of uni- and bisexual (versus mono- and di-), I will go along with quadisexual. If I have committed a linguistic blunder here out of ignorance, I will tell you a small secret: I couldn't care less, and, I'm sure, neither could the Ukolsti.

I was met at the shuttle terminal in Chivakatopran City by a member of one of the two Ukolsti male sexes. The Ukolsti were on the average shorter and heavier than humans, and their skin colors ranged from a pale ice-blue through a dark red-violet. My new companion was the azure of a hazy summer's morning sky in the countryside beside the Danube. He was perhaps considered tall on his world, but he was still several inches shorter than me. However, he looked broader and stronger, and I made a mental note that I didn't really want to put the comparison to any sort of scientific evaluation, such as an arm-wrestling contest in a Ukolsti tavern some night. If the Ukolsti had taverns, that is. That's how little I knew about these people whose hospitality I'd depend upon during my stay.

I knew that I'd also have to rely on the expertise of my guide, a Ukolsti physicist who had for some time been a corresponding alien expert for Waters Plasmonics. His name was Asparatimundic egli don Sagragaratil.

We introduced ourselves when he met me at the gate in the tunnel terminal. "As we will be working rather closely together," he said, "I think it best if we leap directly to the informal terms of address and forms of behavior. We'll have other things to occupy our minds. In that spirit, please call me Mundic."

I learned later that such an invitation to dispense with the rigorous and taxing Ukolsti formalities was something an honor. I suspected as much, because the same thing is the case in many cultures, Earth-derived or otherwise. "And you may call me Ferencz," I said. He dipped his head in a slight bow of acknowledgment. From then on, we concentrated on the death of this unpopular Earthling, a death that bound together for a time the destinies of two planets.

Mundic took one of my two suitcases and led me from the tunnel terminal. "I think we should begin," he said, "with Mr. Tolliver's trial."

"Excuse me?" I said, baffled. "What trial?" Wily Gerhardt Schnellenbogl hadn't mentioned anything about Tolliver standing trial on Ukol.

My warning senses began screaming that I'd walked blithely into something much worse than I'd been led to believe. I'd been set up, in other words. Well, it's happened before, it goes with the business; but then at least I'd been on Earth, where I was comfortable about the local rules. Now here I was, several light-years from Earth, alone among aliens with an entire set of new rules I had only begun to learn.

We left the terminal building. I paused for a moment, set my suitcase on the sidewalk, and looked around at Chivakatopran City. The older-looking buildings were very baroque stone towers, heavily decorated with architectural details whose names I could look up if I felt like it. Lots of small statues in niches and reliefs and structures that stuck up and out.

The newer buildings were higher, but they were transparent enclosures. If more land had been available downtown, they might have been domes. Domes take up a lot of space. These newer buildings were stacks of floors, none of which extended to the outer walls. Each floor was environmentally connected to the others. Light, heat, and air circulated unhindered among them. The structures were like tall, rectangular domes beneath the pink sky.

"My vehicle," murmured Mundic. I grabbed my suitcase and got into his automobile. He leaned forward and gave directions to his driver, then sat back and relaxed.

"As I asked before, what trial?"

Mundic frowned. "I am unhappy that you don't already have this information. It means that I need to do quite a bit of explaining."

"We may blame WP Corporation for that," I said.

"Possibly. Or possibly some individual did not want you to have this information. Perhaps that individual has even prevented WP Corporation from having it."

I gave that a moment's thought. "Some individual, you say. You mean the murderer."

''Possibly,'' said Mundic. I couldn't read his expression. It was always carefully neutral. I'd soon learn that that was common among the Ukolsti.

Fredrick Tolliver had arrived in Chivakatopran City about an Earth month ago. He had been met by Mundic, who had taken him to dinner and showed him around the city. Tolliver had acted the complete boor throughout. Whatever wonder he saw, he was unimpressed. Whatever beautiful or astonishing thing Mundic showed him, Tolliver shrugged and explained how the same thing was done better on Earth. In a few hours, Mundic had had enough and left Tolliver at a hotel where WP Corporation had reserved a suite.

That's when things began to deteriorate at an amazing rate. Tolliver behaved like the worst sort of intolerable visitor from Earth. Before the era of interstellar travel, tourists from one nation would invade another, dumbly insensitive to their hosts' culture. Where there was once, for example, the ''ugly American,'' today, we have the ''ugly Earthling.'' That seems to have summed up Fredrick Tolliver rather neatly.

After Mundic left him at the hotel, Tolliver made himself comfortable in his suite for an hour, and then went out to see what kind of entertainment he could find on this deceptively Earthlike world. This was taken from testimony of the Ukolsti desk clerk from Tolliver's hotel.

Evidently there were indeed taverns in Chivakatopran City, because the next witness who testified against the Earthling was a bartender. Tolliver walked about three-quarters of a mile to the east, and found himself in an era of restaurants and bars. These catered to the local Ukolsti residents rather than off-worlders, who tended to remain near the downtown hotels and the entertainment district immediately to the west.

Tolliver entered a bar called Nightclub #2655. He sat alone at the bar, at the end nearest the entrance. He might have felt hesitant about coming in any farther, into the dimness that even he must have realized covered an alien way of life he did not comprehend. The bartender said he'd been surprised to see a human in his establishment;

it had happened before, perhaps once or twice in the preceding twelve Ukolsti years. Nevertheless, Ukolsti courtesy demanded that the bartender mask his emotions and serve the human.

Tolliver was wholly ignorant of Ukolsti liquors and did not know what to order. The bartender testified that he made a suggestion, advising Tolliver to drink only a locally manufactured fermented beverage that was equivalent to a strong beer. At first Tolliver took the bartender's recommendation, but then quickly and loudly announced that the beer had a repulsive taste that wasn't worth the small kick he was getting from it. He wanted to try some of the stronger stuff.

The bartender said that he tried to talk Tolliver out of it, saying that he couldn't be responsible for the unknown effects the powerful distilled liquors might have on the human. Tolliver insisted. The bartender admitted that by this time, he'd quite grown to dislike the Earthling, and his attitude was to let Tolliver suffer the consequences of his own bad judgment. The bartender further admitted that after he learned what Tolliver had done later, he'd experienced great guilt and swore that he'd never serve another human again.

The bartender set a small glass of light yellow-green liquor beside Tolliver, along with a glass of water. All this time, the human had been rudely forcing himself into a conversation among a four-member sexual grouping—the Ukolsti counterpart of a marital union, which was out celebrating the promotion of one of the females in her corporate clan.

Tolliver swallowed the liquor, gagged, and drank about half the glass of water. He immediately ordered another. "I've tasted worse around the Mediterranean," he said. The bartender obliged. He quoted the following bit of conversation which he could not help but overhearing, even if he hadn't been listening closely in the first place.

"So," said Tolliver, drunkenly, "I understand you Ukolsti got four sexes. What I want to know—what the people of Earth are speculating about—is how that works?

I mean, we only got two sexes, and sometimes even that seems too many.''

One of the males turned to Tolliver and said, with carefully restrained outrage, ''The Ukolsti sexual relationship among the four partners is very different from that of humans.''

''I know, I know,'' said Tolliver petulantly. ''But exactly how? I mean, does one of you—''

''We are somewhat uncomfortable discussing these matters in public with a human,'' said the male. His words seem diplomatic enough on the page, but the bartender said the male was close to striking Tolliver then and there. In fact, according to the bartender's testimony, all four of the Ukolsti were visibly upset, and the bartender himself had to fight down the desire to reach across the bar and grab the Earthling by the throat.

''Aw, c'mon, you blue sons of bitches, what's the big deal? On Earth—''

One of the males growled something in the Ukolsti language. A female vigorously shook her head no. The other male said something. Again the female shook her head. She leaned forward and addressed Tolliver. ''If it will satisfy you and put an end to your unacceptable behavior, I will tell you briefly. The first male, the sperm father, has intercourse with the first female, the egg mother. Then the egg mother has intercourse with the second male, the egg father.''

Tolliver frowned, his brows drawing together. ''Uh huh,'' he said. ''But there's got to be another step. There are four of you, and I imagine you got to make another transfer.''

The four Ukolsti got to their feet. One of the males dropped some money on the bar. The female said in a very tight voice. ''You are correct. The egg mother and the sperm mother must have intercourse.''

''I don't see—'' began Tolliver, but by that time the quadrisexual unit had walked stiffly from Nightclub #2655. The human turned to the bartender. ''What's she mean?'' he asked.

The bartender drew himself up to his full height and

spoke slowly and precisely. "That matter is never spoken of, even among ourselves."

"Aw, bloody hell," said Tolliver. He staggered out into the darkness. It was the bartender's opinion that he was going in search of the four-member unit.

The next important testimony came from one of the males of the unit, the egg father. Evidently, Tolliver succeeded in following the family back to their living quarters. The Ukolsti do not believe in locked doors, and this marital unit lived in one of the open-floored buildings. It was a simple matter for Tolliver to enter quietly and hide himself.

"We did not know of his presence until after we'd begun an intimate and joyous sexual celebration of Shelandariva's promotion," said the egg father. "I heard some noises from a curtained closet area and grew suspicious. I left our bed and went to the closet, where I discovered the Earthling, who'd been spying on us using a pocket mirror.

"My rage overcame my social restraint, and I began to wrestle with the human. The others came to see what the disturbance was about. The human struggled and kicked out, and my other family members tried to separate the two of us. In the chaos that followed, he kicked Shelandariva in the chest. She immediately began to choke and gasp for breath, falling to the floor. Her ribs had been broken, and the fractured bones punctured both her heart and lungs. She was dead before the emergency medical squad arrived.

"We immobilized the Earthling, and he was duly arrested and taken away to jail. He was charged with murder. Various forces I will not name have worked long and hard behind the scenes to ensure that he is not convicted. I do not anticipate that justice will be done."

The egg father's prediction at the trial was absolutely correct: Fredrick Tolliver was found innocent of the murder of Shelandariva, found guilty of an accidental slaying, given a suspended sentence, and released. Justice may not have been done, but in the larger picture it helped to avoid a serious interstellar incident.

I was appalled. "I wish I could somehow present the sincere apologies of my race and my home world," I said. I wondered if WP Corporation had enough influence by itself to get one of its employees off the hook, even on a distant planet. Or did the company have help, perhaps from various human governments that benefited from the company's deliberations and advice? It was impossible for me to say.

"It is not necessary," said Mundic in a wooden voice. "We understand that Fredrick Tolliver was not a typical representative of the human race. We have such individuals among the Ukolsti, as well."

"Then how," I asked, "did Tolliver die?"

Mundic explained, his face as expressionless as always. "Later that day, as he was gathering his belongings prior to release, he was murdered with a blunt instrument. Ukolsti officials, fearing that this, too, might cause an interstellar incident, ruled his death an accident, although it was absolutely clear to everyone that such a thing was impossible.

"All that was found at the scene of the covered-up crime was a pocket mirror—perhaps the same mirror referred to by the egg father in his testimony—a handkerchief with a blue stain that our police labs cannot identify, and a Ukolsti tool that was probably the murder weapon. But, as I've said, as of this moment there is no murder. It was just an accident. Lately there have been a few too many accidents . . ." he said, letting his voice trail off.

Just then we arrived at the hotel. Mundic helped me carry my bag inside. "Is this the same hotel where Tolliver stayed?" I asked.

"Yes, it is. There are floors with rooms for off-worlders. Those rooms all have four walls, unlike the rooms reserved for Ukolsti visitors. We have learned that many off-worlders prefer it this way. They tend to be squeamish about unrailed floors that overlook drops of a couple dozen stories. Therefore we provide enclosed rooms for our guests who are, shall we say, altitudinally challenged."

"Thank you," I said, suppressing a shudder. He accompanied me to my suite, which was very comfortable and fitted out accurately with everything a human traveler might expect to find in a fine hotel on Earth.

Mundic consulted a clock in the suite's sitting room. "I would be pleased if you'd be my guest for dinner," he said. "Afterward, it will still be early enough for you to begin interviewing the witnesses. Or, if you'd prefer, we can put that off until tomorrow morning."

I was a little weary from the traveling. "Let's see how I feel after dinner," I said.

"Excellent. There is a very good dining room just downstairs, if you're agreeable?"

I spread my hands. "I'm completely open to your suggestions," I said. As if I were going to go out wandering about an alien city like Fredrick Tolliver, looking for a place to get something to eat.

We rode the elevator back down to the lobby area, and went into the dining room. We were seated quickly because it was still before the dinner rush. We were also seated in separate booths which were closed off completely by heavy, cream-colored cloth hangings. I was given a menu by a waiter, and when I opened it up I found an excellent selection of human dishes chosen from several different cultures on Earth itself, and three or four from human colony worlds. I decided to reserve judgment until I saw how the Ukolsti chefs handled what were to them alien cuisines.

"I'll have the Chinese potstickers for an appetizer," I said. "Then the Poulet Rochambeau, fresh cauliflower in a cream and pecorino cheese sauce, and boiled pierogies stuffed with sweetened sauerkraut."

"Yes, sir," said the waiter. "Would you care for a beverage?"

"A Coke now, please. I'll choose a wine to go with the dinner."

"Yes, sir."

As the waiter turned to leave, I asked a question. "Pardon me," I said, "but this is my first day on Ukol. Do you take all your meals in privacy?"

The waiter looked uncomfortable. "It is something we

hesitate to talk about," he said. "But yes, most Ukolsti prefer to dine alone or in the presence of their immediately family members only."

"Thank you very much." I watched the waiter leave with my order.

It seemed that the Ukolsti came supplied with a full complement of cultural taboos. I wondered what others there were, and quietly hoped that I wouldn't cause offense through ignorance. Tolliver had, and now Tolliver was dead; of course, Tolliver had not merely transgressed a subtle social pattern. He'd worked long and hard at it.

Despite my doubts about the culinary expertise of the Ukolsti, when the meal arrived every bit of it was excellent. It was an extremely pleasant surprise, but I reminded myself that I was in the dining room of a large hotel that customarily housed off-worlders from many planets. I might not enjoy the food anywhere else in Chivakatopran City. I saw no urgent reason to learn the truth.

When I asked for my check from the waiter, he smiled and told me that my dinner companion had insisted on paying for both of us. That was fine by me. "May I have a receipt, then?" I asked. No point in letting a few EC dollars sleep in Gerhardt Schnellenbogl's pocket when they could be in mine.

I met Mundic again in the hotel lobby. "Mundic," I said, "I owe you my thanks."

"I hope it was pleasant to you," he said.

"More than I'd expected."

"Good." That's all we were going to say about the meal. "Now, Ferencz, do you feel up to speaking to the witnesses?"

Did I? Well, not particularly, but that's what I was getting paid for. "All right," I said.

Mundic nodded. "The most likely suspects are the three remaining members of marital unit. The bartender in Nightclub #2655 is a suspect also, to a lesser degree. It depends on how offended he was by Tolliver's behavior. You must understand that among the Ukolsti, death is the common punishment for gross negligence in observing the social taboos. And anyone outraged enough is permitted to inflict that penalty. We try to make allowances for alien visitors who don't know our culture, but Fredrick Tolliver was, how shall I say—''

"He was Fredrick Tolliver, and that explains everything.'' We left the hotel and got into Mundic's waiting car.

"I've arranged this meeting with Shelandariva's mourning wife and husbands,'' he said. "They've already been questioned many times by the police investigators of both Ukol and Earth, as well as certain other officials. Please remember that they are under no obligation to answer your questions. We have no genuine authority. I had to exert a certain amount of influence.''

"I'm sure WP Corporation is grateful,'' I said, staring out the window as the car moved swiftly through the clean, broad streets of Chivakatopran City. "If I were one of Shelandariva's family, I wouldn't want to have to go through these events all over again.''

"They expressed the hope that this will bring the matter to a close. They want to be left alone in their grief. Please remember that when you speak with them.''

"Of course,'' I said.

Shelandariva's family unit lived in one of the tall, enclosed residential blocks east of the downtown area. Mundic had been here before, so I let him lead me up in the elevator to their apartment. It was cool and dimly lighted within, and even though I'd prepared myself, I couldn't suppress a strong feeling of vertigo whenever I glanced at the edge of the floor, where open air tumbled straight down a shaft a hundred feet to ground level. I didn't want to go tumbling down after it, so I tended to stand nervously in the very middle of the parlor while Mundic spoke quietly with the three distressed Ukolsti in their own language.

Finally, Mundic turned to me. In English he said, "Everything is well, but remember what I've told you.''

"Yes, thank you,'' I said. I turned to the surviving female and the two males. "I want to express my personal condolences to you, and the regrets of my employers on Earth. This was a tragedy that need not have happened. I also want to thank you for allowing me to intrude on your privacy."

"Yes, yes," said one of the males impatiently. His attitude was also markedly belligerent. Perhaps he thought all Earthlings were like Fredrick Tolliver, and he was prepared to penalty-kick me down the airshaft at the first opportunity.

"Kalikun," said the female, "remember your courtesy. We have guests in our home."

The male looked abashed. "I apologize," he said. He would not go farther than that.

"Welcome," said the other male, "and think of this as your home while you are with us. We have Mundic's assurances that you respect our culture enough to want to avoid any unpleasantness. That is all we ask."

"What Mundic has told you is true," I said. "I have a few questions for each of you. I will need to speak individually with all of you, in turn. I will make the process as brief as possible. Is there some etiquette involved with whom I speak to first?"

"No, none," said Kalikun, "but I volunteer."

"You have my gratitude. Is there somewhere we can speak in private?"

"This way," said Kalikun, leading me to their kitchen. We sat down at a large, gleaming aluminum table.

"I know you've answered these questions for the other authorities, but no one provided me with that material. Fredrick Tolliver was killed in the early afternoon on the twenty-first day of Mmach. Where were you at that time?"

Kalikun glared when I mentioned Fredrick Tolliver. When he spoke next, it was with barely-concealed fury. "I am a teacher of young, mentally handicapped children. At that hour, I have a physical training period with them. On the day in question, I was at the school. I believe I organized my class into two teams for sunig. It would take too long to explain the game to you."

I raised a hand. "It's not relevant in any event," I said. I smiled. I felt I had to. The resistance and dislike poured from Kalikun in almost visible waves of energy.

If he felt that way about me, I could only begin to imagine how much hatred he'd felt for Tolliver. Here was a man who could have killed, given the unusual Ukolsti social arrangements and their ideas about society's vengeance against the breaker of taboos. "Then there would be others at your school who could substantiate your alibi?" I asked.

"All this is already a matter of record," he said with a growl.

"No one has given me the record."

"Then, yes, there are many who could and who have vouched for my presence at the school at the time of the killing."

"You did not leave at any time during the early afternoon?"

"No."

I thought for a moment. "Are you the member of the family who spoke so vehemently at the trial about justice not being done?"

"Yes, that was me. And wasn't I correct?"

I felt my shoulders slump a little. "Yes," I said sadly, "you were correct. Thank you for your time."

Kalikun said nothing, but got up and left the kitchen. A moment later, the female entered. She sat in the chair Kalikun had vacated.

"May I ask your name, madame?" I said.

"Venaahelocenai," she said.

"I must ask you the same question I asked Kalikun—"

"Did he give you permission to call him by his familiar name?" she asked.

"No," I said, "I just heard you speak it before. I did not ask him his full name."

She frowned. "That was an error on your part."

I closed my eyes for a moment, then opened them again. I felt too warm. "In any dealings between alien races, there will be errors, even with the best of intentions on both sides. I assure you that I do, indeed, have the best of intentions."

She nodded. "I can tell that you are nothing like that Earthling Tolliver. I am glad of it."

"Then may I ask, where were you in the early afternoon of the twenty-first day of Mmach?"

"I was at my desk at my job. I am a data shunt for a large banking and suicide-control firm. My desk is at the right rear of a large room, and there are scores of people sitting around me who have already attested to my presence there throughout the workday."

"Thank you, madame," I said. "I'm very sorry about what happened, and I'm very glad for your generous cooperation."

"Let this be the end of it. Please, let this be the end of it." She didn't even look at me as she rose and went back to the parlor.

The other male took her place at the table. I asked him the same questions, and he told me that he was a musician who'd spent the afternoon rehearsing for a recital with three others. They had already made sworn statements to back up his alibi.

We walked together back into the parlor. "It was very important for me to conduct these interviews," I said. "I have to ask this, however: I may need to return to ask a further question or two after I've spoken with some other witnesses, merely to clarify small details I may not understand. Is it presuming too much upon your hospitality and forbearance to ask permission to return, if the situation demands it? I emphasize that this may not be the case, but I feel obliged to warn you in advance of the possibility."

"Yes, come," said the female. "You've caused no offense."

Mundic stepped toward me and grasped me by the elbow. "Then we will leave you in peace." He spoke a few words in their language, then steered me to the door. In a few seconds, we were riding the elevator back to the ground.

"Very good, very fine," he said approvingly. "You behaved admirably. I'm sure your conduct reassured them about humans, perhaps just a little."

"I'm glad," I said. As an investigator, I've become

hardened to tragedy over the years, but I felt a strong emotional response to this case.

Once more in Mundic's automobile, he asked, "Where would you like to go next?"

"I'd like to see the holding area where Tolliver was killed. And I'd like to see the tool that was used to crack his stupid head open."

Mundic nodded agreement. "Both are in the same building—the local police have been slow about releasing Tolliver's personal effects, because he had no family or friends on Ukol, and the authorities are not sure to whom to give the items. I've applied, as a correspondent employee of WP Corporation, but no decision's been made yet."

I glanced at my watch, which was still set on Budapest time. The information it gave me bore no relation to where I was now. Glancing out the window, I saw that Proxima Centauri was hanging low above the horizon. It would be night soon.

I told Mundic what the three members of the marital unit had said. He shook his head. "I would've sworn the killer was one of them," he said. "But they all have perfect alibis."

I laughed gruffly. "No such thing as a 'perfect alibi,' Mundi. People in my profession used to be called detectives, because we detected things ordinary people never noticed. Even an airtight alibi may have disguised holes in it. For instance, even though a person claims that he was on a carnival float in full sight of half a million people, as well as being televised to places on five continents, there is still a chance he could've snatched just enough time to get off the float, commit murder, and return unnoticed. Ordinary people tend to forget about routine breaks in a daily schedule—a teacher's open period between classes, for instance, or lunch breaks, or what have you. I've shaken many an unshakable alibi in my time. I haven't crossed any of those three off my list as yet."

"Ah, I see. Well, of course, you're the expert. That's why WP Corporation sent you here."

Our stop at the police holding area—I hesitate to call it a jail—was brief. Mundic and I were taken to the place of confinement, which was a huge room furnished with benches, where the prisoners milled around and held conversations or sat forlornly by themselves. The Ukolsti police didn't use jail cells to segregate their prisoners. They relied on Ukolsti social dynamics to keep order, and for the most part it seemed to work.

"Tolliver was kept here," Mundic said. "After he received his suspended sentence, he was brought to the properties room to collect his belongings. He was killed shortly thereafter."

I looked around. "Where was his body found?" I asked.

"In the elevator to the ground floor."

I nodded. "Now I want to see the weapon itself."

"This way," said Mundic. I followed him through a maze of corridors to a small window with a metal grate over it. Mundic went to the window and conversed for a while with a uniformed woman on the other side. Evidently he'd arranged in advance for me to view the weapon, just as he'd arranged for me to interview the three aliens, because in a few minutes the woman returned from the depths of her domain, carrying a long metal pipe fitted into a circular metal disk. The woman slid open the window and pushed the murder weapon through. Mundic gave it to me.

I hefted it. It was extremely heavy. It made a first-rate blunt object. "What is it?" I asked.

"It's a Ukolsti calibrating device, used with certain types of high-temperature furnaces."

"Uh-huh," I said, giving the thing back to him. He returned it to the officer in charge of evidence. We left the police building.

"Was that of any use to you?" Mundic asked.

"As much as anything else had been so far," I said.

"I suppose investigation is a long, slow process of gathering bits of information. It must demand a particular way of thinking, a certain frame of mind."

"Sometimes," I said. "And sometimes not. On rare

occasions, solutions present themselves gift-wrapped like birthday gifts.''

"Has that happened in this case?"

I laughed. "Let you know when it does."

"Where would you like to go next?" he asked.

"I'd like to speak to the bartender at Nightclub #2655."

"Yes, of course," said Mundic. He leaned forward and murmured his directions to the driver. We headed back in the direction of my hotel.

When we arrived, it was obvious that Mundic was somewhat uncomfortable about accompanying me into the bar, despite the usual lack of expression on his face. Mundic was not a party type of guy. That was all right. We weren't going to be there long.

The bartender was displeased to see another human in his establishment, but Mundic spoke with him, and then he cooperated with me freely. I learned that he'd been hugely angered by Tolliver's behavior, but who hadn't been? The interesting thing was that the bartender had a very weak alibi for the time of Tolliver's killing. "I work nights here," he said. "When that off-worlder was punished, I was at home, in bed and asleep. You can ask my wife."

I took his name and address, and then I said, "Give me one of the drinks Tolliver ordered that night."

"That's a very bad idea," said Mundic, severe disapproval in his voice.

"I'm not going to drink it," I said. "I just want to see it, smell it, maybe taste it."

"If you say so," said the bartender. He poured the yellow-green liquor into a glass and set it before me. Mundic paid for it because I had no local currency. I lifted it to the lights and looked through the sickly-looking fluid. I sniffed it, and it made me gag. I cautiously raised the glass to my mouth and took a small sip. It was the most horrible tasting stuff I'd ever experienced. Even thinking about it now makes my palms sweat and my belly sick. I'm not going to compare the taste of the liquor to anything else; imagine it for yourself.

I thanked the bartender for his help, and Mundic and I left the nightclub. We got back into his car. "Could he have killed Tolliver, do you think? His alibi is the thinnest yet."

"He could've killed Tolliver, depending upon how ferociously outraged he'd become. Anyone could've had access to the elevator in the police building, and the bartender had the day free."

"And the testimony at the trial described how angry the bartender got that evening. Almost as angry as the egg father."

"The case is much less opaque now than when I first arrived," I said. "It won't take much longer to solve. I'm very confident about that."

"Next?" asked Mundic.

"I'm not sure," I said.

"I have a list of minor suspects—waiters, desk clerks, officers and prisoners he came into contact with in the police building. Some of them were rather fierce in their denunciation of Tolliver, but I don't think any of them had as much motivation to kill him as those people you've interviewed this evening."

"I—" I broke off, aware that I was about to become violently sick in the back of Mundic's automobile. I motioned meaninglessly with one hand, at the same time desperately fighting down nausea. I did heave once, but contained it, except for a slight dribble that escaped my lips. I took out a handkerchief and wiped my mouth. I was astonished to see the cotton material stained blue.

"The same thing must've happened to Tolliver," I said weakly. "Except he had a beer and two complete drinks. He must've been monstrously sick, and yet he managed to follow the marital unit to their apartment building."

"And the experience of his horrible reaction to the liquor taught him nothing," said Mundic thoughtfully. "I suppose that to the moment of his death, he never truly understood that he was on another world, among another race, and not back on his familiar home world where he could behave as he'd always behaved.''

There was no doubt a lot of truth in that. "In some ways, he was brilliant," I said. "Otherwise, he couldn't have been hired for his job at WP Corporation. In many other ways, Tolliver was among the stupidest people I've ever heard about."

Mundic nodded. "Now, as to these minor suspects. Do you feel well enough to see them tonight? Or should we put them off until tomorrow?"

I waved a hand. "There's no need," I said. "I'm rather sure I know who killed—let's not dance around the euphemism, the world is murdered—Fredrick Tolliver."

Mundic stared at me curiously. "Who was it, do you think?" he said.

I smiled. "Why, it was you, Mundic. When you heard that Tolliver had killed a Ukolsti citizen, it was enough for you to seek revenge. You met him at the interstellar tunnel terminal, just as you met me. You took him to dinner, just as you took me. You spent more time with him than anyone. I'm willing to bet that he had plenty of opportunities to heighten first your displeasure, then your disgust, and finally your righteous wrath. Even though he was an off-worlder, and you wished to show him every courtesy, when you heard that he'd actually killed one of your fellows, poor Shelandariva, you decided that your socially dictated need for revenge had to be satisfied."

"You are quite right," he said in a composed voice. "You know, he spied on me at dinner with that pocket mirror, just as he spied on Shelandariva and the rest of her family in their most private of moments. Tolliver was spotted by a waiter and asked to leave. Tolliver made such a disturbance that it attracted my attention from within my booth, and I learned what he'd done. I was willing to swallow my anger at that point, but he insisted on aggravating the situation. At last it became too much to bear."

"I suppose I agree," I said.

"How did you know it was me?"

"The weapon was another giveaway. I spent some time

investigating WP Corporation. I recognized the device as something used only by plasmonics engineers. 'High-temperature furnaces,' indeed.''

Mundic's carefully masked expression began to waver. ''I suppose now you intend to hand me over to the police?''

I shrugged. ''Not at all. I was paid to find the identity of Tolliver's killer, not to 'bring him to justice,' in Kalikun's words. I'll make a report to Gerhardt Schnellenbogl. I'm pretty certain that will be the end of it. You're too valuable to the corporation to prosecute. In any event, no one on Earth liked Tolliver in the first place. I doubt if there will be any unpleasantness as a result of my investigation, either here or on Earth. I think they just wanted to know.''

''Thank you,'' murmured Mundic. In a couple of minutes, the automobile stopped outside my hotel. ''I will come by tomorrow morning to take you back to the shuttle terminal.''

''That is most kind of you, Mundic. I hope you realize that I think of you as a friend.''

Ukolsti social conventions that I knew nothing of prevented him from replying. I got out of the car and headed into the hotel. I discovered that I couldn't wait to leave this world of pink skies and blue people, and return home to blues skies and pink, Hungarian people.

DAW

Science Fiction Anthologies

☐ **FUTURE EARTHS: UNDER AFRICAN SKIES**   UE2544—$4.99
   Mike Resnick & Gardner Dozois, editors
From a utopian space colony modeled on the society of ancient Kenya,
to a shocking future discovery of a "long-lost" civilization, to an inge-
nious cure for one of humankind's oldest woes—a cure that might cost
too much—here are 15 provocative tales about Africa in the future and
African culture transplanted to different worlds.

☐ **MICROCOSMIC TALES**   UE2532—$4.99
   Isaac Asimov, Martin H. Greenberg, & Joseph D. Olander, eds.
Here are 100 wondrous science fiction short-short stories, including
contributions by such acclaimed writers as Arthur C. Clarke, Robert
Silverberg, Isaac Asimov, and Larry Niven. Discover a superman who
lives in a *real* world of nuclear threat . . . an android who dreams of
electric love . . . and a host of other tales that will take you instantly
out of this world.

☐ **WHATDUNITS**   UE2533—$4.99
☐ **MORE WHATDUNITS**   UE2557—$5.50
   Mike Resnick, editor
In these unique volumes of all-original stories, Mike Resnick has created a series of science fiction mystery scenarios and set such inven-
tive sleuths as Pat Cadigan, Judith Tarr, Katharine Kerr, Jack Haldeman,
and Esther Friesner to solving them. Can you match wits with the
masters to make the perpetrators fit the crimes?

ISAAC ASIMOV PRESENTS THE GREAT SF STORIES
Isaac Asimov & Martin H. Greenberg, editors

☐ **Series 24 (1962)**   UE2495—$5.50

☐ **Series 25 (1963)**   UE2518—$5.50

DAW

FANTASY ANTHOLOGIES

DAW
Tanya Huff

VICTORY NELSON, INVESTIGATOR:
Otherworldly Crimes A Specialty

☐ **BLOOD PRICE: Book 1** UE2471—$3.99
Can one ex-policewoman and a vampire defeat the magic-spawned evil which is devastating Toronto?

☐ **BLOOD TRAIL: Book 2** UE2502—$4.50
Someone was out to exterminate Canada's most endangered species—the werewolf.

☐ **BLOOD LINES: Book 3** UE2530—$4.99
Long-imprisoned by the magic of Egypt's gods, an ancient force of evil is about to be loosed on an unsuspecting Toronto.

THE NOVELS OF CRYSTAL

When an evil wizard attempts world domination, the Elder Gods must intervene!

☐ **CHILD OF THE GROVE: Book 1** UE2432—$3.95
☐ **THE LAST WIZARD: Book 2** UE2331—$3.95

OTHER NOVELS

☐ **THE FIRE'S STONE** UE2445—$3.95
Thief, swordsman and wizardess—drawn together by a quest not of their own choosing, would they find their true destinies in a fight against spells, swords and betrayal?

DAW

Attention:

DAW COLLECTORS

Many readers of DAW Books have written requesting information on early titles and book numbers to assist in the collection of DAW editions since the first of our titles appeared in April 1972.

We have prepared a several-pages-long list of all DAW titles, giving their sequence numbers, original and current order numbers, and ISBN numbers. And, of course, the authors and book titles, as well as reissues.

If you think that this list will be of help, you may have a copy by writing to the address below and enclosing two dollars in stamps or currency to cover the handling and postage costs.

DAW Books, Inc.
Dept. C
375 Hudson Street
New York, NY 10014-3658